The
STUBBLE
FIELD

The
STUBBLE
FIELD

Mary Nichols

ORION

First published in Great Britain in 1993 by
Orion
An imprint of Orion Books Ltd
Orion House, 5 Upper St Martin's Lane, London WC2H 9EA

A CIP catalogue record for this book is available
from the British Library

ISBN 1 85797 177 9

Typeset by Datix International Limited, Bungay, Suffolk
Printed in Great Britain by Butler & Tanner Ltd
Frome and London

To My Family

Chapter One

'*D*o y'see anyfink? Can y'see him?'

Sarah Jane, who had her bottom in the air and her freckled nose down the rabbit hole, ignored her brother.

'Is he there?' Billie was jumping up and down in his excitement, thin arms pumping and golden curls leaping.

Sarah Jane sat on bare heels and tossed back a veil of long red hair to reveal a perfectly oval, perfectly filthy face and green eyes alight with mischief.

''Course he is,' she said. 'Ain't we just chased him down there?' There were several rabbit holes along the bank which divided the stubble field from the copse, but she had taken careful note of the one the rabbit had bolted down. 'An' if you keep shakin' the earth like that, he'll stay down there. Stand still, do!'

She looked about her for inspiration, just as the animal in question popped up further along the bank and tore off across the stubble field, its white tail bobbing up and down, marking its path. Sarah Jane, who had already pulled the hem of her blue cotton skirt up between her legs and tucked it into her waistband, set off after it. There was no hope of catching it, but she had to make the effort for Billie's sake. The terrified animal turned at right angles. 'Head him off!' she shouted. The rabbit, confronted by Billie, turned again and made straight for Sarah Jane. She dived headlong into the prickly stubble, while their prey disappeared towards the copse. She was winded and had a stitch in her side, but after a minute, she turned over on her back, laughing and wiping away a trickle of blood from a scratch on her cheek.

Billie came and stood over her, blotting out the sun, so that his small, anxious face was in shadow. 'You ain't much good at catching rabbits, Sarah Jane,' he said.

'No,' she admitted.'We shall have to raid the tater field again.'

'I'm sick o' taters, and you said we should have rabbit for dinner. You said we could catch one.'

'Well, I was wrong, weren't I? Ol' Bobtail don't seem to want to be catched.'

It was not a new thing, this mothering of her tousle-haired brother; she had been doing it for nearly three years, ever since her ma's last lying-in. For all they were as poor as church mice and her pa could not really afford another mouth to feed, they had mourned the passing of the little scrap as if he had been the most wanted child on earth. Her mother had never recovered her strength, growing weaker and thinner as the months and years passed, until she was nothing more than skin and bone and hardly bigger than a child herself. It was almost as if their roles had been reversed and Sarah Jane became the mother of the little family, doing all the chores of the housewife – cooking and cleaning, feeding the chickens, collecting the eggs and making up the swill for their pig who rooted around on the patch of grass which belonged to the cottage; all this on top of nursing her ma. As soon as her father had left the house to go to his work each morning, she had washed her and dressed her and coaxed her to eat, and in the evening when Pa came home and took over, she amused her brother, keeping him quiet so that he did not tire the invalid, then put him to bed and cuddled him, telling him stories which she made up as she went along. Not for a single second did Sarah Jane begrudge what she did; she was devoted to her parents and her brother and the house was full of love.

She was not sure if she had been expecting her mother to die; no one ever spoke of it and her father was always cheerful and would allow no gloom to invade their home, but the time came when her mother could no longer leave her bed, could hardly raise her hand to do anything for herself; even then she smiled. She and Pa were holding hands and smiling at each other the day, three months ago now, when her eyes had closed for the last time, and for a minute or two afterwards Pa continued to smile as if his face had stuck that way. And then he had crumpled on the bed and sobbed. Sarah Jane had never seen him weep before and she stood uncertainly, not crying herself though her body was wracked with grief, and then she moved forward and he had drawn her into his arms and Billie had wriggled up between them and the three of them had sat on the edge of the bed and drawn comfort from each other.

These were the last tears her father shed though Billie, only seven, had continued to cry on and off for days. Sarah Jane had taken him onto her lap and cradled his head against her fast developing breasts, rocking him and soothing him. She had wanted to howl too, to give vent to her misery in noisy sobs, to seek comfort in her mother's arms as she had done when she was very little, but there was no comfort to be had and crying would not help her brother. Pa, silently immersed in his own grief, could do nothing for either of them.

He had seemed to grow old before her eyes; the laughter went from his voice and the ready smile from his lips. It was as if a candle had been snuffed out inside him, leaving him in the dark and cold. He moved about their tiny cottage as if he had weights on his feet. He must have been like that at work too, because four weeks ago they had brought him home on a farm gate, gored to death by the big black bull.

'He were too slow,' Farmer Cooper had told her. 'Time was he would ha' bin over that gate and out o' the way in the time it takes to tell it.' He paused, looking round the spruce kitchen. 'There'll be arrangements to make.'

'Yes.' His over-loud voice had intruded on her shocked system; she wished he would go away and leave them in peace. She wanted to talk to Pa, ask him what to do; surely he could still hear her?

'I'll see to it, shall I?' he had gone on.

'Yes, please.'

'What'll you do now?'

'Do?' She had looked up from a numb contemplation of the lifeless figure of her pa, now laid out on his bed, to meet the enquiring eyes of the farmer.

'You can't stay here,' he had said. 'Not . . . not after the funeral.'

'Why not?'

'This is a tied cottage, didn't you know that?'

She had known it, of course, but she had not been able to think of anything except that their pa had left them and there was no one else in the whole world to turn to. 'I can work for you.'

'I need a man.'

Sarah Jane had looked bleakly at Billie, standing beside her with his hand in hers, white-faced and uncomprehending; it would be years before he could become a useful farmhand. It wasn't so bad for her, she was at an age when she could work, but no one would want her brother, whose appetite, like that of all small boys, was good; there was no way he could earn his keep. Somehow she had to make enough for them both. 'What'll we do?' she asked.

'Go to the Union. They're not as black as they're painted, and

3

you'll be looked after there.' The farmer had spoken gruffly, but not unkindly. 'They'll give you food and a bed and work to do and, like as not, there'll be a schoolroom too. Wouldn't you like to learn to read and write?'

She had nodded, too overflowing with misery to take in what he was saying, but after he had gone, she had sat in the high-backed rocking chair by the hearth to think. The chair had been her father's and his father's before him; the head of the house had always sat in that chair and neither of the children would have dared to use it when he was alive, even when he was not in the house. Now there was no one to turn her out of it.

The Union! It was not that she did not know where the workhouse was; everyone knew, and if what she had heard was right, unsubstantiated though that was, it was a place of punishment, not sanctuary. She could remember it being built, not because the building itself was memorable, but because it was opened in a great flurry of importance at the time of her mother's last confinement. It stood, gaunt and forbidding, where the long ribbon of unmade road from the village of Chevington to the hamlet of Penny Drift was crossed by the main road from the east coast to Peterborough and heaven knew where beyond that. It was a tall rectangle of brick with high barred windows. Above the door hung a bellrope and above that, chiselled into the lintel, were some words which Pa, when she asked him, had told her said *Penny Drift and Chevington Union 1837*. She screwed up her forehead in an effort to concentrate on the arithmetic. It was 1841 now, so she must have been nine at the time and Billie three.

Ma, white as a sheet, had sent her to fetch the neighbour who was to act as midwife and when that worthy arrived, wiping floury hands on her grubby apron, Sarah Jane had been left to look after Billie, while her mother's cries had filled their little home. The terrifying sounds had gone on a long time and afterwards she had overheard the midwife telling her pa, when he had been fetched from his work, that it had been a blessing in disguise, what with the state of agriculture and the poorhouses full to overflowing and him having two little 'uns already. She supposed the woman had been trying to comfort him in her clumsy way, but Pa had said it would be a long day a-comin' afore he'd see any of his kin in the workhouse and puttin' up these fancy Unions all over the place wouldn't change his mind on that, and she ought to know better than to mention it. The workhouse was for the blind, the crippled, even the downright lazy, and he was none o' those

4

things. 'This family don't beg,' he had said. And later, when his wife had died and the same neighbour came to lay her out, he had told her, 'I can work and Sarah Jane is a good little mawther. We'll do.' He could not have foreseen his own death.

The day after her father's funeral, she had left Billie to amuse himself and set off to look for work. Though still grieving, she went cheerfully and optimistically, a state of mind which did not last beyond midday. There was no work, or what there was meant living in and everyone in the vicinity knew she had a brother and they would not take them both. Desperate, she had walked all the way to Peterborough – ten miles, so the signpost said. Towns were something new in her experience and she had been so overcome with the size of the place, the bustle and the unbelievable noise, that her courage had failed her and she had turned right round and walked back again, arriving home at suppertime with every limb on fire with fatigue, to find Billie fast asleep in the middle of the kitchen floor with his thumb in his mouth and his arm round an old rag doll which had been his only comfort during the long, lonely day.

The next day Farmer Cooper had returned, bringing with him his new man, whose tactless young wife ran about the little cottage crying out with pleasure at how neat and clean the place had been kept and how well they would do there.

'Go to the Union,' Benjamin Cooper had repeated, seeing Sarah Jane's stubborn expression. 'I want you out – today.'

So they had left, but not to go to the workhouse. Instead they had taken up residence in an animal shelter on the far side of the farm, taking with them a change of clothes, a blanket, a few pots and pans, a stale loaf and half a dozen eggs, long since eaten and forgotten, together with five shillings the farmer had given her for the furniture.

Billie had cried when she first took him there. 'I wanna go home,' he said over and over again, as if repetition would grant him his wish.

'Well, you can't.' She had spoken sharply, not because she was hard-hearted, but simply because her own emotions were brimming over and she could not afford to give in to them. While he needed her, she would fight with all the strength and determination she could muster to look after him.

'Ma! I want me Ma!'

'Ma's dead, you know she is.' She had to be cruel, it was the only way she could bear his sobs. She had squatted down beside him on the floor of the shelter, taking his shoulders in her hands and shaking him very gently. 'Now look here, Billie. Ma is dead and Pa is dead and we can't go back, not ever, so you'll just have to make the best of it. I'm here, ain't I? I'll look after you. From now on, you've only got me and I've only got you.' Then she had hugged him and soothed him until he quieted.

And in the late summer days that followed, he had cheered up no end, treating their new lifestyle as a kind of adventure and leaving the worrying to her. She had tried again to find work, anything at all which would put bread into their mouths, but by this time, their way of life had taken its toll. Her long red hair had become unkempt and her clothes filthy and ragged, and though she tried to wash them, she still looked like the worst kind of gypsy, and there were plenty of clean-living, wholesome girls looking for work. She stood no chance.

While the weather remained fine and the food they bought with the five shillings could be supplemented by scavenging from the fields and orchards, they could manage, but when the long, hot summer came to an end and it turned wet and cold, what then? And if anyone caught them stealing they would be in deep trouble. Hadn't Pa told her what terrible punishment was handed out to thieves? And hadn't she and Billie been brought up to be honest and law-abiding, and hunger no excuse for stealing? But the last of the five shillings had been spent the day before and the time for decisions was not far off.

Billie's voice interrupted her reverie. 'You said we'd catch a rabbit.'

'I'll catch you instead.' She scrambled to her feet and chased him, laughing aloud. He dodged, she followed, round and round, up and down, shouting to each other, until she caught him at the top of the field where the ploughman had already made inroads into the stubble, and they rolled together in the soft earth. She wanted to stay there forever, never to be hungry or thirsty, never to have to make a decision, just lie there with the hot sun warming her face, the skylarks soaring above the fields and the frogs croaking in the ditch almost by her ear. But neither rabbits nor potatoes put themselves into the stew.

'Now, I think I shall put *you* into the pot instead,' she said, laughing and hugging him to her.

'Sal,' he said, suddenly serious. 'I'm hungry.'

'I know and I'm sorry. We'll try again tomorrow, set a trap maybe.'

'Pa said that was poachin' an' if someone catches us doin' that, what happens then?' Poaching was even more terrible than thieving in Billie's eyes.

His words seemed prophetic for when she sat up, she saw a coach had stopped on the road below the field. It was a grand shiny affair in dark green, with a monogram on its side and a uniformed coachman on the driving seat. The door opened and a gentleman stepped out, bending low in order not to dislodge his grey top hat. My, he was grand, she thought, tall and handsome, about the same age as her Pa, perhaps a little younger, but not so *worn*. He was dressed in a lilac-grey frockcoat over a blue striped waistcoat and grey trousers. His blue silk cravat was tied in an elegant bow and held by a pin which sparkled in the sunlight. Taking a step or two towards them, he shouted, 'Hey, you children. Come here at once!'

Sarah Jane had no intention of doing any such thing; she sprang to her feet and, grabbing Billie by the hand, dived for the copse. Once in the cover of the trees, she stopped and turned to look back. The man was still standing in the road, gazing in their direction.

'It's Lord Chevington,' Billie whispered. 'I seed him once afore when I was out with Pa. D'you think 'e can see us?'

'No.'

'Will 'e come up 'ere?'

'No.' She laughed. ''e ain't goin' to get 'is fine shoes mucky, now is 'e?'

It appeared she was right because, after a minute, he shrugged and returned to his carriage and it set off again in the direction of Chevington village. The children emerged from their hiding place to watch it go. 'My, 'e's a dandy and no mistake,' Sarah Jane said. ''ow'd you like to dress like that, Billie, an' ride in a carriage?'

'I'd as lief ride on the box and drive it. I'd wear a top 'at and a coat with *dozens* of capes and brass buttons and Wellington boots an' I'd crack me whip an' make them there 'orses fly.'

'I'd ride inside,' she said, holding her hand across her brow to shield her eyes from the sun, the better to see the fast-diminishing vehicle. 'I'd sit back on the cushions with me silk ballgown spread all round me and satin slippers on me feet and jewels in me 'air and when I got to the ball, all the fine swells would want to dance with me ...' She halted suddenly. 'It's stopping at the farm-gate.'

They watched as the coachman climbed down and hurried up the rutted drive to the farmhouse. ''e's tellin' on us!' Sarah Jane snatched Billie's hand and began to run. 'Let's get outa 'ere.'

They went back to the crude building which had become their home, imagining themselves safe and were taken completely by surprise when, later that day, the farmer's big frame blocked the

7

entrance. Billie, who was toasting his toes at the fire Sarah Jane had built and eating a boiled egg, filched from under one of *their* old hens, turned to look up at him with his mouth covered in egg yolk. Sarah Jane jumped to her feet and Billie bolted the remainder of the egg before it could be snatched from him.

'What are you doing here?' The voice was enough to give Billie the shakes. 'I told you to go to the workhouse.'

'We didn't choose to go,' Sarah Jane said. 'No one can make us, and we're all right here.'

'That you're not, you're trespassing.' He pointed with his cane. 'And what's that?'

'An egg. Leastways, it *was* an egg, now it's only the shell.'

'Stolen, I'll warrant.'

Sarah Jane was silent, but unabashed. Billie's lip began to tremble and she stooped to comfort him, wiping the tears from his cheeks with grubby fingers and making his face even dirtier than before.

'Well, 'tis plain you can't stay here,' he said. 'Come alonga me.'

'Where to?'

'No questions now, just get your things together.' He reached past her to grab Billie's bony shoulder.

'Leave him be!' Sarah Jane shouted. 'You frighten him.'

He smiled suddenly. 'But I don't frighten you?'

'No, you don't,' she lied. 'I ain't afraid of anyone.'

He laughed. 'Well, my brave little miss, afraid or not, you're coming with me.' He stopped to kick out the fire. 'You could have set the whole place alight and been burned to death in your sleep.' Then he propelled Billie outside into the gathering twilight, knowing Sarah Jane was bound to follow.

It was a turning point, she recognised that; they could not go on as they had been doing. She had tried and failed and her failure set her castigating herself but she did not know what else she could have done, nor what she could do now. If only she could find work, if only she had some talent those with money were prepared to buy, but she knew nothing except how to keep a cottage clean and cook a plain meal – and what use was that? Even now, Sarah Jane was not at all sure they would not be better making a run for it, but there was nowhere to run to and the farmer had a firm grip on Billie; there was nothing to do but follow him to the farmyard where he set about harnessing up the pony and trap.

He was in a bad mood; a cow was calving and there was ploughing to be done, and he had to act as nursemaid to a couple of no-good urchins. If it were not for the fact that Lady Chevington was one of the guardians of the workhouse and His Lordship had said he would check up on the children, Farmer Cooper would have run them off the land with threats and left it at that. As it was, he felt obliged to take them to the Union himself and make sure they went in.

The girl was looking at him with defiance in her green eyes. 'A spell in prison would be more to the point than a good home at the workhouse,' he told her. 'And don't tell me you don't choose to go, for we cannot all do what we choose, otherwise I should be out on my fields now, instead of worrying about you.'

'Why are you?' Sarah Jane demanded. 'You didn't afore. You didn' worry about us when ... when Pa died.'

'That was before His Lordship took a hand in the affair. He says you're to go to the Union and no arguments.'

The Union it would have to be, Sarah Jane decided, but promised herself it would not be for long. As soon as she could think of a way to manage, they would be off and no one would stop them. 'I ain't givin' you no arguments,' she said, remembering her father's response to the midwife, and lifting her chin. 'But we ain't beggin', mind. Us Winterdays don't never beg.'

He opened the little door at the back of the trap. 'Get in then, the pair of you. The sooner we go, the sooner I can get on with me work.'

They scrambled up and sat together on one side while the farmer hoisted his bulk onto the opposite seat and glared at them. Sarah Jane, still apparently defiant, though trembling inside with apprehension, stared back at him as the pony trotted out of the gate and turned down the flat fen road. It stretched for miles, straight as an arrow, a foot or two higher than the level fields on either side, which receded, like a calm ocean, into the distant heat-haze. It had seemed endless the day she had walked along it on her abortive trip to Peterborough, but today they fairly flew over the ground and with every yard her spirits dropped.

'Where we goin'?' Billie whispered, pulling on her arm. 'I wanna go back home.'

She turned from contemplating the fields to smile at him. 'We're goin' to find a new home. You'll like it there.'

'How far is it?'

'At the end of this road,' Benjamin Cooper put in. 'A couple of miles.'

Billie was terrified of the big man; he dare not even look at him, much less speak to him. He tried to wriggle himself behind his sister. 'Why do we have to go?'

She sighed. She didn't want to explain, didn't know if she could. It was necessary, that was all there was to it, and admitting that meant admitting her own failure to prevent it. He would not understand. 'Because we do.'

Whether he was satisfied with that answer, she did not know, but he fell to watching the back of the sturdy little pony as it covered the ground at a spanking trot. If his mind had not been full of the knowledge that something important was going to happen, something unknown and therefore terrifying, he would have enjoyed the ride. The last time he had been in the pony and trap was when his pa had been sent on an errand by the farmer and had taken him with him. That had been fun and Pa had bought him a toffee apple in the market. There had been no toffee apples for a very long time now.

The trap slowed down and pulled into the side of the road to make way for an oncoming coach and pair which Sarah Jane immediately recognised as the one they had seen earlier. It rattled past, so close, she could feel the heat from the horses' backs and could see Lord Chevington sitting inside. He was even more imposing close to; his dark hair curled from under his top hat and the sparkling jewel in the pin in his cravat was matched by another on his hand, which rested idly on the top of his cane. He was looking straight ahead; his dark eyes, beneath winged brows, seemed to be brooding on something. There was someone sitting opposite him and Sarah Jane screwed round in her seat to see if it might be Lady Chevington, but all she saw was a dark shape which might have been a young man or a boy.

'I am relieved to see Cooper found those children,' His Lordship said when they had safely negotiated the pony and trap and he had acknowledged the farmer's raised hand with a slight inclination of his head. 'Children should be loved and cared for, not allowed to run wild.'

'Yes, sir.'

The older man sat back in his seat and regarded his young companion as if seeing him for the first time. But for him, Timothy might very well have been like those two children, penniless and unloved, forced to make his own way in a hostile world, but the knowledge gave Geoffrey no satisfaction. He felt deeply sorry for the boy. Brought up by a succession of housekeeper-nannies in a small house in Islington leased for the purpose, he had, in all his seventeen years, never had a mother's love, and His Lordship was well aware how inadequate he had been as a substitute, however much he indulged him with the material things of life. Walton Grange was a case in point. He had bought the small house in a neighbouring village and staffed it so that Timothy could have somewhere to call home, a place to come to during university vacations. 'It will be near enough for me to visit you,' he had said. 'It is time you had your own establishment.' But it did not make the task he had set himself any easier. Timothy was growing into a fine lad, a real gentleman's son, and it was time he was told the truth.

The sight of the girl in the stubble field had finally decided him. She had stirred a memory of another wild, laughing girl, whose laughter had turned to tears when her child had to be given up. 'Get rid of that bastard,' she had been told by those around her. 'Get rid of it or be turned out.' But she would not leave the little scrap at the workhouse door and instead had sent an impassioned plea to His Lordship. Seventeen years ago that had been – years in which Geoffrey had come from acting out of a sense of duty to acting from love, made all the more poignant because he had not been able to tell anyone about it, not even the child himself.

Now the time for prevarication was over and he did not know how to begin. 'You liked the house, didn't you?'

'Yes, sir. It's very generous of you.'

'Before we reach Cambridge, I have something to tell you.' He rapped on the roof with his cane and the coach was brought to a halt. 'We'll take a walk, shall we?'

It was cooler once they had left the vehicle and walked into the shade of a small copse. Geoffrey stopped and faced the boy, clearing his throat. 'Timothy, I have something to say which may shock you, but you have to be told and I think today is an appropriate time. I know you will take it like a man of the world.'

Timothy, at seventeen, already considered himself a man. He was as tall as he was likely to be, which was only a couple of inches below six feet, he dressed like a man, in frockcoat or tails, and he had found out about women through the servant who had cleaned his bedroom at school. He had a generous allowance which permitted him to indulge in manly things like going to the races, gambling at cards and taking the occasional drink. He was hail-fellow-well-met. He had learned early in life that you could almost always buy your way into favour and he had no compunction about doing that, just so long as his companions suppressed their curiosity about his background. It was something he was decidedly touchy about and there had been one or two bloody noses among his schoolfellows before they had been convinced that his generosity had a price.

Now, perhaps, the questions which had caused this sensitivity were about to be answered. He realised, as he waited for His Lordship to go on, that his heart was beating fast and his hands were trembling. He clasped them tightly behind him, saying nothing.

'You may have wondered why I took on the task of bringing you up, of being your guardian.'

'I expect you were asked to do so by my father before he died.' His lack of parents was the hub of his disquiet about himself, but Timothy had never dared to question His Lordship about them; it was almost as if he were afraid that the reality would not live up to what his imagination had painted for him.

Lord Chevington smiled ruefully. 'Timothy, I am not only your guardian, I am ...' He cleared a throat which had suddenly become dry. 'I am your father.'

'*My father?*' The boy stared at the man incredulously for a full minute, then, as the news sank in, his thoughts raced ahead. He was the son of a baron, a man with acres and acres of country estate, a London house and numerous business interests including railway building. He had always known His Lordship was wealthy and more than generous, but to be related to him by birth! The implications were enormous. It was common knowledge that Lord Chevington, though married many years, was childless. Until this startling revelation. If he were the only child ...

Lord Chevington watched the changing expressions cross the boy's face, a face so like his own, with its clean-cut features, a firm, almost stubborn chin, high cheekbones and well-shaped brows. There was shock there and delight – and an ill-concealed avarice that sent ice into the older man's veins. He spoke quickly to cover his dismay. 'Perhaps I should have told you before this.'

'Why didn't you?' Timothy could not keep the excitement from his voice. To inherit not only the wealth of the Chevingtons, but the title too – that would be something, an answer to all the ribaldry and taunts he had endured at school. One day to be Lord Chevington!

'I wanted to be sure you would understand.'

'But I don't. If I am your son, your only son ...'

'You are at this moment.' Lord Chevington lifted his tails and sat on the trunk of a fallen tree. 'Come and sit by me, Timothy.'

Even the boy's movements were like his father's as he obeyed. 'Why haven't I known until now? Why don't I live at Chevington House with you?'

'Because, Timothy, although you are my son, you are not Lady Chevington's. You are not my heir.' He paused when he heard the boy gasp, but ploughed on, unable to stop. 'I had a liaison ...'

The dream faded and left a hollow emptiness in the pit of Timothy's stomach. His racing heart slowed almost to a stop and he felt sick. 'A bastard,' he whispered. 'A penniless bastard.'

'Not quite penniless.' His Lordship attempted a smile. 'You will always be well provided for.'

'In secret! At the mercy of your charity?' He jumped to his feet so that he towered over his father and stood looking down at him. 'Why did you have to tell me? *Why?*' There were tears streaming down his face, but there was anger rather than misery in his voice. 'Why couldn't you let me go on believing I was your ward?'

Geoffrey Chevington stood up slowly, almost wearily, and faced the boy. They were of much the same height though Timothy had the slimness of youth and his hair was much darker. 'You are old enough and man enough to be told the truth.' He wished, with all his heart, he could retract them, but the words had been said and could not be unsaid; all he could do was to try and mitigate the hurt. 'Nothing has changed between us.'

'Nothing changed! How can you say that? Everything has changed. You have ruined my life. I am a bastard ...'

'That is not a word I care to use.' Oh God, what had he done?

'But it's the truth, is it not?' Timothy's voice was loud, echoing among the trees, full of hurt and bitterness. 'You can't wrap it up in fancy words and make it any different, can you?'

Lord Chevington reached out to put a hand on his son's arm, but Timothy shrugged him off. 'I always looked up to you and respected you,' he said bitterly. 'Damn it, I loved you! You were my hero, my benefactor, someone who could do no wrong. Now I learn you are nothing but a ...' He could not think of an epithet bad enough.

'I have erred only once and I do not regret it because it gave you to me and you have afforded me a great deal of joy.' Geoffrey paused, watching the boy's face, but there was no softening in his expression;

his rage was almost tangible. 'And you have not been unhappy, either, have you?'

'Not until now.' It was a cruel answer and the boy felt a certain satisfaction in the expression of hurt which flickered in his father's eyes.

'I knew the news would shock you, perhaps that's why I delayed so long. I am sorry—'

'Sorry! Is that all you can say? In one breath you tell me you have sired me and in the next that you have disinherited me.' It had always been a source of puzzlement, if not irritation, that he was never allowed to visit his guardian's country mansion. Even today, when they had passed the gates on the way to Walton, he had wondered why they had not turned into them. Now the reason was all too clear.

'While Lady Chevington lives . . .'

'Does she know about me?'

'Not that you are my son. She knows I am guardian to the child of an old friend, that is all. It would be unwise for you to meet because you are so like me and I have never been able to lie to her successfully.' The admission was quietly spoken and hid a great deal of regret. He would have liked nothing better than for Constance to know and accept the truth, but her own childlessness was a cross she had to bear and knowing he had a son through someone else would only double the pain. He loved her too much to tell her. 'While there is still a possibility of a legal heir, the situation will not change, cannot change, but you can visit Chevington when Her Ladyship is away. When she stays with her sister in London or goes to Bath in high summer, we can tour the estate and spend some time together. If you are living at Walton Grange, it will be convenient, won't it?' His voice had taken on a placatory tone, which was not lost on Timothy. It made him realise how important he was to his father, that he could, except for the one thing he wanted most, twist him round his little finger.

'Who was my mother? Was her name Myson?'

'No, I called you that.'

'Why?'

'It was all I could think of, that you were *my son*.'

Timothy grimaced; even his name was an invention; there was no family tree, no roots at all. 'Did you love my mother?'

Did he? Lord Chevington didn't remember that so much as the tears pouring unchecked down her cheeks onto the cheap shawl in which the child was wrapped. Her anguish lived with him still. The

14

infant had been asleep and had slumbered on, even when she had run away, leaving him to stare, mesmerised, at the tiny bundle of life she had thrust into his arms, a life his inconsiderate actions had brought into the world. No mother should be asked to give up her child like that; no man had a right to use a woman's body so uncaringly. His own guilt and shame haunted him long after the memory of the girl and his passion for her had faded into nothing. 'No,' he said slowly. 'I do not think so.'

'No. Do you even *remember* her?'

'Yes, I remember, but it was just a passing fancy.'

'A passing fancy! No home, no proper parents, no name even. I am nothing, a nobody.' He was suddenly reminded of the children they had seen playing in the stubble field and His Lordship's interest in them. 'I'm worse off than those urchins. They at least had a name and a proper mother and father.' He stopped suddenly, wanting to hurt and hurt again. 'Or are they your bastards, too?'

'Certainly not. I've never seen either of them before.' It was on Geoffrey's tongue to berate the boy for his impertinence, but he decided not to; he had distressed him enough without adding a scolding. 'I was concerned for them, that's all. Children should be loved and treasured and they clearly were not.'

'And you think you have loved and treasured me?' Timothy gave a bitter laugh. 'Not enough to marry my mother, it seems. Who was she? Did she love me? No, she couldn't have or she'd not have let me go.'

'Timothy, it wasn't like that at all ...' Geoffrey stopped speaking because the boy had turned from him and marched angrily back towards the coach. Slowly he got up and followed him; later, perhaps, he might listen.

They rode on in silence, both brooding, the one annoyed that he had handled things so badly and the other fuming with bitterness and resentment, hating the man on whom he depended so totally. Timothy would have liked to make some theatrical gesture of defiance, to have marched out of his father's life forever, but grown men did not indulge in histrionics when the result could be penury. Besides, he ought to inherit Chevington, the man owed him that, and the only way he could bring it about was to stay on good terms with him. One day his bastardy would not matter. One day he would look the world in the eye and the world would have to acknowledge him.

By the time they had arrived at the lodgings His Lordship had taken for him in Cambridge, Timothy had managed to calm himself. He produced his most charming smile, a smile which could melt the hardest heart, let alone that of a father who loved him. 'I am sorry for my outburst. It was shock, nothing more. I expect I'll get used to the idea in time.'

Lord Chevington let out his breath in a huge sigh of relief, regretting that the boy was now too old to embrace, because he felt like kissing him. Instead he smiled. 'Nothing has changed; we will go on just as before and when you come down from Cambridge there will be a place for you in my railway ventures.'

Timothy was not sure he wanted to work for his living; he was not at all sure he wouldn't just as soon have the carefree life of the Winterday children, who were not weighed down by bastardy, nor concerned with their place in the world. But they were dirty and poor, and poverty was certainly not something he would wish on himself. He had never been short of any of the material things of life and he never intended to be. He followed his father into the lodgings, musing on how he could shape his own future the way he wanted it. The two children in the stubble field, who had unwittingly brought about the disclosure, were forgotten.

Chapter Two

Sarah Jane, made uncomfortable by the scrutiny of the three men and the lady sitting at one end of the large oval table, gripped her brother's hand and stared defiantly back at them. She was acutely aware of the smudges of dirt on her blouse and the creases in her skirt, and that the only comb her hair had seen that morning was ten fingers raked through it. And her brother – her responsibility – looked even more unkempt; his clothes were almost in tatters and his curls were so filthy it was difficult to tell that they were supposed to be blond. No wonder these respectable guardians of the workhouse looked so contemptuous.

But the lady was not contemptuous, and it was she who caught Sarah Jane's attention. She was so beautiful she took the girl's breath away. She had softly coiled fair hair under a flower-trimmed bonnet, blue eyes and pink lips that smiled sweetly. As for her clothes, Sarah Jane had never seen anything like them. She wore a mauve tiered skirt over huge hoops and each tier was edged with lace in a darker shade. There was lace around the neck of her bodice and more on her flared oversleeves. Sarah Jane gazed in wonder, ignoring the other people in the room, and even, for a moment, forgetting her brother.

'Make your curtsey to Lady Chevington,' Matron commanded, digging her in the small of the back. The matron was an enormous woman, six feet tall and almost as broad, wearing a blue silk dress over several layers of stiffened petticoats. Her hair, under a prim white cap, was grey and she had the merest suggestion of a dark moustache. From her belt hung a huge bunch of keys which jangled as she moved. Billie, if not Sarah Jane, was already terrified of her.

Sarah Jane wobbled precariously as she attempted to bend her knee, unable to take her eyes off Lady Chevington. She was so perfect, so pale and squeaky clean and not a hair out of place, she made Sarah Jane feel like a crawling insect, fit only to be stamped on.

'Well my dears, let us have some knowledge of you. Names first.'

17

Sarah Jane dragged her attention from Lady Chevington to the man who had spoken. He was fatter and younger than the other two and had a ruddy complexion and a bulbous nose, topped by a thatch of ginger hair. He wore a brown tweed suit, a canary yellow waistcoat and spotted cravat. The other two were both dressed in an indeterminate grey which made him seem like a parrot between rooks. By the same token, Lady Chevington was a bird of paradise.

'I'm Sarah Jane Winterday and this here's Billie,' Sarah Jane said, straightening her back and tilting up her chin. She had done no wrong and had nothing to be ashamed of; she would not cringe. ''e's me brother.'

'Winterday?' Lady Chevington asked.

'Yes, ma'am.'

'Yes, my lady,' the matron corrected her.

'Never mind,' Her Ladyship said gently, then to her fellow guardians. 'I have heard of the family. His Lordship asked me to look out for them.' She turned back to the children. 'Have you no relatives, uncles or aunts, to look after you?'

'No.' Sarah Jane paused and then seeing the matron's disapproving look, added, 'My lady.'

'How old are you, child?'

'I'm thirteen, Billie's seven.'

'You had better admit them,' one of the grey men said, addressing the matron. 'Send the boy to the infants' ward and find the girl some useful employment.'

Matron turned and left the room, returning a few minutes later accompanied by a very old crone with a long nose and equally long chin. Her hair was white and stuck out at all angles from beneath her cap. She fixed piercing blue eyes on Billie and held out a skinny hand. 'Come you on, boy.'

She advanced on Billie who ran and hid himself behind his sister. When she attempted to lever him out by his thin arms, Sarah Jane pushed her away. 'Leave him be!' she shouted. 'Leave him be! He don't wanna go.'

'He has to,' the old crone said. 'He has to come with me.'

Sarah Jane locked both arms around her brother who had buried his face in her bosom, and faced the two women while the guardians looked on, apparently reluctant to interfere. 'I won't let you take him.'

'You most certainly will,' Matron said through gritted teeth; she would be damned if she would allow this chit to defy her, and in front of the guardians, too. She grabbed Sarah Jane's arm in a grip that made the girl wince. 'Now come with me and leave your brother to Mrs Hewitt. She knows what is best for infants.'

'She don't know what's best for Billie,' Sarah Jane insisted, planting her feet squarely to resist the pressure. 'He has to stay with me.'

'He cannot. It's against the rules.' Both women began pulling and pushing, determined to lever Billie away from the little whirlwind who protected him.

'Enough. Stop this at once!' Lady Chevington hardly raised her voice, but Mrs Hewitt let go of Billie's ear lobe and Matron, who was in the act of cuffing Sarah Jane about the head, dropped her hand to her side.

'I will not have this undignified behaviour,' Her Ladyship said. 'It is not becoming to officers of this establishment. Now, I wish to speak to the children.' She beckoned to Sarah Jane. 'Come here, Sarah Jane, and do not be afraid. '

'Ain't afraid,' Sarah Jane said defiantly, but truthfully; such beauty could not also be cruel.

'I'm glad. How long have you been looking after your little brother?'

'Nigh on three years. Me Ma was sick, you see, and after she died Pa was killed and Farmer Cooper said we wasn't to stay in our 'ouse and we 'ad to come 'ere. We didn't wanna come, but 'e said Lord Chevington said 'e was to bring us.' It all came out in a rush. She smiled, remembering how the farmer had dumped them at the entrance to the workhouse, got back into the trap and driven away as if afraid that once the door had been opened, he would be sucked inside along with them. Well, she could hardly blame him for that. 'If I'd knowed you were goin' to take Billie away from me, I wouldn't 'ave rung that pesky bell an' asked to come in.' She would never forget the sound of that bell; it was like the death knell the church bell had rung at her father's funeral, paid for by Farmer Cooper, as if such generosity made everything right, and it had filled her with foreboding. She should have understood its message and followed the departing Farmer Cooper up the road as fast as Billie's legs could go.

'What would you have done if you hadn't come here?' The gentle voice of Lady Chevington broke her train of thought.

'I dunno, but I'd ha' thought o' somethin'.'

Her Ladyship's smile was radiant and sympathetic; it transfixed

19

Sarah Jane. 'Sarah Jane, could you provide for your brother, protect him from harm, give him the chances in life your father would have given him, had he lived?'

'I'd ha' tried.'

'I am sure you would, but wouldn't it be better to let us give him those chances? Here he will learn to read and write and figure; could you teach him that?'

Sarah Jane, who could not do any of those things herself, except simple money sums involving farthings, ha'pennies and shillings, shook her head glumly.

'And as for you, my dear, you could learn to cook and sew and launder, and that will stand you in good stead when it comes to finding employment. Then perhaps you and your brother could be together. We shall have to see what can be done.'

It sounded almost like a promise to Sarah Jane; at least enough of one to give her pause. If being good brought freedom any nearer, then she would have to try and be good. She prayed that Billie would understand that.

'Look on it as an apprenticeship, something you must do in order to better yourself,' Lady Chevington went on. 'You do want to better yourself, don't you?'

'Yes, I s'pose so.'

Her Ladyship smiled and leaned forward so that her scent wafted across Sarah Jane's nostrils like the perfume of a summer garden. 'It won't happen without some effort on your part, Sarah Jane. We all have to work towards what we want in life. We need a goal, every one of us.'

'Even you?'

'Impertinent hussy!' Matron hissed.

Her Ladyship ignored her and went on smiling at Sarah Jane. 'Yes, even me. It won't be easy, but will you think about what I have said?'

'Yes, my lady.' Sarah Jane looked towards Billie, who stood and glared at her as if she had turned traitor which, indeed, she had. 'Be good, Billie,' she whispered. 'I'll come and see you as soon as I can.' She stooped to hug him and then delivered him into the hands of the little woman, praying that he would understand she had no choice. She had no hope of winning a physical tussle with the two workhouse women, nor the words to argue her case with Lady Chevington. But she was not cowed. Oh no, she would live to fight another day.

Mrs Hewitt gave Billie what she considered a friendly smile, more for the benefit of Lady Chevington than the boy, then she took his hand and led him away. At the door, he turned his head to look back at Sarah Jane. His mouth was trembling and tears stood bright on his lashes, while down his cheeks they had cut canals through the dirt. She could do nothing but watch him being taken from her in a kind of stupor, unable to believe such a thing was happening. It was beyond anything she had imagined.

She was roused by Matron's strident voice. 'Make your curtsey and thank Lady Chevington for her kindness, Sarah Jane.'

Almost before she could obey, the big woman had seized her wrist and bustled her out of the door, along the corridor and out into the yard. Here were several groups of women, all in identical blue and white striped dresses, white aprons and caps and heavy black boots. They left off gossiping when they saw the matron and sullenly made way for her. She sailed between them, looking neither to right nor left.

Sarah Jane looked about for a friendly face but was greeted with blank disinterested stares. These women were lifeless, dull, lacking the vital spark to give them individuality; they were all replicas of each other, scrawny, broken-toothed, mild-eyed. She didn't want to become like that; she might as well be dead. Was that what Lady Chevington had meant about making something of herself? Rising above her surroundings? Being different? Being better? Whatever happened, she must not become like these women. She tried a smile in their direction, but receiving no response, broadened it to a grin.

'Yer'll laugh t'other side on yer face when yer've been here a spell,' someone called.

Matron stopped and turned, searching out the speaker, a girl a little older than Sarah Jane with short spiky hair which stuck out at all angles. 'Lizzie Dunne, come here,' she commanded, and when the girl obeyed, added, 'Sarah Jane has just joined us. Take her to the bath-house and after that direct her to Mrs Garby for work.'

Lizzie smiled at Sarah Jane, holding out her hand. 'Come alonga me.'

'And wash her hair, too,' Matron called after them, as they set off across the yard. 'And if you find even one living creature, you're to tell me and I'll have the barber cut it off.'

Sarah Jane looked puzzled and Lizzie laughed. 'She means yer hair.'

'There's nothin' alive in my hair,' Sarah Jane said indignantly. 'Nor I ain't dirty neither.'

21

'All new inmates have to bath, dirty or not. It's the rule.'

They entered a building on the other side of the yard and into a room where several grubby tin baths were ranged along a white-washed wall. The stone floor was wet and slippery and cold to Sarah Jane's bare feet. She stood in the middle of the room wanting to weep, but the trembling of her lip became a smile. Lizzie answered with a grin of her own. 'That's right, dearie, you've got the right idea. We must all laugh or else cry and what's the use o' cryin'? It don't change nothin'.'

'No.'

'Well then, off with yer clothes. You don't expect to bath with them on, do yer?'

Slowly Sarah Jane shook her head. She had become dumbstruck; everything was so new and strange and her thoughts and emotions so jumbled, she couldn't think of a single coherent thing to say. Besides, she was worried about Billie. Where had they taken him?

'Cat got yer tongue?' Lizzie was busy filling one of the baths from big tin jugs which stood ready.

Sarah Jane's unfocused gaze shifted and cleared. 'No.'

'Get on with it then. The sooner you start, the sooner it'll be done with.'

Slowly Sarah Jane unbuttoned her blouse and took it off, followed by her skirt and petticoat, then her chemie and finally her baggy pantalettes, symbol of her childhood. They were worn and grubby and she longed to be grown up enough to leave them off. Lizzie gave her a piece of coarse soap and a rough towel and left her.

Sarah Jane stepped in gingerly and sat down. The water was cold but it was such a hot day, she found it quite pleasant and began slowly soaping herself. Could she get herself as clean as Lady Chevington, she wondered, and then, how did she manage to *stay* clean? She didn't have to work, that was how; everything was done for her. 'One day I'll be a lady,' she said to herself. 'One day I'll wear silks and satins an' ride in a carriage and people will look up to me and obey me the minute I open me mouth like they do Lady Chevington. Cookin' an' sewin' an' launderin' jus' won't come into it.' She mused for a moment on the prospect of this, then fell to wondering why Lord Chevington had seen fit to interfere in her life. What was she to him? Was she glad or sorry? She supposed she was glad to have the worry of finding food and shelter lifted from her shoulders, and sorry her independence had been taken from her. It would not have mattered so much if Billie could have stayed with her. Did Lord Chevington know they would take her brother from her? Did he have any idea what it was like to have someone you love wrested from your side and be helpless to do anything about it? Had Billie understood she could not help it? She couldn't, could she? It was no good feeling guilty. But she did.

Lizzie returned with a bundle of clothes. 'For someone who weren't so keen to get in, you're taking your time,' she said, picking up more jugs of water and tipping them over Sarah Jane's head. 'You've lovely hair, Sarah Jane, so thick and long. I wish mine were like that; it never grew long again after they cut it off.' Sarah Jane looked up at her and a jug of water was inadvertently emptied over her upturned face. They laughed together, guiltless conspirators against a life they could not change, then Sarah Jane stepped out, towelled herself dry and dressed in the cheap workhouse uniform. She loathed it; it was hot and uncomfortable and fitted badly, and what was worse, the boots pinched. 'Do I have to wear those? I'm not used to anything on my feet.'

'In course you must.'

'How can I get to the infants' ward?' she asked, as she tucked the still-wet hair up into the mobcap Lizzie gave her.

'What d'you want to go there for?'

'They took me little brother there and he'll be missin' me.'

'Mixing ain't allowed. Men, women and infants all have separate places. Yer a woman and Billie's an infant, that's all there is to it. He'll be happy enough when he settles down. You'll have enough to do lookin' after yourself—' She was interrupted by a bell clanging loudly. 'Come on, it's dinner-time,' she said. 'Hurry up, it's meat today, so we must be quick afore it's all gone.' She grabbed Sarah Jane by the arm and tore off out of the door, across the yard and into a huge hall in the main building, hauling the girl along with her.

The room was filled with rows of long tables and crowded with inmates lining up for their meal. Sarah Jane and Lizzie joined the queue and were given a bowl containing two or three pieces of unidentifiable meat and some chunks of vegetable swimming in thin gravy, a hunk of bread and a mug of water, which they took to one of the tables.

At the far end of the room, at a table on a dais, sat the Matron, flanked by a little bearded man with a high-domed head so bald it looked like an egg, and a tall man in a faded black frockcoat and a purple cravat, who might once have been handsome. They were being served from china tureens by two inmates. 'Who are they?' Sarah Jane asked, pointing.

'The bald one is the Master, Matron's husband, the other's Mr Wistonby. He ain't an officer, but he ain't an inmate neither. He's Matron's brother and he can come and go as he pleases. The fat woman beside him is Mrs Garby. She's in charge of the laundry and you must go to her after dinner to be given your work, only watch out 'cos she'll drive you into the ground if you let 'er.'

Sarah Jane scanned the sea of faces. Everyone was attacking their food as if they hadn't eaten for a month. She watched in amazement as the pieces were fished out of the gravy and gobbled up, the gravy drunk from the bowl and the bread used to soak up the rest until the plates were clean and shiny. There was no sign of Billie.

As soon as the meal was over, Lizzie went to her own work in the sewing room and Sarah Jane was set to work in the laundry, deservedly the most unpopular place in the workhouse. It was airless and smelled of boiling linen and unwashed bodies. The heat from the steaming coppers was almost unbearable and water ran in rivulets down the walls, matched by the sweat on the faces of the women and girls who worked there. Sarah Jane, taking her cue from the others, stood over a wooden tub, rubbing with coarse soda and lye at a mountain of soiled garments and bed linen. The tub was too high for her and holding the washboard upright to drape the clothes over it, made the dirty water run down her arms and drip off her elbows. She was soon soaked through in spite of the sacking apron tied round her waist.

When she was finally freed to go to her supper, her hands were raw and her back ached so much she could think only of rest; she even gave away the slice of bread and little bit of dry cheese she had been handed for her meal. The long day had ended at last and she went to bed exhausted and thoroughly depressed. Lying on her straw-filled mattress, squashed between identical rows of wooden beds, the aches drained slowly from her stiff body and she tried to think. There were women about her in various stages of undress, preparing for bed or already between the coarse blankets, for only those in the infirmary were allowed sheets. They called to each other, said their prayers or not, as fancy or conviction dictated, snuffled and snorted and settled down to sleep.

Would every day there be the same, Sarah Jane wondered. If so, the sooner she left the better. It was all very well for Lady Chevington to advise her to stay. *She* hadn't been stuck at a washtub all day and *she* didn't have to sleep in a crowded dormitory without the one person she loved above all other. At home, in the farm cottage, she and Billie had shared a narrow bed, pressed together for warmth and companionship, whispering their secrets to each other long after both exhausted parents had fallen asleep in the bed on the other side of the room. From the day Billie had been big enough to be moved from the cradle at his mother's side, he had slept with Sarah Jane. Where was he now? Was he lying on a bed somewhere, alone and afraid? Was he crying for her? She could not let him weep alone; as soon as her room-mates were all asleep and the long dormitory was quiet, she told herself drowsily, she would creep away and look for him.

It was a bell's insistent clanging which roused Sarah Jane from slumber so deep she could not at first remember where she was. Then it all came back to her and she started up in an agony of guilt. How could she have allowed herself to drop off to sleep like that when Billie needed her? She scrambled from the bed and began throwing on her clothes, fumbling with the ties of her petticoat.

'What's the hurry?' Lizzie's drowsy voice came from the next bed.

'Got to go to Billie.'

'And then what?'

The question brought Sarah Jane up short. When she found her brother, what would she do? Looking down the rows of beds at the women – some with limbs flung out in sleep, others using their chamber pots, some scratching, some dressing without an ounce of modesty – she knew Billie would never be allowed into the room, let alone to share her bed. But she had to talk to him, to reassure him she hadn't forgotten him, if nothing else. 'I must see for myself that he's all right.'

'You'll only make things worse. They don't like people breakin' the rules and that's a fact. They'll beat yer and yer brother too, you can bet on it. The Master's a grand one with a cane an' he likes using it too ...'

'I ain't givin' in,' Sarah Jane vowed as they went to their meagre breakfasts. 'Me ma would turn in 'er grave. I want to know where they took Billie and how 'e's doin'.'

It was Lizzie who found out for her. There was a very efficient grapevine in the workhouse if you knew who to ask, and by the time they broke off for their dinner half-hour, she was able to give Sarah Jane news of her brother.

'Granny Hewitt took him over to the farm,' she said, referring to the compound where chickens and pigs were reared for the workhouse table. 'She locked him in the pigsty.'

'Why?' demanded Sarah Jane.

'Making the punishment fit the crime, 'cos he peed on the floor. She said 'e weren't fit to live with nobbut the pigs.' She paused, wondering whether she ought to tell Sarah Jane the rest, and deciding it might make her realise what she was up against. 'She went and forgot 'im. They brought 'im out this morning.'

'He was out there all night?' shrieked Sarah Jane, making everyone turn towards her in surprise; dinner-time was for eating as fast as you could and was not meant for conversation and certainly not for drawing attention to yourself by hollering. 'Alone?'

'Yes, 'cept the sow and 'er piglets.' Lizzie could not refrain from smiling, though she could see how agitated Sarah Jane was. 'By the time they fetched 'im, 'e looked like one 'isself. And stunk like one too. They threw a couple of buckets of water over 'im and went over 'im with a yard broom afore they'd let 'im indoors.'

Sarah Jane sprang to her feet but Lizzie pulled her down again. 'Don' worry, Sarah Jane, 'e's been bathed and fed and sent to the schoolroom. 'e's all right, really 'e is.'

But Sarah Jane would not listen. She hurried from the room, leaving Lizzie to finish what was left of her dinner, and hurried across the compound, making for a building where earlier she had glimpsed children of Billie's age. She had no coherent thought, no plan except to find her brother and take him out of the clutches of that dreadful old woman. She was peering into the schoolhouse window, trying to see Billie among the thirty or so pupils who bent over their slates, when she felt a heavy hand on her shoulder. 'What are you doing, girl?'

She turned to face the matron, defiant. 'I came to see me brother. I told him I would.'

'I am afraid you cannot. He is happy among his new friends and wants for nothing.'

'I don't believe it. 'e was locked in the pigsty and they threw water over 'im and ...'

'Who told you that nonsense?'

'It's not true?' Just for a moment, Sarah Jane wavered; in her experience, adults did not lie.

'Of course it's not true.'

'I want to see for meself. I want 'im to tell me 'e's 'appy.'

'He is happy, why shouldn't he be?' The matron nodded towards the schoolroom. 'He's in there. Can you hear him making a fuss?'

'No, but ...'

'Go back to your work.'

'No!' Sarah Jane stamped her foot in its heavy black boot. 'I hate it here. It's a terrible, terrible place. You can't make us stay. Bring him to me and give me back me own clothes ...'

'Be silent!' Matron dragged her away from the window in case Billie should hear her and make his own protest, though she doubted he would. Granny Hewitt's methods would not be approved by Lady Chevington but they had the desired effect; the boy was completely subdued. 'You will upset them all with your tantrums.'

'I want to leave,' the girl persisted, pulling herself away from the matron's steel-like grip and running to the classroom door. It crashed back against the wall as she flung it open and thirty small bodies skewered round on their benches and thirty pairs of eyes turned to look at her in silence. She scanned them, trying to pick out Billie's blond locks, not realising they had only a couple of hours before been swept from the floor beside the barber's chair and he was as bald as a coot. Before she could spot him, she had been dragged outside again and the door shut.

'Go back to your work, miss. In here if we are defiant and ungrateful we are punished, but if we are good and obedient, we are happy and content; it is a lesson you would do well to learn early. Your brother has already learned it.'

'Well, I won't. I want to take Billie away and never come back.'

'And pray, where would you go? How will you live?' The big woman was actually smiling. It was a grin of triumph because she knew there were no answers to questions like that.

Incensed, Sarah Jane advanced in a flurry of flying fists and began beating a useless tattoo on the woman's ample front. It had no more effect than a puff of wind, except to dislodge her cap and attract a crowd, who stood around gaping, speculating on what would happen next.

'That's enough, girl,' the woman said, dragging Sarah Jane across the yard away from the infants' section, away from Billie, who had suddenly become aware of what was happening and was yelling her name at the top of his lungs while Mrs Hewitt hauled him back to his seat. 'We shall see what's to be done with you. You've a mite too much spirit for one in your circumstances.' She pulled up short when they reached the main building on the other side of the compound and met the Master coming out. 'Alfred, we have a rebel here. She has attacked me. What shall we do to teach her manners?'

'Well,' he answered slowly, as if the punishment needed a great deal of thought. 'For an unprovoked attack on you, my dear, who are the very essence of kindness and compassion, nothing less than a beating will do.'

'No,' Matron said quickly, making Sarah Jane look up in surprise; she would hardly have expected the big woman to object to that. 'Beating's too quick. The attic, I think. Let us see if she is ready to apologise tomorrow. If not, she will stay there until she does.' She turned to Herring, the workhouse odd-jobman who was also Matron's eyes and ears when it came to knowing what was going on among the inmates. 'Take her up. And she's to have bread and water for supper and nothing else. Is that understood?' To Sarah Jane, she said, 'Go and ponder on your wickedness. Perhaps tomorrow you will be penitent.'

Resisting the temptation to answer back and because there was nothing else she could do, Sarah Jane followed the little man into the main building, up two flights of stairs and along a corridor to some steps which disappeared through a hole in the ceiling.

'Up you go,' he said, pointing.

Sarah Jane hesitated. 'What's up there?'

'Only the roof. If you behave and say sorry tomorrow, you'll be let down.'

'Well, I won't, so there!'

He laughed. 'We shall see. We shall see. Now, up you go or shall I give you a helping hand?' He leered at her and his hand went up her skirt and groped over her bare bottom, now without the worn pantalettes. She gave a little scream and scurried up the steps to escape him, pulling herself through the trap door out of his reach. He followed part of the way up, then she heard the door being pulled across and bolts being pushed home on the other side and she was alone in a tiny room, tucked between the rafters under the slates of the workhouse roof.

She was seething with resentment and a huge sense of injustice. It wasn't fair. She sat on the floor and leaned back against one of the heavy roof trusses, hugging her knees to her chest and screwing her eyes tight shut in an effort to hold her tears at bay. She must not cry, she must not, weeping would not help Billie or herself, but oh, how she wished she could bury her head in her mother's lap and feel her gentle hand on her hair, soothing her with quiet words. But her mother was gone, her father too, and now Billie had been wrested from her and she had no one, no one at all. Why had she allowed Farmer Cooper to browbeat her? Why had she listened to Lady Chevington who had lulled her with soft words and gentle smiles into trusting her? Why had she been so gullible? She should have tried harder to find work, she should have been prepared to beg and steal, anything to stay out of this terrible place. It was no more than a prison and neither she nor Billie had done anything to deserve it.

The tears fell at last, streaming one after the other down her cheeks and dropping, unheeded, off her chin onto her arms – tears of sheer misery, of self-pity, but most of all, of remorse. She had failed Billie, broken her promise to look after him and she could not forgive herself. 'Ma,' she sobbed. 'Oh Ma, what shall I do? What *can* I do?' But there was no one to answer her and eventually she slid down to the floor and fell into a troubled sleep and did not wake until she heard the bolts being drawn and Herring's head appeared through the trap, and by that time she had decided to apologise.

It was not so much the chilly, cramped quarters and the loneliness – especially the loneliness – but the realisation that there was nothing to be gained by making a stand; stamping her feet and demanding rights she knew she did not have would do no good at all. She would have to learn patience and so would Billie. But she would have her revenge. One day Matron, and all those like her, would have to look up to Sarah Jane Winterday, just as they did to Lady Chevington. *She* would be able to command *them*. But to do that she must think positively. 'Blessed are the meek,' she said to herself, quoting an almost-forgotten Sunday-school text, then added, with a wry grin, 'But not for long.'

Matron's sitting room was a clutter of furniture with small lace-covered tables, dark mahogany chairs, glass-fronted cupboards filled with china, and on every available space stood an ornament or a picture or a potted plant. Sarah Jane wondered how the big woman managed to squeeze herself between them without knocking anything to the floor.

'Good,' Matron said, when Sarah Jane had delivered her apology and promised, with tongue in cheek, to turn over a new leaf and be a model inmate. 'There will be no need for us to acquaint Her Ladyship of this, for to be sure, she would be very disappointed in you if she knew. Now go back to your work. If you do well, it will be all the better for you when the time comes to go outside.'

Sarah Jane seized on the word 'outside' and clung to it like a drowning man to a lifebelt. Outside meant roads and trees and hedges and houses; it meant sunshine and wind and bare feet, but above all, it meant freedom. Outside was the answer to everything. With every appearance of cheerfulness she returned to her work in the laundry and at midday took her plate of broth and sat beside Lizzie at the meal table.

'You're back, then.'

'Yes, but I've got to see Billie somehow.' She wanted to tell him of her new policy of patience, to convey a little of her own optimism so that he could share it.

'You'll see him in church on Sunday, might even get to sit near him. You could slip him a note.'

'I can't write. And if I did, Billie couldn't read it – not yet anyway; perhaps when he's been at his lessons longer.'

'Then yer'll just 'ave to bide yer time.'

Time! She had all the time in the world and no time at all. Every day she stayed in the Union was a day of her life lost, every day was a day wasted, a day of drudgery. It was not that she was lazy; she was prepared to work as hard as anyone if it meant release, but her labours availed her nothing – no praise, no blame, no pay, no further-ance of her goal. Fame and fortune would be a long time coming if she waited for them to come to her; something had to be done. But first she had to make contact with Billie.

The inmates left the confines of the Union each Sunday to walk, crocodile-fashion, to the village church for morning service. The follow-ing Sunday, Sarah Jane found herself sitting a few rows behind her brother. She longed to rush up to him and hug him, but his spiky blond head was bent dutifully over his clasped hands and he seemed unaware of her. After the service, the younger children trooped out first and they caught sight of each other. She had expected him to try to speak to her or at least to show he was pleased to see her, but he had done nothing but smile slowly and that had wrung her heart. She ached for freedom, longed to kick the dust of the Union behind her and go out into the world, and she had assumed that Billie felt the same. But he hadn't looked unhappy. It was as if Lizzie and Matron and everyone else had been right; he no longer needed her. She didn't like the feeling at all.

In the months that followed she saw little of him. On Sundays he was in his pew a few rows in front of her and during the week she sometimes caught a glimpse of him crossing the compound with his slate under his arm, or playing tag with his classmates, and though he always raised his hand to her if he saw her, his manner was impersonal; he had become a stranger to her.

Occasionally, through the grapevine, she heard that he had been punished for some misdemeanour, usually for failure to learn his lessons and one day, driven by a rumour that he had been given a severe beating by the workhouse master, she tried once again to go to him, but was hauled back to her own part of the compound, her mission unaccomplished.

'You have been warned,' Matron had said sternly. 'Do you want to be locked up again?'

'No, Matron.'

'Then go back to your duties. I promise you your brother is quite content.'

'Then why was he thrashed? What did he do?'

'He is a wicked, ungrateful boy and that is all you need to know. He deserved his punishment. Now go back to your work or it's the attic for you and bread and water, do you hear?'

Angry and frustrated, she had returned to the drudgery of the laundry, wondering how long it would be before Billie forgot she was his sister and had promised to look after him. What an empty promise that had been!

Her only hope, she decided, was to make some progress towards her ambition. It was an ambition she revealed to no one, not even Lizzie, because she would have laughed at her. How could she, an unlettered pauper with no family background, hope to reach the dizzy heights of being a lady? But even to make a start, she needed basic accomplishments, an education first and foremost, for whoever heard of a lady who couldn't read?

The only volumes to be had in the workhouse were the Bible, religious tracts and simple moralising stories – these so tattered with being handed round and round, squabbled over, wept and laughed over, they were hardly legible. Some even had pages missing, and what cries of frustration and annoyance that caused. The more she thought about it, the more Sarah Jane realised what she was missing, not only in practical ways like writing letters, but the sheer pleasure reading afforded. She had seen them, those who could read, quietly tucked in a corner of an evening or hunched on their beds, making the best use of the last minutes of summer daylight, completely immersed in the written word. It was as if nothing existed outside the pages of their books.

The answer lay in the infirmary. The sick wards were on the ground floor of the block which divided the men's from the women's quarters and there were two, one for men and one for women. She had been sent to the men's section with a message from Matron to the visiting physician a few weeks before and had paused to chat to the inhabitants of the long rows of beds. They were old or handicapped rather than ill and had been so obviously pleased to see her, she returned whenever she had a spare hour after her day's work was done. She listened to their complaints, heard their life stories, tucked them up, ran errands for them and smuggled in the occasional bit of tobacco or jug of beer. She was always willing, always cheerful, and they loved her and teased her to make her laugh. Her laughter brought sunshine into their lives and made them feel young and whole again. The rough women who did the nursing became used to seeing her there and made no effort to stop her.

She had seen Matron's brother there, moving from bed to bed, helping the patients with their correspondence. She intended to ask him a favour, but she would have to choose a time when there were no attendants about because talking to him was bound to be an infringement of some rule or other which merited punishment. She was learning to be wily. And patient.

Chapter Three

*T*he man in the infirmary bed might have been any age. His toothless cheeks were sunken and wrinkled, his bony hands, clutching the clay pipe Sarah Jane had filled for him, were distorted with arthritis, and yet his eyes held a spark of something that said he was a man still and not too old to appreciate a pretty girl; to savour the long white neck and firm young breasts of a fifteen-year-old approaching womanhood, to picture the trim waist and long limbs which he knew were hidden beneath the unflattering workhouse uniform. The trouble with being old was that your mind refused to come to terms with the frailties of your body. 'If I were in my prime . . .' His voice trailed away as his imagination painted what he could no longer have in reality.

Sarah Jane laughed, tossing back her mane of beautiful red hair, freed from the damp white cap she wore all day in the wash-house. 'I must go now, I've me work to do.'

'You'll come back?'

'Yes.' She stood up, straightened the bedcovers and walked down the length of the ward, unaware of the effect she had on the occupants of the beds she passed, which ranged from simple admiration to undisguised lust.

Thomas Wistonby, who sat with a patient near the door with his writing materials on his knee, watched with wry amusement. The girl carried herself with a natural grace and held her head up, unlike so many of the inmates who slouched around with lacklustre expressions. She was likely to turn into a rare beauty and he could wish himself a few years younger, though at thirty-eight he did not consider himself old, not by any means.

Seizing the longed-for opportunity, she stopped in front of him. 'What are you doing?' she asked, knowing the answer perfectly well.

'Writing a letter for this poor unfortunate.' He indicated the one-legged man in the bed.

She sat down on the end of the bed. 'Can I watch? I want to write to me brother. They won't let me talk to 'im.'

'Who won't?'

'Matron and Granny Hewitt. She once shut 'im in the pigsty all night, I know she did. And scrubbed him down with the yard broom. There weren't no cause to do that.'

He smiled because her anger was still so evident it made her cheeks pink and the lovely green eyes blaze. 'What do you want to say to him?'

'I want to tell 'im I ain't forgot 'im, that I'll get 'im outa 'ere as soon as I'm able. I want to know why 'e was thrashed. 'e's not a bad boy and he's missin' me, no doubt. When I'm ready to leave, I mean to write and tell him, 'cos 'e 'as to come too.'

He smiled, unwilling to put her off because he found himself wanting her company. Her green eyes had a life in them he had not seen in a woman's eyes for many a year, and her red hair, long and uncontrolled, shone so that he felt an almost overwhelming urge to reach out and touch it. She had the innocence of youth and a natural vivacity which aroused desires he thought had been suppressed forever; it was deliciously disturbing. 'And you think watching me will help?'

'Yes.'

'Then stay and welcome, is that not so, Jacob?'

'Aye,' the man in the bed agreed, 'but let's get on with it.' He stumbled over what he had to say, but Wistonby, dipping his quill in the bottle of ink he had taken from the leather bag slung from his shoulder, continued to write with a flourish, oblivious to the pauses and changes of mind of the man who was dictating. It was as if one bore no relation to the other, although both ended simultaneously.

'There,' Wistonby said, turning the paper round and handing it to the patient. 'Put your mark at the bottom.' He pointed with the feather of the quill, before handing it to him. 'Just there.'

His client looked dubiously at the letter. 'It's a long letter.'

'Do you want me to shorten it?' Wistonby demanded. 'For if you do, just say which words you don't want.'

'That's not fair,' Sarah Jane objected, knowing Wistonby usually charged by the word and because few inmates had any money, his payment was often taken in kind, in a plug of tobacco or a small piece of jewellery. 'How can he know which is important and which ain't?'

'Fair or not, it's business,' Wistonby said. 'Without it the world of commerce grinds to a halt, the wheels of industry stop turning.' And as Sarah Jane opened her mouth to protest: 'It's no good pleading for him. I've a living to make; if I felt sorry for everyone I did business with, I would be ruined.'

Sarah Jane grinned mischievously. 'I thought you was already ruined, else why are you in here and not riding round in a grand carriage with four fine horses and a new suit of clothes to your back?'

'Ah!' He took the letter, sealed it with wax softened with the help of a taper from the pot-bellied stove and put it in his leather bag with the ink, taper and wax. 'Perhaps one day I might tell you the story of that, but let's just say I was too soft, that I didn't press for my bills to be paid and that's why I'm brought so low. 'Tis only temporary. I shall soon be on my feet again.'

Sarah Jane was not at all sure she believed him, but realised it would be tactless to say so. 'I want to do business with you,' she said.

'You want a letter written to your brother?'

'No, I want to learn to read first. I'll get nowhere till I do.'

'And you mean to get somewhere, do you?'

'Yes, I do, and don't you go tellin' me I can't.'

'You can do whatever you've a mind to,' he said, as an idea came to him which he found exciting. 'But 'tis a lengthy business, learning to read. It cannot be done overnight.'

'I know that, silly.'

'It is also very costly. How do you propose to pay me?'

'I can work.'

'At what? What can you do in here, that anyone will give you ready money for?'

For a moment Sarah Jane was nonplussed, but she quickly recovered. 'Couldn't you wait until I get out and find a situation? After all, if I can read and write I'll have a better one, won't I?'

'I must look on it as a long-term investment, is that what you're saying?' He was smiling now, teasing her, knowing how much she wanted what she was asking for and wondering how far she would go to obtain it. 'There is something you could do for me, if you've a mind ...'

'What's that?'

He took her arm and drew her towards the door, speaking softly. 'You could be kind to an old man.'

'But I *am* kind. I'm kind to all the old men in here, you know I am. I run errands and sit with them and hold their hands when they ask me ...'

'And will you hold my hand?'

She looked at him with a puzzled expression which made him laugh. It wasn't that she knew nothing of the sex act – you couldn't sleep in the same small room as your parents and not find out about it; if he had been more explicit, she would have known immediately what he meant. 'Do you need someone to hold your hand?' she asked.

He was suddenly serious. 'Very much. It's many a long year since someone did that for me.'

''Tis the same for all of us in here,' she said softly. 'This is such a cold place and there is no love in it.'

'No love,' he repeated, unable to resist the temptation to put a bony finger up to stroke her cheek. 'How right you are. So, my little one, will you give me love in exchange for reading lessons?'

'Oh yes,' said Sarah Jane promptly.

'Tomorrow, then.' He paused as they arrived at the end of the corridor where the infirmary wing joined the main building. 'Come to my room after dark tomorrow. Do you know where that is?'

'No.'

He pointed to a stairway. 'It is on the first floor above the infirmary at the end of the corridor. I will leave the door ajar.'

Sarah Jane returned to her own section, bright-eyed and elated, and the next evening after her work was done, made her way stealthily to his room, telling the curious Lizzie she was going to help in the infirmary again.

Matron's parlour had been a clutter of knick-knacks; Thomas Wistonby's room was full of books. A whole wall was given over to them and more lay on the table; there was a pile on a desk, which was also littered with papers, as if she had interrupted some important work. Apart from the desk, there was a worn leather armchair and a sagging sofa covered in chintz and, in a corner, a four-poster bed with its curtains drawn. A good fire blazed in the grate, for it was autumn again. It was like stepping into another world and Sarah Jane stood and gaped.

He smiled. 'Come in, my dear. Do not be afraid.'

She advanced slowly. 'Can you read all these?' The sweep of her arm encompassed the books.

'Of course, and if you are diligent, you shall read them too.'

'What are they all about?'

'Almost every subject under the sun, but many are law books.' He took off his coat and hung it on a hook behind the door, before shutting it noiselessly. Then he untied his cravat and flung it on a table behind him. He was, she realised, seeing him newly shaved and in his shirt-sleeves, a well-proportioned man and nothing like as old as she had at first thought. His rather scruffy appearance and the way he slouched round the workhouse had led her to believe he was old and decrepit. He looked at her and his brown eyes suddenly lit with humour. 'Come and sit by me,' he said, sitting on the sofa and patting the seat beside him.

'You want payment in advance?'

He laughed aloud. 'Are you anxious to have it over and done with?'

'No,' she said, obeying. 'It's nice in here, warm and cosy.'

'Cosy,' he repeated, realising he would have to take things very slowly. But he was in no hurry. Her innocence was so refreshing, he was almost reluctant to despoil it. But he needed her, oh how he needed her! She would brighten days which had become wearisome in the extreme. It was not that he was ungrateful to Elizabeth for giving him a home when he was down on his luck, but here he had no social contact at all; the visits of the guardians afforded his sister and brother-in-law an occasional diversion, but the guardians did not know he lived under the Union roof and Elizabeth had told him it would be better if they did not learn of it. Now, here was this nubile beauty, unafraid and anxious to please, and he was going to make the most of it.

'You will not,' he said, stroking her hair with gentle fingers, 'tell anyone about your visit to me?'

''Course not. I ain't a fool.'

He laughed. 'Indeed you are not. Now, what shall we start with?' He stood up to look along the shelves for something fairly simple. 'Ah, this will do. I had forgotten I had it.'

'Why have you got so many books, Mr Wistonby?'

'Call me Thomas, my dear.' He turned suddenly from browsing through the book's pages, realising he did not even know who she was; he had been thinking of her as Clara. 'Tell me your name.'

'Sarah Jane Winterday.'

'Well, Sarah Jane, I have so many books because I am a lawyer and a scholar.' He returned to the sofa, sitting down very close to her.

'Why do you live here?'

'Why not?' He did not want to open old wounds. 'It is peaceful and it suits me.'

'Peaceful!' Her laughter rang out and he put his finger to his lips, turning his eyes to the door. 'Sorry,' she whispered. 'But it ain't peaceful, oh no it ain't.'

'Before you learn to read, my dear, perhaps you should learn to speak.'

'Can you learn me that too?'

'Teach you,' he corrected her. 'You learn, I teach. I can but try.'

'Will it take long?'

He smiled and put the back of his hand up to touch her cheek. 'Oh, a long, long time.' And his voice was wistful.

'But I ain't got the time.'

'"Haven't", not "ain't". Say, "I haven't the time".'

'I haven't the time,' she pronounced carefully, then giggled. 'That's how the gentry talk.'

'So it is.'

'Can you learn ... teach me to be a lady?'

'A lady? Now there's a thing!' He smiled and picked up her hand, putting the palm to his cheek. 'So soft,' he murmured. 'So soft.'

'That's 'cos me hands are always in the washtub,' she said disconcertingly. 'Tell me, can I get to be a lady?'

'My hands, not me hands.' He sighed and reached over to kiss her cheek, holding his breath for her reaction, but she did nothing, being too concerned about having her questions answered. 'I like you the way you are.'

'But I am a nobody.'

'There are advantages to that,' he said, remembering Clara. She had not been a nobody, that had been the trouble. Everything she did, everywhere she went, was noted and talked about, romances with young lawyers included. Sarah Jane might look up to him as a gentleman, but there were degrees of gentility and a struggling lawyer whose education had been paid for by a bachelor uncle, should not have aspired to the hand of the daughter of a Lord Justice. 'But how do you define a lady?'

She laughed. 'Why d'you use such long words all the time?'

'I suppose it is because I read a great deal,' he said. 'The more you read, the more you learn. Now, answer my question: why do you want to become a lady?'

'Because they are so shining clean and they smell nice and they can *make* people do things.'

He smiled. He had expected her to say something about being rich and elegantly dressed but Sarah Jane, he soon discovered, never did what was expected of her. 'Do what things?' he prompted.

'Like Lady Chevington does. If I was a lady, I'd make everyone do what I want.'

'So, it's power you're after. Why?'

'So's I can help Billie. I'd make the Master stop beating him. I'd look after all the little children a deal better'n in 'ere. They'd 'ave a proper school and warm clothes and puddin's and pies and meat every day.' Her eyes were bright with eagerness. 'An' the old men and women too.'

'Don't you want anything for yourself?'

''Course. Do you think I like slaving in here with nary a thank you, let alone bein' paid for it?'

'Things like that cost a great deal of money.'

'If I was a lady, I'd have money, wouldn't I?' she retorted.

'It is possible to be a lady and have no money, just as it's possible to be rich and powerful without being titled and, anyway, ladies are born, not made.'

'You mean I can never be one? Not even if I try real 'ard?'

'You might, in years to come, be able to pass yourself off as one, but goodness me, it will take a great deal of hard work. You might not consider it worth the trouble.'

'What sort of 'ard work? I ain't afraid o' work.'

He laughed. 'Oh, my dear Sarah Jane, I adore you.'

She looked at him, puzzled. 'Why are you laughing?'

'Because you make me happy.'

'I do?'

'Indeed you do. Now let us begin your first lesson.' He opened the small volume of mythical stories for children he had chosen and began picking out the letters for her. It was not a particularly practical book as a first primer, but Sarah Jane was an apt pupil and she soon became fascinated by the tales of Pegasus and Hercules, the Wooden Horse of Troy and Jason and the Golden Fleece. Her face disappeared beneath the veil of her hair as she bent over the pages.

After half an hour, he took her shoulders in his hands and turned her towards him, pushing the unruly locks away and holding her face in both hands. 'Sarah Jane,' he said gently. 'You know what I want from you?'

'You want me to be kind to you and hold your hand.' She paused, searching his face. 'But it is you who are kind to me, kinder than anyone has been since Ma and Pa died, and I 'ad to come in 'ere.' There were tears on her lashes. 'I don' know what I've done to deserve it.'

He couldn't do it, not then; the hard rising of his passion would have to be stilled for the moment but he could not restrain himself indefinitely. 'I think you should go now,' he said, standing up and moving away from her. 'You've done enough for one night. Come again tomorrow.'

'That's all?' She sounded surprised.

He could take her now, he told himself. He could satisfy the hunger for love which had plagued him ever since they had dragged him from Clara's dead body. Sarah Jane would never dare complain, and wasn't her desire to learn as great as his to possess her? She would acquiesce.

But was acquiescence what he wanted when he could have so much more with a little patience? He reached out and put his hand under her chin to raise her face, then stooping, put his lips to hers. They tasted of soap and salt – soap because she had washed extra carefully before coming, and salt because that was what she used to clean her teeth. 'Go now,' he said, opening the door and making sure there was no one in the corridor. 'Take care. And remember, not a word to anyone.'

She slipped out and he shut the door and sank back onto the sofa, put his head into his hands and groaned softly.

Sarah Jane could hardly wait for work to be finished the next day, so that she could return to her lessons. If Lizzie thought anything of her preoccupation or heightened colour, she made no comment, and Sarah Jane, mindful of her promise to Wistonby, told her friend nothing, except that she had to make another visit to the infirmary. She went to the lawyer's room the next night and the next, and each time she learned a little more, and on the third occasion, how the lessons were to be paid for.

He was gentle, curbing his own impatience, talking soothingly as if she were a nervous deer who might take fright and disappear from his life altogether, and that he did not want. He explored her body slowly, savouring the feel of the smooth young flesh, the firmly developing breasts, the flat belly, ankles, knees, thighs. 'My lovely girl,' he murmured. 'Be kind to a lonely, distracted man.'

She had been endeavouring to ignore what he was doing, continuing to read aloud, stumbling over some of the words, which he corrected mechanically, hardly listening, but now she turned to him with a smile and kissed his cheek. 'I am, but why are you distracted?'

'Because of you. Do you know you are nearly a woman?'

'Indeed I do.'

'And women love differently from children?'

'Do they?'

'They *make* love.'

'Oh, that!'

It was such an unexpected reply, he was taken aback, but then he could contain his frustration no longer. He took the book from her and put it on one side, then cradled her face in both hands. 'Oh, Sarah Jane, my tormentor. It's been so long, so long ...' He kissed her mouth very gently, then adding pressure, parted her lips and forced his tongue between her teeth, making her whole body tingle in a way which excited her. His mouth ranged over her face and into her neck. 'My sweet girl, my saviour,' he murmured, unbuttoning her blouse and burying his face in the cleft between her fast-developing breasts, which peaked dark and hard as he cupped them in his hands. 'Meet me halfway, please, my little dove.'

Slowly, oh so slowly, he asked a little more of her in the way of response until her whole body shivered and there was a queer warm sensation between her thighs, an involuntary opening of her most private self. She found herself clutching at him, digging her fingers into his back and winding her legs about his thighs, arching towards him in anticipation of she knew not what. When, at last, he thrust into her, she welcomed him joyfully. There was no calculation, no guile, unless it was the skilful way he brought her to a climax; there was nothing but a simple act of union, a mutual hunger to be satisfied. Oh, she had her reasons and so had he, but they were submerged in the pleasure of the moment. No one had ever told her it was wrong; morals didn't come into it. She gave because it was her generous nature to give.

Thomas had needed to prove himself still a man, not an empty, dried-up shell and, for him, it was like the easing of a long-endured pain. The relief was blissful enough to overcome guilt. If he had any regrets, it was that he had taken her virginity, which she had not seemed to prize as she should, but he consoled himself with the thought that someone would have taken it sooner or later, perhaps even one of the unsavoury inmates straying into the women's compound, and she might have lost it violently, and if not violently, then uncaringly, and he had surprised himself with how much he cared.

Sarah Jane herself seemed unconcerned and the lessons continued, though not every evening, otherwise she would not have been able to stay awake during the day. Sometimes they made love first, sometimes afterwards, sometimes not at all, but he blessed heaven that she seemed to have retained her innocence, and he realised nothing could sully that, because it was part of her nature; the learning to read and understand the ways of the world were more likely to corrupt her than he was. She made him happy, happier than he had been since Clara's violent death.

And Sarah Jane blossomed, and it was not so much their sexual activities, which she owned she enjoyed, but because of her growing self-confidence. Not only was she learning to read, she was learning about life – life in the country, life in the city, a little about government and social welfare and why workhouses were needed more than schools and, as far as Thomas Wistonby was able to tell her, about why people behaved the way they did. She could understand – or almost – why Billie had seemed to turn his back on her.

'He is growing into a man,' Thomas said one day, when she mentioned her brother. 'He has to stand tall among his fellows and not be tied to his sister's apron strings.'

'He ain't tied to me apron strings,' she said, forgetting the careful speech he was trying to instil in her; she always forgot it when she was worked up about something.

He smiled and threw up his hands. 'I give up. There is no point in spending hours teaching you when everything flies out of your head the minute something happens to bother you. Why are you upset?'

'I'm not. I saw Billie across the yard today and he hardly noticed me.'

'What did you expect? Billie has his own life. He is happy, just as you are, only in a different way. You are happy, are you not, my little dove?'

'Oh yes, but Billie does not have you.'

Her answer warmed him. 'He has made his own friends,' he said slowly, deciding to say nothing of what he had discovered about the latest beating; it would only reawaken her desire to leave and that he could not bear. If she knew that Billie had been thrashed for trying to run away, there would be no holding her, especially if she knew of his brother-in-law's perverted sense of justice. Bare backsides were not only beaten, they were used. He smiled suddenly; according to Herring, who had been watching through the keyhole and was so filled with glee he had to tell someone, Billie had saved himself by peeing all over the Master's groping hand and so enraged him, he had let the boy go. He could not tell Sarah Jane that. 'He was very young when he came in here,' he said, idly running his hand along her bare arm and up into her neck, making her shiver. 'He has become conditioned to it sooner than you.'

'Well, I shan't ever get used to it. I wonder you can stand it.'

'I can go out if I want to.'

'Yes, but you never do.'

'There's nothing to go out for.'

She wriggled herself closer to him and laid her head on his shoulder. 'You've got all you want in here, isn't that so?'

He kissed the top of her head. 'Yes, little one.'

'Have you ever been married?'

'Yes, a long time ago.'

'What happened?' When he did not reply immediately, she added, 'Don't you want to talk about it?'

'No.'

'When Ma died, Pa didn't want to talk about it, either. It was like he had wrapped himself in a big thick cloak, as if he was cold, and he had no room for anyone else in it. I wanted to talk to him, 'cos I could see he was hurting bad, but he wouldn't have it.'

'What happened to him?' he asked, forgetting to correct her.

'He died too.'

'Would that I had.'

'Oh, Mr Wistonby – Thomas – you must not talk like that, it's wicked.'

'But I am wicked. I killed her.'

'Killed her?'

'Oh, do not look so horrified. I did not murder her, I killed her with shame and disgrace.' He lived again the horror of those dreadful days. In order to impress Clara and pay court to her and, after their marriage, to maintain her in the style he thought necessary, he had borrowed. And when his debts had become due he had juggled his clients' accounts, manoeuvring the apostles they said, robbing Peter to pay Paul, convinced he was clever enough to cover up his illegal dealings and she would never need to know about them. He should have known he could not keep it up, that sooner or later, both Peter and Paul would want a reckoning on the same day. And when it had happened, he could not face her. He had left her a note and attempted to disappear.

They had pursued him, of course – her father, his creditors, other lawyers, the police. They caught him because he had had no preconceived plan for such an eventuality. And they told him Clara had tried to follow him on horseback, had loved him enough to want to stand by him and help him, but she had never reached him. Her horse had thrown her and she had died within hours. His lovely Clara, his adored wife was dead, and it was all his fault. While others set his house in order for him and her father paid his debts to hush it all up, he had been frozen with shock and could do nothing to help himself.

After the funeral, his father-in-law had turned from the open grave to face him. 'Now, sir, if you please, be gone from my sight, I never want to see you or hear your name mentioned again.'

He should have gone to prison, but it seemed he was to remain unpunished, for the family's sake. Elizabeth, bless her, had offered him a home and Chevington Union had been his prison and his refuge ever since; he rarely left it and had allowed himself to drift along, trying to forget why he was there, waiting for death to release him. Until Sarah Jane. Dear child, she deserved better than him, but he could not give her up. While she remained in the Union, he would continue to enjoy her, but he would never wantonly do anything to hurt her.

'I'm sure it was not as bad as that,' she said stoutly, accepting his reluctance to talk about something which he obviously found painful; she did not want to make him sad. 'I was moved to the kitchen today.'

Her voice brought him back from his reverie and he shook his brooding thoughts from him. 'You'll not learn much about cooking there.'

'Oh, but I can cook already. I often did when Ma was ill, not grand meals with lots of courses, but good simple food, better than we get in here, and that's a fact. Mrs Garby was pleased. She said I could help prepare the meals for the officers' table tomorrow.'

'I shall look forward to that,' he said gravely. 'And since you have finished your book, let us find you another. We will combine reading with cooking, shall we?' He ranged along the shelves until he found what he was looking for. 'This belonged to my mother, but you may have it.'

'To keep?' She took the book from his hands and opened its pages. It was not a printed book at all, but a notebook, written in a beautiful copperplate.

'It is my mother's receipt book,' he said. 'She enjoyed cooking, too.'

She flung her arms about him and kissed him. 'Oh thank you, thank you. I shall take very great care of it.'

'Mind you do.' Although he had said nothing to Sarah Jane, he realised that, sooner or later, their association would have to end, for nothing in life lasted forever and he wanted to give her something he valued, something to remember him by. 'It will help you to read handwriting as well as the printed page. Let us see how you manage with it.'

Sarah Jane, glowing with health and happiness for the first time since arriving at the Union, found it harder and harder to keep her secret. She had to tell someone or burst, and the only person she could trust was Lizzie Dunne. In any case, Lizzie had been remarking on the way she was speaking nowadays, although, according to Thomas, there was hardly any difference.

'You're getting to be a reg'lar madam,' she said, one evening when they were sitting together in the dormitory. 'Pickin' over yer food, though I suppose in the kitchen you get the leftovers from the top table, and mincin' about like you thought you was a lady.'

'Do I?' Sarah Jane asked eagerly.

'Do you what?'

'Behave like a lady?'

'Pretendin' don't make you one.'

'No.' She was silent for a minute, then she brought her book out from under her pillow. 'See what I've got.'

'Where d'you get that?'

So Sarah Jane told her. 'It was worth it,' she finished. 'He's a gentle old goat and I've become quite fond of him.'

Lizzie's mouth, already open in shocked disbelief, fell open still further. 'You mean you've done it more than once?'

'Oh yes,' said Sarah Jane cheerfully. 'I haven't got much of the reading yet, and I want to learn to write too.'

'But don't you know that's how babies are made?'

Sarah Jane laughed. ''Course I do. Didn't I help me Ma ...' she paused to correct herself ' ... my mother when Billie was born and the other little one who died?'

'Supposin' you was to, you know – have a baby?'

'Mr Wistonby thought of that. He gave me something, a little sponge. I soak it in vinegar ...'

'And it works?'

45

'Has done so far.'

'But whatever will Matron or the Master say if they find out?'

'They're not to know, for who's to tell them? No one goes to Thomas's room after supper.'

'Sarah Jane, how can you talk so?' Lizzie didn't know whether to be frightened or envious. 'It's wicked. You shouldn't oughta do it afore you're married. Don't you know enough to know that?'

'What's marryin' got to do with it?'

'Everything. Oh Sarah Jane, you're supposed to save yourself for yer husband! A man expects his wife to be a virgin.'

'What's that?'

Lizzie sighed. 'A girl what's never done it.' She looked at Sarah Jane's puzzled face. 'You know – *it*. Once it's done, there's no undoin' it. Don't you want to find a man who'll marry you?'

She had, Sarah Jane noticed, implied that any man who married her would be doing her a favour; it just showed how differently they viewed life. She began to have doubts about the wisdom of saying anything to Lizzie. Had she horrified her friend to such an extent that the enormity of the secret was beyond her ability to keep? 'Promise you'll not say a word to a living soul,' she urged her. 'Swear it.'

'I swear, indeed I do.' Lizzie crossed herself fervently and although she kept her promise, it didn't stop Sarah Jane's secret from coming to light.

One autumn evening almost a year later, Matron, looking for her brother to ask his advice about something she could not afterwards remember, came to his room and discovered Sarah Jane, not only in his room, but in his bed, and both were completely naked. Her astonishment was so comical, Sarah Jane burst into laughter and made matters infinitely worse.

'You wicked, wicked girl!' Matron exclaimed, when she managed to find her voice. 'Heaven knows what is to become of you! Put your clothes on and take yourself to the attic. Stay there until you are sent for. We can't have you corrupting the others.'

Without a word, Sarah Jane scrambled into her clothes and fled, her boots in her hand. Behind her, she heard Thomas begin, 'But Elizabeth ...' and the matron reply, 'Oh, I don't blame you, Thomas. She's no better than a whore, but there's no doubt about it, she must go.'

Herring was sent to make sure she went to the attic and it was Herring who unlocked her attic prison every morning to let her out to wash and go to the privy, and locked it again when she returned. And three days later it was he who escorted her to Matron's sitting room and left her at the door.

'Come in, Sarah Jane, come in.'

Sarah Jane had expected another tirade and a penalty so dire she could not even imagine it, but Matron's soft, almost friendly voice, took her by surprise. She pushed open the door and advanced cautiously, only to discover that Matron was presiding over the tea trolley while Lady Chevington sat in the best armchair, sipping from a fragile china cup. The Master stood by the window, looking uncomfortable.

'This is the girl,' Matron said, as Sarah Jane made her curtsey. 'She is full grown and strong and has worked in the laundry, the kitchens and the infirmary and is well trained in all these tasks. She can also read and write a little, but not so much as to get above herself.' She presented the last piece of information in such a way that the administrators of the workhouse were given the credit, making Sarah Jane smile.

'Come here and let me take a proper look at you,' Her Ladyship said suddenly. 'I feel I should know you.'

'You were here when we were admitted, my lady,' Sarah Jane enunciated carefully.

'We?'

'My brother and I.'

'Of course, Winterday, I should have remembered when Matron mentioned your name. My goodness, what a change there is in you!' She smiled. 'How like a wild cat you were, defending your little brother and standing up to everyone. How is your brother?'

'I have not spoken to him since we first arrived,' said Sarah Jane, grasping the heaven-sent opportunity. 'Every time I tried to see him, I was stopped—'

'Allowing them to meet would have been too disruptive, my lady,' Matron put in before Sarah Jane could elaborate; she did not want Her Ladyship probing into Billie's beating, for she knew perfectly well what had happened. 'It would have upset the boy when he had settled in so well. We must have these rules. It is not that we want to separate them . . .'

'No, I understand,' Her Ladyship murmured. 'But as Sarah Jane is shortly to leave here, I think it would be in order for them to have a few minutes together, to say goodbye.'

'Of course, my lady, I will arrange it.' Matron gave Sarah Jane a black look and the girl returned it with a broad grin, savouring the one and only moment of triumph of her whole stay in the Union.

'You will take her then?' the Master asked. He had been in favour of giving Sarah Jane a beating, but Elizabeth had other ideas, perhaps because she knew his weakness. She wanted to unload the girl onto an unsuspecting employer, and the only one they could think of who might be gullible enough to take her without asking too many questions was Lady Chevington.

'Yes, I think she will be very suitable. Send her to Chevington House at the end of the week.' Her Ladyship put down her cup and saucer and stood up. 'Thank you for the tea, Matron. I will let you know how Sarah Jane is coming along when the guardians meet. I am sure you will want to keep in touch with her.'

'Oh, indeed, yes,' Matron said. 'We like to know how all our young people do.'

'Begging your pardon, my lady,' Sarah Jane put in. 'You said you'd see what could be done for Billie . . .'

'Did I?'

'Yes, my lady. You said that when I found a position we might be able to be together. Don't you remember?'

'Impudent girl!' Matron almost exploded with wrath. 'Ungrateful wretch!'

No, Matron.' Her Ladyship held up a kid-gloved hand to silence her. 'Sarah Jane is thinking of her brother and that is commendable.' She turned to the girl. 'Billie is not yet of an age to work, is he?'

'No, my lady, but . . .'

'When he is, we will see what can be done. Much depends on how well you settle in and if there is a vacancy.' She smiled and picked up her parasol. 'You must be patient, my dear. Now, I must go.' She turned to the Master, who sprang forward to escort her to her carriage.

As soon as they were out of earshot, Matron turned on Sarah Jane. 'I never heard such impudence! How dare you speak to Her Ladyship like that. It was a wonder she agreed to take you at all. I could have died of shame, that someone who had been in my care and taught good manners should speak so disrespectfully. Do you realise how fortunate you are?'

'Yes, Matron.'

'You will be fed and clothed and housed and for that you must work hard and put this unfortunate business behind you.'

48

'Billie,' Sarah Jane put in, just in case the matron chose to ignore Her Ladyship's instructions. 'Lady Chevington said . . .'

'I know what Her Ladyship said,' Matron snapped irritably. 'You will have five minutes with your brother on the day you leave.' She paused, eyeing the girl as if deciding whether to say what was on her mind, what had been on her mind ever since she had caught the girl in her brother's bed. 'You will speak of what happened to no one, do you understand? *No one.*'

She's afraid of something, Sarah Jane thought. She hasn't told Lady Chevington the real reason she's sending me away because she dare not. Her Ladyship would certainly want to know who the man was and she could not tell her because her brother was living at the Union by courtesy of the Poor Rates and the guardians didn't know that. If Sarah Jane were to tell Her Ladyship she had been seduced . . . There was no question of betraying Thomas who had been so good to her, but for the first time in her life, Sarah Jane tasted real power and allowed herself a small smile of satisfaction.

If only she didn't have to leave Billie behind. It seemed just one more failure on her part – another act of betrayal. It made no difference that she had no choice, any more than she had had a choice when she brought him here in the first place. In any case, she could do nothing for him while she remained in the Union.

'I'll write to you, Billie,' she promised when he came to Matron's sitting room to say goodbye. He seemed so vulnerable, standing in the middle of the cluttered room, his large blue eyes clouded by indifference. 'And when you are old enough to work, you can come too.'

'Who said so?' Although it was a year since his last visit to that room, he had come reluctantly, expecting another thrashing and what the Master chose to call his reward for taking his punishment like a man, but he had not liked having his private parts mauled and though his bladder had come to his rescue then, he dreaded a repeat performance. It had not occurred to him that the summons could have anything to do with his sister and he had been surprised when he was ushered into the room to find Sarah Jane standing in her outdoor clothes and a basket at her feet; it seemed that she was going out into the world and leaving him behind. Not by the merest flicker did he betray his disappointment. His face took on the wooden expression he had learned to adopt ever since that night in the pigsty had sapped his vitality; it frustrated the adults about him and proved an effective armour against being hurt.

49

'Lady Chevington.' He was not the Billie Sarah Jane remembered; he seemed unresponsive, lost inside himself, and she was not sure if that was all part of growing into a man or not. He had left his childhood behind and she had missed the going of it; nothing she could do now would make up to him for that. 'And when you're old enough to work, you can come too.'

He did not believe it; nowadays he believed very little of what adults told him. His stoic acceptance was more than she could bear and with a stifled sob she hugged him to her and then, unable to look at him again, picked up her basket and ran from the room.

Chapter Four

Sarah Jane left the ugly building which had been her home for the past three years in a mood of optimism. The small basket she carried contained a fresh set of underwear, a flannel, a hairbrush and the late Mrs Wistonby's notebook which, together with the plain new dress and boots she was wearing, were the sum total of her possessions, but that was of little consequence, she decided, as she made her way to the crossroads to await the arrival of the carrier's cart. She would do well in her new life; it would be the first step on the ladder. Her only regret was for the people she had left behind, Thomas particularly for he would miss her, Lizzie, who had been her friend and confidante, and Billie. Billie was a problem, but what else could she have done? Did he know how much it grieved her to leave him – had he understood that she couldn't help it?

The cart came rumbling up the road and stopped beside her. 'Chevington House, if you please,' she said cheerfully, offering the carrier the sixpence she had been given for her fare and settling herself on the seat beside him. 'I'm to be apprentice there.'

He smiled as he pocketed the coin and commanded the horse to walk on. If she had come from the Union, no wonder she smiled. Anything was better than that.

A gang of railway navvies, making an embankment alongside the road, stopped their work to call good-day as the cart went by, and Sarah Jane shouted a cheerful greeting.

'Railways everywhere,' the carrier said. 'They're doin' me out o' good business with their penny a mile.'

'Is that all it costs?'

'If you take the Parliamentary.'

'What's a Parliamentary?'

'A special train for poor people. Course, if you go first or second class you pay more.'

'But the railways don't take people right up to their doors,' she said with unanswerable logic. 'If you waited at the station for the trains to come in, you could get your business taking them home.'

'I have me route,' he said stubbornly.

She shrugged; it was not her concern if he was too set in his ways to change with the times.

He put her down at the end of the drive leading to Chevington House. The big iron gates were flanked by brick pillars topped by roaring stone lions, and beyond them the long drive was bordered by trees, planted by some earlier generation of Chevingtons in a countryside which supported very few trees. The early autumn sun shone, the sky was blue, and the leaves, just turning to red and gold, had begun to carpet the ground. She moved off the path to shuffle through them. This was her idea of 'outside'; this was what she had been dreaming of all the long years. If this was punishment for her crime, it was no deterrent. Besides, she felt no guilt; she couldn't see that she had harmed anyone. Thomas had said she had been good for him and she was glad about that.

The house, when she came upon it, dazzled her. It was a square building with hundreds of windows, all reflecting the light of the sun. Creeper hid its brickwork and huge fronds of blue wisteria hung over and about the great oak door. At one end was a tower, covered with ivy, part of the house and yet separate from it, as if it had been built as an afterthought. She stood looking up at it, lost in wonder, until a voice behind her shouted, 'Hey, girl! Go round the back before someone catches you.'

She followed the direction of the gardener's pointing finger, between the side of the house and a long low building which turned out to be stables and tackroom, and found her way to the back door which stood open to allow a cool breeze into the overheated kitchen.

'I'm Sarah Jane Winterday,' she told the scullion who came in answer to her knock. The girl was about twelve or thirteen, and had such a pronounced squint Sarah Jane could not tell where she was directing her gaze. 'I'm to be apprentice here.'

'You'd best come in and I'll tell Mr Wilkins you're here.'

Sarah Jane stepped inside and was immediately in a world of cooking stoves, washtubs and kitchen sinks; her high spirits sank as she realised she had exchanged one place of drudgery for another.

'I'm Tilly Compton,' the girl said, leading the way through the kitchens to a room beside the pantry. 'No doubt you'll be working with me.' She knocked on the door and pushed Sarah Jane into the room.

Mr Wilkins was a plump grey-haired man in black breeches, stockings and tailcoat who stood with his back to the fireplace. He was about forty-five, Sarah Jane judged, and not particularly tall, but he had an air of authority which brooked no argument. After a desultory questioning of her about her background and abilities, he dismissed her. 'Tell Tilly to give you Meg's uniform,' he said.

She found her way back to the kitchens and the scullion conducted her up two flights of back stairs. 'You'll share with me,' she said, throwing open the door of one of the attic rooms. It was sparsely furnished, but it did have a cupboard and a chest of drawers with a mirror on top, besides a washstand with a jug standing in a bowl and a double bed with a flock mattress. It was more than she had ever had before, shared or otherwise. 'You can have the bottom drawer of the chest and this side of the cupboard.' She looked down at Sarah Jane's luggage. 'Shouldn't think you'll need more than that.'

'Mr Wilkins said I was to have Meg's uniform,' Sarah Jane said. 'Who's she?'

'The girl who was 'ere afore you. She was about your size.' She flung things about in the cupboard until she found a linen dress, an apron and cap. 'Put 'em on and come back to the kitchens. Can y' find yer way down again?'

She disappeared and Sarah Jane sank onto the bed in a daze. Would her life here be any better than in the Union? At least in the workhouse she had had friends, someone to talk to and laugh with; here there would be no Thomas and she didn't think Tilly would ever take the place of Lizzie. She sighed, got off the bed and put on the second-hand dress which was too short and showed her ankles, and a cap which was so filled with starch she had difficulty prising it open far enough to get it on her head. After a quick glance in the mirror which did nothing to make her feel any better, she made her way back to the kitchen and her new life. It was not a time for regrets and she would not be downcast. Life was all about seizing opportunities and making the best of them, and if they didn't come as readily as she hoped, why, then she would make them happen. Thomas had taught her that.

The butler, she learned from Tilly, was responsible for the below-stairs staff and the smooth-running of the household; he ruled with an unbending discipline and no one dare disobey him. He worked immediately under the steward, a gentleman Sarah Jane was to hear about, but never see, and he gave his orders through the cook. Cook was decidedly fat; her face was always bright red because she was never away from the fire, and she had a breathless way of speaking, as if she was in a perpetual hurry. There were a great many others, but no one saw fit to introduce Sarah Jane. The only one who bothered with her was Tilly with whom she was to share her duties.

There were to be guests for supper and the kitchen was a flurry of preparation; chickens were being roasted, puddings boiled, sauces thickened.

'You'd think the Queen was coming,' Tilly, stringing beans, grumbled. ''stead of only Mr and Mrs Townsend.'

Sarah Jane, who was sitting on a stool peeling potatoes, scooped out an eye with a knife worn down to a sharp point, and asked, 'Who are they?' before throwing the potato into a saucepan and beginning on the next.

'Mrs Amelia Townsend is Lady Chevington's sister and Mr John Townsend is a Member of Parliament. I don't doubt the men will spend the evening talkin' railways and boring their wives to death.'

'Why railways?'

''Cos His Lordship has become very rich by them.'

'I thought he was rich already.'

'So he was,' Tilly said. 'Now he's *richer*.'

'It must be very satisfying to be able to spend money and not have to worry whether you can afford to,' Sarah Jane said wistfully.

'It don' stop 'em frettin' if they think we're bein' wasteful,' Tilly said, looking at Sarah Jane's peelings. 'Cook will have somethin' to say if you don't pare 'em thinner than that.'

'Will we get to eat any of that?' Sarah Jane jerked her head in the direction of the kitchen whence delicious smells drifted into them. 'I'm hungry.'

'After the family have had their supper, we'll have ours and you'll be able to eat your fill.'

In the matter of meals she would certainly be better off than in the workhouse, Sarah Jane decided, when later that evening she sat with the other servants on benches down each side of the long table in the servants' hall to have supper. The food was good and plentiful, even if most of what they ate had been sent down from the dining room and been reheated.

Afterwards Tilly, her arms up to the elbows in hot washing-up water, told Sarah Jane what she would be doing the next day and every day after that. She was to clear out the fireplaces in the day rooms each morning at such an early hour that no member of the family could possibly meet her unless they were sleepwalking, light the fires and make sure the coal scuttles were full. 'Twice a week, we have to black the grates,' she said. 'An' you have to get into all the crevices, 'cos Wilkins will inspect 'em afterwards. An' we have to get it done afore His Lordship comes down.'

'What happens if he does?'

'You'll be for it, I can tell you. We do the breakfast room first so that it's warm when His Lordship comes down, then the morning room for Her Ladyship and after that the library and the drawing room. When we've done that, we wash the pots in the kitchen until His Lordship is at his breakfast, then do his bedroom grate and empty the chamber pot into a bucket and carry it down the back stairs to the midden heap at the bottom of the kitchen garden.'

Sarah Jane grinned. 'And I suppose I'm to make sure I'm not seen with that either.'

Tilly giggled and Cook snorted her disapproval of scullions who answered back.

'When you've done that, you can have your breakfast.'

'And after that?'

'Same as today,' Cook said. 'You'll be kept busy in the scullery and the laundryroom, and you'll not leave except to take the washing into the kitchen garden and peg it on the line or to ask one of the gardeners to fetch in fruit and vegetables, and there'll be no dallying over that. Now best get to bed or you'll be useless in the morning.'

It seemed to Sarah Jane that she had only been in bed a few minutes when Tilly shook her into wakefulness again. Reluctantly she rose and dressed and followed the other girl downstairs.

In the half-light of dawn, it was difficult to see very much; the candles they carried only lit the area where they worked and Tilly was not disposed to let Sarah Jane dawdle. A red Turkey rug stretched the whole length of the hall and there were spindly-legged chairs ranged along the walls between the doors. These opened onto rooms which were all huge and beautifully carpeted and furnished, and each had a fireplace which the girls set about cleaning out and re-lighting. But it was the library which fascinated Sarah Jane the most. It was a very large room with hundreds of books ranged round its shelves, many more than Thomas Wistonby had. They were beautiful books too, not tattered like Thomas', but then his books had been well used and wasn't that what books were for? She could not resist the temptation to wander, candle in hand, to look at them.

'If you drop hot wax on the carpet, you'll be for it,' Tilly said.

Sarah Jane ignored her. Among the serious books on religion, philosophy, biography and history, her eye caught titles she recognised – *Robinson Crusoe, Gulliver's Travels, The Vicar of Wakefield*. Mr Dickens seemed well represented and there was Jane Austen's *Pride and Prejudice*. She reached out and took *The Pickwick Papers* from the shelf and opened it.

'For goodness sake put that back!' Tilly's voice was a horrified whisper.

Reluctantly Sarah Jane returned it to the shelf. She had begun reading it with Thomas and found it quite difficult; Mr Dickens used long words and complicated sentences, but her avid interest in the fortunes of the characters had carried her along, until the lessons had come to an abrupt halt. 'I wish . . . '

'What? D'you wish you could read?'

'I can. I just wish I could borrow some of these.'

'Oh, do forget the dratted books and let's get on,' Tilly said when Sarah Jane showed no sign of getting down to work. 'I ain't goin' to do it all by meself, y'know.'

Sarah Jane sighed, dropped on her knees in front of the grate and took the blacking brush Tilly handed her.

Sarah Jane soon realised Tilly was not to be trusted; the scullion told Cook about the incident with the book and earned her a scolding, and whenever Sarah Jane transgressed – by day-dreaming or talking too long to the under-gardener – she would know the sharpness of the cook's tongue. It was Tilly who, catching Sarah Jane one Sunday afternoon completely absorbed in *The Pickwick Papers*, told Wilkins that she had taken one of His Lordship's books. While Sarah Jane was outside picking up windfall apples for a pie, he searched their room and carried off both the borrowed book and Mrs Wistonby's notebook which he assumed had also been stolen, taking both to His Lordship, with the result that Sarah Jane was summoned to the library.

His Lordship was standing near the window, looking thoughtfully out onto the garden, his hands clasped behind him under the skirt of his blue coat. He turned as she made her way into the room and walked over to his desk. She could not stifle her gasp when she saw the two books lying on the papers scattered there, and what worried her most was not that she had been caught, but that he might not return the precious notebook to her.

'You may well look surprised,' he said. 'Do you not know that it is wrong to steal?'

'Yes, sir ... me lord.' Her speech, so carefully nurtured by Thomas, slipped as it so often did when she was flustered. 'But I ain't stole nothin'.'

'These books were found in your room.'

'Mr Wilkins had no right to go through my things,' she retorted hotly.

'Indeed he has if he suspects you of dishonesty.' Lord Chevington paused. 'He was right to do so, wasn't he?'

'The notebook is mine, sir. It was given to me.' She stopped, realising it would be unwise to mention Thomas.

'And this one?' He picked up *The Pickwick Papers* and weighed it in his hand.

'I only borrowed it. I'd have put it back when I finished it and you'd have been none the wiser.'

'Why did you want it? Can you read?'

'Yes, my lord.' She had recovered from her agitation and was prepared to face him out. 'But if I don't practise I shall forget how to.'

'And is that important?' He seemed to have forgotten the theft and was looking at her as if suddenly seeing the real person beneath that characterless uniform.

'Yes, it is. How can I get on if I can't read and write?'

'You want to get on?'

'Of course I do. Doesn't everybody?'

'Well, Sarah Jane, I commend your ambition, but taking books which do not belong to you is certainly not the way to do it. You should have asked.'

'Asked?' queried Sarah Jane, with a smile. 'How could I, when I am not allowed to speak to you unless you address me? And if I'd mentioned it to Mr Wilkins, he would certainly have refused.'

He acknowledged the truth of that with a laugh. 'You have not been here very long, have you?' he asked, wondering why he thought he ought to know her; he rarely took much notice of the servants, leaving their hiring to Constance. 'Where were you before you came here?'

'In the Union, my lord.'

'How long were you there?'

'Three years, my lord. Ma died and Da was gored by Farmer Cooper's black bull. You told him to take us there.'

The memory clicked into place but he could hardly believe it was the same girl he had seen disporting herself in the field; it was surprising what a little soap and water and good food could do. Almost a woman now, she was strikingly beautiful and self-assured for someone with her kind of background. There was a positive quality about her, as if she knew she would always rise above the knocks life dealt her; she was vibrantly alive.

'Three years,' he said, remembering. 1841 was the year he had begun his railway investment, the year Timothy had gone up to Cambridge, the year he had told the boy the truth. They had been three busy, profitable and mostly contented years, but for one thing; Constance had still not given him his longed-for heir and yet he loved her and would not, for all the world, hurt her. Timothy had, perforce, to remain in the background, a secret he could not share. The boy had changed too, though he supposed that had been inevitable. He had grown into a slightly embittered young man. Oh, it was not immediately obvious because he could be charming and attentive when he chose and sometimes, when he laid aside the air of indolence he had adopted, there could be glimpsed the man his father always hoped he would become. What Timothy needed was a nice girl to set him straight, someone from a loving, uncomplicated family who could bring out the caring man who lurked beneath the façade.

Impatient with himself, Geoffrey looked across the desk at the girl; her frank green eyes were regarding him as if she understood his thoughts. But how could she? How could anyone? He flicked through the pages of the book he held. 'Have you finished reading this?'

'No, my lord.'

'Would you like to?'

'Oh yes, my lord.'

'You know how to look after a book? You know you must not turn down the corners of the pages or open it so flat you break its spine?'

'I would not dream of doing such a thing.'

He picked up the receipt book and handed both to her. 'Then you may continue to borrow books from this shelf.' He pointed. 'The rest you must not touch.'

'Oh thank you, my lord.' The green eyes lit up with pleasure and the thought crossed his mind that pleasing her would be a gratifying occupation for some lucky young man.

Clutching the books to her bosom, Sarah Jane left him and ran up the back stairs to put them in her room, before going back to the kitchen to face Tilly's curiosity. She was too pleased with the outcome of the interview to be angry with her, but she would be careful not to give her an opportunity to sneak again.

The servants were allowed two hours of freedom on Sunday afternoons and although Sarah Jane did consider going to the Union to see Billie, the journey could not be accomplished both ways in the allotted time, and besides, she had sworn never to set foot inside the place again and standing outside hoping to catch a glimpse of him would be a waste of precious time. She wondered if she dare ask for writing materials so that she could write to him. His Lordship would give them to her, she was sure, but she dare not seek him out for such a little thing.

Instead she spent her free time exploring the countryside and when winter was over and the days warmer, she liked to find a grassy bank under the shade of a tree and read one of the books from His Lordship's shelves. The more she read and learned the more she realised how little she knew; each tiny taste of knowledge led her on to savour more. She ranged the shelves, moving on from fiction to geography and history and from there to politics and economics. She understood little, but she was greedy for learning and soaked everything up like a sponge.

One Sunday she discovered a brook on the far side of the estate. Its green bank, where it joined the larger river, sloped gently down to clear water which, in the heat of that June afternoon, was too inviting to ignore. She began by removing her black boots and stockings and paddling in it, holding her skirts above her knees and letting the cool water soothe her aching feet. When her skirt and petticoat began to trail, she took them off and flung them on the bank. Before long she was splashing joyful and naked, and singing chirpily to herself, alone in a world of blue skies, green grass and cool water.

She did not hear the clop of hooves on the path above the bank, nor did she realise she was being watched as she clambered out and began drying herself with her petticoat.

At the sight of the naked girl, Timothy reined his horse to a stop, and the scowl which had been spoiling his handsome features for the last two hours changed to a smile. The striped dress, cambric underwear and black shoes and stockings scattered about the grass, marked her as a servant, and servants, particularly Chevington servants, were fair game. The fact that this one had the figure of a goddess and hair the colour of the setting sun, was an additional enticement, if enticement were needed, for him to dismount and approach her.

Sitting on the bank absorbed in drying herself, she had not heard him arrive and was startled into crying out when he seated himself on the grass beside her. 'Oh!' Green eyes wide, she recoiled from him, clutching her damp petticoat to her body.

He tugged the petticoat away from her, and she was torn between covering her nakedness with her hands and trying to retrieve her dress, just out of reach on the grass.

'Touch me and I shall scream.'

He laughed and picked up the striped uniform and put it behind him. 'Who would hear you? And besides, would it be wise? After all, you are the one who is naked. I am fully dressed and looking perfectly respectable.'

There was no denying that; he wore an expensive riding jacket and breeches, shiny leather boots and a yellow silk cravat. 'Then go away. Please, please go away.' She had learned a great deal while listening to Tilly's gossip, much of which was about the liberties the gentry took with servant girls. According to Tilly, many a girl had lost her position because she dare not refuse the attentions of the master or some younger member of the family intent on trying his wings where they were unlikely to be scorched. She did not know if he were part of the Chevington family, but she needed her job; it was the only thing keeping her out of the workhouse. And it was the only way she could go on educating herself.

'You don't really want me to leave, do you?' He ran the back of his forefinger slowly down her spine and was rewarded with an involuntary shiver of response. 'We have only just met.'

'We have not met at all, and I want to get dressed.'

'Oh, no, it would be criminal to cover such perfection. You are not real, are you? You are a water nymph, Aphrodite rising from the waves ... '

'She was a goddess.'

'So she was,' he said, surprised that she knew. 'The goddess of love, the most beautiful of all.'

She laughed suddenly. 'That's what Paris said, and look at the trouble that caused.'

'What trouble?' He had been arguing with Lord Chevington about his new role in the Chevington business empire; his father wanted him to start in a very humble way, working in the office, when he wanted to be out and about, to see what was going on and have some managerial responsibility. He had lost the argument because he had remembered, just in time, that his whole future as a Chevington lay in not biting the hand that fed him. He had taken his horse and his smouldering resentment to the Chevington estate to gallop away his black mood and remind himself why he had to knuckle under. The girl was a welcome diversion.

'The Trojan War. Aphrodite promised him the most beautiful woman in the world if he gave her the golden apple, but that was Helen and she was already married.' Why, she asked herself, was she allowing him to draw her into conversation, unless it was to distract him enough to snatch her clothes and escape?

'We won't risk a war if we sit and talk a bit, will we?'

She laughed. 'I'm not so sure of that. If I don't get back to work on time, there might well be a battle, and one I would be sure to lose.' She enunciated her words carefully, making him smile. He had never met a servant girl who was not overawed by his attentions and was prepared to answer him intelligently when he spoke to her; few he had met could read at all, let alone a translation of the *Aeneid* like the one that lay on the grass beside her nor, for that matter, one who was so addicted to cleanliness. This girl positively sparkled; her green eyes were full of life and her hair was the thickest, the reddest, the shiniest, he had ever seen.

He reached out to push back the tresses which veiled her shoulders and cupped one plump breast in his hand, running his thumb over the nipple and making it pout. Her whole frame quivered. 'Perfect,' he murmured. 'Perfect.'

She made herself ignore the message her body was giving her and shrugged him off. 'Go away. I want to dress.'

'What! Would you have me deny myself the pleasure of gazing at the most beautiful woman in the world?'

She was flattered, in spite of the warning voice in her head which told her to beware. 'That was Helen. Make up your mind, a minute ago you were talking about Aphrodite.'

'Beautiful woman, beautiful goddess, it's all one.'

'What do you want with me? Find one of your own sort.'

'What sort is that?'

'You are a gentleman.'

She had touched his Achilles heel and he was suddenly morose. 'I am no more a gentleman than you are a lady.'

'But your clothes are ...'

'Clothes do not make a gentleman. If that is all there is to it, we will

61

be equal.' And to her intense surprise he took off his jacket and flung it on the grass, then began to untie his cravat.

'No! No!' she shrieked. 'Please don't! Please let me dress and go back. I'll be in awful trouble if I'm late.'

'Stay just a few minutes longer.' He reached over to kiss her, but she pulled herself away from him.

'Do you take me for a fool? If you was thinking what I think you was, you can forget it.' She was very agitated now and her careful speech had slipped.

He lay back on the grass and roared with laughter. 'You are priceless, do you know that?'

She had been hoping for an opportunity to grab her clothes, but now he was lying on them and short of wrestling with him for repossession there was nothing she could do; she couldn't run back to the house naked.

'Aphrodite was immortal,' she said, trying to tug her dress from under him. 'I am merely human or I would cast a spell on you, strike you blind, or set you a task so difficult that you would never come back.'

He smiled. 'But whatever it was I would accomplish it, if it meant I could spend the rest of my days with you.'

'You are talking nonsense and I am getting angry,' she said, though his nonsense pleased her and she wasn't really angry. In an effort to snatch her clothes, she abandoned the remnants of her modesty and, kneeling up, pummelled him in the chest and abdomen.

Her flying fists were getting dangerously close to a part of his anatomy which was already giving him some trouble. He grabbed her wrists and, in one swift movement, turned her over on her back, sitting astride her and pinning her arms down beside her head. She struggled a moment and lay still. He looked down into green eyes that suddenly filled with tears, and found himself unaccountably wanting to reassure her. 'I won't hurt you, my dear. I only want ...'

'I know what you want, right enough, I ain't stupid, but you can go and find someone else to play your silly games with.'

'But there ain't no one else,' he said, mimicking her speech. 'There is only one you. And I need you.'

'Please ...' She was begging now and she did not like herself for it, especially as her body was speaking a different language to her lips and she knew its meaning. The physical desire was there and she must keep the fact from him or she was lost.

'If I give my word not to touch you unless you want me to, will you stay and talk to me?' It was going to be difficult but he would enjoy the conquest all the more for his restraint.

'Y ... yes, if you let me dress first.' It was better than giving in to him, but she would have to make up some excuse for being late back.

He sighed melodramatically. 'Very well, if that is the only way. Take your clothes.' He moved off her and she grabbed her dress and petticoat and tore off behind the bushes. He laughed. 'Why hide, my dear? I have already seen all there is to see.'

'I hate you!' she shouted. 'Go away!'

He lay on his back smiling up at the soft blue sky and cotton-wool clouds, knowing she would have to pass him on her way back to the path. A moment or two later, she emerged, demurely dressed in the striped cotton, but she had not put her stockings on and her hair still tumbled about her shoulders. If anything it increased his desire for her. He sat up and patted the turf beside him. 'You must keep your word and I will keep mine.'

Gingerly, she sat down. 'What do you want to talk about?'

'Anything. I like the sound of your voice. What's your name?'

'Sarah Jane. Who are you?'

He smiled. 'Me? Why I am the nobody my dear father has made me.'

'That's a funny answer. I meant what is your name?'

'Nobody's don't have names.'

She laughed, showing even white teeth. 'You must be called something.'

'Give me whatever name you like. It will be the better coming from your lovely lips.'

She laughed. 'Then I shall call you Paris.'

'Paris of the golden apple. That will do very well.' He smiled and took her hand in his. Her hands were the only things about her which betrayed the work she did; the nails were broken and ingrained with stove blacking. 'How old are you?'

'I shall be seventeen next Sunday.'

'And where did you learn to read?' He picked up the book and idly turned its pages.

'Mr Wistonby taught me in the Union.'

'Did he teach you anything else?'

'Oh yes, to speak like a lady and to write a letter and he told me all about London and politics and things like that.'

'I am already very jealous of Mr Wistonby.'

She giggled. 'He was old.' Then realising she was being unfair, as well as inaccurate, she added, 'Well, older than me, but I was very fond of him.'

'I am older than you.'

'Not by much, you're not.'

'I'm twenty-one, but there are times when I feel as old as Methuselah.'

She laughed. 'But much more handsome.'

'You think I am handsome?'

Sarah Jane hesitated, but she had always been truthful. 'Yes,' she said.

'Will you come here again next Sunday?'

'Perhaps,' she said, tantalising him with a flash of trim ankle as she scrambled to her feet and picked up her shoes and stockings and the book which had to be returned to His Lordship's library. 'You'll have to wait and see.'

He surprised himself by letting her go. Reluctantly he stood up, retied his cravat and put on his coat. He felt empty, as if a goddess had truly passed his way, and taken his manhood with her. If he wanted it back, he would have to see her again and prove to himself that she was only flesh and blood, that once his passion was spent, she would return to being nothing more than an ordinary servant. But even as he thought it, he realised that there was nothing ordinary about Sarah Jane. Besides being a beauty with a sublime figure and green eyes that shone like emeralds, she was so full of life; it poured out of her and wound itself about him so that he felt its energy uplifting him. He felt as if he could move mountains.

He had the run of the Chevington estate for most of the summer because Lady Chevington had decided to spend a month at Bath with her sister, and might afterwards have a week or two in London. It was not an arrangement he liked, but it was, for the time being, as near as he was likely to get to what he had come to look on as his inheritance and he had to put up with it, or not come at all. He smiled; seducing one of his father's servants would add a piquancy to his visits, a kind of secret revenge. They had a surprising affinity, as if they had been moulded by the same hand, and yet their backgrounds were so different. Backgrounds, yes, parentage he was not so sure of, because his father refused to have the subject mentioned; he might be the child of a servant just like Sarah Jane.

He shook that thought from him as he returned to his horse, quietly cropping the grass where he had left it with reins trailing. His imagination had always produced a mother who was gentility itself, the wife of a well-known aristocrat who was head over heels in love with his father, but whom, for reasons of *noblesse oblige*, she could never marry. It made him feel a little better about his bastardy. But only a little.

Sarah Jane spent the week building fantasies about the young man she thought of as Paris, and wondered if she could have behaved any differently, but there wasn't a lot you could do if you were stark naked. And he had been right – screaming would only have landed her in trouble, not him. She wondered who he was and where he lived and if he knew that he was trespassing on Lord Chevington's estate. He must have done; everyone knew His Lordship. She dare not voice her questions to any of the other servants, nor even hint that she had had an adventure while she was out; it would involve her in a cross-examination and that would make the whole thing tawdry and spoil the magic, for magical it was.

No one had ever called her beautiful before and though she told herself a thousand times that he had meant none of it, she really wanted to believe he had been sincere and that he really was interested in her. After all, he had been prepared to sit and talk to her after she had persuaded him to let her dress. Not since she had been caught in Thomas' bed, had anyone put their arms round her or kissed her or, indeed, said anything affectionate to her. She could have had the pick of the young male servants, if all she was after was a romp in the hay, but she wanted more than that. She wanted emotion, a heightened awareness of her own self, the giving and receiving of more than just a lustful passion. More than anything, she wanted the closeness of another human being; she hungered for it. She ached with the need for someone to love, someone to love her.

Paris was a gentleman for all his funny talk, and her dreams soared into the realms of the impossible. She imagined him riding up to the front door of Chevington House in a carriage at least as grand as Lord Chevington's, and saying, 'I have come to claim Sarah Jane. Fetch her to me at once!' And then he would take her away to a life of love and leisure, where she would not have to lift a finger, except to summon a servant. And they would have lots of beautiful children and Billie would come to live with them and they would be happy ever after.

But it *was* only a dream and she ought not to indulge herself with it, and she should certainly not return to the brook the next Sunday. But when the time came, she found her feet taking her there of their own accord. She had dressed with especial care in a green flowered dress which Cook had found for her in one of the trunks in the attic. 'For you to wear of a Sunday,' she had said. It was better than her uniform and with her hair brushed until every strand shone like a filament of red gold, she ran pell-mell to meet her fate.

She stopped when she saw his horse tethered to one of the trees; if she took another step she would commit herself to whatever lay ahead, pleasure or pain, and she was half-afraid. On the other hand, her life was so empty, so devoid of affection and he had made her feel good about herself, so what had she to fear but disappointment? She would guard herself carefully against that by keeping a cool head. Slowly she went forward, ducking beneath the overhanging willow to the water's edge.

Chapter Five

'*S*arah Jane!' The voice came from the water and she looked across to see his dark head surfacing out in the middle. 'Come and join me.' He began swimming towards her and when he reached the shallow water, sat on the bottom, smiling at her.

He was just as she had remembered him– dark, handsome, smiling. His teeth were white and his eyes were almost as black as coal and his hair, when it was wet, curled round his ears and flopped over his forehead.

'Are you ... have you got any clothes on?'

'Do I look as though I have?'

'No.'

'Come on in, the water is just right.'

'I can't do that, it wouldn't be proper ...'

'Don't tell me you are going to be coy about it, not after last week.'

'That was different.'

'How different?'

'I was already undressed when you arrived.'

'And this time, I am undressed and that makes us even. If you don't, I shall come out and throw you in with all your clothes on, and how would you explain that when you got back?'

He stood up, dripping water off a figure that was lithe and young and slimly muscular from his broad shoulders to his tapering hips and firm thighs. His flesh was smooth and slightly tanned, nothing like Thomas' had been and it stirred her more than ever Thomas' rather flabby white torso had done ... Unable to look at it and keep her resolve to remain calm, she gave a little cry and covered her eyes with her hands. He laughed and she heard him wading out to stand in front of her. 'Am I so ugly, Sarah Jane, that you cannot look at me? Am I not fit for a goddess?'

She opened her eyes and found his dark eyes looking into hers with an intensity that almost burned. 'Sarah Jane, don't you know you

67

have been driving me insane all week?' He put his arms about her, so that his hard wet body was pressed against her and dampened her dress, and ran his mouth down her neck from her ear to the hollow of her throat, making her shiver. 'My thoughts have been so full of you, I haven't been able to concentrate on anything else at all.'

'Me too,' she said. 'I got a ticking off for day dreaming.'

'Daydreams are the best kind to have. Dreams in the night have a habit of ending badly and turning into nightmares.' He began undoing the buttons on the front of her dress. 'Get these wretched clothes off. My fingers are all thumbs with impatience.'

'Did you mean it when you said you needed me?' she asked suddenly, as if his answer would dictate whether she obeyed or not.

He recognised the implied condition and bent his head to touch her lips with his. 'I have never needed anyone so badly in my whole life.' And at the moment he said it, he meant it; he was rigid with need. His lips roamed over her face and neck and, when the coarse striped dress finally came off, he buried his head in the cleft of her breasts. Then he pulled off the rest of her clothes and, picking her up in his arms, carried her to the water and dropped her in. Her hair floated round her and then she surfaced, sitting on the silt of the bottom and laughing up at him. He knelt beside her to push her hair back and kiss her wet face. 'You are adorable.'

She answered by tugging him down beside her and throwing water over him. They laughed and kissed and wallowed for several joyous minutes and then he picked her up again and carried her to the bank, where they lay side by side like a pair of basking seals.

He rolled over and began kissing her wet body, exploring it with his mouth and tongue, until her overflowing sexuality and his obvious need of her made her throw the remnants of her doubts and inhibitions away and she lost herself completely in the pleasure of the moment.

Her response took him by surprise. She was no simpering servant girl with pretensions of modesty, nor was she a shameless wanton. She was a perfect lover, with just the right blend of shyness and forwardness which, if he had been more experienced himself, would have warned him that he was courting disaster. He drowned himself in her sensuality, allowed it to engulf him, so that he forgot his frequent arguments with his father, forgot that he should not be hankering after what he could not have; Sarah Jane he *could* have and he gloried in her. To his surprise, he found himself murmuring, 'I love you, Sarah Jane, love you, love you.'

And when it was over and he lay spent beside her, he knew that his hunger had not been assuaged, that far from getting her out of his system, she had only whetted his appetite for more. He wanted to be with her for more than an hour or two, he wanted time to explore that lovely body, to find new ways of loving her, to exhaust himself on her, to own her. She was something his father could not dictate to him about because he would never know, and the thought that she was His Lordship's servant only added to the piquancy. 'Do you have to go back?'

'You know I do,' she said, wishing she could stay because he made her feel so happy. In the euphoria of the moment she ceased to be Sarah Jane Winterday, scullion, and became a beautiful and desirable woman, a woman who was loved.

'But I want you to stay. I need you.'

She rolled over on her stomach and propped herself on her elbow to kiss his lips and then each brow in turn. 'And I need my job.'

'How can you speak of your job at a time like this?'

'Why not?' She began dressing slowly.

'You'll come again next week?' He pulled on his riding breeches and reached for his shirt.

'You want me to?' She seemed surprised.

'Of course. I shall think of nothing else until we meet again.' He jumped to his feet and ran off through the trees to his horse. She was beginning to wonder why he had left so hurriedly when he returned.

'You said today was your birthday. I've brought you a present.'

She had finished dressing and was pulling her fingers through her hair in an effort to dry it without tangles. With shaking hands she opened the small box he put into them. It was lined with velvet which cradled a tiny golden apple. 'See,' he said, touching the golden stalk at its centre. 'It opens.' Inside, on a bed of tortoiseshell, lay a single beautiful pearl.

'Oh, it's lovely!' She raised her eyes to his and he noticed, with an uncharacteristic pang of guilt, that they were glistening with unshed tears. 'No one has ever remembered my birthday since Ma died. Oh, Paris!' And she burst into noisy sobs.

He wiped the tears away with the back of his finger and kissed her. 'Don't cry, for heaven's sake.'

'But I'm so happy.'

'Then what do you do when you are sad?'

'I grin and bear it,' she said, smiling again. 'But I can't accept this.'

'Why not?' He had brought it as a bribe in case she proved difficult, and though that had not been necessary, he decided to give it to her anyway. For several glorious minutes he had been content and because he was too proud to admit it, he wanted to give her something which would make her think of him when she was not with him; it would bring her to him again. 'Let's just call it a token of my appreciation of your favours.' He paused and laughed. 'And in the hope of more to come.'

'More?' she queried mischievously, dodging as he reached for her again.

'Can you doubt that? I shall expect you next week. You'll come, won't you?'

'I'll see.' She laughed and put the little box in her dress pocket, before reaching up to kiss him. 'Thank you, Paris, oh, thank you.' Then she hurried away, back to the real world of drudgery in the kitchens and bedrooms of Chevington House.

If anyone noticed the extra sparkle in her eyes, or the lightness of her step in the following weeks, they did not say so, and if Lord Chevington noticed that her taste in reading matter had veered from history and economics towards romance, he saw nothing out of the ordinary in that. Paris had become a very necessary part of her existence and their abandoned coupling was the high spot of her week. His lovemaking was nothing like Thomas' had been; he made love with eagerness and impatience and a kind of wild ecstasy which always found an echo in her own craving, set her heart racing and her limbs responding. The romantic novels she had borrowed had opened the world of falling in love to her and she was sure she was in love with Paris because the thought of never seeing him again filled her with panic. And she thought he loved her because he had told her so and she had no reason to disbelieve him, especially as he demonstrated it so forcefully every time they met. He could not have enough of her and, as far as she was concerned, that was proof enough.

She knew gentry did not marry housemaids and although he spoke and dressed like a gentleman, she was not completely sure he was one; there was something about him, an insensitivity, a lack of the good breeding which was an integral part of Lord Chevington's character, the only real aristocrat she knew. Perhaps like her, Paris had ambitions to be something other than he was and she did not blame him for that. It did not occur to her that while he might fulfil her ambition, she could be an insurmountable obstacle to his.

The weather blessed them for four consecutive Sundays but on the fifth it was overcast and threatening rain and he took her to an empty gamekeeper's cottage in the stand of trees which had been planted a century before to house game and shield Chevington House from the prevailing east wind.

'That's not where you live, is it?' she asked, as they approached it. 'Not in a gamekeeper's house?'

His laugh was a little cracked. 'No, even I am allowed something a little better than that. But it is near at hand and convenient and no one is likely to come here.'

'How do you know?' she asked. 'You don't belong round here, do you?'

'Belonging,' he said. 'Now, there's an interesting subject. Do I belong? If so, where and to whom?'

'You talk in riddles. Tell me, where do you live?'

'Oh,' he said airily. 'I live in the clouds, especially when I am with you.'

The gamekeeper's cottage had been empty for some time and was full of dust and cobwebs. The usable furniture had long since been taken out and all that was left were a few broken chairs, a kitchen table and a single bedstead with sagging springs and no mattress. Even in summer, it was cold and had a forlorn air about it as if it were peopled by unhappy ghosts. 'Let's leave,' she said, shivering a little. 'I don't like it.'

'What's wrong with it?' He seemed tense and irritable, the tenderness had gone from him. His grip on her arm was tight enough to bruise and his voice had an edge she had never noticed before. 'It's got four walls and a roof to keep off the rain.' He laughed. 'It even has a bed.'

It was not just the place that felt wrong; he was different. He was bitter about something he could not speak of, and hating her because he needed her in the same way as she needed him – for comfort. It frightened her.

'It's dirty and, oh, I don't know, it doesn't feel right. It was someone's home once and we have invaded it. I think they are watching us.'

He laughed. 'Watching? What nonsense! It's been empty for years.'

'Who lived here?'

'How should I know? A gamekeeper, I expect.'

'Where is he now?'

'Dead, I suppose. There's a new cottage over the other side of the wood where the latest keeper lives. Do stop prosing on about other people, Sarah Jane. We've more important things to do.' He took her in his arms and kissed her lips but the kiss had little warmth; heat, yes, but not warmth and she was aware of the difference. And the impatient way he pulled open her bodice annoyed her.

She moved away from him. 'Stop it.' She was aiding in the destruction of her most cherished fantasies and yet she could not help herself.

'Stop?' he queried. 'What's the matter with you, Sarah Jane? You've never told me to stop before, you couldn't get enough of me.'

'You were gentle before. You said you loved me.' It was all slipping away from her, the healthy lustiness, the loving tenderness, the joy of just being together and exploring each other, and with it went her hopes and dreams and she felt like howling.

'Did I?' He could not remember it. 'A man will say all kinds of things in the heat of the moment.'

'You mean you lied to me?' She looked up at him, dry-eyed; the tears were deep inside her and that was where they had to stay.

'No, of course not.' His need of her was tangible and urgent and the sight of her standing there, green eyes bright with a passion she was trying to withhold from him and her perfect body promising so much and ready to give so little was enough to enflame him. He took her shoulders in his hands as if he meant to shake her, but then realising he would have to go carefully if he wanted to enjoy her, just once more, held her at arm's length and looked into her eyes. 'God, Sarah Jane, must you torment me so?' He laughed uneasily. 'You are my Aphrodite, my goddess. I need you as I have never needed anyone before.' He pulled her down onto the creaking bed and her anger melted away. He knew just how to arouse her. He held her close as his tongue flicked over her ear and down her neck; his mouth, hungry and demanding, searched for hers and, finding it, forced it open; his hand slid her skirt up to her waist and ranged over her belly; his knee, caressing, parted her thighs.

She gave in, defeated, but somehow they could not recapture the magic of the river bank. Her mind was too troubled to release the passion she felt for him and both were left disappointed. Their lovemaking was mechanical, contrived, like a habit difficult to break, and instead of giving joy, it made her miserable. Without his love, her life became meaningless because there was nothing else to fill it and nothing to look forward to. She tried to force him back to the old loving relationship, tried to make him respond in the same way, and though his body complied, his mind had already left her. Physical love, she realised with a sudden insight which broke her heart, was not enough and she had been a fool.

While he had wanted her, she would have done anything to make him happy, but he was not happy now and she would not cling to him, would not beg; her pride would not let her.

'I will look for you in the usual place on Sunday,' he said when they parted, kissing her without passion.

'If the weather is fine,' she said, pretending a light-heartedness she did not feel; something in her bones told her he would not be there. 'Summer will soon be over.'

She knew her dreams were over too, though, for the life of her, she did not know why. Nothing had happened, they had not really quarrelled, she still needed him, and strangely enough, she knew he still wanted her as passionately as ever. So what had gone wrong? At no time did she connect the change in his attitude with the return of Lady Chevington.

She went back to the river bank the following Sunday, but the sky was overcast, threatening rain, and a cool wind ruffled the water, turning it to a muddy brown; the magic had gone. She had known, deep in her heart, he would not come, and she had no desire to linger. She turned and went back to her attic room, hoping the pages of *Oliver Twist* would help her forget the young man with the intense dark eyes.

Twice more she went to their old haunts but he was never there and she returned home fighting back tears. He was hateful, she told herself. He had taken all she had to give and when she had nothing new to offer, no greater excitement than her continuing devotion, he had left her, empty and alone once more. And now it was worse than before; it would have been better never to have known him. 'Fool!' she told herself. 'Fool to be so easily taken in.' If she had been a lady, he wouldn't have used her so; if she had been a lady, he would have courted her properly and asked her to marry him, but because she was nothing but a servant, he had played with her like a toy and now he had discarded her in the same way. It took a long time to come to terms with the truth of that and when she did, she made up her mind no one would ever do that to her again.

She tried pretending it had all been a dream but the presence of the golden apple hidden under the newspaper lining of her dressing table drawer was proof it had not been a product of her sleeping hours. At first she brought it out in private moments when she knew Tilly was busy elsewhere, ran her hands over it, smiling as she released the catch and touched the pearl, so white, so pure, pure as her love. But she fetched it out less and less often now, for what was it but a tawdry gimcrack, a symbol of nothing but her own gullibility? But she could not bring herself to throw it away. When she began to be sick into her slop bucket every morning, her flat, muscular belly grew rounder and her waist disappeared, the dream turned to nightmare and she knew she was in trouble.

There wasn't a single person in the entire household in whom she could confide, no one who could, or would, help or understand her. She struggled on, toiling up and downstairs with scuttles of coal and buckets of slops, driving herself far harder than ever her demanding employers expected, hoping all the while that her physical exertions would end her misery. But the child within her grew and she knew it was alive because it kicked, quite strenuously sometimes, so that she had to put down whatever she was carrying and wait until it had settled down again. Her visions of becoming a lady diminished in direct proportion to the increase in her girth, until the one faded altogether and the other demanded her full attention. She found an old pair of stays that Cook had thrown out and laced herself into them so tightly she could hardly breathe. She felt sick and giddy, and at her wits' end. And she hated the man who had brought her to this; instead of making her dreams come true, he had shattered them – and for what?

'Come out of the clouds, girl! I spoke to you.'

Sarah Jane, whose daydreaming had given way to a desperate fretting which occupied all her waking thoughts and most of her sleeping hours, turned to face the cook, who was sitting near the window peeling apples; a long corkscrew of thin skin hung from the knife in her hand.

'Come here by the window and let me look at you.'

She knew her secret was a secret no longer, and felt nothing but an enormous relief as she moved to obey.

'Well, my girl, how long have you got to go?'

'I don't know, about a month, I think.'

'Merciful heaven, only a month! Why did you say nothing before? Did you think it would go away?'

'No ... I don't know, I just hoped ...' Her voice trailed to a halt. How could she explain to the middle-aged cook what it was like to feel wanted, how good it felt to be loved? But he had not loved her after all, and she had been an idiot. How could she have forgotten her ambition, all she had been working towards with her reading, all the grand plans for being a lady and wielding the power that only position and money could give her? How could she become a lady when she had a child with no father? She wished, oh how she wished, she had not gone back to the brook a second time.

'Wilkins must be told. Apprentice or not, you'll not stay another night under this roof.'

'But where will I go?' Her voice was a monotone; the question was not a new one, it had been nagging at her for weeks.

Cook looked at the girl who was little more than a child and felt an unexpected wave of compassion. Sarah Jane had slumped on a high-backed chair, with her head drooping and her lovely hair scraped back into her working cap, looking the picture of dejection. Why, oh why, had her mother or the workhouse authorities not given her some instruction? How could she be expected to deal with lusty men if she did not understand what it was all about? She stood up, put the bowl of apples on the table, and went to put her arm about the girl's shoulders. 'Who is the father?' she asked gently.

'He never told me his proper name,' Sarah Jane wailed. 'He was a gentleman, and handsome. He had black hair that curled a little in his neck and dark eyes and his mouth ...' His full sensuous mouth she could not describe.

'How old was he?'

'He said he was twenty-one.'

Cook was going to suggest that the young man should be made to face up to his responsibilities but Sarah Jane's description had made her doubt the wisdom of that. Better let sleeping dogs lie. 'Is there no one you could go to?'

'No.' Sarah Jane delved into her apron pocket for her handkerchief and moped her streaming eyes. 'Me little brother's younger than me and in the Union in any case.' For the first time for months, she thought of Billie and was filled with guilt because in her selfish pursuit of happiness she had forgotten all about him. How could she help him now, when she could not even help herself?

'You must return there yourself.'

'Oh, no! I can't go back there.' She didn't want to give up what little freedom she had, and besides, babies born in the workhouse bore the stigma all their lives. And they would take her child from her and put him in the infants' ward so that she could return to work; it would be like parting from Billie all over again, only much worse because she had come to realise she wanted to keep this child of hers. Lizzie had said, 'Don't you know that's how babies are made?' How confident she had been, how sure of herself! Too late she had remembered her friend's admonition to save herself for the marriage bed. It had always been too late, Thomas had seen to that. Thomas, what of him? Was he still there, still reading and writing letters and giving good advice?

'There might be someone,' she said slowly. 'I'll write to him. Please don't tell Wilkins yet. Please give me a little longer.'

'He'll soon not need telling,' Cook retorted, going to the dresser drawer where she kept a notebook for jotting down menus and her orders for the day. She tore a few pages from it, picked up a steel pen and a bottle of ink and handed them to Sarah Jane. 'Here, take these and write your letter.'

Sarah Jane retired to a corner and set about writing to Thomas, then returned to her work, to wait for his reply; if he was still living at the Union, he would reply, of that she was sure. Three days later her faith in him was rewarded when he appeared in person. She flung herself into his arms with a joyful cry and hauled him into the kitchen. 'Oh, you don't know how pleased I am to see you.'

'I hope you can help her,' Cook said after Sarah Jane had introduced them. 'She can't stay here and won't go to the Union, so what's to be done?'

'Can you spare Sarah Jane from her duties, so we can talk privately?' he asked.

'Yes, take her for a walk, make some arrangements for her future. We can't have a lying-in here.'

Sarah Jane led him out of the house towards the wooded section of the park, though she was careful to keep away from the empty cottage and its memories. He said nothing until they were well away from the house, then he stopped and turned and took her hands in his, holding her away from him so that he could look her up and down. Pregnancy had made her lovelier than ever; there was a bloom about her, her hair shone as never before and her eyes, looking so hopefully at him, were huge and bright. 'You are a silly little addle-pate, aren't you?' She nodded and he went on, 'Now, tell me how it came about, and don't leave anything out.'

So she told him, expecting him to upbraid her again, but instead he chuckled. It was good to hear his laughter and she joined in, though her situation was certainly not funny.

'Why didn't you remember what I told you, prevention is better than cure?'

'But I left my sponge in your room – I didn't have anything. And besides, this was different.'

'Different? How different?'

'I don't know, I can't explain. He was so handsome and bright, like a new penny . . .'

'He was a gentleman?'

She smiled wryly. 'He weren't no gentleman, but he . . . oh, he made me feel special, as if I really mattered to him. He said he loved me.'

'A real charmer, in other words. Oh, Sarah Jane, how could you be so deceived?' But knowing Sarah Jane, he already had the answer to that. She always believed the best of everybody; it wasn't so much that she was particularly gullible but that she was so honest and straightforward herself, she expected everyone else to be the same. The truth must have been a bitter blow. He smiled, aching to hold her in his arms again, to taste the pleasure and the pain of possessing her. He had always known that he was a kind of father figure to her, that the feelings she had for him were not those he had for her. She had given him back his youth and will to live; he had given her comfort and affection. He had hoped that he had also given her the ambition to want to make something of herself and he cursed the man who had spoiled that. 'He must be found.'

'Don't you think I haven't tried to find him? But I don't even know his proper name. In any case, what's the use? He would not marry me.' It was the first time she had acknowledged that, even to herself, and it was the bitterest pill of all. 'I hate him. I could kill 'im with me bare 'ands.' In her agitation, she slipped back into speaking with the flat vowels of the fens.

'You are hurt and disappointed, but you're not vengeful, Sarah Jane. Besides, what good would killing him do? You need him alive.' He had taken care to preserve Sarah Jane's guilelessness and treat her like the lady she so desperately wanted to be, and now this young whippersnapper had ruined everything for her. He would make him pay, and pay generously. 'Now we must decide what's to be done.' He had a germ of an idea, but first he had to find the young man and persuade him to stand up to his responsibilities financially. 'But you must be a good girl and go back to the Union while I make the arrangements.'

'No! I won't go back there, I won't! I thought you'd help me, but if tha's all you c'n say, I could've saved meself the bother of writin' to you.'

He took her shoulders in his hands and looked down into her face. 'Sarah Jane, infants need somewhere to be born and the Union is better than the hedgerow.'

'But they will take my baby from me.'

'No, they won't. I will write to my sister and she will let you have my old room until I return.' He knew he was deceiving himself; Elizabeth would never comply with such a request, but he had to say something to persuade her to go. He would make it up to her later.

'She'll never do that,' she said scornfully.

'Yes she will, because I shall tell her that we are going to be married.'

'Married?'

The look of surprise on her face was so comical, he chuckled. 'Why not? It would be the answer to your problems, wouldn't it? I promise I'll come and fetch you out as soon as I can and we'll find somewhere else to live.' He smiled, as the idea grew on him. 'I might even go back to practise as a lawyer. We could have a good life, you and I and the little one.' He told himself he was being practical and sensible and ignored the fact that his insides were churned up at the prospect of having her in his bed again, all legal and above board.

'You would be a father to my child?' she asked in astonishment. 'Why should you do that for me?'

'Because I care for you,' he said. 'And I am sad to see you in such straits.'

She flung her arms around his neck and sobbed. 'Oh, Thomas, I do not deserve your kindness.'

He took her in his arms, with the bump of Timothy's child holding them apart, and kissed her into being calm. 'Then you agree?'

Knowing he was right, she still hesitated. Some part of her still yearned for Paris, for the happiness they had known; he had given her a glimpse of another world and she was loath to let go of it. Marrying Thomas meant surrendering her dreams and placing her future in his hands, and though she was still very fond of him, she was not at all sure that that was what she wanted, but the realist in her argued that she would be a fool to turn Thomas down, and she ought to be thinking of her child's future, if not her own. And Thomas was a proper gentleman for all his funny ways. 'Must it be the Union?' she asked.

'Yes, until I have found your erstwhile lover.' He turned back towards the house, as if there were no more to be said, and she trailed reluctantly after him. 'He must pay for his pleasure and your broken dreams. Trust me, Sarah Jane.'

'Oh, I do,' she cried, sorry for her ingratitude. If her future lay with her old friend, then she must turn her back on the bitter-sweet memories of a summer of love. 'I'll go back to the Union if you think that's best, and perhaps it won't be so bad, if it's not for long.'

'Good girl. I'll ask my sister to let your brother stay with you, shall I? He will be company for you until I come back and when we're married, Billie can come and live with us.' He was aware, even as he promised to include her brother in his plans, that it all hinged on finding her lover and, what was more to the point, making sure he could afford to be generous. Sarah Jane had implied he was a gentle-man, and her impression had been that he was rich, but her idea of rich could be way off the mark and in any case, young men often sported the appearance of wealth with nothing to back it. He smiled wryly to himself, remembering his own pretensions as a young man. Perhaps he should not have told her his plans until he was sure of their success, perhaps he had buoyed up her hopes for nothing, but it hurt him to see his laughing green-eyed girl so unhappy and he wanted to help her. 'Now, go in and collect your belongings and I will see you safely onto the carrier's cart.'

'Today?' Now the time had come she was sorry to be leaving. Living at Chevington House had given her an insight into how the more affluent members of society lived, fuelled her ambition and taught her a great deal, more than even Thomas had been able to, but it was no good dwelling on impossible ambitions, she must make the best of what she had. And what she had was a friend. She was very fond of Thomas; his command of the situation relieved her of the need to think for herself or make decisions, and her flagging spirits revived. Whatever was to come could not be worse than what had gone before and she had survived it. But oh how she wished it had all been differ-ent.

She left him in the kitchen while she went up to her room and tied her possessions into a pitifully small bundle and when she returned he was alone, writing a note for her to take to his sister. He stood up and smiled reassuringly. 'Come, my dove, our future awaits us.'

They walked slowly down the drive to the lion-guarded gates and in less than half an hour, the clip-clop of hooves and the creaking of a cart told them the carrier was rounding the bend. He stopped abreast of them and grinned at her as Thomas helped her climb up on the seat and handed over her fare.

It was almost two years since she had travelled that road and very little had changed except that the railway had pushed its iron ribbon further into the countryside. On the plains of the fens, it ran on an embankment for miles, dividing the fields as once the road had divided them. The navvies had gone, moved on down the track to carry on their work, mile after mile, passing through villages, skirting towns, tunnelling through hills and bridging valleys; they moved forward and didn't look back. And she must not look back.

But at the sight of that gaunt building standing at the crossroad, she found herself hurled back to a long ago summer, when she had been forced into that dreadful decision. She had not known what it meant then, but she did now. She knew exactly what was on the other side of that heavy door with its message over the lintel and its frayed bellrope, and she did not see how she was going to endure it. And if Thomas did not keep his promise to come back for her, what then? She had a sudden vision of years and years of living in that awful place, working in the laundry or among the pots and pans of the kitchen, with no hope and no love, always doing as she was told, until she grew old and wrinkled. Her courage failed her, or perhaps she found a new courage; she could not afterwards have said which it was.

'Stop!' In her agitation, she stood up and nearly fell from the swaying cart. 'I want to get off.'

He shrugged his shoulders and pulled on the reins. She climbed down, resolutely turned her back on her only refuge and set off down the road which led westwards, knowing that she had cut herself off, not only from the shelter of the Union, but from Thomas too. He didn't deserve such off hand treatment, but she couldn't help it. 'Forgive me, Thomas,' she said. 'But I couldn't go back there, not even for you. An' I couldn't marry you, 'twouldn't be right.' She had to be in charge of her own destiny, to live her own life, to make her own decisions, be they right or wrong, to bring up her child in freedom.

Her one idea was to put as many miles as possible between her and the workhouse, and the sun was low in the sky before she began to think of finding shelter for the night. But the weather was fine, a hedgerow would do; it bothered her more that she had not eaten since breakfast and hunger pangs gnawed at her insides. She stopped and pushed her fingers into her stomach, willing the pain to go away. It did, but when it returned, the strength of it took her by surprise, and she was forced to acknowledge that this was no hunger pang. It brought to mind her mother's last confinement, the agony she had suffered, the heartrending cries which had filled their little home and made Billie cry, and the dead child, so still and perfect.

There was a small spinney ahead of her and, curling up through the trees, a thin spiral of smoke. She stopped, waiting for another spasm to pass, and then ran in among the trees, stumbling as she went, scratching her hands and face on the undergrowth and not even noticing. Through tears of fear and pain, she saw people, men and women about a campfire, heard voices and laughter as if from a great way off. 'Help me. Oh, please help me,' she pleaded, as she stumbled among them.

'Mercy be,' said a plump woman in a grubby brown skirt and a faded blouse. 'She's havin' a bairn. Bring her over here where the ground is soft and leave her to me. James, stir up that fire and put the pot on again. Daisy, you find something to wrap the child in, an old shawl or a blanket – a soft one, mind.'

They helped her to a bed of bracken a little way from the campsite and then the woman shooed the others off and knelt beside her. 'Bless ye, you're no more'n a bairn yourself,' she said gently, stroking the tangled hair from Sarah Jane's face. 'Is it full-term? Do ye know the date it should be?'

'It's nigh on a month early.' Sarah Jane screwed up her face as another pain began. 'Does it matter? Will it ...'

The woman smiled. 'I'm sure it will be fine. Now, be a brave lass and push when I tell ye, it won't be long now.' And as Sarah Jane opened her mouth to shriek, she pushed a piece of harness between her teeth. 'Bite on this. We don't want to frighten the little'ns, do we?' The pain subsided again and Sarah Jane smiled weakly. 'I'm sorry ... sorry to put you to all this tr ... trouble.'

''Tis nothin', m'dear. Come on, get ready for the next one, I c'n see its head.' And when, a moment later, Sarah Jane spat out the leather and opened her mouth again, she added, 'Hold onto me and save your breath for pushin'.'

Sarah Jane thought her whole body was being ripped apart as the pains came thick and fast, and then suddenly it was over, and she flopped back exhausted. There was a sudden hush in the clearing as if humans and animals alike were waiting with bated breath, and then the silence was pierced by the wail of an infant.

' 'Tis a beautiful laddie,' the woman told her, deftly cleaning the blood and mucus from the child. 'A mite small, but as healthy as you're like to meet.' She wrapped Sarah Jane's son in a shawl and handed him to her. 'There, lass, give 'im a cuddle.'

Sarah Jane took the child and held him in the crook of her arm, gazing down with wonder at the soft, almost-white hair, the screwed-up face and the tiny fingers poking above the shawl and was overwhelmed by her love for him. This little child was hers, her flesh and blood, part of her body, part of Paris too. What would he say if he knew their love had produced this new little being, this innocent child? Would it have made any difference? She prayed for the strength to keep him at her side, to look after him, day by day, and watch him grow to become a man, tall and straight, in pride and love. For his sake she must grasp whatever life had to offer, pleasure and pain, and make something of herself. She must not fail him as she had failed Billie; he had to come first, before lover, husband, brother, or anyone else who came into her life. This she promised herself.

She had not thought of a name for him but now she murmured, 'Jason', as if she had known it all along. 'Jason. And your mam will find the golden fleece for you.' She put her finger in his hand and he clutched it firmly, making her laugh delightedly. The sound made him open his eyes and she knew then that he would be a constant reminder of the man who had given him to her; he had inherited the wide, dark eyes of his father.

While her midwife tidied up around her, Sarah Jane sat and held her child, overcome by the wonder of his birth. 'He's mine,' she whispered. 'He is, isn't he? He's all mine.'

'Ye'll know that when he starts keepin' you awake of a night with his teeth.' The woman laughed. 'And when he starts walkin' and gettin' into mischief, ye'll ha' no doot who's responsible for the little laddie.'

It was a responsibility both awesome and delightful and hers alone; no one – neither Thomas nor Paris nor anyone in the future would take it from her, ever. Jason was hers, her penance and her blessing, her shame and her pride. Her son.

Chapter Six

*T*he group had obviously been in the clearing for a day or two because there was an order about the rough canvas shelters which housed them and the table by the fire where the meals were prepared. They seemed, at first, to be one big family, but when they crowded round to look at the baby and introduce themselves, she discovered there were two, the McBrydes and the Barnabys. James McBryde, by virtue of the fact that he was the older man and physically the more powerful, was their leader. He wore moleskin trousers, a gaudy waistcoat and a floppy-brimmed felt hat that had once been white. The plump woman who had attended Sarah Jane so skilfully was his wife, Maggie. They had a son of about ten called Ned, lanky and growing out of his clothes, but healthy for all that, and a pert little six-year-old daughter called Celia, with dark ringlets and merry eyes. Joseph Barnaby was a smaller version of James, dark where James was fair, and his wife, Daisy, thinner and sharper-featured than Maggie, was mother to twins, Ben and Jon, who were a little younger than Ned.

Sarah Jane tried to voice her gratitude. 'I don't know what I'd have done without you,' she said, 'but I've no money to pay you.'

'Bless ye lass, we don't want paying,' Maggie said. 'We'd have done the same for anyone.'

'I've only got this.' Sarah Jane delved into her bundle and took out the box containing the golden apple. She no longer needed it to remind her of carefree summer days and a man whose constancy had been blown away on the wind like the seeds of the dandelion; she had his son. She held it out to Maggie. 'Take it, please. I don't think it's worth much, but it's all I have.'

Maggie took the box and opened it, then gasped. 'How did you come by it?'

'I didn't steal it,' Sarah Jane said defensively. 'It was given to me by ...' she paused, fumbling for the right word ' ... by Jason's father as a birthday present.'

'Are you sure it's not valuable? It looks like a real pearl to me, and I'll swear that's gold.' Maggie handed it to James, who looked at it and gave it back to Sarah Jane.

'Keep it lass,' he told her. 'Ye never know when ye might have greater need of it than now.'

'But I want to give you something for helping me.'

'No call for that,' he said. 'Now, tell us your plans. We're railway folks as you might ha' guessed, and we're on the tramp for work. The *East Fen* section behind us is finished and we're looking for a place where they're taking on men. We sent our son, Duncan, on ahead to scout for us, and when he comes back, we'll be moving on.'

She was gripped by panic. Her foolhardiness had landed her among them, but it was almost as if it had been ordained, and now they were talking of moving on. She ought to move on, too, in case Thomas came looking for her; he could be very persuasive and she knew that it would be wrong to marry him just because he felt sorry for her. Pity was something that did not last. And if he insisted on her going back to the Union, it would be a backward step and she did not want to take it; she must go forward, always forward. But where to?

'He's been gone over a week,' Maggie added. 'We're expecting him any day now.'

'D'ye want us to send for someone?' James asked. 'The bairn's father, mebbe?'

Sarah Jane did not want to think of the handsome young man she called Paris and their careless lovemaking by the river; it seemed so long ago it was like a dream. What had he said about dreams turning into nightmares? This was a nightmare, and no mistake, and it would have been worse but for these people who sat round the clearing, waiting for her to speak. Their obvious sympathy made her feel a cheat, but she could not explain how she had conceived her child; they could not be expected to understand. 'I have no idea where he is,' she said. 'He ... he just disappeared.'

'Where were you headin' when you came upon us?' Daisy asked, idly putting her finger into Jason's hand and watching him grip it.

'I ... I was going to visit friends. I didn't realise the baby would come so soon.' She looked at the small bundle cradled in her arms; he was enveloped in one of Maggie's shawls, the lower half of him pinned into a square of cotton torn from one of Daisy's old petticoats. He needed proper clothes and soon he would need food and later schooling; he needed so much and how was she ever to obtain them for him?

'They'll be worryin' about ye,' James said gently.

'No, they weren't expectin' me.' She was, she knew, a very poor liar. 'Can I stay until your son arrives? I still feel a little weak.'

'Aye, lass, 'course you can,' Maggie said. 'Duncan will help you along the road to your friends when he comes. Now, ye had best feed the wee one, for I can see he is stirring himself to let rip. We'll leave ye in peace.'

The clearing was suddenly filled with the crying of a hungry infant and they smiled and drifted away to see to their own affairs. She opened her blouse and held her child to her breast where he nuzzled about until he found the nipple. She watched him sucking, feeling the pull of his firm little mouth and smiled. 'Oh, my darling babe, what are we going to do?' she whispered, bending her head over his. 'Where can we go? How will we live?'

The questions tumbled over each other, but she had no answers except: 'Go back to the Union.' Perhaps she had been a fool not to take the way out that Thomas had offered; at least then she would have had a roof over her baby's head and someone to take care of them both. Now she was alone and there was no one to turn to. Tears, she had taught herself never to shed, began pricking her eyelids.

But she *did* have someone, she scolded herself. She had Jason – and she had no business wallowing in self-pity. She bent to kiss the top of his head, plucked him from one breast and turned him round, where he clamped himself to the other. Jason had given her something to live for, to work for, and she would, too. She could read and write and cook and clean; there must be someone somewhere who needed her talents, few as they were. But to do that she had to stay out of the Union and out of the clutches of anyone who wanted to dictate the course of her life. Could she stay with the navvies, just until they reached a place where she could find work? Wherever they were going was bound to be better than Chevington Workhouse, and wherever it was, she would find other opportunities.

As soon as everyone was awake the following morning, the ritual of rising and breakfasting began. The women left the clearing to wash in the stream running through the meadow alongside the spinney, while the men gathered wood, raked out the fire and set it to blaze again. When their wives returned, they went to their own ablutions and the women cooked breakfast. When they called her to join them Sarah Jane left Jason still sleeping in the warmth of her bed and stood up shakily. She felt thin as a reed and light as a feather as she crossed the clearing; it was almost as if she had just been born herself, that what had gone before had been another, different, darker life. Everything was bright and new and she was ready to begin again.

Three days later her optimism received a jolt when she left her bed and discovered a newcomer had arrived during the night. It was obvious this was Duncan McBryde; he was a golden-haired replica of his father, slimmer and perhaps an inch or two taller, but he had the same finely arched brows and cornflower-blue eyes.

'It's Duncan back,' Celia told Sarah Jane triumphantly. Then to her brother, who was busy taking down the rough canvas shelter which housed their belongings and loading everything onto the donkey-cart, 'This is Sarah Jane, an' she's got a new baby.'

He stopped what he was doing to smile and offer Sarah Jane his hand. 'Aye, so I've heard.'

'Pleased to meet you,' she murmured, feeling his great strength in the firmness of his handshake. 'Your people have been very kind to me.'

He grinned. 'From what I hear ye gave them little choice.'

She was inclined to be annoyed, but seeing the twinkle in his eye, smiled. 'No, I didn't, did I?'

'Where were ye going?' he asked.

'To visit friends.'

'On foot? Alone?'

He was, she noted, very tall; the top of her head barely reached his shoulder. 'Why not?' she demanded, tilting her head up to look defiantly into his clear eyes. There was humour there, and understanding, and an indefinable something that warmed her heart. It was almost as if he could see right into her head and knew exactly what was going on there. He knew she was lying, but there was no condemnation in his gaze.

'Duncan.' The imperious voice of his sister piped up. 'Tell Sarah Jane she can come with us.'

'Perhaps she doesn't want to,' he said mildly.

'Oh, she does, don't you, Sarah Jane?'

'Yes,' she said, realising that she wanted it more than she could say; they seemed so contented, so at peace with each other. It was something she had not seen since her mother had died, this oneness. It certainly did not occur in the Union, nor, as far as she could tell, among the occupants of Chevington House. 'Just some of the way.'

'What about your friends?'

'I lied. There are no friends.'

'Have ye nae folks?'

'No. I thought if I stayed with your people I could find work. Anything – I don't mind what it is.'

Maggie, carrying a pile of blankets she had just folded, stopped on her way to put them in the cart. 'Do ye want Duncan to keep ye company on the road a spell? He can catch us up later.'

'She wants to come with us,' Duncan said.

'With us?' Maggie repeated. 'Whatever for?'

'For company,' Sarah Jane said. 'Just a few miles, 'til I can find somewhere to work.'

'We canna delay,' James said. 'We leave as soon as we're ready.'

'I'm ready now,' she said, acutely aware of Duncan watching her.

'If ye canna keep up,' Joseph put in, 'then someone else'll beat us tae the jobs and we'll all be the poorer.'

'I'll keep up. I'll wager I can walk as far and as fast as any of you.'

'What if the bairn ails?' Daisy queried. She knew all about ailing bairns; she had borne five and only the twins had survived. 'What then?'

Sarah Jane saw a glimmer of hope. She looked from one to the other, and then turned green appealing eyes on Duncan. 'He's strong and healthy, he won't ail. Please take me with you. Just as far as the next town.'

They laughed and Maggie said, 'Bless ye, lass, we won't be going near towns. Railways is laid in the country.'

'I'm sorry,' Sarah Jane said, hoisting her child higher in her arms. 'I shouldn't have asked. I'm sorry I put you to so much bother. Thank you for all you've done.' With a last despairing look at Duncan, she turned and began to walk slowly towards the road.

'Wait!' She heard Duncan's voice behind her and stopped, holding her breath. 'Wait a minute.' He turned to his parents. 'If ye let her go, ye'll worry yourselves sleepless about what's become of her, and dinna bother denying it. Let her come – I'll look tae her.'

'Ye, lad?' his father queried in surprise.

'Aye, why not?' It had been an impulsive gesture on the young man's part, made up of a mixture of admiration and pity, and he hoped he would not regret it, but the look in Sarah Jane's eyes as she turned away had torn at his heart. He had so much and she had nothing.

'Oh, thank you,' Sarah Jane cried. 'You'll not regret it, I promise you.'

'There's naught to thank me for,' he said, tugging at the corner of a straw mattress which poked over the top of the cart he had been loading. 'Ma wouldna have left ye, whatever she said.'

The decision made, Jason was settled on a soft bundle of clothing in a corner of the cart and Celia climbed up beside him with instructions to keep an eye on him. Their remaining possessions were packed into bundles and distributed among them for carrying, and then they set off, using the nearby railway track as a guide and heading northwest, away from Chevington, away from the Union, from Paris and Thomas and Billie. But Sarah Jane couldn't help that: her fear, her intuition – every fibre of her mind and body had told her not to go back to the Workhouse, and it wasn't just that she hated it. Her future did not lie in that direction, nor for that matter with the navvies, but she had to take one step at a time. 'I'll make me own way,' she whispered, as she trudged beside the cart, hardly taking her eyes off Jason, who slept contentedly. 'I will too, you'll see.'

Walking alongside her new friends, listening to their chatter, her depression lifted. Her feet were bare, her head uncovered and there were no more grates to blacken or slop buckets to empty. She took off her boots and hung them round her neck so that she could feel the soft grass beneath her feet as she had done when she was small. Life, for the moment, was good again.

James called a halt at noon and thankfully they rested, eating bread and cheese and cold sausages. Sarah Jane fed Jason, watched by the curious Celia, and within half an hour, they were on the move again. In some ways, she wished they had not stopped; her limbs had become stiff and the tiredness she hadn't noticed when she was walking engulfed her and made lead of her feet. But she had promised to keep up, and keep up she would. She forced her way forward and in a little while her movements became automatic, one aching foot before the other, numbed into a kind of walking sleep.

'Tired?' Duncan asked, as they picked their way between the railway and a river, taking the straightest and therefore the shortest line.

She liked the soft burr of his Scottish accent, the gentleness of it, the quiet strength of his presence walking beside her, mile after mile. 'A little.'

'Ye'll get used to it,' he said. 'A couple of days on the tramp and ye'll be hardened like the rest of us.'

'Yes.' She had to believe that or she would give up, right there and then.

'Tell me about y'self,' he said, trying to take her mind off her aching muscles. 'I want tae know everything about ye.'

She hesitated, knowing there were some things he would not like about her, but she could not keep them from him; he deserved her honesty. So she told him about her parents and Billie, who must surely have forgotten her by now because she had broken all the promises she had ever made to him. She told him about Thomas Wistonby and her education, about Chevington House and even about the handsome young man who had fathered Jason. She told him without emotion, without excuses, apportioning no blame. He listened and said nothing. 'Now you know,' she finished. 'I should have told you all this before you took me on, but I was afraid you'd turn me away.'

His smile crinkled the tanned skin around his eyes and made them seem even bluer. 'It changes nothing. The past is past and should be forgotten.'

'Then why ask about it?'

'Because it helps me to know ye,' he said simply. 'We canna offer an easy life, because 'tis far from that, and ye'll be expected tae do your share of the work, but we stick together and help each other.'

'Will you be telling the others?' She nodded towards James and Maggie, walking side by side ahead of them.

'No.'

They walked twenty miles before making camp, eating a frugal meal and dropping into an exhausted sleep where they sat. They were not far from a town – Sarah Jane had seen its spires and chimneys across the fields – but nothing was said about her leaving them and she was glad of that. She did not think she could bring herself to plead with them again.

The next day they walked another twenty miles and, determined not to complain, Sarah Jane plodded on with the protective Duncan beside her. They left the fens behind; the dark flat fields gave way to hills and valleys, the reeds and sedge became trees and meadows, the lark replaced the willow warbler. Cutting a swathe through it all was the railway track, seemingly endless, with the sun glinting on its shining steel for miles ahead. Sarah Jane knew that when it came to an end, they would have reached their destination. But she was in no hurry. Her walking had developed a kind of rhythm which helped to keep her going, the weather was dry and warm and her son behaved perfectly. Both families seemed to have accepted her as one of the

89

group, though she sensed Maggie had reservations. She was Duncan's mother and protective of him, and Sarah Jane was not such a fool as to be unaware of her own sex appeal, but she had other things to think about now she was a mother herself, and she was careful not to offend any of them. While they were on the tramp she was a drain on their limited resources, but that was a situation she intended to remedy at the first opportunity; in the meantime she repaid their kindness with a willingness to do anything they asked of her. She helped pack and unpack, put up the shelter, prepared vegetables, looked after Celia as well as Jason, and amused the boys with her stories of the Ancient Greeks. Later, if they would let her, she would do more, and when they arrived wherever they were going, she would look for work to pay for her keep. And when she had money saved, she would move on.

They reached Scarside five days later and the serenity of their journey was suddenly shattered. Here was all the noise and clatter and bustle of a railway works – trucks, barrows, pile-drivers, ropes, chains, sleepers, rails, wagons and horses, men and boys.

Sarah Jane and Duncan, walking ahead of the rest of the party, paused to watch the men laying the line in the wake of the navvies who were building an embankment and preparing the ground. One team laid the heavy wooden sleepers, followed by another carrying the rails. With the precision of a drill learned through long practice, they dropped them exactly into place.

'They're called iron men,' Duncan told her, pointing to the men with the lines. 'After them come the spikers to drive the spikes into the chairs which hold them on the sleepers, then the screwers finish spiking and bolting the joints.' He pointed again to men with crowbars who followed the teams. 'They're the trackliners. They make sure all the rails are in a perfect line.'

'Is that what you do, lay the lines?'

'I can turn my hand to most things,' he said, and to Sarah Jane it did not sound like boasting. 'But it's usually excavating.'

'Who says where the line goes?'

'The surveyors and engineers, but in the end 'tis all down to economics and investment, who wants a railway, where and why.'

'And investors expect a quick return on their money?' She remembered something of Thomas's tuition on economics. It hadn't meant much at the time, but now she could see it in practice, it was easier to understand.

'Of course – wouldn't you?'

'Will you get work here?'

'We'll try.' Duncan looked about him as they moved on past the platelayers, then he said, 'It looks like a well-run works. They're working in a rhythm, there's none loafing or drunk, nae fighting either.'

'Do the men sometimes fight and get drunk?'

'If the pay is poor and the truck bad or the beer watered, then ye can be sure, sooner or later, they'll go on a randy.'

'Why is the pay better in some places than others?'

He grinned at her. 'Ye are a curious one, aren't ye? Why all the questions?'

'If I am to live among you, I want to know what to expect.'

He laughed. 'Ye need have nae fear that Da or Joseph will come home drunk, nor me neither.'

'I didn't think you would. Why don't the owners treat the men all alike?'

'Because there's good owners and bad owners and because some work is harder than others. Rock is difficult and tunnelling is the nearest you'll get to hell on earth and viaducts are treacherous; they must all be paid for at different rates. The contractor is employed by the owner and he lets out subcontracts. The subcontractor arranges the price with the gangers, either for a set, that's a truckload, or by the day, and the ganger passes it on to the men in wages.'

'Who's the ganger here?'

He pointed to where wagonloads of spoil had been brought from a cutting further back along the line and hitched to horses which were hauling it up a temporary track to the apex of the embankment. 'He's the one directing the boys running the tip.'

Sarah Jane watched as the leading horse, ridden by a boy and walking beside the rails, not between them, was urged into a gallop. She cried out, convinced that wagon, horse and rider would be pitched over the edge to certain death, but at the last minute the youngster who controlled it, slipped the harness and horse and boy turned aside, while the wagon careered on under its own momentum until it hit a sleeper laid across the very end of the line. Jolted to a stop it tipped up and deposited its contents neatly over the top. 'It looks dangerous.'

'It can be, but then nearly all navvying is dangerous.'

Directed by the ganger, the navvies scrambled down and used their shovels to level out the mountain of soil. In the heat of the day, the men worked without their shirts and their brown backs gleamed with sweat.

'Don't they ever stop?' she asked, in awe of the power of those rippling muscles. Looking up at Duncan, standing so close she could feel the warmth emanating from his body, she fell to wondering if he looked like that when he was stripped. She had never seen him without his shirt but, looking at him now as if seeing him properly for the first time, she realised that his body must be every bit as magnificent as theirs. The thought sent a familiar shiver through her limbs which was as unexpected as it was pleasurable and for one brief moment she allowed her imagination to run riot, before she pulled herself together and took a step away from him and the temptation to put out a hand to touch him.

He smiled, unaware of the effect his nearness had on her. 'They must drink and eat and attend to nature, o' course, but the work goes on; they leave it in turns. When it's too dark to see, they all go home.'

'Where's home?'

'Oh, anywhere. Some go to the shanties, that's the big huts you can see over there.' He pointed to a group of wooden buildings. 'Some have their own small huts alongside the line, a few take lodgings in the villages nearby, but they're usually too dear and too far from the work.'

'What work do the women do?' She had seen one or two of them moving about between the huts.

'They look after the men, cooking, washing, all the usual things. Some serve in the shop or the tavern.'

'Could I do that?'

He looked at her sharply. 'Indeed not!'

'Why not? I must do something to repay you and your family . . .'

'Ye have the bairn and that will keep ye busy. And ye can help Ma.'

'But it's not enough. I must bring in a wage.'

'There'll be time enough tae think of that later,' he said. 'The little one's nae yet a week old.'

When the rest of the party caught up with them, they were standing together, with his arm casually across her shoulder, and although it was more protective than possessive, it was as if it belonged there.

Sarah Jane followed as they made their way onto the site, led by the elder McBryde. 'We're three good men and three strong boys,' he told the ganger. 'We heard there's work here.'

'Where you from?'

'We've been working on the *East Fen*. We're experienced men and the boys are good with the horses.'

'I could use you for a few months, can't promise anything after that. Pay's two and six a day and half that for the boys.'

James shook hands on the deal and they set about finding a home. There were no permanent dwellings in the neighbourhood because the railway cut straight through the countryside and so they began a weary trudge from door to door of the already crammed shanties. 'We've room for one man,' they were told at one, and at another, 'We can take a couple, but no children.'

They would not be separated, and so went to look at a cave they had seen when they came down the hill to the site. To Sarah Jane it seemed out of the question, just a hole in the rock face, but James said, 'It'll do.'

Sarah Jane, who had taken Jason from the cart to feed him, watched while everyone moved off as if they had been drilled to the jobs allotted to them. Daisy swept the cave, Maggie lit a fire with wood gathered by the children and soon had the cooking pot on its cleft stick above it, while the men set off down the hill back to the works.

'Come and help me,' Maggie said, when Sarah Jane had pulled her bodice back over her breasts and buttoned it again. 'Put the bairn down, Celia will watch over him.'

Sarah Jane settled her son under the shelter of a bush and went to help with the preparation of the meal. 'Where have the men gone?' she asked. 'Surely they don't have to begin work tonight?'

Maggie laughed. 'No, they've gone to get tommy tickets.'

'Tommy tickets?'

Maggie handed her a pot and a spoon. 'Here, stir that. You'll soon learn that life on a navvy site is lived on credit. You spend your wages afore you get 'em. The ganger gives the men tommy tickets against their future wages and they must spend them in the tommy shop. The shop belongs to the contractor, o' course. Duncan has gone with his father and Joseph to get tommy tickets to buy wood and hammers and nails and canvas, and if such a thing can be had so late in the day, a loaf of bread and some tea.'

'Can't you shop anywhere else?'

Maggie smiled ruefully. 'If you've got ready money and if there's a store nearby, you can do what you like, but they're mighty big ifs.'

'I was thinking of trying to find work down there.' She nodded her head towards the site. 'You have all been so good to me and I don't know how else to repay you, but Duncan doesn't want me to.'

Maggie looked at her sharply. 'Sarah Jane, we're all very fond of ye, ye know that, don't ye?' She paused, deciding that now was the time to speak her mind. She was worried about Sarah Jane's past and the father of her child. Only a wealthy man could make a present of the like of that golden apple which, if Maggie's guess was correct, was worth a deal of money. Even then he would not give it to a servant girl he had casually tossed in the hay; there was more to it than that. Duncan, she knew, was on the way to being smitten and how would he feel if the man turned up again? 'Sarah Jane, I ask ye, please tae have a care. Duncan is young and he's never had a lass afore and I wouldna have him hurt.'

'Hurt him? How could you think I would do such a thing?' Maybe it was unfair of her to take advantage of them and Duncan in particular, but then life was not fair; a girl had to live, especially if she had a child to look after. Duncan was her lifeline but that did not mean she would do anything to make him unhappy. 'I'd never hurt him, or any one of you. What made you say that?'

'We never pried into your life before you came to us, did we? 'Tis plain as a pikestaff ye're no' a little innocent. An' Duncan's too young to be takin' on a ready-made family. Big and strong he is, on the outside, but inside, he's a great big softie, ready to listen to any tale of woe.'

'I ain't told 'im no tale of woe, though he does know everything about me, 'cos I ain't 'eld nothin' back.' As usual when she was agitated, Thomas' tuition flew out of her head and her speech reverted to the fen child's flat vowels and dropped consonants. 'An' no one said anythin' about takin' me and Jason on, not 'im nor me. We're just friends, just as you an' me and the Barnabys are friends, and I'm ready to work for my keep. I told you that, but if I ain't wanted, then I'll leave.'

Ignoring Maggie's protests, she got up and ran out to where Jason lay and picking him up, started off down the hill towards the shanty village. How foolish she had been to think they would allow her to stay until she chose to go. She was not ready to go, not yet. Duncan had been right, Jason was too young to be left. But she was not going to beg again. She should remember she was a Winterday. Hadn't Pa said, 'This family don't beg?' She had done too much of that already. She stumbled in among all the paraphernalia of railway building – lines, sleepers, wagons, stables, shanties – but had no idea where she was heading and stopped to take her bearings.

'Well, and who 'ave we 'ere?'

She turned at the sound of the voice and found herself being examined from top to toe by two women who had come from one of the huts, one thin as a rake, the other short and plump. Their woollen shawls, draped carelessly over their shoulders, covered clothes which, although shabby, were gaudily coloured. One wore a cottager hat tied on with a kerchief and the other a huge-brimmed bonnet with a sweeping plume. Their fashionable shoes had seen better days and their coloured stockings were full of holes, but it was their vividly painted faces which amused Sarah Jane most, and she could not suppress a smile as she retorted: 'What's it to you?'

'Where yer from?' demanded the thin one.

'If it's any o' your business, from Chevington way.'

'Who's yer man?'

'Who says I've got a man?'

They laughed and the plumper of the two dug her in the ribs. 'Well, you certainly had one once.'

'And what business is it of yours?'

'Oh, 'tis our business, all right. Just try takin' one of our men and yer'll larn soon enough ...'

'Why should I wish for one of yours?' she said, looking down her nose at them. 'If the looks of you is anything to go by, they don't do so well.'

'This is our pitch an' we don't allow no poachers. Now git while yer can still walk.'

Although she did not understand them, their threats annoyed her and she stood her ground. 'Who do you think you are, telling me to leave? I go where I please.'

The taller of the two grabbed her shoulder, making Jason wail. Sarah Jane pulled herself away and bent her head to soothe him. She felt a stinging blow on her bottom and fell forward, only just managing to avoid falling on top of Jason. Furious on his behalf, she put him on the grass out of harm's way, before scrambling to her feet and turning on the women, forgetting any pretensions she might have for ladylike behaviour. 'Frighten me baby, would yer? Well, let's see what yer made of, shall we?' She flailed into them both, arms turning like windmill sails. They retaliated and very soon all three were punching, kicking, pulling hair, scratching. A crowd gathered, shouting and cheering.

Suddenly Sarah Jane felt herself being dragged off and hauled bodily to her feet. Her anger was white-hot and her hair covered her face so that she could not at first see who held her. 'Let me be!' she shouted, straining against her captor. 'Let me get at 'em.'

'Leave 'em alone, man,' someone called cheerily. 'I ain't had such entertainment since me ol' granny's wake.'

'Calm down, Sarah Jane, calm down.' It was Duncan's voice and it was he who held her. 'Just what do ye think ye're doing?'

'They started it.' She struggled ineffectually.

'Ye shouldna be fightin' the likes o' them. Ye shouldna be fighting at all.'

She stood still and confined herself to glaring furiously at her adversaries, who were picking themselves up and dusting themselves down. Sarah Jane twisted round to face Duncan and realised that he was having difficulty in suppressing a grin. This annoyed her still further. 'I have to find work,' she snapped, flinging back her hair to reveal a face covered in scratches. 'An' it's not funny!'

'*That* kind of work?' He jerked his head towards the backs of the women who were strolling away with their arms round two navvies.

'I wasn't doing anything. They just started on me for no reason, asking questions and laughing at me. And when they knocked me over and made Jason cry ...' She was burning with resentment. 'I ain't 'avin' that.'

He stooped to pick the child up, cradling him carefully on one arm. 'Keep out o' their way, d'ye hear?'

'Why? Who are they?'

'Whores,' he said briefly.

'What's a whore?' she asked, suddenly remembering that Matron had called her that when she discovered her in Thomas' bed. She hadn't understood the word, but there had been no one to ask, and until now, she had forgotten it.

He smiled indulgently. 'Sarah Jane, ye are a simpleton sometimes. They serve a certain need among the men, a physical need for which they are paid, but ye're not to have anything to do with them, d'ye hear? Keep away from them or ye'll be tarred with the same brush.'

So that was what it meant! She wasn't a whore, was she? She'd never been paid, not exactly, though Thomas had given her lessons. Did that make her one? 'Does your mother think I'm a whore?'

'Whatever gave ye that idea?'

'She said I was no innocent.' It was, she knew, her guilt which had made her react so violently to Maggie's words of warning, guilt, not only at making use of them, but because she had recognised her own sexuality. Maggie had seen it too and Maggie had been afraid. 'Maybe I'm not, but that doesn't make me one of those, does it?'

'Certainly not.'

'She thinks I mean to hurt you, though how she thinks I can do that I do not know. I wouldn't do anything to harm any of you. I owe you.'

There was something about the way he was looking at her that stirred a memory. She had a fleeting glimpse of Thomas wanting her so badly that he was prepared to chance his sister's wrath to have her, and another of Paris offering her gifts for her favours, and the under-gardener at Chevington drawing her into the shadow of the stable to steal a kiss. It was the same sort of look except there was a kind of shyness about it; he was less sure of himself than they had been. But the message was unmistakable. Coming so soon after the revelations of her own body not a couple of hours before, she was taken aback.

'A man canna be trapped unless he wants to be.' He laughed suddenly, apparently unaware of her tumultuous thoughts. 'Six foot two I am, and still she thinks I'm her wee bairn.'

'But you're not, are you? You're not a child.'

'What a question!' He grinned down at her. 'There's a time and place for everything, Sarah Jane, and it's not this moment. Now, come away.'

'But I have to find work and lodgings.'

'We've been through all that, Sarah Jane.' He turned and took hold of her arm. 'I'll hear no more about it, d'ye hear? Besides, who'd look after the bairn if ye went out to work? Ye couldna take him with ye. Ye both belong with us and that's an end of it.' It was the first time she had seen him even slightly put out and her thin body shivered beneath his huge hands. It was not fear which gripped her, she knew that, but the reawakening of desire. It must be subdued; it had been her undoing twice before and she was not going to risk it again.

'Come on home.' He smiled down at her. She was half-child, half-woman, so innocent in some respects, so mature in others, and she flitted from one side of her nature to the other without warning. She was, he decided, like the stream along whose banks they had walked; when it came to an obstacle like a boulder or a tree trunk, it went over or round, whichever was the easier, and continued on its way. It was a little sullied at the edges by reeds and stagnant pools and the decaying rubbish of its contact with man, but its centre bubbled on, clear and sparkling. Without too much self-analysis or too many tortured doubts, he went straight to the spring. Inside she was pure and already he loved her.

'Home?' The word was like music to her ears.

'For as long as you want it.'

She laughed suddenly as if she had just discovered the world was a beautiful place. She slipped her hand into his and together they went back up the hill to the cave.

James and Joseph had stopped only for a hurried meal and were busy putting the building materials they had bought to good use. Duncan handed Jason to Sarah Jane and went to join them. Wooden posts were hammered into the ground and slats and canvas nailed to these, so that a large living room was created in front of the cave mouth; the cave itself was to become their sleeping quarters. Tarpaulin was used to roof the new structure and to make an entrance curtain. It was far from draughtproof, but it provided them all with shelter and they were all snugly inside when the first few heavy drops of rain tested their workmanship.

Happiness was to be found in such unexpected places, Sarah Jane decided, and when you least expected and deserved it. Chevington and her life there seemed so long ago, so far away, and though she had had a real roof over her head there, warm clothes and proper food, she would not now trade it for what she had. She would write to Billie and to Thomas. Thomas had taught her about seizing opportunities and he should understand why she had done what she had. But supposing he found Paris, supposing Paris tried to take Jason from her? Would he? Could he? She would fight to her last breath to keep him, but what if she lost? She was a nobody, love alone could not overcome those who had more power in society than she had, and if Thomas were on the side of the powerful ... She would write to him because he deserved some explanation, but she would not tell him where to find her.

Chapter Seven

*H*alf his life seemed to be lived in a railway carriage these days, Geoffrey thought as he settled himself in a first-class compartment of the train taking him home to Chevington. It was becoming increasingly inconvenient to be tied down to the public timetables; he would buy his own train, then he could come and go as he pleased. After all, if railways were to become his main enterprise he should have a carriage of his own, and an engine, too. He would call it *The Lady Chevington* – that would please Constance.

His original intention when agreeing to back the *East Fen Railway Company* had been to confine his activities to the immediate neighbourhood of his country seat and, once the railway had been completed, to dispose of his interest to those who were to run the finished line and return to the life of an English gentleman. But he had found he enjoyed the cut and thrust of business: it added a zest and purpose to his life and when the opportunity had arisen to take over the *West Fen Company* he had seized it enthusiastically. The line had since become as profitable as the *East Fen*. Now Jack Miller, his engineer, had suggested further expansion – which meant ploughing back his profits into what looked like an ailing company, and Geoffrey was not sure of the wisdom of it.

According to Miller, the trouble was due to inefficiency and a dishonest subcontractor who had been selling inferior goods in the tommy shop. The men had rioted, gone on what they called 'a randy', set fire to the shop and destroyed the track and the contractor had no funds to begin again. 'Redress their grievances and offer them a fair wage and they'll settle down,' he had said.

Lord Chevington looked up from reading his engineer's report, to gaze at the houses, farms and fields beside the line, but he did not see them. His mind was on their conversation. Should he or shouldn't he? The iron wheels running so smoothly on the track echoed his thoughts – *should he or shouldn't he?* If he lost all his profits, he'd be none the worse off; he would still have his home and estates, and what a challenge it would be! It would also benefit his son, for if Timothy took an interest, he could make his way in the business world and that might mitigate his obvious disappointment over lack of an inheritance. But it was more than disappointment, Geoffrey acknowledged. It was bitter resentment; Timothy had never recovered from the blow of learning of his bastardy. Geoffrey sighed. He should not have told the boy; it should have remained a secret, taken to the grave. There was nothing he could do about it now except to be as understanding as possible.

Ever since he had told Timothy the truth, Geoffrey had been trying to make it up to him. He had spent more time with him, increased his allowance, made the house at Walton over to him, leased him a modest London apartment, bought him horses, a carriage, a wardrobe that would have been the envy of Beau Brummel, and encouraged him to become involved in the railway enterprises. He had given Timothy almost anything his heart desired, except a public acknowledgement of his kinship. This was a sticking point Geoffrey avoided discussing because it always ended in a heated argument which left him exhausted and depressed.

He wanted to give in, to bring the young man home to Chevington and adopt him as his heir. Legally, he could do so, for the estate was not entailed, but there was Constance to consider. He could not talk to her about it, not even to please Timothy. It was funny that she had never shown either interest or curiosity about the boy. As far as she was concerned, her husband was doing his duty by a dead friend. Timothy wanted for nothing and there was no need for her to concern herself with his welfare when the workhouse children needed her more.

He stood up as the train drew into Chevington station. It was a small halt which had been built expressly for his own use and any guests who might come to Chevington House, and there was only one employee – a stationmaster, porter and ticket-collector, all in one. That worthy ran to take His Lordship's bag as soon as he saw him descending from the train. 'Good afternoon, my lord,' he said cheerfully. 'Lovely day again. Trains all on time and the gig's waiting for you outside.'

His life ran like clockwork; there was an ordered routine which meant that whenever he arrived at Chevington Halt, there was always a vehicle to meet him. If he wanted to ride, there were mounts; if he wanted to shoot or fish, there was always plenty of game. If he wanted to entertain, the rooms readied themselves and food appeared as if by magic. He could command with a flick of a finger, so why did he have this vague feeling that he was missing something? Whatever it was, it drove him to risk more, to work harder, than any of his contemporaries. His wife did not comprehend it any more than he did; it was difficult to put into words and that was his fault, not hers.

Constance was still a very beautiful woman and every bit as desirable as when he had first met her, and his only regret was her childlessness and the fact that his fatherhood had to be kept from her. It wasn't that he feared her anger, he could take that, but he could not bear the thought of hurting her. At least he could try and talk to her more about his business interests, show her how important they were to him.

'Both fen sections are all but finished,' he told her over dinner which they took at the now popular time of seven o'clock. Constance sat beside him and not at the foot of the table separated by several feet of polished oak; he could reach out and touch her if he chose. 'There are a few looplines and connections and a station or two to be built but, by and large, the area is now adequately covered. It has been a very profitable venture, even disregarding the side benefits.'

'I am pleased to hear it. Now perhaps we can return to normal.'

'Normal, my dear?' He raised one eyebrow at her but he knew perfectly well what she meant.

'You are an aristocrat, not a tradesman. You should leave things like that to those who are paid to look after your interests, not go chasing all over the countryside doing everything yourself. I can't think why you do.'

He had tried to tell her before, but she never seemed to take it in. 'You know we had a surplus of milk and when I heard about the experiments in canning and evaporating, I decided I wanted to be involved, but before the railway line came through Chevington it was impossible to keep the milk fresh enough to reach the manufactories where the canning is done.' He paused to smile at her. She was wearing an evening gown of heavy green silk which enhanced the creaminess of her bare shoulders and matched the emeralds in her necklace. 'There were other benefits too – the transport of grain to the flour-mills and animals to the slaughterhouses. You know when they are sent by train, they arrive in far better condition than when they are driven on the hoof. And passengers, of course. I could not have returned to you so quickly if I had been obliged to arrange a post-chaise or come by the mail.'

She was leaning forward, a morsel of white fish covered with creamy sauce on her fork, poised to pop into her mouth. He was riveted by the tip of her tongue, pink and sensuous, curled to take the food. His senses reeled. It was all the more disturbing for being unconscious; she was completely unaware of the effect it had on him. He pulled himself together, raising his glass to her.

She smiled an acknowledgement. 'I understand that but it does not answer my question, does it?'

He had forgotten the question, but he had to go on, or ravish her on the table. The idea of doing that made him smile. 'Railways afford a reliable and speedy means of communication between the farms, the manufactories and the cities to the benefit of all. Even you must own that the advantages outweigh the disadvantages.' He reached out and covered her hand with his own. 'Constance, there is a quiet revolution taking place in this country of ours. The old order is changing and I want to be a part of it.'

'But it is hardly the life of a nobleman,' she said, withdrawing her hand in order to ring the bell at her side for a servant to clear the first course and bring in the next.

'I have been thinking of expanding my interests,' he went on. 'There is another line . . .'

'Expanding! Oh Geoffrey, you are taking things too far. Quite apart from the fact that I have no idea how I will explain it to our friends, who think you are quite mad already, you could overreach yourself.'

'Nonsense, my dear. I believe buying up the line adjacent to the West Fen is a great opportunity. It means I will control most of the network linking the fens to the Midlands, and that could have some significance in the future.'

'But surely you could invest without actually working?'

'It's more than being an investor,' he said, standing up to carve a joint of beef which had just been put on the table in front of him. 'It's being involved every step of the way from the first drawings to the last rail. I choose to work and that is no bad thing.'

'Yes, but if you like being occupied, you could work about here and do the things that someone in your position should do. You could take your seat in the Lords.'

'One member of the family in politics is enough.'

'If you mean my brother-in-law, that's not the same. He is an elected Member of Parliament and could easily be thrown out at the next election.'

'I doubt it! He is making quite a name for himself, as Amelia has no doubt been quick to tell you.'

Knowing she was losing that argument, she changed tack. 'If you don't want to do that, you should involve yourself in local affairs. Why did you turn down that appointment as a magistrate?'

'I do not feel in a position to pass judgement on my fellow men. "Let him that is without sin ..."'

'Oh, Geoffrey, sometimes you exasperate me! Someone has to mete out justice and charity. We cannot all stand back and wash our hands of the evil in this world.'

He watched her take a tiny helping of vegetables from one of the many tureens which had been put on the table in the wake of the beef. 'You take care of that very admirably, my dear, with your work at the Union.' He piled his own plate with food and smiled at her. If only she had children of her own to bring up, this frantic busying of herself with other people's affairs would not be her life's work, he thought, and if they had had children together, then they might be closer. 'So, tell me the latest news of that citadel to man's inhumanity to man.'

'That's not fair! The poor would be a great deal worse off without it, though I own I am sometimes disappointed by their behaviour after we have done our best for them. Sarah Jane Winterday is a case in point ...'

'Sarah Jane? Isn't she one of our servants?'

'She was. Wilkins had to dismiss her.'

'Why?'

'She was ... in an interesting condition.'

He laughed at the euphemism. 'One of the menservants?'

'Possibly, though she wouldn't say.'

'Perhaps you shouldn't condemn her out of hand. It takes two, you know.'

'I'm going to the Union on Friday, when I shall speak to Sarah Jane and try to find out who the father is. If she wouldn't tell Wilkins, she might tell me.'

'She has gone back there?' He remembered the young girl standing in his library, head erect, green eyes full of life, as he handed her one of his books. She had been very different from the normal run of servants, graceful and beautiful in an untamed sort of way, and so unafraid. She had spoken up for herself and laughed at his surprise that she could read. Few servants would consider hours spent in reading as time well spent. Now someone had ruined it for her. He was suddenly filled with an overwhelming pity. 'Was that necessary?'

'Where else could she go? We can't be seen to condone such immoral behaviour, can we? If she had been prepared to name the father, something might have been arranged, but as it is, she must pay for her folly. She will be looked after in the Union and so will the infant.' She laid aside her napkin and stood up. 'I shall wait for you in the withdrawing room. Don't be too long.'

She left him fiddling with the delicate stem of his wine glass and musing about the way they lived their lives, each doing what interested them most with very little reference to the other. Tonight was the first time they had really talked for months and he felt closer to her than he had done for a very long time. But more than anything, he wanted to make love to her. He took only one glass of brandy with his cigar and hurried to join her again.

She was sitting on the sofa embroidering a tapestry for what she fondly imagined would become the top of a stool, but which he knew would find its way into the ragbag along with numerous other items begun but never finished. She had little patience with the mundane occupations with which a woman in her position was expected to fill her time, the embroidery and endless gossip, the rounds of visiting for visiting's sake, riding out in the carriage to show off her newest gown or hat. Like her husband, she preferred to be profitably busy, but at no time would she have thought of making the comparison.

She looked up and smiled as he entered. 'Talking of the Union,' she said, 'has reminded me I had a strange caller today.'

'Oh.' He sat down beside her, took the embroidery frame from her hands and laid it aside. 'How strange?'

'He was a lawyer.' She paused and gave a light laugh. 'At least, he said he was a lawyer and he spoke like a cultured gentleman, but he wasn't like any lawyer I have ever met; he looked so unkempt.'

Geoffrey grimaced. 'Constance, I know you meet all sorts when you go to the Union, but should you be entertaining such people here, when I am away from home?'

'He didn't come to see me, he asked for you. He seemed quite put out when I told him you weren't here.'

'What did he want?'

'He wouldn't say.'

'What was his name? Where did he come from?'

'He said his name was Thomas Wistonby and he came from the Union, at least when I said I thought we had met, he told me he worked among the inmates who needed help of a legal kind and I might have seen him there.'

'But I have no business with the Union.'

'I don't think it was Union business. Anyway, he said he would return tomorrow, so you'll find out then. I've said he may call at ten o'clock.'

'Very well,' he said, rising and holding out his hand to her. 'Now, can we forget unions and business and whoever is coming tomorrow and go to bed?' He bent his head to kiss her. 'I love you, Constance, as I have always loved you and if I have sometimes neglected to tell you so, then I am penitent.'

She flushed with pleasure and allowed him to lead her up the stairs to his bedroom, where he dismissed his valet and the maid who hurried along the corridor to help her, and, ushering her into the room, shut the door on them.

'Geoffrey, you've shocked them,' she said. 'And I can't manage my buttons myself.'

'I'm not entirely helpless,' he said. 'Turn round.'

They laughed together as he fumbled with the tiny buttons at the back of her dress, then the ties of her petticoats, then the crinoline cage, until she was standing in her drawers and shift. 'Why do women have to wear such a multitude of clothes?' he asked.

'To protect us from the cold,' she said, giggling like a girl. 'And from assaults such as this. You have to be pretty determined to breach the defences.' She was naked now and the glow of the fire played over her smooth skin, shone in her fair hair and was reflected in her eyes, so that she seemed to be alight from top to toe.

'I *am* determined.' He pulled off his own clothes, scattering them about the room, then picked her up and laid her gently on his bed. 'Now, I shall breach the defences,' he said, lowering his head to her abdomen.

'I have none,' she said softly. 'Not against you.'

His hands and mouth roamed over her body until she moaned with pleasure. He entered her swiftly and allowed the passion he had been trying to control all evening to overcome his normal restraint. It was over too quickly, he knew that. He ought to have stemmed his impatience. Now she would be disappointed and probably think that his one aim was to beget an heir as quickly and unemotionally as possible. And nothing was further from the truth; tonight he had wanted her as any virile man would want his wife. He rolled over onto his side and drew her towards him, kissing her with the tenderness he should have shown at the start. 'We should do that more often.'

105

She smiled slowly. 'The remedy is with you, dear Geoffrey. You are away so much . . .'

'Yes, I am sorry. I shall try to be at home a little more.'

She wriggled closer to him and laid her head in the hollow of his neck, so that the scent of her hair filled his nostrils. 'How little you have changed in twenty-two years,' she murmured. 'You are still the impatient young man I married and I still feel the same as when we first met, head over heels in love with you.'

He laughed and kissed the top of her head. 'And I with you. The years have sped by so quickly, haven't they? It seems like yesterday you came down the aisle in that magnificent wedding gown and I nearly burst my breeches with love and pride. What a catch you were!'

'Not so much of a catch as it turned out,' she said quietly. 'I haven't been able to give you an heir.'

'There is still time. Perhaps tonight . . . '

'No, Geoffrey, it's too late.' Her voice broke and she swallowed. 'I did so wish for a child, not only to give you an heir, but because I wanted to be a mother, to hold children of my own in my arms, to watch my sons grow to manhood and my daughters into beautiful women. I would have given almost anything for that.'

He propped himself on his elbow and turned to look down at her. 'I've been selfish and unthinking. I didn't realise how much it meant to you.' He took her hand and turned it over slowly to kiss the palm. 'Would you like to adopt a child?'

'No!' she said, so sharply that he looked at her in surprise. 'No,' she repeated quietly. 'I am past the age when looking after an infant comes naturally.'

'An older child, then – a boy coming into manhood?'

'No, Geoffrey, it would not be fair on all the other children at the Union to pick one out. In a way they are all my children, don't you understand that?'

Was she being deliberately obtuse, he wondered. How could she imagine he meant a workhouse child? Could he tell her that he had a son? Could he persuade her that Timothy really belonged to them both, that the woman who had borne him had been a surrogate for her, no more?' No, he decided. Telling her that would be like boasting that their childlessness was no fault of his and he couldn't do it. He cradled her in his arms and murmured endearments, soothed the sad thoughts from her, told her it did not matter, assured her that she was everything to him and thrust Timothy to the back of his mind. Poor dear, trusting Constance, how could he deceive her so? And how could he not?

Constance had been right about the man's appearance, he decided, when a footman showed Thomas into the library the following morning, although it seemed he had made some effort to tidy himself. His trousers had been pressed, and his cravat – albeit a hideous purple – had been carefully tied, but neither disguised the down-at-heel shoes and overlong hair. Geoffrey, determined to keep the interview short, did not ask him to be seated.

'Good morning, Mr Wistonby. Lady Chevington tells me you have urgent business with me.'

'Yes, my lord.'

'It would have been better if you had come to my office.'

'It is not that kind of business, my lord. It is of a personal nature.'

The fellow had come to beg, he knew it. 'Then let's hear it,' he said.

'It's about your son.'

'Mr Wistonby, you are mistaken. Lady Chevington and I have no son.'

Thomas smiled at the way His Lordship had avoided telling a direct lie; it encouraged him to go on. 'A slip of the tongue, my lord,' he said easily. 'Of course, I meant your ward, Mr Timothy Myson.'

'What about him?'

'It is also concerning a young lady ...'

'Get on with it, man.'

'I know young gentlemen like to have their fling and who can blame them? But the poor, dear girl is quite ruined and completely bereft ...'

'Are you telling me a young lady has been compromised by my ward?'

'Yes, my lord, exactly so.'

'Who is she?'

'Her name is Sarah Jane Winterday, my lord. She was a servant in your household.'

'Oh.' How had Timothy met her? Had he come to the house, knowing it was forbidden to him? Had Constance seen him? How much did this man, Wistonby, know? 'If you have come to tell me she is expecting a child, I know it,' he said carefully. 'My wife informed me that the girl had been dismissed because of it.' He did not for a moment doubt that Timothy was capable of bedding the girl and he did not blame him, except for the embarrassment of having someone like this lawyer fellow coming to him for money. No doubt he would threaten a scandal if he did not pay. He felt like telling him to go to hell, that girls like Sarah Jane asked for trouble, but he could not do that. There was Constance to be protected for one thing and the girl herself had not struck him as being promiscuous. Oh, Timothy, you fool, why could you not have had a care for the consequences and why take Sarah Jane, who deserved better than to have motherhood thrust upon her before she had left her own childhood behind? 'But how can you be sure the culprit is my ward? Did Sarah Jane name him?'

'No, my lord, not exactly, but from the description she gave, it can be no other.'

'A description is hardly proof, Mr Wistonby. What other evidence have you?'

'I have spoken to others . . .'

'What others? Name them, if you please.'

'No, my lord, I don't think that will be necessary.' Thomas didn't want to divulge the source of his information. Tilly would be dismissed and that wouldn't be fair, considering he had pumped the story from her with two sixpences and several glasses of gin at the local hostelry – hardly adequate compensation for losing her job.

'Gossip, Mr Wistonby. That will not do.'

'My lord, Mr Myson was at Chevington at the relevant time and not skulking about like a stranger, and on one occasion he was seen talking to Sarah Jane in the grounds.' He paused, watching His Lordship's face before going on: 'Her Ladyship was away for some time last summer and it is common knowledge that when she is away, Mr Myson spends a great deal of time here, though I gather he does not come to the house.'

The inference was obvious and Geoffrey looked at him sharply. 'And how did you come to interest yourself in Sarah Jane's affairs?'

'I met her in the Union, where I sometimes give aid and advice to the inmates. She came to my notice being such a good, helpful girl. She spent much of her time in the infirmary tending the sick and most grateful they were too, as many of them told me. I taught her a little reading and writing and how to speak properly, so what could be more natural than she should seek help from me when she is in trouble?' Lord Chevington was no fool, but Thomas was banking on the fact that he would be anxious to hush up the affair for the sake of his wife; he was fairly sure she did not know the truth of the young man's relationship to her husband. He smiled confidently. 'Your Lordship is renowned for being a fair man, so you will surely not deny the assistance the poor girl has a right to expect.'

'Right, Mr Wistonby? You are saying she was entirely blameless?'

'No, my lord, but when a young and innocent girl is seduced by someone so obviously her social superior, what choice has she but to comply with his wishes? It has happened before, times without number, but Sarah Jane is not the usual run of servant girls, my Lord. She is bright and ambitious, or at least she was until this unfortunate affair. All that will be stifled if she has to remain in the Union. And she is worried about the child. I am sure you know they will take it from her. Your grandchild will be born in the workhouse and will never have the kind of love, more fortunate ... ah, children ... enjoy.'

He meant more fortunate bastards, that was obvious, and he was referring to Timothy. He could not have said anything more calculated to sway Geoffrey into doing something; he could not allow any kin of his to be subjected to that degradation. But what could he do? He could look after the infant when it was born, just as he had taken care of Timothy, but he dismissed that idea immediately as impractical; having another ward to hide from Constance would be just too much. 'The child of my ward would not be my grandchild, Mr Wistonby,' he said quietly, hoping he had been mistaken in his assessment of the situation.

'Not officially, my lord, but ...'

So it *was* blackmail. He wouldn't have believed Sarah Jane capable of it; the lawyer had undoubtedly put her up to it. 'I have yet to be convinced,' he said, treading warily. 'I will speak to my ward and if he acknowledges he is the father of the child, then we shall see what can be done.' He was suddenly reminded that Constance was going to the Union on Friday and had declared her intention of seeing the girl then; he couldn't risk that. 'Come to my London office the day after tomorrow and bring Sarah Jane with you. I'd like to speak to her myself.' He took a purse from his tail-pocket and handed over two guineas, leaving the lawyer in no doubt that he fully understood him. 'This will ensure your attendance at my office. There will be no more until we have spoken again on Friday. Good-day, Mr Wistonby.'

Thomas took it and bowed his way out, looking very pleased with himself, something which annoyed His Lordship intensely. It wasn't the money he cared about, nor that he was expected to support Sarah Jane's child, it was the fact that now there were more secrets to be hidden, more skeletons in cupboards and it was all because Timothy had been careless. He would have to return to London to speak to him. He ordered the carriage to take him to the station and went in search of his wife to tell her he had been called away.

He felt guilty, not only at leaving her again so soon, but because it was on account of Timothy and he could not explain it to her. If it turned out that his son had nothing to do with the expected child, he would be decidedly angry at having wasted his time.

It was late in the day when he arrived at the offices of the *East and West Fen Railway Company*, which were on the first floor of an old building in Euston Road, chosen for its proximity to where the main line termini of railways coming from the north were being built. A clerk was still at his desk, scratching away at a ledger with a quill which needed sharpening. Scattered about him, both on the desk and on a table, were innumerable books, maps and plans. A model of a steam engine stood in a glass case on the mantelshelf and above it hung a portrait of His Lordship as a young man. Glancing at it, he was struck by his own likeness to Timothy; no one who had known him when that was painted could be in doubt of their relationship. He would order its removal and replace it with one of Constance.

'Is Mr Myson in?' he asked the clerk who had sprung to his feet.

'No, my lord. He left to go to the House of Commons and said he would go directly home afterwards.'

Because railway entrepreneurs were expected to provide a public service and needed the power to purchase land compulsorily, each project had to be incorporated in an Act of Parliament. Hundreds of these bills were in the process of becoming law and *The London Gazette* had been obliged to print a daily supplement to list them all. Each set of plans had to be drawn up and deposited with Clerks of the Peace in the counties through which the line was to pass and each separate piece of land listed, together with the name of the owner, the lessee and the occupier, and there was a time limit set for its purchase. The process often involved protracted negotiation and compensation for damage and disturbance.

John Townsend had suggested that listening to the debates on new railway bills would be a good way for the young man to learn about what other railway companies were planning, companies like the *London and Birmingham*, the *Great Northern*, the *Midland*, as well as the hundreds of smaller concerns who were vying with each other for the chance to build lines all over the country. 'I'll go to Kensington and wait for him there,' Geoffrey decided. 'You can fetch me a cab and then go home.'

The cab deposited him outside Timothy's apartment just as the young man himself arrived back from the Commons. 'Father! I thought you had returned to Chevington.'

'Something came up which I must discuss with you.'

'The proposal for the new line? Jack told me of that. I think you should go for it. Come in and I'll tell you what I learned today because it has some bearing.' The door was opened by a manservant, their hats and coats were taken and borne away while Timothy continued to talk about the latest railway bill going through Parliament, but Geoffrey's mind was too much on other things to care very much what George Hudson, the so-called Railway King, was up to. 'If he can do it, we can,' Timothy was enthusing. 'And if we add Ashley Green ...'

'Ashley Green?' Geoffrey came back from his reverie. 'How did you know about that?'

'Miller told me. After that there's Hailey Common. If we can get that too, it will make us the biggest railway concern in the east and as other lines fail, we will take them up until we'll wield more power than even George Hudson.'

So it was power the young man craved – and Geoffrey could hardly blame him for that. Power was to be his compensation; power could overcome his bastardy. Sarah Jane would hardly fit into that scheme and as for her child ... Sighing, he followed his son into the drawing room. 'We?' he queried.

'You and I.' Timothy smiled easily. 'You did promise me more shares and greater responsibility.'

'Be patient, Timothy. You are very young and you need more experience of how to deal with people before you can take an executive role.'

'I've learned all I need to know watching you. Let me take on the Ashley Green section, I won't disappoint you.' Timothy had overcome his naturally indolent nature by reminding himself why he had to work, why he had to make himself indispensable to his father. Since coming down from Cambridge he had discovered he was a good negotiator; he could talk easily with anyone, from the most influential financiers down to the lowest navvy and he had an eye for detail which was almost finicky. He had learned to confer knowledgeably with engineers and contractors, concerned himself with the price of land, the cost of sleepers, chairs and rails and drove a hard bargain when it came to navvy piece rates. Much to his own surprise, he discovered he enjoyed the cut and thrust of it all. He gained an almost sensual pleasure watching an adversary capitulate, in seeing the defeat on his face, the sweat beading his brow, the frightened eyes, the slack mouth. And the greater the man's fall, the greater was Timothy's sense of wellbeing.

'We haven't acquired it yet and I didn't come to talk about railways. We can do that in the office.'

Timothy grinned as if certain of having his own way. He pointed to the decanter and glasses. 'Help yourself to whisky while I go and change.'

'I think we should talk first.'

Timothy, halfway to the door, turned in surprise. 'Can't it wait?'

'No. Best get it over with.'

'That sounds ominous. We had better start with a drink, then.' He went to the decanter and poured out two generous measures. 'Sit down, Father. You will look less forbidding seated.'

'Do I look forbidding?' Geoffrey accepted the glass Timothy held out to him and sat in an armchair by the fire. 'Perhaps it's because of what I have to say.'

'Oh?' He slumped into the chair on the other side of the hearth, throwing his legs over its arms.

Geoffrey resisted the temptation to reprimand the young man on his untidy way of sitting. 'I believe you went to Chevington last summer?'

'You know I did. Her Ladyship was not there.'

'And you met a girl called Sarah Jane with whom you had an affair, is that not so?'

Sarah Jane. Timothy had wanted her the minute he had set eyes on her. There had been something about her he could not resist, an animal magnetism, a sexuality which shone like a beacon; she was both child and woman, guileless and seductive. He would always remember those few weeks of passion with a smile because it had eased another, even greater craving. It was a pity it had had to end so abruptly. 'You seem well informed,' he said.

'I am being asked for money.'

'How can that be? I was careful not to let her know who I was and, besides, it would never enter her head to try and extort money as a result of a few hours of pleasure.'

'Not even if that pleasure resulted in a child?'

'A child?' He sat up with a jerk.

'So my informant tells me, a fellow by the name of Wistonby who seems to be her protector.'

'Wistonby, did you say?'

'Yes. Do you know him?'

'No, but Sarah Jane mentioned him. I believe they had been lovers.'

Why did that shock him, Geoffrey wondered. Why had he thought Timothy would be her first? 'She told you that herself?'

'Yes. Is she with him now?' Timothy felt a sudden anger, as if Sarah Jane had cuckolded him.

'No. She was sent back to the Union and Lady Chevington is determined to speak to her there and find out more about how it happened.'

'Oh, I see.' The young man smiled suddenly as the implications of that came to him. His father was being blackmailed. It was something he had often considered himself, but there had been no reason for it because he could have almost anything he wanted without it, although if his father proved sticky on the subject of his management of the railway building project, he might give it a try – gently, of course, because he didn't want to alienate him.

'I can't have a grandchild of mine born in that dreadful place,' Geoffrey went on. 'I've asked the lawyer to bring Sarah Jane to the office on Friday. I want to be sure the child is really yours.'

'There's no way to be sure, but if it was conceived in July or August last year, then it's possible.'

'Timothy, why did you do it? Why did you have to disgrace one of my servants? Why?'

Timothy smiled at the memory of the laughing red-haired girl with the lively eyes. 'Because she was beautiful and I found her bewitching – reason enough, I should have thought.'

'Why did you leave her in that condition?'

'I was unaware of her condition. Besides, Her Ladyship returned.'

'Oh.' Geoffrey did not want to go into that again. Timothy was banned from Chevington when Constance was there and that was all there was to it. 'If the girl is carrying your child, then perhaps you should do the honourable thing and marry her.'

Timothy considered this suggestion for the time it took to remember what he considered his rightful inheritance and to realise that Sarah Jane certainly did not fit in with his plans for that. She would make an admirable mistress, but certainly not a wife. 'Marry her?' he queried. 'What a ridiculous idea! I did not take her virginity. She was an experienced lover which, if you had taken the trouble to question your informant, you would have discovered. She, is after all, only a servant.'

'But not too lowly for you to take to bed.'

'That was different. Good God! Any number of gentlemen amuse themselves with girls of a lower order but they do not make wives of them.'

'You have no call to look down your nose at her,' Geoffrey said, recognising the truth of what Timothy said, but somehow unwilling to apply it to Sarah Jane. 'Your own mother was ...' He stopped suddenly.

'Yes, Father? My own mother was what? Don't you think it is about time you told me who she was?'

Geoffrey had never intended to answer that question but Timothy's attitude annoyed him. He drained his glass. 'She was a gypsy.'

Timothy stared up at his father with a look of horror. It was a moment or two before he could speak. 'I don't believe it.'

'Why not? Gypsy or scullion what's the difference?' His disappointment in his son made him want to hurt him. 'Now you know that much, do you want to know the rest?'

Timothy wanted to shout 'No!' at the top of his lungs, but a kind of masochistic fascination made him look at his father and smile. 'Tell me all.'

'I heard that a tribe of gypsies had camped in one of the meadows on the home farm and I went there to turn them off. I saw her washing pots down by the river and stopped to speak to her. She told me about her life and how difficult it was to find somewhere to stay. There is no need to go into details, is there? I did not know she had a child until she sent a message to me to meet her in the old gamekeeper's cottage on the estate. She had you with her. You were about two weeks old.'

Timothy remembered the keeper's cottage, grubby, festooned with cobwebs. Sarah Jane had been convinced it was haunted; invisible eyes had been watching, she had said. His father. His mother, a black-eyed gypsy. He shivered. 'What happened to ... to my mother?'

'I never saw her again. I believe she married one of her own tribe.'

'You didn't keep in touch with her at all?'

'No, we neither of us wanted it. It was best to make a clean break; she had her life to lead and I had mine.'

'No wonder you don't want Her Ladyship to know about me,' Timothy said bitterly, getting up to help himself to more drink and tipping it down his throat in one mouthful. 'You've always enjoyed making me toe the line, haven't you, telling me I should always be aware of the feelings of others, making me hide myself away because you didn't want to hurt your precious wife. How dreadful it would be for you to have to confess to adultery with a ... a gypsy. Would she forgive you, do you think? What would you tell her? That you had fallen madly in love and couldn't help yourself?'

'It wasn't like that ...'

'No? Then why am I here, tell me that.'

'Your mother gave you to me.' The flat statement hid a memory he could not erase, but it was not one he could share. 'Her family didn't want you and—' He paused. 'I did. Now the subject is closed and we will never refer to it again.' He tried to smile but didn't quite succeed. 'We were discussing Sarah Jane and what is to be done about your dilemma.'

'*Your* dilemma, Father.'

Geoffrey ignored the barb; his son had been sorely wounded and only time would heal. 'I think the best thing would be for me to make you an extra allowance so that you can properly do your duty by her. The lawyer will see to everything. Shouldn't be surprised if he didn't marry her himself.'

'You expect me to pay him to take her off my hands and bring up my child, is that it?' For some unfathomable reason Timothy didn't like that idea.

'Why not? It would be the best thing for Sarah Jane, wouldn't it? Respectability.'

'I doubt Sarah Jane cares much for respectability.' He laughed and drained his glass. He did not see why Sarah Jane should not accept what could not be helped just as he had to. He would have her for a mistress and the thought of renewing their hedonistic relationship excited him. 'Do you want me to be present on Friday?'

'I think it might be as well.'

'And we'll also talk about Ashley Green? Once we've settled the Sarah Jane question ...' He left the sentence unfinished.

Geoffrey knew what he meant. Give in to him or have Constance told, not only that he had a son but who had mothered him. He felt as if his arms were tied to his body and he was being stifled by a thick blanket. 'I'll think about it,' he said, knowing he had no choice.

Chapter Eight

*T*he navvies worked hard, harder than the agricultural labourers with whom they were often compared, but for the railway builders there were no tied cottages and little patches of ground for their own use, and because they went where the rails went, they never put down roots. They were nomads; they did their work and took their pay, and spent their spare time in carousal of one sort or another – a party to celebrate a birthday, a wedding, or even a wake, or sometimes simply because it was pay day and they had money burning a hole in their pockets. Sometimes a group of them would go into the nearest town on a randy. The shopkeepers, seeing and hearing them coming, would board up their windows, while the tavern-keepers, unwilling to turn down good business, emptied their public rooms of all but the cheapest furniture, hid away the best crockery and glasses and waited for the onslaught. Occasionally Duncan would go with them, but he kept his word; in all the six months Sarah Jane had been with the navvies, he had never come home rolling drunk.

Although bigger and stronger than any man she had ever encountered , he was also gentle and kind. She had known nothing like it since her parents died, not even from Thomas, whose kindness had been motivated by his own sexual and emotional needs. Duncan asked nothing in return. But there were still, in the depths of her being where she kept all the secrets of her soul, all the old yearnings, the unfulfilled passions, a longing to be something that she was not, nor could be. She had not entirely swept away her dreams of becoming a lady, and because those dreams were as unattainable as ever, she sometimes found herself weeping. Duncan would kiss away her tears and stroke her hair and beg her not to cry, and then, just as suddenly, her mood would change and she'd take both his hands in hers and whirl him round, laughing. They were like children, and their love had the innocence of childhood; not once had he done more than hold her in his arms and give her a brotherly kiss. Sometimes she wished he would do more, sometimes she was glad that he did not, because she was afraid. It was as if the very act of union would shatter her fragile security, as it had done twice in the past. The rest of the family had accepted her as another sister or daughter, and if that was how Duncan saw her, then so be it. She told herself that she was content. No one bullied her, no one made any demands on either her body or her intellect. She willingly did the chores expected of her, everything she had done at Chevington House and more, with even less in material reward, for there were no leftovers from grand dinners and no books to feed her hunger for an education. If she felt bored or frustrated, she pushed the feeling deep inside her and refused to acknowledge it.

And she had her darling son. Jason was extraordinarily beautiful with soft, very fair hair and wide dark eyes. Jason was content to lie in the cradle Duncan had fashioned for him and chuckle up at her, showing two tiny teeth which nipped her painfully when he sucked at her breasts. She was starting to wean him, but the longer she could breastfeed him the better, because he would be another mouth for whom food had to be bought and Duncan had stuck to his determination that she would not go to work on the site. She accepted his decision because, if truth be known, she did not want to leave Jason in anyone else's care while she went.

It was a source of great wonder to her that he existed at all; she had pushed all memories of Paris to the back of her mind as if by so doing she could deny he had ever been, that they had ever lain together and produced this miracle. In spite of Thomas she had been a child at the time and she did not want to remember that she had been foolish enough to give her love and trust to someone who was not man enough to tell her the affair had ended, nor be reminded that she had been angry and hurt enough to swear vengeance. She did not think vengeance was part of Duncan's philosophy.

Jason, with his blond curls and happy nature, reminded her of Billie, Billie who was shut up in Chevington Workhouse, away from the woods and fields and open skies she enjoyed; she had failed him badly and the fact that she had had no reply to her letter was no excuse. And it was nearly Christmas, a time for families. Determined to make amends, she bought paper, pen and ink from the tommy shopkeeper and, leaving Daisy and Maggie to finish their shopping and do a bit of gossiping, returned to the cave to write to her brother.

She was so absorbed in what she was doing, trying to put on paper all she knew and felt about her life with the navvies, that she did not at first hear Ned arrive back from work a little ahead of the others and was startled when he spoke. 'What are you writing?'

He was standing beside her, thin and gangly, with his head on one side. She smiled. 'A letter to my brother. I'm telling him how happy I am with you and wishing he could be here with me.'

'I wish I could read and write,' Ned said, wistfully.

She looked up from her letter. 'Has no one ever taught you?'

'Duncan went to school before Ma and Pa started navvying and I was to go when I was old enough but then we went on the tramp and after that . . .' He stopped. It wasn't his parents' fault his father could not make a living in the Scottish village where he had been born.

Schools were something else the navvies needed; even the children in the workhouse received a better education than those on a navvy site. Sarah Jane smiled suddenly. Duncan might forbid her to go out to work, but this was something she *could* do. 'Would you like to learn to read and write?'

'Yes.'

'Me too,' said Celia, from the floor where she was tickling Jason. His gurgling laughter filled Sarah Jane with a great feeling of tenderness towards them all.

'I'll teach you, and Ben and Jon too, if they want to learn,' she said. 'We'll have an hour's schooling a day, if your ma and pa agree. But I'll have to buy books for the reading.'

Books! She had promised herself she would find a job so she could buy books, books to continue her education – and here was Ned asking for the same thing. How many others were there, she wondered. And how many parents would be willing to pay a few pence to have their children learn to read and write? Duncan had said that if she wanted books, he would get them for her, but not wanting him to spend his hard-earned money on what the others would consider frivolities, she had dropped the idea; but now her sleeping ambition stirred. She could do something with her life, after all. She would learn all she could about this business of building railways, right from the start – the money it needed, how much went on equipment and stock, how much for the men's wages, how much the owners themselves got out of it, the law of it all, the rights and wrongs. And why tommy shops were needed more than schools. She could help these people who had been so good to her.

'Read what you've written,' Ned said, nodding towards her letter.

So she did, pointing to the words and saying them syllable by syllable until he had grasped the meaning of what she had written. He wanted to know all about Billie. He had not known she had a brother and it was past his comprehension that they were not together; as far as he was concerned a family was a single unit. 'Why don't you send for him?' he asked.

She smiled. 'There's nowhere for him to sleep, is there? Perhaps later, when we move to something bigger.'

She sealed her letter and put it into her pocket ready to post, as everyone came in for their evening meal and the cave was soon a hubbub of conversation and laughter. She would broach the subject of teaching later, after the young ones had been put to bed.

She loved the twilight hours when the long working day came to an end, when the clang and clatter of working men, of horses being urged on by boys, of women shouting their gossip from hut to hut, was stilled. From their vantage point, they could see lights twinkling here and there at uncurtained windows, but they were too far away to hear more than the occasional slamming of a door, or the neighing of a tethered horse. 'Ned wants me to teach him to read,' she said, leaning her head against Duncan's rough coat as they sat round the fire that evening.

Maggie, who sat close to the rushlight in order to see to sew, looked up at her over the top of a pair of steel-framed spectacles and dropped the shirt she had been darning into her lap. 'D'ye want to do it, lass?'

'Of course I do. It will be a way of repaying your kindness. You'll let me, won't you?'

'I don't see why not,' James said.

'Good.' She took a deep breath for the next step. 'I fell to wondering how many others on the camp couldn't read and write.'

Duncan laughed. 'Most, I should say.'

'Would they pay me to teach them? A penny a time, something like that.'

'Mayhap,' he said. 'But why d'you want to do it?'

She smiled. 'You won't let me take an ordinary sort of job, will you? But this isn't ordinary and you wouldn't mind that, would you?' She looked up at him, pleading. 'Say you wouldn't.'

Duncan, who could deny her nothing it was in his power to give, capitulated. 'You'll be wanting a schoolroom next,' he said, chuckling. 'And slates and books and a bell to ring the scholars in.'

He was teasing, but she chose to take him seriously. 'One thing at a time, Duncan. First, I have to find enough pupils and somewhere to do the teaching.'

They put a notice on the tommy shop door and paid the shopkeeper sixpence to point it out and read it to anyone who showed an interest. Two days later, Sarah Jane had a nucleus of a class, mostly children, but there were one or two adults, who came in their midday break. Books and slates were ordered from the travelling journeyman; they arrived a week later and Sarah Jane began her lessons in the cave, which was quiet during the day. Maggie and Daisy preferred to do their washing and cooking out of doors when the weather was fine.

The school was a great success but that did not mean she was excused other work; she was still expected to help with the chores and take the men their midday meals. She would pick her way across the mud carrying a large can of soup, six tin mugs and some bread wrapped in a clean cloth to where the men shovelled earth into wagons beside the new embankment. She never ceased to marvel at their strength, the fluidity of the muscles rippling along their arms and across their backs, the way each clod of earth landed accurately with its own heavy crump on top of the one before. They hardly noticed the change in the seasons, except that now it was winter they worked harder in order to make their sets in the shorter daylight hours. Their only concession to the changing temperature was to keep their shirts on as they worked, and Sarah Jane's was to wear boots and a woollen shawl Duncan had bought her.

A few weeks into the new year, she found them talking to a wiry little man carrying a bundle tied in a kerchief at the end of a pole, who had just walked into the camp.

'From Ashley Green, are ye?' Barnaby asked, nodding towards the path over the distant hill.

'Came through but didn't stop,' he said. 'The men was on a randy and what a randy, I've never seen the like.'

'What's it about?' Sarah Jane asked, as she set down the mugs and began serving out the soup.

He turned to her and smiled. My, she was a beauty with her red hair and flashing green eyes and those voluptuous breasts with her blouse straining over them. The men were lucky devils; he hadn't had a woman in a twelvemonth, had nearly forgot what it was like. 'The contractor's lit off with the wages and the guv'nor's sent for the militia.'

'Soldiers,' said Ned, eyes wide. 'I saw some soldiers once, Highlanders they were, marching with pipes and drums and their kilts swaying. Would these be Highlanders?'

'No lad, just farmlads dressed in fancy uniforms,' the little man said. 'They'll not be an ounce of good.'

Sarah Jane left them talking but she was reminded of that conversation later in the day when she went to fetch water for the family wash. The stream ran down the hill and into the valley where the men worked and she had to climb above the site to where it was clean enough to use.

Here, on the barren hillside she was alone except for a kestrel hovering overhead, keen eyes sweeping the gorse-covered slopes. She stood and watched as it swooped suddenly, to rise again with a small animal in its talons. In no time at all it was a tiny dot in the distance, free as the air which was its element. She was free too, free to stay or to go; there were no ties to bind her to the navvies except those of her own choosing. She had made her choice and that was that. But up here, in the hills, away from the sights and sounds of a navvy encampment, she could dream her dreams in privacy. Here, away from eyes that seemed always to be watching her, Maggie's and Daisy's in particular, she could indulge in the fantasies which had kept her going in the workhouse. Oh, they were childish and irrelevant now, for hadn't Duncan said 'a home for as long as ye want it'? And hadn't she been happy to accept?

Her musing was interrupted by the sound of laughter and she looked up to see Ned and the twins scampering over the rise above her. 'Ned! Boys!' she shouted, setting down her buckets to hurry after them. 'Where are you off to?'

Unaware of her, they continued climbing, sometimes running, sometimes walking, and though Sarah Jane stayed on their trail, she could not close the gap between them. Twilight had turned to night by the time they topped the hill and could look down on the shanties of the Ashley Green site. Half the huts were burning, others had smashed windows and broken doors; wagons had been overturned and their contents spilled and trampled over; women and children ran about with buckets of water ineffectually trying to smother the flames. She saw the boys disappear into the mêlée and ran after them, pushing her way through the throng of angry men, who brandished whatever weapons they had managed to pick up – shovels, picks, crowbars, knives.

Someone shouted, 'Here they come!'

121

Towards them marched a troop of militia in blue and white uniforms, armed with muskets and accompanied by an officer and a civilian on horseback. The horsemen stopped and the two groups stood and faced each other in silent hostility. Sarah Jane, craning to see above the heads of the men who surrounded her, saw, not the uniformed officer who led the troops, but the elegantly clad man who rode beside him. For one heart-stopping moment she was transported to a bank beside a stream on a warm summer's day. Above the roar of the inferno behind her, she heard happy laughter and the sound of splashing water, felt warm kisses on her neck and breasts and the murmured words, 'I love you, Sarah Jane. Love you, love you.'

She could not move, her limbs would not obey her; she could only stare at him, her thoughts churning and her pulse racing. She had pushed him to the back of her mind, pretended he had never existed and yet here he was, towering over the crowd on his magnificent horse, looming like a great stormcloud, threatening her happiness. But he was not the laughing young man who had loved her with such passion. There was a hard look about his face as if hate had replaced love along the way and it wasn't just that the situation demanded severity; the look was ingrained in his features. He sat his horse arrogantly, looking down his long nose at the surging crowd, as if the men were ants to be crushed, but she could tell by the set of his jaw and the way his hands held the reins, that he was afraid. These navvies, these coarse, rough, tough men could destroy him. It came as a revelation to her; she had thought him invincible, like the heroes of the ancient myths which had been her favourite reading matter in those dreamlike days.

'Who is that?' she asked the man standing next to her.

'That bugger! That's Mr Timothy Bloody Myson, the owner's puppy dog. Does a lot of yapping, but 'e ain't got no bite.'

'Timothy Myson,' she repeated slowly. 'What is he doing here?'

He laughed hoarsely. 'Come to see his pretty soldiers do their duty.'

'What about our pay?' someone yelled at him. 'We done the work and we want our wages.'

A slight smile curled Timothy's lip. 'And who pays for the damage to the workings? Those rails.' He pointed with his crop. 'They have to be paid for. And the wagons too. And the goods from the shop. It'll cost more than you're owed to set that to rights.'

'An' the contractor gets off scot-free, does he?'

'No. We will track him down.'

A roar of laughter greeted this. 'Pull the other one, Mr High-and-Mighty.'

Hemmed in by the mob, Sarah Jane could do nothing but go with the tide as they surged forward, urged on by someone shouting louder than all the rest. 'Come on, lads, they won't fire. Let's show 'em who's guv'nor.'

The officer looked at the wall of angry men bearing down on him and then turned in the saddle to speak to his companion. Timothy nodded, the officer gave the order and the soldiers raised their muskets to their shoulders. It was in that instant Sarah Jane caught sight of Ned, eyes agog, perched high in the branches of a tree. Her relief turned to horror as a fusillade of shots was fired over the navvies' heads and Ned flung out his arms and pitched head-first into the crowd.

'He's hit! They shot an innocent child!' Now nothing could hold the angry crowd. 'Murderers!' Sarah Jane, carried helplessly along, found herself at the spot where Ned lay and fell on her knees beside him as the mob carried on past her, threatening to engulf the small company of militia. Unable or unwilling to discharge their weapons again, they tried to make an orderly retreat, but it soon became apparent that they were not going to be allowed to do that; they turned and fled. Their officer rode after them shouting at them to stand firm, and Timothy, finding himself alone, stayed a moment as if he meant to take on the navvies single-handedly, but then thought better of it and cantered after them, with the navvies cheering his defeat.

Sarah Jane had no time to worry about his fate; Ned needed all her attention. The ball had passed through his arm just above the elbow, tearing the flesh and muscle, leaving a gory mess. She knew what she ought to do because she had once seen it done in the workhouse infirmary when one of the inmates had caught his hand in the machine used to cut up the pigfood. Swallowing bile, she tore a couple of strips from the hem of her petticoat, bound the wound with one and tied the other firmly round the top of his arm and, pushing a small stick through the knot, twisted it tightly. The bleeding slowed to a trickle, but she was left with the problem of getting him over the hill and back home. And where were the other two? She looked around her, terrified that something might have happened to the twins and breathed a sigh of relief when she saw Ben's tousled head peering round the side of one of the overturned wagons.

He emerged slowly, trembling and white-faced, followed by Jon, clinging to his shirttail. She took a hand of each and smiled. 'Ned's been hit,' she said. 'Do you think you could run and fetch his Da or Duncan, someone to carry him?'

Ben nodded, eyes wide with fear. 'What are you goin' to do?'

'I'll stay here and look after him. Be as quick as you can, won't you?'

They set off at a sprint she knew they would not be able to maintain, but if they could keep going at even half that pace, the men would be with her in a couple of hours. 'Stay together!' she shouted after them.

The rioting navvies returned, arguing among themselves, unsure whether they had won a victory or not. Routing the militia had made them feel good for a while but it did nothing to redress the wrongs they had suffered, nor to restore the stolen pay. And they were incensed about the child being shot. One of them brought her a dirty brown blanket that smelled of smoke. She wrapped it around Ned. 'Your da'll come soon,' she said.

'I came to see the soldiers,' he muttered. 'I weren't doin' no harm.'

'I know.' She looked down at him, taking his good hand in both her own, willing her strength into him. His eyes were feverishly bright and his face paper-white; even his lips had lost their colour. 'Don't talk, there's a good boy. Just lie still and listen while I tell you a story. Once there was a king called Midas . . .'

An hour later she heard the sound of pounding feet and looked up to see James and Joseph running towards her, their great chests heaving.

'Thank God,' she said. 'You got here quickly.'

'We were already halfway when we met the boys,' Joseph panted as James dropped to his knees beside his son.

'I only wish I'd caught them up before they got here,' Sarah Jane told them. Then she would not have seen Paris, would not have been reminded of something she had been trying to forget. 'The owner's puppy dog' the man had called him. She had thought Paris was a gentleman and had never questioned how he came by his money and would not have understood if he had told her. Now she did; he was one of those who grew rich on the hard work of others, who didn't care how many people were hurt as long as they made a profit. She had been held in his arms, had borne his child and, heaven help her, she had once loved him and because of that she felt personally aggrieved, as if he had turned against her.

It was nearly day when they arrived back at the cave. Maggie and Daisy had long since talked themselves out but they were not asleep; huddled watchfully round the fire which Duncan had kept going, they waited in silence. Maggie, sitting nearest the door, saw them first and rushed out to meet them. James, who had relinquished his burden to Joseph for the last mile, put his arm around his wife. 'Wish't ye,' he soothed as she tried to take Ned from Joseph's arms. 'He took a ball in his arm, but it's nae as bad as it looks. Let's get him inside.'

The twins, who had been given supper and put to bed as soon as they arrived home, scrambled up and crowded in the doorway. Daisy shooed them away to let Joseph pass with his burden and Sarah Jane, her job done, slipped away and wandered over to a copse of pines that overlooked the site.

The men were already at work; wheels rumbled, chains clanked, horses whinnied. The horses would miss the boys today, she thought, for even the twins were too weary to work and would be left to sleep off their adventure. As for Ned, there was no telling when he would be fit to work again; a boy with a useless arm could not become a full bodied working man; he would have to earn what he could by doing odd jobs, dependent on his family. The only alternative was the Union and knowing what that was like, she wept. She wept for Ned and for Billie and for everyone condemned to a pauper's existence. She wept because the tranquil unhurried existence she had been enjoying had turned out to be a myth and now she was faced with a reality which frightened her.

She could not shake off the images – Ned moaning in pain, the fires, the angry navvies, the frightened militia and the man on the horse. Paris. Timothy Myson. It was strange that it had taken two years to learn his name. She had loved him once and he could still arouse powerful emotions in her. There was something between them which could never die, an unbreakable thread, stretching between them, made strong by the existence of their son. She told herself it was hate, but she knew it was not. Supposing he were to come to Scarside? Supposing he and Duncan came face to face, would Duncan realise who he was? And Jason, what would happen to Jason? Telling herself that the man had not seen her and would not have recognised her if he had, and would certainly not want to acknowledge Jason as his own, did no good at all. She still felt threatened.

'Sarah Jane.' She heard Duncan's soft voice behind her. 'Sarah Jane, what are ye doing out here?'

'Nothing.' She scrubbed at her eyes with the back of her hand. 'Just thinking.'

He came and stood beside her, putting his arm about her shoulders. She laid her head on his broad chest and felt comforted as she always did when he was near. 'Ye worked a miracle,' he said, stroking her hair. 'Ned will be good as new. Don't grieve, my love.'

'I'm not grieving,' she said, unexpectedly. 'I'm plain furious. It should never have happened, none of it should. If there had been no randy, our boys wouldn't have gone looking for excitement and Ned would not have been shot.'

'No, but be fair, love, the soldiers fired over the navvies' heads. How were they to know Ned was in the tree?'

'They shouldn't have fired at all. Why don't the owners pay the men regular? Why don't they make sure the contractor is honest before they give him the men's wages? And with all the riches they've got, why do they have to squeeze more out o' the workers with their stinking tommy shops? If the men had their wages in cash ...'

'Mayhap ye're right, but the men need the work and the owners know it. Ye canna change it.'

'Let's leave, Duncan. Let's go somewhere else away from all these troubles.'

'There are no troubles here, my love. This is a good site.'

'But when the line joins the one at Ashley Green, what then? Anything could happen. If Jason ...'

He laughed. 'What could happen to Jason? He's only a wee bairn.'

She could not express her fears in a way he would understand. Instead she said, 'Don't you want to get on?'

''Course I do.'

'But you can't do it if you stay here, can you?' she persisted.

'No,' he said slowly, wondering what was in her mind. 'But what about your school? Isn't that enough for ye?'

'Daisy or Maggie will carry it on and I can always start another. There should be schools on all sites.'

'Are ye so unhappy here?' He sounded hurt.

'No, Duncan, no.' She rejected the idea outright. 'I love you, you know that. It's just that ... Oh, I don't know what I mean.' Overcome by emotions too strong to analyse, she burst into tears.

'Oh, my dear lass,' he said, holding her close and brushing the tears from her cheeks with a gentle finger. 'Dinna cry, I canna bear it.' He waited until her sobs had subsided, then he took her face in his hands and tilted it up to his. 'Without ye my life is not worth a farthing. If ye decided to go back to your other life ...'

'My other life?'

'Ye know what I mean, to Jason's father.'

It was uncanny how he had hit on that notion. She wanted to tell him Paris had never existed except as part of a girlish dream which had no substance, but Jason was living proof of his existence and hadn't she seen him, not so many hours before and hadn't he stirred up such a mixture of emotions, she didn't know how to cope with them? But how could she expect Duncan to understand that? She hardly understood it herself. 'You are all I want,' she said.

'Shall I stay here with ye, a wee while?'

She nodded, and he sat down and leaned against the trunk of the tree, patting the ground beside him.

She sank down beside him and he put his arm round her and cradled her head against his shoulder with a huge gentle hand. She looked up at him, seeing him for what he was, a simple man, a good man. Beside him Timothy Myson was a dwarf, not physically because he was almost as tall, but in spirit; he could not reach out to others, as Duncan did, and make them all the better for knowing him. Duncan's humanity embraced the universe, Timothy's was confined to Timothy.

Duncan was one of that rare breed of men who know true contentment and never yearn for what they cannot have. He got on well with his workmates, was respected by the ganger and unwilling to cause a stir when he was not convinced it would do any good. There were plenty of others to do that, he told her, and a right mess they were making of it. Telling him that he could succeed where others failed weighed with him not at all. He was not a coward, being quick to defend his own and Sarah Jane in particular, and he was not afraid of stating his opinion if it was asked for, but his ambition was limited to what was achievable; it made him the kind of man he was, easygoing and slow to anger.

He deserved someone better than she was, a woman to walk beside him all through his life and set her pace to his, someone as pure and good as he was. She was not pure, not even her thoughts were pure, because what she wanted more than anything at that moment was to have him inside her, to demonstrate what she could not express, to meet tenderness with tenderness and passion with passion; not lust, never that. Now she understood what Lizzie had been saying; she had thrown away that most precious of commodities, her virginity, and she wished it could have been otherwise. He was too good for her, she knew that, but if he were ever to discover that for himself and send her away, she would be lost. She loved him, oh, not in the tempestuous way she had loved Paris, but quietly, trustingly. The joy he gave her was returned tenfold; one kiss paid for ten, one smile produced a day of laughter, one tender word a look of adoration which was more eloquent than any speech. It was too wonderful, too awesome, and she feared nothing so much as losing it all.

'I love ye too,' he said, covering her mouth in a kiss that was far from brotherly; it expressed a vibrant and virile need for her which took her by surprise. She did the only thing she knew how to do. She reached up and put her arms round his neck, drawing him closer, telling him without words that she meant to put the past behind her, to suppress her own longings, her ambition, in order to further his. He held her close, stroking her hair, her cheeks, her neck, comforting her, loving her, breathing life into her, slowly rousing her from the torpor of her exhaustion, until passion surged through her veins and found silent expression in her moving hands and lips. He was gentle and undemanding, patient and caring, and there was no past and no future, but a single moment of time which was theirs alone.

Maggie found them there, half an hour later, fast asleep in each other's arms, and knew that in the saving of one son she had lost the other. She crept away, grieving silently.

'I've a notion to go to Hailey Common,' Duncan said, one evening a couple of weeks later.

'Why?' his mother demanded.

He had known there might be an argument and was ready for it. 'I want to get on,' he said. 'I don't want to take unskilled wages all my life. I want to be a ganger, maybe a subcontractor. I owe it to Sarah Jane and Jason to make a better life for us all.'

'Jason isn't your bairn,' Maggie said.

'He is now.'

Sarah Jane felt a great surge of triumph and then deliberately squashed it. 'Duncan, if you're saying that because of anything I said ...'

He smiled at her. 'But ye meant it, didna ye?'

'Yes, but ...'

He reached out and covered her hand with his own. ''Tis what I want, too.' He paused and looked around the group. 'Hailey Common sounds like the sort of place a man can make his way up. It's a few miles north of Derby. They're going to build a line to link up with the *Midland* and take it through to Manchester. I heard it from a tramping navvy, not two days since.'

'When will ye go?' James asked, puffing gently on his old clay pipe.

'Tomorrow.'

'Tomorrow?' echoed Maggie, bleakly. 'Why so soon?'

'There'll be others after the good jobs, and I don't want tae miss my chance. If the prospects are good, I'll send ye word tae join us.'

'In that case, it's time ye jumped the broom,' Maggie said. She had known she had lost her influence over her son the day Sarah Jane had joined them. It had been difficult to come to terms with that, because that golden apple, with its perfect pearl, still worried her. Only Duncan knew the truth behind that and he had brushed aside the questions she had diffidently voiced, telling her that Sarah Jane had been ill-used and that was all she needed to know. But what if Jason's father came back? What then? Would the lure of gold prove too much for her?

She sighed; Duncan was a man grown, he must be left to make his own decisions and his own mistakes, and she had been a soft fool to think otherwise. And she supposed he could do worse than Sarah Jane. The lass kept herself clean as a new pin, she was industrious and could make an appetising meal out of the most unpromising ingredients; she had all the attributes a woman could wish for in a son's wife, except virginity. She looked up to see Sarah Jane's green eyes regarding her as if she knew what she was thinking. She smiled nervously.

Sarah Jane turned from Maggie to Duncan. 'What does that mean?'

'Ma thinks we ought tae be wed,' he said quietly. 'I'll say yes tae that if ye will.'

Marriage was something Sarah Jane had never considered, though she ought to have done. Duncan was not the kind of man to take her for granted. If she married him she must stifle her discontent, deny her dreams, forget the grand plans she had made for herself and concentrate on him. There would be no knight in shining armour, no grand house in which she could display her taste in good furniture or please guests with her fine cooking, no horses and carriages, but to refuse him would hurt him dreadfully. She looked up to see him watching her, waiting for her answer. 'Yes,' she said, reaching out her hand to his. 'Yes, I would like that very much.'

'Do it tomorrow afore you go,' Maggie said, making a brave effort to still her fears.

'How can we do it tomorrow?' Sarah Jane asked, her mind full of church-bells and solemn vows.

James laughed. ''Twill be a navvy wedding, none o' your fancy words in church, but it will be real for all that, leastways, among the navvies.'

'I've a dress that will do and Daisy will lend her best bonnet,' Maggie said, looking at Daisy, who nodded in agreement. 'We'll trim it with flowers, Celia can gather those. Come, let's make a start.' She went to her bundle which she kept in the depths of the cave and produced a flowered dress with long sleeves and a deep frill at the hem. 'It'll need taking in a bit,' she said, shaking it out. The men had been watching with tolerant amusement, but now she turned on them, 'Out with you! This is no place for grinning men.'

James laughed and stood up. 'We'll go and tell the folks over a quart of ale.' He jerked his head at the other two and they disappeared, leaving the women to deck Sarah Jane out in the makeshift wedding dress.

'I shall miss you all,' she said later, as she took off the dress and prepared for bed.

'An' we'll miss ye, lass,' Daisy said, because Maggie was too overcome at the thought of Duncan leaving her to speak. 'Now best get to sleep, you've a busy day ahead of ye.'

She had only just drifted off, or so it seemed, when she was awakened by Maggie. 'Come, lass, Duncan wants to make an early start, so up with ye. He's waiting down by the tommy shop.'

So was the whole population of the encampment. Grouped about the open space in front of the hut, they stood and cheered as she approached, escorted by Maggie and Daisy and attended by Celia, carrying a posy.

Duncan, his hair neatly brushed and a new kerchief at his throat, stepped forward and took her hand. He led her to where a besom broom had been set across two low stools. 'All ye have tae do is jump over the broom with me,' he whispered. 'Hold up your kirtle so ye don't fall.'

'Is that all?'

'That's all. Are ye ready?'

She clung to him with one hand and lifted her skirts into a bunch with the other, while the onlookers started to clap, going faster and faster. Hand in hand, they ran the last twenty yards to the makeshift barrier and jumped, then fell into each other's arms, laughing helplessly. Celia pulled her posy to pieces and threw the petals over them, a new barrel of ale was tapped and a fiddler began to play a dance tune. Sarah Jane, standing in Duncan's encircling arms, turned her face up to be kissed. 'Now we're wed?'

'Aye, now we're wed, until death us do part. One day I'll buy ye a ring and say that to ye in church.'

'It doesn't matter,' she said, her heart full to bursting. 'This means just as much to me. And I wouldn't trade you for a thousand churchified husbands.' Looking down at the simple homespun dress she wore, she smiled to herself. What was important was Duncan's love for her and hers for him. It would last through fire and water, through joy and tragedy, through life and beyond; she did not doubt it. Their home, wherever it was and whatever it was, would be a castle, simply because he was in it, and if she had to walk instead of ride, what did it matter? She would not mourn her lost dreams.

'All the same, that's what I'll work for,' he went on. 'And a proper home and everything ye want.'

'All I want is you, forever and ever.'

'God grant your wish,' Maggie said, coming to kiss them both, and handing Duncan a bundle she had made up to start them off in their married life, containing a few pots, some bedding, a little food. He bent to embrace her and she buried her face in his coat, not wanting him to see her tears. 'God bless you,' she murmured, too choked to say more.

James came with two glasses brimming with ale, which he handed to Duncan and Sarah Jane. 'A toast afore ye go,' he said, drawing his wife away and standing with his arm protectively round her, knowing how she felt.

They drank to each other and to all navvies everywhere, and danced a while, until Duncan took Sarah Jane on one side. 'We'll leave them to their celebrating now, for they'll keep it up all day.'

While he went to the contractor's hut to collect the wages he was owed and to pay off his tommy ticket debts, Sarah Jane ran back to the cave and changed into her workaday dress of brown wool topped by a fringed shawl, then, picking up her bundle, she returned to say goodbye to everyone. 'We'll write,' she cried, as Duncan took the year-old Jason from Daisy's arms. 'And if a letter comes from my brother, will you send it on?'

131

''Course, lass.'

Side by side they set off, over the distant hills, looking back now and again to wave to the watchers in the valley, until the brow of the hill hid them from view. Then they turned and faced the future with the optimism of all young couples newly married.

Chapter Nine

*T*hey reached Hailey Common in the late afternoon of the following day, having spent their wedding night at an inn. In the middle of a valley between two rolling hills they came upon half a dozen huts surrounded by machinery and trucks, piles of railway sleepers and lengths of line. Stretching from the door of one of the buildings stood a queue of patient men. Duncan joined them and Sarah Jane took her son and their bundles to a patch of grass a little way off and sat down to wait for him, tickling Jason's toes and laughing when he giggled.

'Why, look what the cat's brought in.'

Sarah Jane's glance went from two pairs of flimsy shoes and two pairs of laddered silk stockings, over creased taffeta crinolines to the painted faces of the whores she had tangled with a year before.

'Where's yer man?' the tall one demanded.

'My husband,' said Sarah Jane carefully, savouring the sound of it, 'is just coming.' She nodded to where Duncan strode towards them.

'My husband!' they jeered, mimicking the refined tone she had adopted. 'Don't yer go puttin' on yer airs and graces 'ere, Lady Muck, for yer'll soon be pegged down to size if yer do.'

But they stood aside when Duncan arrived, openly admiring his broad shoulders, which tapered down to slim hips and long muscular legs. 'If Lady Muck gives yer any trouble,' the fat one said, putting a grubby hand on his arm and peering up into his face, 'yer know where to come.' They drifted away, laughing.

Sarah Jane stood up with Jason in her arms. 'Oh, why did they have to come here too and spoil everything?'

'Like the men, they go where the work is,' he said. 'Ignore them. If they think they can rouse ye, they'll bait ye all the more.' He smiled. 'Now we must get busy.'

'They've taken you on, then?'

'Yes, starting tomorrow. Today I help build huts.'

'We'll have our own?'

'Not yet, I'm afraid. It would cost too dear and take too long. We'll have tae share tae start with.' He had been in shared huts before and he didn't like it, but here there were no houses, no cosy hillside caves, only huts built by the men themselves with wood and tarpaulin and old doors supplied by the tommy shop which, apart from the contractor's hut, was the first building to be erected. Now, under the banging and hammering of the navvies, others were growing, springing up like mushrooms all over the site. Duncan pointed to one which was already completed. 'Go to that one and say Charlie Bender sent ye. I'll be there as soon as I've finished work.'

The shanty was ruled by a tiny ill-tempered shrew of a woman called Emmy. She was so thin as to seem nothing more than skin over bone; she had lank brown hair and lacklustre eyes and an enormous beak of a nose which would have looked large on a man. Her clothes were the product of several dresses gleaned from her many begging sorties to the houses of the well-to-do and put together haphazardly. Her bodice was a vivid red, her skirt sky-blue and one leg o' mutton sleeve was cream and the other green. She looked like a character from a comic play, though Sarah Jane soon learned she had nothing to say worth laughing at. She scowled at the girl over an evil-smelling pipe clamped between broken teeth.

'Mr Bender said you'd find room for us,' Sarah Jane said, standing uncertainly in the doorway holding Jason in her arms. 'My husband will be here directly.'

Emmy removed the pipe. 'A shillin' a night and help me with the work. And,' she added threateningly, 'The first sign o' trouble and out you go.'

'There won't be any trouble,' Sarah Jane said confidently. 'My husband will look after us.'

'Then you'd best come in and settle your bits and pieces.'

Sarah Jane picked her bundles up from the ground where she had dropped them and stepped inside her new home.

The hut was divided into three; the only door led into the large middle room, which was called the living room but which, judging by the heaps of untidy bedding on the floor, was also used for sleeping. To the left was a smaller room containing nothing but bunk beds, tiered three high, a couple of chests and a chair; to the right was another room used as a kitchen and washroom. It contained a large pot-bellied stove on which the cooking pot and the laundry boiled side by side. Bacon and joints of meat hung from the rafters. There was a row of wooden cupboards, each fastened with a padlock, the keys for which dangled noisily at Emmy's waist. A large barrel of beer stood on a frame on its side in one corner and the tap of that was locked too. Water had to be fetched in buckets from the stream and that was nearly half a mile away, so it was small wonder that everyone, children included, drank beer.

Sarah Jane moved to a corner of the big room and set down her bundles on one of the beds – a couple of blankets, their clothes, some crocks, a few bits of coarse soap and a paper parcel of food, while Emmy eyed her malevolently, darting about, poking at her things, like a scavenging bird.

'The men will be in soon and they'll be hungry,' she said, nodding towards the kitchen, where Sarah Jane could see the blackened cooking pot and steam curling its way upwards through the hole in the roof which served for a chimney. 'We must have their food cooked.'

'What are you cooking?'

'Come and see. There's beef for Randy Joe and a bit of bacon for Big Bill, some have sausages and some 'taters and the like. Bring your'n with you if you want it boiled.'

Sarah Jane took the piece of mutton she had been saving for their dinner and followed Emmy into the kitchen. She didn't like the idea of dropping it in the pot along with everything else, but they couldn't eat it raw and now was not the time to insist on separate cooking arrangements, so in it went, tied by a bit of string to a stick on the handle.

Several hours later, Duncan came in with a dozen other men and the hut was soon a babble of voices which rose and fell about her like the waves on the shore, filling her ears with meaningless sound so that she felt like screaming. The men fished their own food out of the cooking pot, slapped it on tin plates and sat round the table to eat, gobbling at it and talking while they ate. Their manners, Sarah Jane decided, were disgusting; they ate like pigs. Already she hated it. There was no feeling of being a family, no closeness as there had been at Scarside, where she had enjoyed her own niche in the community, had been able to teach the children and have a little time to herself. Why had she encouraged Duncan to leave? What had made her think that he should be the one to change the face of navvying, when all he wanted was to go on in the way he had always done?

She found their mutton in the dregs of the pot, put it on one of the plates Maggie had given them, together with some potatoes, and set it in front of him; she had never served such an unappetising meal in her whole life, not even in the workhouse, and she was ashamed of it. 'I'm sorry about the dinner,' she said, leaning over him so that only he could hear – not that it mattered, for no one had any interest in what she had to say.

He looked up and smiled. 'We're together, aren't we? And that's all that matters.'

'Together!' Her voice was almost a squeak. 'How can we live like this? How can we eat and sleep and bring up Jason in this rabbit hutch with no place to be private in? Everyone will see whenever ... '

'I've nae fancy for an audience every time I want a kiss either,' he said, smiling at her in the teasing way he had. 'I'll try and do something about it tomorrow. Can ye not be patient until then?'

The following day he did his best to remedy the situation by building a partition across the corner of the room they called their own. He bought a bed, a couple of chairs and a chest from a man who came into the camp with a horse and cart loaded with furniture. An enterprising salesman he; the goods were all secondhand and mostly rubbish, but he went away with an empty cart and a full pocket.

Sarah Jane knew she had to accept what could not be changed and, for Duncan's sake, she tried to be content. She was a navvy wife and nothing could be further from being a lady, though Emmy and the two prostitutes, whose names she learned were Alice and Kate, always referred to her as 'Lady Muck'. It was a nickname that stuck but she would not demean herself by protesting. If that was how they thought of her, then she would do her best to live up to it; she would behave with as much refinement as she could muster. Everything she did, every gesture she made, every word she uttered, was directed towards that end. She would *be* Lady Muck.

It was almost impossible to keep clean and there was no water nor privacy for a bath, but she would not be beaten; she took Jason regularly to bathe in the river when she knew the men were at their work and would not see her, and their clothes were washed ten times more frequently than anyone else's. It made her stand out among the other inhabitants of the site; she shone like a lone star on a dark night.

Sometimes, while she worked, she imagined what she would do if she suddenly became rich. She would do something about the small children who swarmed around the works, dirty because keeping clean was almost impossible, unschooled because there was no one to teach them, ill-fed and coarsely spoken. There were many more here than at Scarside, and she supposed their parents had been drawn by the lure of better working conditions, though she could not see any material evidence of this. If she had money she'd get rid of tommy; there'd be bright clean shops selling good food at fair prices. She'd put a school and a shop and a laundry on every site, and a properly run boarding establishment for the single men. Without moving half a mile from where she was, she would make a vast change. She couldn't understand why it had not been done already; it was so obvious what was needed.

If she were rich, if she were really a lady ... The permutations of the dream were endless and sometimes she would talk to Jason about it. 'We'll have a fine house one day,' she would say. 'A grand house full of lovely furniture polished until you can see your face in it.' She would laugh at his puzzled expression and go on describing Chevington House, its upholstered sofas and spindly-legged chairs, its heavy silk and velvet curtains, the Brussels carpets, the porcelain figures and cut glass, the leather-bound books, French clocks and the big gilt-framed portraits of generations of Chevingtons which lined the wide staircase. 'We'll have lords and ladies come to call and we'll have servants – oh, we'll have a servant for every little thing. You'll have a nursemaid.' She would stop at this and gather him into her arms and smother him with kisses. 'No you won't, though. Your Mam will always look after you.'

'And Da?' It was the first word he had learned to say and it tickled Duncan no end.

Duncan was his father and her husband, there could be no other and if her dreams were to come true, they would have to come true through him, but it didn't stop her longing for a home they did not have to share.

Until they had accomplished that, Duncan would not send for his parents. She supposed it was a matter of pride; he had left them to better himself and until he had proved to his own satisfaction that he had done that, he would not ask them to join him. 'They couldn't live in this hut,' he told Sarah Jane. 'We must wait until we can build our own.'

And for that reason too, she could not think of teaching again; Emmy and the others would scoff such an idea into oblivion. Neither could she ask Billie to join them; there was nowhere for him to sleep. And because there was nothing she could do about it she settled down to a life which was very different from the one she had planned for herself and her son. Not that Jason felt deprived; dirt did not bother him and so long as he had his mother to love and spoil him, he was happy.

All through a hot summer when the earth was baked hard and the insides of the shanties were like ovens, through a bitter winter, when the navvies had to cope with snow-drifts as well as earth and rocks, Sarah Jane helped the bad-tempered Emmy with the housekeeping for eight navvies, which number grew to eleven the following spring, as the cutting progressed and more men were taken on. The huddle of shanties spread outwards to accommodate them and their families, until the whole area resembled a small town, a town without adequate water, without drainage, without policing. Owned by Lord Hailey who had a mansion a few miles away, it was ruled by Charlie Bender, the subcontractor, and those he chose to promote.

Duncan was made head of a butty gang, which meant he was in charge of the men who worked at the head of the cutting. They burrowed into the hillside like frantic rabbits, digging out a huge cave until the roof threatened to fall in, then one of them would climb on top to watch for cracks or movement in the surface in order to warn the men below to run clear. They seemed to delight in leaving it until the last minute and the first time Sarah Jane saw them scuttling to safety as tons of rubble fell and opened the cave to the sky, she shrieked and clapped her hands over her eyes, convinced that Duncan and his whole gang had been buried alive.

''Tis the quickest way to do it,' he said, pulling her hands from her face and laughing. 'Now all we have to do is cart away the crock.' He took his midday meal from her and patted her bottom affectionately. 'Go back to the shanty and do your work and leave me to mine. We know what we're at, believe me.'

As time went on, she learned not to worry about him so much, but she wished he could be taken off that butty gang and set to do something safer. But he had come here specifically for advancement and she had wanted it for him, so it was no good grumbling, there were plenty of others doing that; conditions and pay were always cause for complaint.

Lacking books, she learned about railway building by watching and asking questions and though she was laughed at – for what did a woman want to know things like that for? – she began slowly to acquire the knowledge she was certain would come in useful one day. She learned about the equipment and supplies and how they were brought to the site, the housing and provisioning of the army of men and women who came there to work, about the different skills needed and the wages for each. What no one seemed to know, for the information was the province of the owner and his agents and not available on the site, was how the railways were funded and how much profit the shareholders made. It was an important part of the whole puzzle because if the navvies wanted to bargain, they needed that information. Duncan smiled indulgently, neither encouraging or discouraging her; if it pleased her to show an interest, then he would not depress her by saying she was wasting her time. So long as his meals were cooked, the washing and cleaning done, he could get on with the business of earning their daily bread.

The cooking was done under conditions which precluded making any food appetising and, try as she might, Sarah Jane could not please all the men. Emmy she could not satisfy at all. The men's complaints were made largely from habit, not because they expected anything better, nor knew they could obtain it elsewhere, but simply to breathe some life into their non-working hours, to see how far they could provoke Sarah Jane before she turned her naturally fiery temper on them, which she always did in the end, however hard she tried to control it. Ladies didn't lose their tempers, she knew, but no lady had to put up with what she had to endure.

'They're no better than animals, the way they gobble up their food,' she told Duncan one day, when they had been especially infuriating. 'They don't leave any, so it can't be all that bad. And I can't help it if the stuff in the tommy shop has gone off. I'm the best cook on the site and they know it.'

''Course they do, my love,' he said gently. 'They just like to tease.'

She wondered what she had done to deserve him. She shouldn't grumble so much; he always took it to heart and because what she wanted was beyond his ability to provide, he was unhappy. Her guilt weighed heavy on her; she wanted to do something to please him, her way of saying how sorry she was, not only about the meat but about everything, for dragging him from his parents, making him hoard all his spare cash so he had no enjoyment, making him want to take her to bed, for she had done that on that first day, she knew; she had made use of him. But she had come to love him too, fiercely and with a passionate loyalty, but because there were no words to describe it she had not told him so. What could she do to please him, other than get on with her work in a cheerful frame of mind, and cook and wash for him and put up with Emmy's lodgers?

As soon as she had given Jason his breakfast and cleaned the hut, she put a shawl round her shoulders against the keen March wind which blew along the valley bottom, and went out, picking her way carefully across the muddy workings to the tommy shop. Jason was safe enough playing on their bed with an old rag doll Celia had given him.

The tommy shop was a hut about the same size as the one they lived in, the front room of which was the store and behind it the living quarters of Charlie Bender, the subcontractor. He had once been a navvy himself, but he had been ambitious and had saved enough to set himself up as a subcontractor. The main contractor provided all the materials, including the wagons and the drilling equipment, and he was responsible for the rails and fittings, the horses and labour. He strutted about full of self-importance, glorying in the power to hire and fire, and enjoying the proceeds from the tommy shop, which besides making a huge profit for the main contractor, furnished him with a sizeable extra income.

He was a thin little man with a high-domed head, bald at the front but with long mousy hair at the back which fell, straight and greasy, to his shoulders. He had a hook nose, little currant eyes and a droopy moustache. For some reason that Sarah Jane could not fathom, he fancied he had a way with the ladies and she didn't like entering the shop when no one else was there, unless she knew Mrs Bender was in the back room; then he always behaved with scrupulous correctness.

The shop was a clutter of foodstuffs, flour, sugar, cheese, tea. Meat and bacon, covered with flies, hung from a beam at one end, and jars and packets of this and that were ranged on shelves round two walls. There were also buckets, brooms, lamps, candles, lengths of rope, a couple of rolls of coarse calico, tea kettles and knick-knacks of all sorts.

Clutching her tommy tickets, Sarah Jane pushed open the door, but hesitated on the threshold because Charlie was serving Alice and Kate and she knew that if she went in, they would torment her as they always did. But to retreat would be to admit she was afraid of them and Sarah Jane was no coward. She stepped inside and moved over to examine a cheese on one end of the long table which served as a counter, doing her best to ignore them.

'Well, if it isn't Lady Muck,' Alice said, making a mocking curtsey. 'Good morning, my lady, do go before me.'

'I can wait,' Sarah Jane said sharply.

'But supposin' our business is private and for Charlie's ears alone?'

'This is a shop, isn't it?' Sarah Jane snapped. 'And it's open for business, isn't it? If you want to talk in private, go somewhere else.'

'Now, now, ladies,' said Charlie Bender, holding up his hands. 'I'll serve you all in turn.'

The whores giggled at the unconscious joke and then roared aloud when Sarah Jane said, 'That's all I'm asking.' She understood her slip, but she would not smile; instead she looked up to inspect a side of beef which hung above her head. It looked flyblown.

'Oh, pay no heed to Lady Muck,' Kate sniffed. 'She's no better than the rest of us; there's twelve men in her hut and eleven of them know what she is.'

That was too much! Sarah Jane turned on them with a cold-blooded ferocity which took them by surprise. It was a moment or two before they could collect themselves, but when they did, they retaliated like a couple of prizefighters. Charlie Bender watched in horror as bottles and jars went flying and a half-empty tea chest tottered and turned over. He righted it, trying to scoop up the tea from the floor with his hands, before giving up and wading in to break up the fight. 'Ladies, please,' he said, ineffectually plucking at the sleeves of one and trying to take another by the arm. 'Please, ladies, not in here.'

No one noticed Mrs Bender arrive, but they felt the weight of the broom she brought down on their shoulders and buttocks. 'Get out!' she screamed. 'Get out before I run you off the site. Get out!' She laid about her left and right. The whores seized their purchases and retreated, leaving Sarah Jane sitting on the floor rubbing the spot on her arm where the broom had landed.

'Up, if you please,' said Mrs Bender. 'Get off home before I give you another taste.'

Sarah Jane, crawling on hands and knees to look for her tommy tickets, ignored her; without the tickets she could buy nothing.

'Is this what you want?' Mrs Bender demanded, bending to pick them up and shaking the flour from them.

'Yes, thank you.' Sarah Jane scrambled to her feet and took them from her as Charlie began tidying up the mess.

''Tis a good thing I came home when I did,' Mrs Bender said. 'Get it cleared up.' She turned to Sarah Jane. 'As for you, your man will have to pay for the damage.'

'But it wasn't my fault!'

'You started it. Tell your husband I'll be along to see him after work tonight.'

'No!' The last thing she wanted was to add to Duncan's problems. 'If you must be paid, then I'll pay. There's no need to go to Duncan.'

Mrs Bender smiled. 'Well, I don't blame you, for it's a beating you'd get from him, that's for sure. But tell me, how can you pay?'

'That's my business, I'll get the money. Just give me time.'

'You can have 'til the end of the week.'

Sarah Jane hurried from the shop, forgetting she had gone in there to buy provisions. Now she was in a mess. How was she going to find enough to pay for the damage without going to Duncan? And all he had was the money they had been so carefully saving for a home of their own. But there was an answer; in fact, it was the only answer.

As soon as she returned to the hut, she went to their corner of the living room and rummaged among the clothes in her drawer, until her hand closed on the little black box which held the golden apple. She sat on the sagging bed with it open in her hand and for a few moments was transported back to a sunny day by a river bank and heard her own laughter; how long was it since she had laughed like that? She had loved Paris that summer and been pathetically grateful for his gift. Even now, she could feel the warmth of his hand as he gave it to her and her ecstatic response. He had bought her with it, just as the navvies bought Kate and Alice, for sexual gratification. Fancy being grateful for that! She didn't need that bauble to remind her of the man who had betrayed her, even supposing she wanted to remember him, which she didn't. Duncan was her husband, he loved her and she loved him and that was the most important thing in her life, next to Jason. If Maggie had been right and the apple was gold, then it should fetch enough to pay the Benders and buy themselves a little fresh meat; she would decide what to tell Duncan when the time came.

A sound from the kitchen roused her and, thinking it was Jason getting into mischief, she put the apple in its box and stuffed it into her skirt-pocket before hurrying to see to him.

He was standing very still in the middle of the room with his thumb in his mouth, watching Randy Joe – so-called for his partiality to drunken brawls on pay day – who was on his knees in front of the cupboard where she kept her food. Flour, sugar and tea were scattered about the floor. She reached down and turned Jason around, patting his bottom to send him back into the living room before turning to the navvy.

'Just what do you think you're doing?' she demanded. 'That's my cupboard. '

He was obviously very drunk. 'I'm looking for me beer ticket.'

She was worried by the waste of food; first the trouble in the shop and now this. 'You'll have to replace all that,' she said, grabbing his shoulder and trying to pull him away. He threw out his arm to shrug her off and she fell against Jason, whose curiosity had brought him back into the room. More frightened by their raised voices, than hurt, he began to bawl.

Furious, she scrambled to her feet, seized Randy Joe's shoulders from behind and jerked him backwards, shoving her knee into the small of his back. She had hurt him, she knew, because he grunted in pain, but not enough; he lumbered to his feet and turned on her. 'So it's a fight you want, is it?' He grabbed her upraised arm and slapped her face, first with the palm of his hand and then with the back, and then again and again, until her head rocked. 'Where's my ticket? He slapped her again. 'Bitch! Thieving bitch!'

With her hands imprisoned, she could only retaliate with feet and teeth, and she used both effectively. She did not hear Emmy come in and begin shrieking behind them, nor Big Bill arriving off his shift, until she suddenly became aware that he had weighed in to her assistance. Other men followed him and took sides according to personal bias and the shanty soon became a shambles of broken furniture, spilled food and torn-up bedding.

They were no longer interested in her or why it had begun; it was a fight, and a jolly good one, and that was reason enough. Sarah Jane crawled on hands and knees to Jason, for he was in imminent danger of being thrown across the room with everything else that was portable and, picking him up, she made for the door.

One of the navvies snatched up a lamp and hurled it across the room, where it burst into flames and set fire to a pile of clothing. Instantly everyone ran for the only exit as fire engulfed the hut and Sarah Jane, nearest to it, was sucked out like a stopper from a bottle. She fell, sobbing, into the arms of a breathless Duncan who had seen the first tongues of flame as he was leaving his work and run all the way, his mind painting lurid pictures of her being burnt to death. Relieved to find her unhurt, he led her to safety and left her sitting on the grass, nursing Jason, then went back to join Big Bill and Randy Joe who stood side by side, beating at the flames with their coats, their quarrel and the reason for it forgotten.

The sky grew dark in the hills around them, but the shanty village was lit up like day, with people milling about, hurrying from one place to another, and then stopping to stare helplessly as the flames licked round the windows of the hut. Inside was an inferno; there was nothing they could do to save it. Dry wooden walls and old furniture burned fiercely until the tarred roof melted in the heat and, shimmering like black glue, dropped into the holocaust. Sparks flew upwards, landing on adjacent roofs. The firefighters abandoned the original blaze and turned to save the other huts. There was no water to be had, so they used blankets and brushwood, scrambling over the sloping roofs to beat out pockets of fire, burning their hands and scraping their knees, leaving the occupants of Emmy's hut to fend for themselves.

By morning the fire had burned itself out and then it began to rain, a few big drops at first, hissing on the still-hot timbers, like a laundrymaid spitting on her flat iron, but soon it became a deluge and the ashes at their feet turned to black mud. The firefighters lifted their faces to the sky and cursed its timing. 'Too late!' they cried. 'Too bloody late!'

There was nothing more to be done and the men found their shovels and returned to work, ignoring Emmy's high-pitched voice, blaming Sarah Jane for the loss of her home and the income it provided.

Sarah Jane had crawled beneath a disused wagon, where Duncan found her, crying softly and holding her son close to her breast, sheltering him with the heavy veil of her hair. 'There ye are,' he said, dropping down beside her. 'I've been looking everywhere.' He took her chin in thumb and forefinger to turn her face towards him and, in spite of everything, smiled broadly.

'What's so funny?' she demanded, sniffling.

'Ye are, my lovely. Ye've a face as black as an undertaker's topper and do ye know ...' He paused to lick a finger and smooth it along her brow. 'Ye've scorched eyebrows. All ginger and curled up, they are.'

She laughed through her tears. ''Tis no worse than you. The rain has made dirty streaks all down your face.' She reached up to kiss his cheek and then was serious again. 'How can you sit and laugh about it?'

'It's better than crying, Sarah Jane.'

'But it *was* my fault, 'cos I can't keep me temper. What are we going to do, Duncan? Where are we going to live?'

He smiled the tired smile of a man who worked too hard and relaxed not at all, and pinched her cheek gently. 'We'll have to start again. It was lucky we had our savings in a tin box, for I picked over the débris and found it. Scorched on the outside it is, but the contents are safe.' He held it out to show her.

She looked at it dully, consumed by guilt. 'But it will take all that to buy clothes and bedding and . . .' She burst into fresh weeping.

He brushed away her tears and took her face in his hands to look closely into eyes red-rimmed from weeping and smoke and lack of sleep. 'It could have been much worse. Ye could have been burned tae death, ye and Jason, and I thank God for your life. The rest doesna matter a farthing. With a few more tommy tickets, we'll manage.'

The mention of tommy tickets reminded her of Charlie Bender and the money she owed. Would he refuse Duncan credit until it had been paid? She had the answer in her pocket. 'We don't need tommy tickets,' she said, fishing it out. 'I've saved this. We can sell it.'

'No.'

'Why not? It means nothing to me.'

'I'll have nothing tae do with it. I don't even want tae see it, d'ye hear? It's my job to look after ye. Do ye think I'm not man enough tae do it without that bauble?' He knocked it from her hand, really angry for the first time since she had known him, and not over the loss of their home, but because she wanted to help him financially. 'I dinna need another man's generosity tae provide for my wife and bairn.'

Even in her misery, she smiled, because he seemed to have forgotten that Jason was not his child. And he was jealous!

'But that's all it is,' she cried, bending to retrieve it ' – a bauble. It means nothing to me and I don't think it's valuable, but if it saves you havin' to ask for more tommy tickets . . .'

'I said no and I meant it. Ye will nae mention it again.' He got up and strode to the tommy shop.

She watched him go, this tall, proud man of hers and she wished, oh how she wished, she could put the clock back. She had made use of this gentle giant, taken all he had to give and given nothing in return except a sharp temper and a body she had thought so little of she had given it to the first man who had asked her for it. And yet he treasured even that. He was not demonstrative, but she understood the love in what he did, the way he thought of her before all others, the way he looked towards her when he had a decision to make, the lifting of one eyebrow as if consulting her, even if he said nothing aloud. And if she protested at anything he did he, more often than not, desisted. Without him life would be unbearable and yet she still did impulsive things which hurt him. She should have controlled her temper and not pitched into the whores or Randy Joe, and she should have had more sense than to mention the apple. His pride was just as easily wounded as hers.

When he reappeared, he was wheeling a handcart loaded with wood and tarpaulin, a door and a couple of windows, and she breathed a sigh of relief. Charlie had obviously said nothing about the ruined stock, but their plan to break out of the vicious circle of tommy tickets and debt to the subcontractor had taken a severe blow from which they could not easily recover, unless the apple was sold.

She followed him as he pushed the cart up the hill a little way, distancing himself from the other dwellings, where he set about building them a new home 'Can I help?'

'Later, when I've got the roof on. Now go and give Jason his breakfast. And find somewhere tae sleep for an hour or two.' There was no anger in his voice, but neither was there any joy. Emmy's accusations she cared nothing for, but Duncan was another matter. His displeasure, his hurt, his disappointment were like knife wounds in her side and she longed for the healing balm of his forgiveness. 'Duncan,' she said. 'I'm sorry, truly sorry.'

He sighed. 'So am I, lass, so am I.'

She turned and walked slowly to the tommy shop. Charlie Bender smiled broadly when he saw her; it was the smile of a cat who'd found the cream. 'Could I come with you into Derby when you go with your cart?' she asked him.

'I don't see why not.' He looked at his wife, careful to keep the eagerness from his voice. 'But what d'you want to go there for?'

'To get the money I owe.' She knew they would draw their own conclusions. In their minds, there was only one way an impoverished woman could earn money in a hurry.

Mrs Bender shrugged. 'Take her if it means we'll be paid.'

'I'm going this afternoon,' Charlie said. 'I have to fetch replacements for the goods that were spoiled yesterday and what with the fire an' all and people wanting building stuff, I'm a fair way to being cleaned out.'

Sarah Jane looked down at her son; she could not take him with her and she would not leave him in the care of any of the navvy women. 'Would you look after Jason while I've gone, please? He'll be good, he always is.'

Mrs Bender hesitated, but the loss of stock was large in her mind.

'Very well, but you get back as fast as you can and no keepin' Charlie waiting, 'cos when his business is done, he'll want to come home.'

'I won't,' she promised. 'But please don't tell Duncan where I've gone.'

An hour later she met Charlie at the bridge where the road from the site crossed the river just above Hailey village. He grinned as she climbed up on the cart beside him. 'I'll have to do my errands first,' he said, as he flicked the reins and urged the horse forward. 'But after that I know a tavern where they serve a fair meat pie and a good drop o' ale. We'll have a good time, shall we?'

She did not answer. Though she had registered what he said, her mind was on her errand. The sooner it was done and the sooner Duncan was persuaded it had been for the best, the happier she would be.

Once they were away from the scar of the railway works, the countryside was beautiful. Rolling hills, green valleys, sheep, cattle, farmhouses were spread on either side of the road like a painted canvas. The rain had stopped and a weak sun shone on the dripping trees, making emeralds of their newly burgeoning leaves and the air was heady. In any other circumstances she would have enjoyed the ride but as it was, she sat silently immersed in a worry which excluded everything else. Supposing the apple was worthless? Supposing Duncan was so angry he threw her out?

Derby turned out to be a fine town, full of grand buildings and busy streets, but instead of being overawed as she had been by Peterborough, she hardly noticed it. They rode along to a provision merchant's, where the subcontractor stopped the cart. 'I'll go and see to my business,' she said, climbing down. 'I'll see you later.'

'There's no call for you to go looking for business when it's right here, under your nose,' he said. 'A debt can be as easily cancelled as made.'

She knew what he meant right enough. 'And what would Mrs Bender say to that idea? I fancy she wants to see hard cash, don't you?'

He grinned. 'Mayhap you're right, but it don't stop us getting together and having a jolly time, does it? I'll meet you in the Black Boar in half an hour.'

'Make it an hour.' The conceit of the man was beyond everything, Sarah Jane decided as she hurried away to find a shopkeeper who would give her a fair price for the apple. The trouble was, she had no idea what a fair price should be.

She dodged down an alley and found herself in a narrow cobbled street lined with shops, one of which displayed the three golden balls of a pawnbroker. The bell above the door rang tinnily as she entered. The room was low-ceilinged and dark; shelves were piled with clothes, shoes and hats, the floor with furniture and musical instruments. A glass case held ornaments, jewellery and watches.

A tubby man in a faded frockcoat looked up and quizzed her through a tiny pair of spectacles. 'Mornin', miss.'

She put the black box on the counter, determined to argue, on the assumption that whatever he offered was bound to be far less than its worth. 'How much will you give me for this?'

He picked up the box and took out the apple, weighing it thoughtfully in his hand. She watched without speaking as he released the spring and the top opened to reveal the pearl. He looked at her over the top of the spectacles and she recognised the avarice in his eyes, even though he was doing his best to hide it. 'Where did you get this?'

'It was a present from ... from an admirer.'

'You think this admirer of yours valued your charms at the going rate of gold and pearls?' he enquired, putting the apple back in its box and pretending indifference.

'That's my affair,' she said. 'Tell me what you'll give me for it.'

'It isn't real,' he said. 'But it's an attractive little trinket. Ten pounds and that's being generous.'

Sarah Jane stifled her gasp of delight and said, 'Don't give me that. I know it's worth a lot more.'

He looked up from his examination of the apple and saw her doubts mirrored in her expressive green eyes. 'Come now, miss,' he said. 'Don't try pulling the wool over old Uncle's eyes. It wasn't worth the effort of stealing it.'

'I didn't steal it.'

'And if it was a gift, the donor did not think as much of you as you thought he did.'

Sarah Jane had a mental picture of Paris giving it to her. Its worth had not been important then, and it was only important now in so far as it could pay off the Benders and buy a few luxuries. 'You can manage more than ten pounds,' she said obstinately.

'Twelve,' he said, opening the drawer of a desk behind him. 'Not a farthing more.'

'Very well. I'll take it.' She would not admit that parting with the apple was a wrench, that she had sold her dreams for a mere twelve pounds. What were dreams anyway, she asked herself, blinking back tears, but so much empty air? And Duncan was real. And the coins clasped so firmly in her fist were real and what they could buy would be real; she should have no regrets.

She looked back once as she left the shop, and saw the little man clear a space in the middle of his window and set the open box on a velvet cushion, where it shamed all the clutter around it into shabby tawdriness.

Chapter Ten

'*W*here's Charlie?' Mrs Bender demanded, when Sarah Jane returned, laden with purchases – provisions, a joint of beef, clothes for Jason, a shirt and trousers for Duncan, a summery cotton dress for herself, enough flowered curtain material to cover two small windows, some notepaper, pen and ink, a bundle of books from a second-hand stall, half a dozen school slates and some chalk.

'Isn't he here?' she asked, feigning surprise. Rather than meet the subcontractor at the Black Boar, she had set out to walk the six miles home, but when the drayman had come up behind her and offered her a lift she had been glad enough to take it; her parcels had been getting heavier with every step. 'I missed him when I finished my shopping. I thought he had tired of waiting for me and come home.'

Mrs Bender had a good idea where Charlie had gone, but the fact that he had separated from Sarah Jane mollified her. 'Did you get your business done?'

'Yes.' Sarah Jane put down her parcels and fished into her pocket for what was left of the twelve pounds. 'Here's enough to cover your losses and redeem our tommy tickets. And there's no call to say anything to Duncan about the trouble with those two whores.'

'He was here an hour since.' Mrs Bender smiled thinly as she searched in the drawer of the counter for the tickets, which she handed over almost reluctantly. Navvies who were free of debt were more difficult to manipulate. 'Wanted to know where you were and why I was looking after Jason.'

'What did you tell him?'

'I told him you'd gone into Derby on business. Did you expect me to lie to him?'

'No, of course not. Where is he now?'

Mrs Bender pointed to where Duncan was sitting on the roof of the almost-finished hut, fixing the tarpaulin into place. Even at that distance, Sarah Jane could tell by the frenzied banging of his hammer, that he was finding it difficult to control his emotions. 'Best get up there and make your peace – if you can.'

Duncan looked up as she approached. She had Jason on one arm, a parcel under the other and more packages dangling by their string from her wrists. If he had not already guessed, the expression on her face would have told him what she had done; it was alight with childlike eagerness. He laid aside his hammer and climbed down.

'Well, Sarah Jane?' He stood and surveyed her with his head on one side. 'So ye went against me and sold it?'

'Yes.' She gave him a wide smile intended to disarm him. 'And I've redeemed your tommy tickets and bought lots of things we need ...'

'So I see.' He would not capitulate that easily.

'You're not really angry with me, are you?'

'Ye knew how I felt about it and yet ye did it anyway.'

'Oh, Duncan, don't be a crosspatch. I didn't want the silly old apple, truly I didn't.' She put Jason down and he toddled through the doorway which, as yet, had no door, to investigate his new home.

'Where did ye take it?'

'To a pawnbroker in Derby. He gave me twelve pounds for it.'

She was so obviously delighted that he could not tell her he thought she had been cheated. 'And did he give you a ticket?'

'No, what would I want a ticket for? We don't want it back, do we?'

A ticket would have stated the price he would have to pay to redeem it; without it, the pawnbroker was free to sell it as soon as he liked and charge whatever he could get for it. Even so, it would have to be bought back just as soon as he had saved enough money. 'One day, ye might.'

'Never.' She laughed suddenly. 'We're on our way up in the world, Duncan McBryde. We don't need gimcracks like that, except to see us through this bad patch ...'

He smiled wearily. 'Bad patch?'

'That's all it is, isn't it – a little hitch. We'd be a lucky pair indeed if we never had a setback. We'll get over it, just so long as you're not angry and stubborn and too proud to see that I love you more'n anything else in this world.'

He laughed and put his arms about her. 'Och, Sarah Jane, what am I going tae do with ye?'

'Do? Why, nothing. Take me as I am, the most loving, grateful and contented wife you could possibly imagine.'

'Contented?' he queried, picking her up in his arms and carrying her over the threshold into the hut. 'Now, that doesna sound quite like my Sarah Jane.'

She nuzzled her head into his shoulder. 'No, but if I'm not, 'tis only 'cos I want things to be better for you and Jason and I'll strive for that as long as I've breath in me body.'

He kissed her and set her down. 'Ye don't want them any more than I do. Now, I must get back to work.'

'Don't you want to see what I've fetched?'

'Later. I must get the roof finished before it rains again, and ye'd better see tae Jason. He seems tae have found a mud-bath.'

With a cry of dismay, she ran outside to rescue her son from the puddle in which he was paddling. Then she took a broom from the handcart and swept out the hut.

'What'll we do for furniture?'

'There's boxes on the cart,' he called down from his perch on the roof. 'I'll make a few bits when I've time. We must make do.'

And make do they did. They were both exhausted by the time they were able to go to bed. The hut was small and crude, but it was home, a quiet refuge from the world of the navvy, the rough behaviour, the coarse voices, the cramped living. Duncan had carved the words *The Haven* on a piece of board and nailed it to a post outside the door because that was what she had called it.

'Oh, Duncan, this is lovely,' she said, snuggling up against him on a straw palliasse on the floor. 'No Big Bill snoring his head off, no Randy Joe shouting, nor Emmy going on at them all like a fishwife and teaching Jason words he never ought to hear. 'Tis so quiet you could hear a pin drop.'

'So we might, if you stopped chattering long enough to listen.'

'We ought to have done it long before now.'

'We didna have the wherewithal, still haven't got it,' he murmured, pretending to be half-asleep. 'Things have tae be paid for; cash or kind, a debt is a debt.'

'We have no debts, not now.' She propped herself on one elbow and traced the outline of his stubbly chin with her finger. 'You're not still mad at me, are you?'

'Furious,' he said, but his tone belied the word.

'No, you're not. You're warm and comfortable and, if you told the truth, you're glad to see the back of that crew in Emmy's hut.'

'They're good men.'

'To work with maybe, but for bedfellows?'

He chuckled. 'Mayhap ye're right.'

'And if a useless bauble achieved it, so much the better. Admit it.'

'It was your insurance against a rainy day.'

She laughed, leaning over him so that her bare breasts were inches from his face. He lifted his head to kiss them one by one, but she refused to be sidetracked. 'It rained hard enough yesterday, and that's a fact.'

He looked up over her naked body to her face, framed by its veil of heavy hair. She was as beautiful as ever, and her lovely eyes looked down into his with an expression that was both mischievous and adoring. She was like a light in a dark tunnel and he never ceased to thank God for her; she made a dull existence one of life and laughter, she made hard work a pleasure and anger insupportable. 'Do you ever think of him?'

'Who?'

'You know who. Jason's father.' His eyes, reflecting the moonlight, shone with an intensity she found unnerving. 'Do you ever wish you could go back to him?'

'Never! Never! How can you lie there like that and even think it? You are my husband and I am your wife, your very loving wife. Without you I am nothing and nobody.'

'Ye will never be a nobody, with me or without me, but I tell ye this, together we can move mountains.'

She laughed, thinking of the excavating. 'Quite literally.'

'You know what I mean. We won't always be on the bottom rung of the ladder and with every step up, life will get better for us and the men under me.' He put his hands up to cup her face and draw her head down to kiss her lips. 'But if I was tae lose ye tae your dreams and your memories . . .' He could not go on.

'My dreams are all about you,' she lied easily, because it was what he wanted to hear. She couldn't help her dreams, could she? 'I've forgotten I ever had a life before we met.' She spread her fingers across his chest and moved them slowly down his torso to his muscular belly. He lay still, trying not to let himself be roused by her exploring hands, but it was already too late. 'An' I vow to keep me temper in future. I'll be the lady, I promise. I'll hold me tongue whatever anyone says to me and we'll be so cosy here.' She giggled as her hand found evidence of his arousal. 'An' I thought you were too tired . . .'

He laughed and pulled her down onto him, moving slowly beneath her until she picked up his rhythm. Their fatigue fled as they quickened, only to return a few minutes later when they rolled apart. Sarah Jane, assured that she had been forgiven, fell into a deep sleep almost at once, but Duncan lay awake for a long time.

When that damned apple had been in Sarah Jane's possession, it had been a thorn in his flesh, but now it was gone and he was benefiting from the proceeds of its sale, it was more than a thorn, it was a huge festering sore. He had to get it back, if only to prove they did not need it. Sarah Jane would think he had retrieved it for her, but he knew it was because of his pride and his jealousy. Perhaps one day she would understand how he felt, what drove him on to work harder than anyone else, to save every spare farthing, why they had so little pleasure. He wanted for her what she wanted for herself, a home and not a hut, some standing in the community, to be looked up to. She wanted to be a lady, he knew that because she had told him of that early ambition, thinking to amuse him. He had laughed dutifully at the time, but it had rankled. He would get her what she wanted even if he had to do the work of ten men.

Tomorrow he must begin making some furniture. He'd come home for his dinner half hour and do a bit each day. Drowsily he went through the items they would need in order of importance, but long before he had finished, he was asleep.

Charlie Bender arrived at the door the following morning after Duncan had left for work, bringing with him a large chunk of hard cheese, a few ounces of tea, a small joint of bacon and a bag of biscuits. He pressed them on Sarah Jane, contriving to keep his hands in contact with hers a full minute before releasing them.

'What's this for?' she demanded.

'You. 'Tis a little gift.'

'I don't want anything from you.' She thrust the package back into his hands.

'You were glad enough of my help yesterday, m'dear, weren't you? Took you into Derby, I did, and you let me down. I waited at the Black Boar for an age.'

'I spent so long shopping I thought you must have gone home,' she said, repeating the story she had told Mrs Bender.

'I've got more patience than that, my little one, much more, as you will see.'

'What do you mean?'

'Nothing. You paid for the spilt food and I know for a fact that Mrs Bender swept some of it up to sell again, so 'tis only fair.'

'Is that the truth?'

'I swear it.'

'Why didn't you wait until I came down to the shop again?'

'Mrs Bender wouldn't understand, would she?' He paused and smiled his oily smile. 'Take them, my dear, and give your man a treat. It'll be our secret, won't it?'

'Secret?'

He laughed. ''Twas you said you didn't want Duncan McBryde to know about your little trouble in the shop, wasn't it? 'Tis only what you asked.'

She would never have accepted if what he offered had been costly or for her alone, but she was still rankling over having to pay that compensation and if Mrs Bender had cheated her, then it was only fair. She allowed her desire to please Duncan with good food to overcome her doubts about the subcontractor's motives; she accepted the food, ignoring the warning bells in her head which told her she was storing up trouble for herself.

She watched him going back down the hill and in among the huts and wagons of the site and then turned back to her son. 'Let's forget the silly man,' she said, fetching out the books and slates she had bought the day before. 'We've more important things to do.' She took his hand and led him out of doors to the shade of a lanky fir which she loved for its resinous smell and bright colour when everything else about them was grey. 'Dreams only become real if you work at making them happen, and the sooner we make a start the better.'

Duncan, coming home for his dinner and finding her there with Jason beside her, bent over one of the books, chuckled. 'He's too young for that, my love, he's not four yet. He just wants to play.'

'We've been sitting here for ages and he wants to learn, I know he does. So do the other children. Mrs Macnamara's little girl was up here, earlier.'

'Curiosity.' He shrugged.

'Isn't that how we all learn? I told her she could come back tomorrow and bring the other children if they wanted to come. You don't mind, do you?'

'Of course not, as long as the little beggars behave themselves.' He had guessed why she had bought so many books and slates. If she wanted to begin teaching again, he would not discourage her, but he questioned what the other women would think of the idea. Hailey Common was different from Scarside and Sarah Jane was no more accepted by them now than she had been when they first arrived, simply because she was different. He knew they called her Lady Muck. It was funny, but she didn't seem to mind; in fact, she bore the name with a certain pride, as if they honoured her.

She busied herself cutting bread and a generous hunk of the cheese Charlie Bender had given her. 'The children here are far worse off than those at Scarside. Their parents make no effort to teach them, either good manners or reading and writing . . .'

'Probably because they can't.'

She turned to look at him. He was sitting on one of the upturned boxes they were using as chairs, his hands dangling between his knees and his head down. He looked exhausted, and small wonder. She went over to stand close to him and held his head against her side, stooping to kiss his forehead. 'I'm sorry, Duncan.'

He put his arms around her waist and looked up at her face, 'Sorry for what?'

'For making you so worried.'

He laughed. 'Ye don't worry me, Sarah Jane. I reckon I can handle ye.' He gave her a playful smack on her bottom. 'But the work, that's another matter.'

Sarah Jane knew that the cutting they had been working on had given way to tunnelling and the navvies were driving through solid rock, every cubic foot of which had to be blasted out, loaded onto wagons and carted away. She had heard explosions, always presaged by a bugle call, every day since it began and though she had been nervous of the way the ground rocked, Duncan had assured her there was nothing to worry about: the navvies knew what they were doing. 'There's trouble?' she asked nervously.

'The men can't earn their piece rates and they're complaining of Charlie's shop prices – twenty per cent above Derby prices they are, and that for shoddy goods. There's talk of a strike. Big Bill's stirring them up.' Big Bill was a hardened combination man; he had been making speeches and trying to enrol the men for years, but he had not been as successful as he would have liked. Although giving lip service to his ideas of a united workforce, they had gone on in their time-honoured way, seeking out work on their own account and taking what was offered. When drunk on randy days, they shouted loudly enough about their slavery and would have lynched any employer foolish enough to go near, but on sober reflection, they returned to work as they always had. But if the Hailey Common men were growing mutinous, Big Bill might find ready listeners. Duncan, normally disinterested, was arguing against withdrawing their labour. No one, he maintained – not navvy, not owner – gained by it.

'But he's right, isn't he?'

'Nay, lass. They'd be worse off if they did that.' He sighed. 'There are rumours of the company going bankrupt if the line isn't finished in time to start bringing in revenue before the investors demand a return on their capital. If the men strike, they'll lose everything. Lord Hailey will just give up and then they'd not even get the pay they've already earned.'

'Does Charlie Bender know where you stand?' She didn't know why, but she felt a sudden cold wind blowing round her heart and she shivered. 'Will he take it out on the men who cause trouble?'

'Aye, but not while the men keep working. He's too much tae lose himself.'

'Can't you do anything? The men will listen to you.'

'Only if it suits them.' He smiled wearily. 'I've been trying to calm them down but why should they listen to me? I've no authority to promise anything. Besides, I'm one of them myself, aren't I? I can't tell them that I'm working my way up so that I can help them, they'd never believe that. If I side with the bosses, I'll be branded a scab. And yet I know that striking is not the answer; it will destroy them.' He put his empty plate on the floor beside him and stood up. 'Don't look so worried, my love. Nothing bad will happen if I can help it.' He bent to kiss her. 'You go on with your teaching and I'll go on with my excavating.'

She stood in the doorway and watched as he swung Jason up over his head, making the child laugh and shriek for more, then he put him down and strode off towards the tunnel. If anyone could take the heat out of the situation, he could; the men liked and respected him and, if it weren't for Big Bill, she didn't think there would be any trouble. Not that she had any time for the owners but if they went bankrupt, they took the men down with them.

'I've heard the line's been sold,' Duncan told Sarah Jane a few weeks later, as they relaxed outside the door of their hut. The sun was a huge red ball, sitting on top of the distant hill, streaking the sky with flame. She had watched it set like that many and many an evening and she never tired of it. 'But whoever's bought it, they need someone a deal more competent than Charlie Bender as subcontractor.'

She smiled. 'You think you could do better?'

157

'I know I could. To start with, I'd—' He stopped and laughed, realising she was teasing him. 'I'd stop women asking foolish questions.' He stood up and offered her his hand. 'Come, my love, it's time for bed. The work doesn't get any easier and I need my rest.'

The next morning Charlie came to him just as he was setting off into the tunnel, and took him on one side. 'I want you to come into Derby with me to the company office. I'll be leaving with the cart in half an hour, so be ready.'

'What for?' Duncan demanded. If the man wanted him to back him up in some scheme to get the men working harder, he would be disappointed. Just because he encouraged the men to keep at work, didn't mean he was a company man. 'I haven't the time tae waste on jaunts into town.'

'This won't be a waste of time, I promise you. We've got a new owner and a new contractor too and he wants a few words with you personally.'

Duncan shrugged his shoulders and obeyed, but when, just over an hour later, he was shown into the contractor's office, he could hardly drag his eyes away from the paperweight on the desk, to look at the man who sat behind it. The golden apple gleamed there, along with the inkstand, the blotter and a bone-handled paperknife.

It seemed to have a life of its own; it accused him with its brilliance, it stood between him and his hopes. It mocked him.

He had tried to buy it back. A few weeks before, he had gone into Derby on pay day and found the pawnbroker, only to be told its owner had come and claimed it. 'I had to hand it over or have the constable fetched,' the man had said. 'So you owe me twelve pounds plus my profit, or the girl does, I don't care which.'

It had taken weeks to save the money, but his inclination to argue had been stifled by the almost certain knowledge that if he refused to pay, Paris would be informed and he couldn't take that risk. The man had always been a dimly perceived figure to Duncan, the figment of Sarah Jane's rosy-hued recollections. He was jealous of him, because he had a place in Sarah Jane's past, but if it was not of the past he had to beware but the present, what then? He had nothing to offer to induce her to stay with him, nothing but a broad back and a willingness to work for her and her child to the end of his days. He had handed over fifteen pounds and left the shop, to return empty-handed to Sarah Jane who, in any case, had known nothing of his real errand.

'Now Lord Chevington has taken over the Hailey Common line,'

Timothy was saying, 'there will be some changes.' Duncan forced himself to attend, to look into eyes which exactly mirrored Jason's; there was no doubt in his mind of that. 'Yes, sir.'

'Not all at once, you understand, but there will be no more management from a distance. Lord Chevington has put me in as manager and I mean to get the line moving forward and moving forward quickly.' He paused and leaned across to pick up the golden apple and play with it in his hands. Duncan knew by the unthinking way he did it, that it had become a habit. 'If changes are needed, changes there will be. That is one of the reasons why I have taken this office in Derby, to be near enough to make sure the line progresses on schedule.' Was another reason for staying close to the works his intention to find Sarah Jane, Duncan wondered. And if he did, what would he do? More to the point, what would she do? The big navvy shook himself like a wet puppy; he mustn't think of that, he must concentrate on what the fellow was saying.

'You shake your head. You do not agree?'

'I agree, sir. It will make all the difference.' Duncan waited for him to come to the point, wishing he would put that damned apple down.

'One of the problems is the length of the tunnel. It's airless and foul with the dust from the blasting. And there's too much of that, considering the meagre amount of spoil it produces. We intend to drill, to sink shafts at intervals right through hillside and work outwards from each. You understand?'

'Yes, sir.'

'You have been recommended as a good man to lead a drilling gang. Do you think you can do it?'

In any other circumstances Duncan would have been thoroughly pleased with himself; it was just the promotion he needed, a chance to prove himself, to make a start on the climb upwards he and Sarah Jane had planned. He wanted to be the one to give her everything she wanted, to grant her wish to be a lady. But if Timothy Myson came to the site, he could not fail to notice her; she stood out like a shining beacon, not only because of her red hair, but by her manner, the way she carried herself, the way she spoke. And if the man was actually looking for her? Should they leave, he and Sarah Jane? Could he persuade her they should take Jason and go somewhere else? She would want to know why and he could not tell her.

'You've no doubts about being able to do it?' Timothy asked. 'You seem unsure of yourself.'

Duncan came out of his reverie. 'I can do it.'

Perhaps he was worrying for nothing; the man could have picked up the apple from almost anywhere, could have bought it simply because he wanted an ostentatious paperweight. It did not mean that he had ever been Sarah Jane's lover. But those eyes! So like Jason's, so dark, so deep they seemed to be able to search out secrets from deep inside you, and they would search out Sarah Jane if he ever came to the railhead. She would have to be told. But when? And how? And what would he do, how could he go on, if he lost her?

He had no answers and because he had no answers, he stopped plaguing himself with questions. But he felt like snatching that bauble away and poking the fellow on the nose, just to see what he was made of.

'The equipment will begin arriving in less than a week,' Timothy continued. 'It will have to be hauled up piecemeal and assembled on location. Your first task will be to take on men. I want good men, not afraid of hard work.'

'They'll be working on piece rates?'

'Naturally. It will be up to you to negotiate those with Mr Bender.' He shut the lid of the apple with a sharp click and set it back on the blotter.

'Sir,' Duncan hoped the effort needed to be polite wasn't obvious. 'Mr Bender's rates . . .'

Timothy smiled. 'I know, the men have been grumbling, but he is governed by the economics of the thing, just as we all are. The drilling should make it easier for everyone, so it's down to you. And before you complain that he is making too great a profit, just remember it was he who recommended you.' He picked up a sheaf of papers, bringing the interview to an end. 'Good-day to you, Mr McBryde.'

Duncan opened his mouth to tell him he could not be bought that easily but, in his present state of mind, he could not trust himself to argue rationally. If he refused the job someone else would take it, someone who did not care what happened to the men and their families. He muttered 'Good-day, sir,' turned on his heel and left, followed by the grinning Charlie Bender.

The navvy had looked as though he was about to give him an argument, Timothy thought, as he crossed the room to gaze out of the window on the busy street where McBryde was climbing onto the subcontractor's cart, but like all labourers everywhere, he knew which side his bread was buttered on. He would do as he was told. He was big and strong and, according to Bender, capable of making the men turn to and do an honest day's work. He knew they couldn't make their piece rates and were demanding a new agreement, but he had no intention of giving in to them. He needed strong men like Duncan McBryde, men who needed to be grateful to him, if the line was going to be made to pay. And he had promised his father it would.

Jack Miller had told them months ago that he believed Lord Hailey might find it difficult, if not impossible, to complete the line on time and within budget. 'There's no doubt that the stretch between Ashley Green and Hailey Common is a very important link in the whole system,' the engineer had said, speaking to Lord Chevington in the London office. 'But it won't go smoothly, not the way they're doing it.'

'What's the problem?'

'It's mainly millstone grit and they've chosen a particularly bad route through; levelling off the gradient alone means tunnelling two hundred feet down, right through the hill. The work is falling so far behind it's likely the time will expire for buying the next stretch of land before they are anywhere near it. If that happens the delay in getting another bill through Parliament will bankrupt the company.'

'Did Lord Hailey tell you this?' His Lordship had asked.

'No, indeed not. He takes very little interest in the line, apart from asking the contractor for a report now and again. And the contractor has sublet the contracts on a fixed price and is rarely seen. The line was costed at twenty thousand pounds a mile and it's likely to exceed that by several thousand, unless some more forward-looking management is put in.'

'Do you think the time is right to make our move?'

'I think someone should go up and scout around.'

His Lordship had sent Timothy, who had, together with the golden apple, brought back a favourable report, though whether his judgement was clouded by the desire to return to the area and locate Sarah Jane, he could not afterwards say. She was nothing but a whore! She had the body of an angel and she made love with a consuming passion and even thinking about her, all this time later, made the muscles in his belly tighten.

He went back to the desk and spread a map out on the surface, using the inkstand and apple to hold it down. The map showed a network of railway lines, thousands of miles of them – some completed, some in progress, others hardly started – crisscrossing the whole country like a giant spider's web. Every town of any importance was, or soon would be, connected to its neighbour, but there was still no overall national system; it was often necessary to take to the roads to make a connection from one line to another. The rivalry of hundreds of different companies, some of whom duplicated routes while leaving vast areas without lines at all, stood in the way of progress. It was left to farseeing people like George Hudson and Lord Chevington to try to link the lines. The map was marked with little copies of the Chevington crest, thick on East Anglia and the East Midlands, more scattered as the Chevington lines moved north and west, towards George Hudson's *Midland Railway* empire. This time next year they would have plugged the gap between Hailey Common and the *Midland*. At last things were going his way and before long he would have everything he wanted, everything – inheritance, Chevington name and all.

The frantic buying up of shares which had taken place over the previous few weeks had left Lord Chevington's *East and West Fen Railway Company* in overall control of the Hailey Common line, but Lord Hailey had retained enough to be a potential nuisance. He had just spent a weekend at Hailey Manor as His Lordship's guest and as a result Timothy himself had become the owner of Lord Hailey's remaining shares. And he had met Caroline Hailey.

She was about seventeen and doll-like in her prettiness, with a rosebud mouth, pink cheeks and blonde ringlets which bobbed over each ear. 'I'm so pleased you could come.' She had fluttered her eyelashes at him. 'It gets dreadfully dull in the country sometimes and Papa is always worrying about his railways or the hunt or something. I prefer to ride without the encumbrance of a pack of hounds – so much more enjoyable, don't you think? Perhaps we can ride together while you're here.'

There had been something in her eyes which startled him, a mischievous gleam, an invitation almost; they were certainly not doll-like. He had begun to enjoy himself.

They had thrown off the rest of the party the next morning and ridden up onto the moors where he had dismounted and lifted her from the saddle. Standing with his hands spanning her corseted waist, he had realised she expected him to kiss her, for she had tilted her head up and shut her eyes. He had put his lips to hers while she stood impassively, neither struggling to be free, nor responding. It was like kissing a doll. If she was like that in bed, heaven help him!

But her family was one of the oldest and most respected in the country and she would make a very suitable wife. It was time he married. Not that he led a life of celibacy, nor was he averse to marriage itself, but no one, no one at all, matched up to the red-haired, green-eyed beauty he had known one summer. Every young lady to come to his notice had been subconsciously compared with Sarah Jane – subconsciously because, until he had seen that apple in the middle of the pawnbroker's window, he thought he had forgotten her. But ever since then the memories of her lusty lovemaking had come flooding back and tormented him. He needed to have his mind free to pursue other avenues – money, power, a good marriage. The marriage was particularly important, because it would be his entry into society, but then, so was the money, because without it no woman of any consequence would look at him. If his name had been Chevington and not Myson, it would have been a different matter; that fictitious name festered like a sore.

He sat down and idly picked up the golden apple. What had possessed him to buy it back and, what was more, to pay over two hundred pounds for it, twenty pounds more than he had laid out originally? He had questioned the pawnbroker and been told the girl who had brought it in had been alone and shabbily dressed. She had been a stranger to the old man, but it was his guess she came from one of the navvy encampments. If Sarah Jane were with the navvies, did he really want to find her? Wouldn't it be better to remember her as she was, young, beautiful, vivacious and sparkling with cleanliness? After any length of time with the navvies, who brutalised everything, she would now be none of those things. Perhaps if he saw her in the degradation of a navvy encampment, he would be so repulsed, it would lay the ghost forever. But their child, what of their child? Was there one, being brought up by a man like McBryde, who had no other thought in his head but pay day, randies and women? One woman. Why couldn't he get her out of his head?

Chapter Eleven

*T*he hooves of the horse thundered in her ears, its rider towered above her, and it was as if he had two heads, one smiling, the other scowling. She cowered in a corner, clutching her son to her. The man bent down and tugged at her hair pulling her head back, then seized Jason from her and rode away, laughing triumphantly. Sobbing, she started to follow and fell into a pit which opened at her feet. She could feel herself falling, unable to save herself. A disembodied hand appeared out of the ether and she strained to reach it, but it seemed to be drifting further and further from her and though their fingertips touched, she could not grasp the hand and it disappeared. Her own terrified shrieks woke her and she found herself sitting up in bed in Duncan's arms.

'He took Jason,' she sobbed. 'He took Jason.'

'Who did?' he asked, stroking her hair from her face with gentle fingers.

She could not tell him, especially after that incident over the golden apple and the way he had asked about Jason's father. He felt threatened, needlessly to be sure, but it would hurt him to know that Paris still came to her in her dreams, even though they were frightening nightmares. 'I don't know. A man.'

"Tis naught but a dream,' he said. 'See, Jason is safe and sleeping, though 'tis a wonder ye didn't rouse him.'

'It was so real.' She shuddered, unable to shake it off. 'He took him away on a horse. And I lost you. I couldn't find you.'

'I'm not lost,' he said, kissing her. 'I'm here, and so is Jason. Go back tae sleep.'

He held her against him, wishing he dare tell her what had been troubling him ever since he had returned from Derby, but he was afraid to; the nightmare haunted him too but in a different way. Was she subconsciously wishing that her dream man, who could only be Paris, would take her and her son off to a better life than he could give her? Was she torn between her love of the man who had fathered her son and her gratitude to him for looking after them both? He didn't want her gratitude; he wanted her love. He would adore her and care for her for the rest of his life and he would look after Jason as if he were his own, but the spectre of her dream came between them and, in Duncan's view, it wasn't so insubstantial as Sarah Jane supposed. He wanted to tell her about his interview with Myson, to ask her to stay with him, not to go chasing rainbows, if rainbows were offered. But Jason, what of Jason? Would the father claim the son? If that happened, Sarah Jane would not hesitate; she would go too. Could he stand by and let her go? He brought himself up short. He was being a fool, for why should Myson want anything from her? In his eyes she was not a beautiful woman to be cherished, but a common labourer's wife, a servant in shabby clothes, to play with in idleness, just as he had played with the apple; he was worrying over nothing. 'I love ye, Sarah Jane,' he said.

'I know you do. And I love you.' She turned her head to look into his eyes. 'There isn't anyone else for me, Duncan McBryde, nor ever could be. You are my husband and my love, I'd have no other.'

He kissed her tenderly. She was far too sensible, he decided, to allow whatever had once been between her and the mythical Paris to be rekindled; it was past and gone. Tell her about Timothy Myson having the trinket, he told himself, make a joke of it so that we can laugh about it together. But he couldn't bring himself to mention it. Besides, she had gone back to sleep, and by morning he had changed his mind again.

Instead of going to work in the tunnel, he fetched wood from the tommy shop and set about building an extension on the side of the hut. He had paced out the ground and was driving in a sturdy corner post, when Sarah Jane, hearing the hammering, came out to see what he was doing. With the coming of daylight, the nightmare had lost its terror and faded to nothing more than a shadow which would disappear as the chores of the day claimed her attention.

'There's plenty of room to build on here,' he said, waving his arm vaguely round the area.

'Why? It's big enough as it is.'

'Not now. A new company has taken over the line and they're going tae begin drilling down into the tunnel from on top and I'm tae be in charge of the first shaft.'

'Oh, Duncan! And don't you deserve it too, keeping the men

working an' all.' She ran and flung herself into his arms. 'Why didn't you tell me last night?'

Now was the time to speak out; if he didn't do it now, he never would. He took her hand in his and looked into her face, gathering his thoughts to begin, but his courage, so readily available when it came to excavating a butt and blowing up rock, deserted him. 'I had to think about it.'

'Think about it?' She looked puzzled. 'What is there to think about? Isn't it what you've wanted all along? Isn't that how you said you could help the men?'

'Yes, it's a step in the right direction, the next rung of the ladder. If we can save a bit so's I can branch out on me own, do a bit of subcontracting, make a bit more, then we're on our way up, my love.'

She was delighted. 'You'll be someone important now, won't you? You'll be a gentleman and I'll be a lady.'

She was only teasing, but it was something he found difficult to joke about since seeing Timothy Myson. He smiled slowly. 'One step at a time, my darling.'

'Someone once told me that ladies are born, not made,' she said. 'But I'm going to make myself one.' She laughed and kissed him. 'I wouldn't want you to be ashamed of me when you're an important railway owner, would I?'

He laughed. 'Ye are already my own dear, darling lady, and I wouldn't change ye for a countess.' He found himself wondering if she would change him for an earl, or even a gentleman – Timothy Myson, for instance – but he pushed the thought from him. 'But before we can do anything, this accursed tunnel has tae be finished. I need more workers, men like Pa and Joseph ... '

'Do you know where they are? It's nigh on four years since we last saw them.'

'I know, but there was a tramping navvy in camp yesterday who said he'd seen them tramping out Birmingham way.'

'Is that far?'

'Fairish, but I reckon they'll come if I can get a message to them.'

'Oh, it will be lovely to see them again,' she cried.

He smiled at her enthusiasm. He had been afraid she might object; she had been so pleased when they built their own place and could live by themselves, she might not have wanted to share their haven with anyone else. 'Ye don't mind?' he asked in order to be reassured.

''Course I don't, silly. I can't think of anything I'd like more.' She paused.

'Now we've a home of our own, could we make room for one more?'

'One more?' he echoed. He had taken great care not to increase their family, believing that in their present unsettled situation another child was more than Sarah Jane could cope with. 'Ye aren't ... '

She laughed. 'No, I meant Billie. I've got so much, so much love, so much happiness, so much of everything and he has nothing. He could learn to work the horses like the other boys.'

'Of course, my love, but he didna answer your other letter, did he? Perhaps he isna at the Union.'

'Maybe he didn't write because I told him I would send for him. He's doubtless been waiting to hear.'

He reached to kiss her. 'Write once more, then. Tell him we'll send him money for a rail ticket, if that's what's holding him back.'

She flung herself on him and showered him with kisses. 'Oh, Duncan, thank you, thank you.'

His message to his parents was sent in the time-honoured way, by a navvy on the tramp, but when it had not borne fruit two weeks later and the drilling equipment arrived, he was obliged to take on strangers and, once again, Sarah Jane found herself with lodgers.

In spite of her efforts to please, the men grumbled. They grumbled about the food, the cramped quarters, the holes in their clothes, the tools they had to work with, the truck and the bosses, and without the shrill-tongued Emmy to scream at them with a vocabulary which easily matched theirs, they often reduced Sarah Jane to angry tears. But if they were to do the work at all, they needed something to enliven it, to ginger their morale and make them forget about that airless tunnel; grumbling about their lodgings was a safety valve and she ought to be used to it by now.

Her only escape was her school. Her enthusiasm and obvious sincerity had, at last, won over most of the children's parents who were glad to have someone to take their offspring off their hands for a few hours a day. And Sarah Jane, in the process of educating the children, was educating herself. Slowly but surely, she was rising above her environment; she became more self-assured, less likely to fly into a temper. Duncan, who had begun by humouring her because he wanted her to be happy, found himself admiring her determination. 'Together we can move mountains,' he had told her. How he wished it were true! As far as he was concerned, this particular mountain was immovable.

It would soon be autumn again and he knew that progress would become even slower as the days shortened. He was concerned on behalf of the men; he could see their living standards dropping almost daily, their wives becoming more slatternly and their children more ragged. The attendance in school dropped to half; the penny a day Sarah Jane charged was better used elsewhere. And Charlie Bender was no help.

'If the men want more money, they must shift more crock,' he said, when Duncan searched him out in the tunnel where he had gone to make yet another inspection. He might go a dozen times a day, and a dozen times a day he would see the progress measured in inches, not yards; instead of doing a dozen sets a day and earning good wages, the men were working desperately in appalling conditions for a pittance. His watchfulness did nothing to improve their morale or make them shift a single shovelful more, but it didn't stop him from goading them to redouble their efforts. 'I can't work miracles.'

'Neither can they.'

'I'm sick of their bloody complaints,' Charlie snapped. Things were going badly wrong and he was on his beam ends. It wouldn't have been so bad, he told himself, if Lord Chevington had taken charge himself; he would have been prepared to negotiate for extras, but his young ward was out to make a name and a fortune for himself and he refused to make allowances for difficulties not included in the original costings. 'And you, of all people, should be loyal to those who put you where you are.'

'There's loyalty and there's loyalty,' Duncan said, doggedly following him down the length of the tunnel. The air was full of choking dust caused by the last explosion and their feet paddled in a few inches of dirty water. It hadn't been there earlier in the day and Charlie looked down at it, puzzled. Duncan stooped and dabbled his hand in it. 'It's spring water,' he said.

They hurried forward, pushing past half-laden trucks, and sweating, begrimed navvies, until they were confronted by the rock face on which the men worked. Torches, stuck in brackets on the walls, flared and smoked in the air coming fitfully from the tunnel entrance, and lit up the wall of rock, where water was gushing from a fissure about six feet up. Clean and pure, it splashed on the men's shoulders down to the rough floor, where it became muddied before running away down the tunnel. They were short of fresh water on the site and had to haul it from the river in the valley; spring water in the right place would have been a great boon, but this was the last place it was wanted. Charlie stared at it with his mouth agape.

'How long has that been coming through?' Duncan asked.

'Came through with the last blasting,' one of the navvies said. His eyes were bright in the semi-darkness, but his voice was flat, indifferent.

'Good God, man, why didn't you report it?'

'It's only a trickle,' Charlie said.

'How do you know that?' Duncan looked round at the watching men who, having no faith in the subcontractor, had turned to him. 'It might be an underground river or even a lake, something big like that ... '

'Don't they know?' one demanded. 'Did the bloody surveyor do his work in his sleep?'

Duncan turned to Charlie. 'Don't you think you should get the engineer down before you let them go any further?'

'I'll have Mr Myson down on me like a ton o' bricks if I stop them working,' Charlie said. 'He's already grumbling because we're so far behind.'

'But he'll nae gamble with men's lives.'

'Oh, won't he?' Charlie said. 'What does he care for the likes of us when it's his profits at stake?'

'He would if there was an accident and an enquiry,' Duncan said. 'He'd try blaming you to get himself out of trouble. You'd be the scapegoat, not him.'

Charlie could see the wisdom of that. He turned to the men. 'I'll send for Mr Myson. When you've cleared up the loose stuff, pack up and wait for orders.'

'What about our wages? We can't afford to stop.'

'I'll see what I can do, but I can't promise. You can have extra tommy tickets to tide you over ... '

'What's the use of that?' They were crowding round him now, threatening. 'What we want is a fair wage, we're nigh on starving. You go and find bloody Lord Whatshisname and tell him what we're saying. You get us a living wage, it's more important than a trickle of water.'

Charlie turned to go, but Big Bill, head and shoulders taller than any of the others, took hold of his shirt-front and lifted him off his feet. 'If you want to keep this here job o' yourn, and all that goes with it, you'll see to your men, or I'll not answer for the consequences. We've had our bellies full of slaving our guts out for naught and our women and children having to eat that tommy rot you sell in that shop o' yourn, and paying dear for it too. You go and tell that to the owner and the engineer and anyone else you like. We'll bring the whole lot out on strike, every single man, and that includes the drilling men and the platelayers. So don't you come whinin' back here till you've done summat.' He gave Charlie a push which sent him stumbling back against Duncan. 'And as for you, Duncan McBryde, you'd better make up your mind which side you're on, afore you interfere again.'

'Come on, McBryde,' Charlie said, thankful Duncan was with him, though not even he would be a match for a dozen angry navvies if they became violent. 'We'll send for Mr Myson.'

They emerged into the fresh air of a warm September evening and it was then Duncan spied his father and mother and the Barnabys coming into the camp, leading the donkey cart with Celia perched on top. He left Charlie to send word to Mr Myson and hurried to meet them, hugging and kissing his sister and mother and shaking the others by the hand. Not until now did he realise how much he had missed them. 'Come, let's go home,' he said, leading the way.

Sarah Jane, who had just sent her pupils home and was tidying up their books and slates, fell upon them joyfully. 'How are you? Are you going to stay? There's work here, Duncan will tell you that. Oh, I can't wait to hear all your news.'

'Hold hard,' Duncan laughed, as she turned breathlessly from one to the other with her questions. 'They've only just arrived, let them get their breath.'

He poured everyone a mug of beer, while Sarah Jane put Jason to bed, then busied herself moving from cupboard to fire with pots and pans, making a more than passable stew which the newcomers attacked with relish. When they had eaten their fill, she sat on a stool and took Celia on her knee, nuzzling her face into the child's soft hair. It was like old times, but now she was no longer the newcomer, the interloper; this was her home, hers and Duncan's, and she was the one offering hospitality. And because she had learned to live on a navvy camp, she could count herself one of them and it made her feel good.

'I've missed you all so much,' she said. 'And the children have grown so; the boys are nearly men.'

'How long did ye stay on the hill?' Duncan asked his father.

'A couple of months, then we moved on to Ashley Green. Things changed there after the riots, Lord Chevington saw to that.'

'Lord Chevington?' queried Sarah Jane in surprise.

'Yes, he owned it.'

'This is a Chevington line now,' Duncan said. 'Though I can't say that I've noticed much improvement.' He was addressing his parents but he was painfully aware that Sarah Jane had fallen into thoughtful silence.

'The owner's puppy dog,' that was what the man had said, but she hadn't known who the owner was, had she? 'You didn't tell me that.'

He shrugged. 'Didn't I? I didna suppose ye'd be interested.'

'Of course I'm interested,' she said. 'I'm interested in everything to do with railway building, you know that. I thought Lord Chevington was a kind man and I'm surprised at him not doing something to help the men here, if he owns the line.'

Duncan did not say His Lordship was only part-owner and the real fly in the ointment was Timothy Myson. Surely she knew who Timothy Myson was? How could she *not* know he was Lord Chevington's ward? Had she been less than honest with him? It was a doubt he didn't want to face. He turned back to his father, anxious to change the subject. 'How long were you there?'

'Two months, then we were paid off. We set off on the tramp, but work's not so easy to come by now and we had to go north.' He paused to stuff a small clay pipe with cheap tobacco and light it, filling the room with its aroma. 'I think railway building is all but done and we'll have to find other ways of making a living.'

Duncan laughed. 'It's not the end yet. At the rate this line's going, it will never be finished.'

'I heard it was slow,' James said.

'You could say that,' his son commented. 'Time enough tomorrow tae learn about that. Tonight we'll have a party. I'll go and buy a barrel of beer and tell the folks.'

Charlie, going over to The Haven to tell Duncan that Mr Myson could not be found, couldn't believe his eyes and ears. A few hours before, everyone had been depressed and gloomy and now, here they were, enjoying themselves as if they hadn't a care in the world. He shrugged and turned away; tomorrow would do.

He rose late the next morning and walked over to the tunnel, where a gang was preparing to go in and begin another day's work. Amid loud protests, he told them to stop and then hurried up the hill to the drilling rig where he knew he would find Duncan.

''Tis a great storm over nothin',' commented Big Bill, as soon as he was out of earshot. 'What's a trickle of fisherman's daughter? Why,

I've worked knee-deep in it many a time and been expected to get as much muck out as if it'd been dry as old bones. There's always springs in these hills, it don't signify.'

'There's water and there's water,' another said. 'We shouldn't take risks.'

'An' sure, don't we take risks every day of our lives?' retorted an Irishman. 'An' don't Bender know that? He don't mean us to stop, he's just coverin' hisself, on account of what McBryde said. The contractor will put us back as soon as he gets here.'

'Let's blast it out,' Randy Joe said. 'It'll tell us one way or another.'

'And have the whole hill fall into the tunnel and a year's work gone for naught?' said another. 'The contractor would be ruined and we'd lose the pay we've already earned.'

'And little enough that is,' shouted Randy Joe. 'What have you got to lose? I say, let's blow it.'

The argument changed from whether they should work, to whether they should blow up the rock face around the fissure, not knowing what lay the other side of it. They were joined by others on their way to the drilling rig, from work further back along the line where the rails were being laid in the wake of the tunnellers, from the shanties; even the women who, realising the men were not working, came to find out why. If they were preparing for an impromptu randy they would have to be stopped; randies were all right on pay day when wages were good, the women approved and even joined in then, but on a weekday when there was no money in their purses and no food in their larders, that was different. They would make sure the men kept hard at it, using tongue and tooth and claw, if necessary. But as soon as they learned what was happening, they joined in the debate and became just as heated as their men.

Randy Joe, losing patience, shouted above the din, 'This ain't doin' a ha'p'orth of good. I'm going to blast. Who's with me?' Without waiting for an answer, he strode off to the contractor's hut, carelessly left unlocked by Charlie Bender, picked up a box of dynamite and detonators and went into the tunnel. One or two started to follow, but changed their minds and returned to continue milling about in the growing heat of a late summer's day, uncertain and leaderless.

The brewer's dray climbed the steep road from the village and stopped at the tommy shop, but the drayman, finding no one there, moved on up the hill, until he was within hailing distance of the crowd. 'Hey up!' he called. 'What's afoot?'

They turned towards the sound and suddenly discovered a thirst in urgent need of slaking. The barrels were rolled off and tapped, while the helpless drayman could do nothing but protest uselessly. 'Where's Charlie? He'll have to pay for this lot.'

But no one knew or cared where the subcontractor was, still less were they concerned as to who should foot the bill for the beer. They drank thirstily, while the sun poured down from a cloudless sky, and before long, they lolled about half-asleep, the urgent need to work forgotten, the reason for their idleness gone from their minds. And away up on the hill, a heat haze shimmered round the metal girders of the rig where Duncan supervised the drilling.

Charlie, coming to find him, mopped his brow on his shirt-sleeve and watched him with envy. The young Scotsman had had no sleepless nights, no lecherous dreams, no nagging doubts about his own ability; he was completely in command of himself, his men and the job in hand. If Charlie could puncture that cockiness, he would, and the only way of doing it was through Sarah Jane. He hated the navvy for being able to make her happy, hated him for his ability to lead his men, hated him for his self-confidence and unswerving cheerfulness. But he needed him to keep the men going and while he needed him he would have to keep on the right side of him, which was why he had not pushed Sarah Jane too far.

He did not know how much longer he could refrain from touching her because with every day that passed, she became more desirable. One day he would have her, one day, when the tunnel was through the mountain and he had all the money due to him from the owners and the extra he had made by cutting corners, he would feel her glorious naked body against his and be inside her and she would thrill to him. She was no different from any other woman; offer her money and presents and she would give in. Had she not already taken little gifts from him? Didn't that show she was willing? 'Hallo there, Duncan McBryde,' he called. 'How are you this fine morning?'

'I'm well,' Duncan said, wondering why he shouldn't be; he was used to tommy shop food and beer that was off.

'It's good to have your folks with you again, isn't it?'

'Aye.'

'There'll be nothing for them if we can't work in the tunnel.'

'I realise that.'

'Have you come across water in the shaft?'

'No, but we're not all the way down yet. If we can get down to that level, it might tell us what's behind the tunnel wall.'

'It might. On the other hand, it might cause more trouble.' Charlie's head ached and he was not disposed to be optimistic. 'Some o' the men wanted to go in again, but I've just stopped them. They're in a black mood but if the tunnel's dangerous, we can't work on it, can we?' It was almost a plea.

'Ye sent for the contractor?'

'Yes, last night, but the boy couldn't find him.'

'What have you done about it?'

'Nothing. I had a look at the tunnel and it doesn't look any worse than last night. Not any better, either.'

'God, man, why waste time coming up here? Go and get Mr Myson, he'll likely be back in the office this morning.'

'Aye, but what about the men? They're turning ugly.'

Duncan was becoming more and more irritated by the man's indecisiveness. 'I'll see to it myself,' he said, striding off down the hill. He would stop on the way and speak to his father and Joseph, who were resting in the hut; he could rely on their common sense and experience to guide him and if Charlie Bender didn't leave off his childish wavering, he would take over himself; someone had to.

Charlie was quite content to let him do this and although nothing was said aloud, he mentally abdicated in favour of the handsome young Scotsman and, relieved of responsibilities which were too burdensome for him, found a quiet corner in the shade of an elder bush and went to sleep, while Duncan sent another messenger into Derby on the bare back of one of the horses. The boy found the office still closed and no sign of Mr Myson and he returned with the letter undelivered.

Timothy's courtship of Caroline Hailey had become a serious pursuit over the last few weeks, and he had been a constant guest at Hailey Manor. She had made no effort to hide her delight at his interest and he had come to the conclusion that he would be doing the expedient, if not the right thing, to marry her. Once she was his wife, all doors would be open to him, all except that of Chevington House, the most important of all, and that would yield to his knocking in the end. Once he had an aristocratic wife his father would no longer be able to keep him hidden away and Lady Chevington herself would hear about him and be forced to recognise him. After that, the rest would follow – the inheritance and the name. Timothy Chevington. He savoured the sound of it. Anyone with a name like Timothy Chevington could not possibly be a bastard.

174

Today they were on a family picnic but Lord Hailey, knowing he wanted to gallop, had encouraged him to ride on ahead and Caroline had followed, ignoring her mother's cries for her to come back. Aware of her behind him, he did not call a halt until they were alone on the highest part of the moor. Here was rough heather and gorse and sparse grass being cropped by sheep, but no people. He dismounted close to a lone tree which afforded a little shade and handed her down.

'It's too hot,' he said, smiling and taking off his riding coat and cravat and throwing them on the ground.

She was shocked. 'Mr Myson . . .'

'You do not mind, do you?' he queried, raising one dark eyebrow. 'It's so unseasonably warm. Why don't you do the same?'

His intense dark eyes were boring into her, making her tense with apprehension. 'Oh, I could not.'

He sat against the bole of the tree and held out his hand to her. 'Then at least take that hat off and sit down by me.'

She hesitated. What had Mama said about gentlemen who came courting and how she should behave? 'With propriety,' Mama had said, 'but you may encourage him a little without being too forward.' She smiled and slowly removed the hat with its trailing feathers and then her riding jacket, revealing a white silk blouse buttoned up to her chin.

He smiled. 'That's better, isn't it?' He patted the ground beside him. 'Now sit down.'

Her answering smile was wobbly as she put her jacket on the ground with the hat on top and dropped down beside him. She was not just being naughty, she was being very, very wicked. It was a delicious feeling. She made no move to prevent him putting his arm about her shoulders, and when he leaned over and kissed her on the cheek, she giggled.

He wanted to tell her to shut up, it made her sound like a child and a silly one at that, and he was not in the habit of coupling with schoolgirls. He wanted a woman.

'Mama and Papa would die of shock if they knew,' she said.

She was most certainly correct there, Timothy thought, but he was not about to propose to their daughter without a foretaste. 'Who is there to tell them? We are alone.'

'Being alone is bad enough,' she said.

'Don't you like being kissed?'

'I . . . I don't know.'

'Don't know?' He affected surprise. 'Do you mean you have never been kissed before? I can't believe that. Someone as pretty as you would surely have many admirers.'

She smiled. 'Yes, but I've always been chaperoned ...'

'You are not being chaperoned now. You may kiss me and no one will be the wiser.'

Kissing she could understand, kissing was a normal everyday occurrence; she kissed her mother and sisters and her very dear friends, and she kissed her father, who was a man, like Timothy. She raised her face to his and got the shock of her life. His lips crushed hers, his tongue found its way between her teeth and set up such a quivering in her limbs, she could not sit still.

He lifted his head and smiled down at her, realising she was terrified and felt a thrill of satisfaction; he liked people to be afraid of him, it made him feel good about himself. But he must be careful. He reached out and deftly undid the top two buttons of her blouse.

'That's cooler, isn't it?'

'Y ... yes,' She could hardly speak for the tumult in her body; her every nerve tingled.

He laughed and slid down to lie on the ground, pulling her down beside him. 'Relax, my dear,' he said, undoing the next button. She put her hand up to close it again. He took it away very firmly. 'It's better if you relax.'

'Oh, Mr – Timothy – whatever are you doing?' she cried, as he skilfully undid the rest of her buttons and his flicking tongue roamed down into the cleft between her breasts. She shivered. 'Oh, do stop ...'

He raised his head to look at her. 'Stop, my dear? You can't mean that.'

'I don't know ... it isn't proper.'

He sighed. 'If you're going to worry about being proper when there is no one to see us, we'll never get to know each other.'

'And you do want to get to know me?' She was pleading for reassurance. 'You are serious about that?'

'Of course I am. Would I be wanting to kiss you if I weren't? I have a very high regard for you ...' He could not bring himself to say he loved her.

'But if you are going to ... to do ...' She did not know what he was going to do and made a feeble attempt to push him away.

He sat up and turned to look down at her, affecting hurt. 'Don't you trust me?'

'Yes, but I'm sure Mama and Papa ...'

He laughed and cupped one breast in his hand. It was small and only half-formed, but the nipple hardened at his touch. 'This has nothing to do with your mama and papa, it is between you and me. It is our secret.' Her nipples were pink and inviting and he felt his own hard arousal as he kissed each in turn. There was no stopping now. 'Trust me,' he whispered. 'I won't hurt you, I would never hurt you. All I want is to show you how much I need you, to prove that we are made for each other. We are, aren't we?'

'Yes.' Her voice was a whisper because he had lifted her skirts and his hand was moving up between her thighs and she was holding her breath for what might happen next.

His lips roamed all over her neck and breasts, as he grappled with the skirt of her riding habit and the lace-trimmed petticoat beneath it, pulling them up to reveal the soft roundness of her belly and a tuft of fair curly hair. 'Beautiful,' he murmured, lowering his head to kiss it.

'Oh, Timothy, oh,' she cried. She felt warm and damp and her back was arching of its own accord, as if to bring his mouth nearer to the core of her. 'Oh, please ...'

'Darling Caroline,' he murmured into the softness. 'This is my secret place, mine alone.' Deftly he undid his own clothing and, standing, stripped himself naked. She lay absolutely still, her eyes tight closed. 'Open your eyes,' he said, kneeling astride her. 'Look at me. I want to see your eyes.'

She opened her eyes and her gasp of astonishment at what she beheld was so comical, he laughed. 'Oh, my sweet innocent, there's proof of how much I need you. I can't control it.' He bent over to kiss her again, searching her mouth with his tongue, making her claw hold of the hair in the nape of his neck, to arch her body towards him, to part her thighs and offer herself to him, crying out as he entered her.

Then she lay still, while he worked himself to a climax. It was very businesslike and dispassionate and he knew he had left her bewildered and tantalisingly disappointed.

It served her right, he thought, as he rolled off her. She had been flirting with him for weeks, teasing him with her eyes, finding ways to slip away from whoever had been set to chaperon them, dropping hints about weddings and where she would like to live, behaving as if he had already proposed. Well, he hadn't, but he supposed he would have to now. It was a pity she was so passive about it; you could get more satisfaction from a whore. Or Sarah Jane.

Why had he suddenly thought of her again? Would he never be able to lay the ghost? After all this time why did those green eyes and that graceful body still haunt him? He realised with a start that Sarah Jane had been younger than Caroline when he had first taken her, but oh, so very different. She had been woman not child, able to gratify him as well as herself and they had been like two halves of a whole – one body, one spirit. Did he still want her? Angry with himself, he scrambled into his clothes and walked away.

Caroline straightened her own clothing and followed him, weeping. 'Have I disappointed you?'

He forced himself to speak lightly. 'No, of course not. Come, let's walk a little until you are calmer.' He took a handkerchief from his pocket and dabbed at her wet cheeks. 'Our secret, yes?'

'Y ... yes.' How could it remain a secret when guilt was written all over her face? Suddenly she smiled, a secret little smile of triumph. Timothy would have to marry her now because they had been alone together for ages and with no more adequate explanation than they had stopped to rest the horses. Timothy was so handsome, so clever and so rich; he could afford to indulge her every whim, which was something poor, dear Papa could not do at the moment, what with failed investments and repairs needed to Hailey Manor and three daughters to marry off. If there was no proposal in the very near future, this very evening, in fact, Mama would want to know why. She smiled and slipped her hand in the crook of his elbow and together they walked to the top of the ridge where they found themselves looking down on the Hailey Common works.

The line had been laid in a cutting dug through a cleft in the hills, but stopped short of a steep rise, where the men had begun tunnelling. Grouped about the end of the rail were all the familiar trappings of a navvy site, trucks, horses, ramshackle huts, piles of wooden sleepers, shining new rails. Now it was his to make into the success he confidently expected it to be, Timothy surveyed it with pride, almost as if he had toiled side by side with the men who worked there. And yet he didn't know a single one of them by name, except the subcontractor and that big ganger, McBryde, and although he had visited the works once when his father had sent him to look it over, he had no wish or need to go again. Unless ... he paused to savour the thought. *Unless Sarah Jane was down there.* He'd have to find out; he would need someone lively to lighten the boredom of being married to Caroline Hailey.

'They're not working,' he said suddenly. 'There's not one of them lifting a tool.'

'They've probably gone on strike. Papa used to say they were deliberately uncooperative, but that seems silly to me. They must work or they don't get paid, so it doesn't make sense to strike, does it?'

Her voice startled him; he had forgotten she was there. 'I think we should rejoin the others,' he said, turning back to the horses. He didn't try to explain why navvies stopped work, although he understood it very well, but strikes had to be broken, if the owners – and that included him now – were going to come out with a profit. He'd send for Charlie Bender as soon as he returned to the office and in the meantime he would try to behave like a lovesick suitor.

Chapter Twelve

*T*he day was unusually quiet, but that suited Sarah Jane's mood. Jason had been left playing happily with Celia and she was alone and, for once, she was glad of it; she had a slight headache from the drink she had taken the night before and was feeling too lethargic to do anything but sit on the hill above the workings and let the time slide by. It was her favourite place. Sometimes she brought her pupils up here for their lessons, away from the distractions of the shanty village, sometimes she would bring only Jason and then she would sit in the shade, with her son playing nearby, and indulge in daydreams.

On the opposite hill, where an iron gin stood like a gaunt giant against the skyline, marking the spot where the first shaft was being sunk, she could see men moving about; Duncan's men, she thought, and her heart swelled with pride. They would work, both of them, work for each other, for a better life for the navvies, for their children and their children's children. And she would not let anything spoil that, not Paris, not Charlie Bender, nor the spiteful Alice and Kate. Her ambition to be a lady would be met through Duncan because she would never leave him, not for anyone. She was so preoccupied she was not immediately alarmed when she saw Charlie Bender making his way over the boulders towards her, and she made no move to get up.

'Hallo, Sarah Jane,' he said, dropping down beside her. ''Tis a warm day, wouldn't you say?'

'What are you doing up here?' she asked warily. 'Shouldn't you be down at the shop or the works?'

'The missus is minding the shop and Duncan's gone down to the tunnel for me.' He put out a hand to touch her ankle but, deciding the gesture was premature, let it fall to the ground.

'Why has Duncan gone to the tunnel for you?' she demanded, her puzzlement outstripping her worry about why Charlie Bender was there. 'Is something wrong?'

'Nothing to speak of, just a spot of bother with the men. Naught to worry your beautiful head over.'

It didn't sound right; Duncan's work was on the rig. She looked up at it, shielding her eyes with an upraised hand, trying to search out his tall figure and reassure herself that all was well, but the workers were too far away for her to pick anyone out. 'But why Duncan? Can't you handle it?'

' 'Course I can, but it's the first chance I've had to be alone with you since you ran out on me in Derby ...'

'I don't know what you mean.'

He laughed. 'Oh Sarah Jane, don't be such a little innocent. You know very well what I want – what we both want.'

'No, I don't.'

'You know that I'm mad for you and I know 'tis the same for you and you can't deny it.'

'There you are wrong, Mr Bender,' she said coolly. 'I do deny it, absolutely.'

He grinned with maddening self-confidence. 'Why, you would say that, just to tease, but I know you aren't averse to selling your charms, if the need arises, and perhaps when it doesn't arise too. You are a warm and generous woman and you wouldn't deny me, who's done you more than one little favour.'

She was busy looking for a way of escape and did not answer. 'I'm mad for you,' he went on. 'I can't sleep for thinking of you.' He reached out and put a clammy hand on her ankle, sliding his hand up her leg and groping under her skirt to her knee. 'You've tormented me long enough. I want you. Now.'

'Well, I certainly don't want you!' Angrily she hitched herself away and tried to scramble to her feet. He grabbed her ankles in both hands, forcing her legs apart and making her fall back and crack her head against the rough ground. The blow almost stunned her; she felt sick and dizzy. 'Come now, Sarah Jane, fair's fair. You owe me and you've teased me long enough.'

'I owe you nothing.' She tried to fight him off, desperation giving her strength, but for all he wasn't very big, he was strong and wiry and more than usually determined. 'Duncan will kill you,' she grunted, trying to pull herself free. 'He'll cut you up into little pieces.'

'But he'll never know, will he? You wouldn't be such a fool as to tell him, now would you?' His little currant eyes burned with a fire that no argument could quench. 'Besides, you're no more than a doxy,

181

just like Kate and Alice, though they don't pretend to be anything else than what they are. Duncan McBryde is a fool if he don't know that.'

'Let me go! Get your filthy hands off me!' She lunged at him, trying to kick him in the groin where it would hurt most, but he saw it coming and moved sideways. She tried to rise, but he pushed her back.

'Why did you think I gave you presents? Did you suppose it was from the goodness of my heart?' He threw himself on top of her now, squeezing the breath from her, holding her down with the weight of his body and one hand, while the other struggled with the buttons of his trousers.

'You said Mrs Bender had cheated me,' she panted. 'And I was fool enough to believe you.'

He laughed and, pinning her hands to the ground either side of her head, lowered his mouth to hers. She thrashed her head from side to side to avoid his tainted breath, calling him names which were certainly not ladylike. He let go of her long enough to slap her face hard, but had regained his grip before she could do more than writhe beneath him. 'I will have my way,' he muttered. 'You are a whore and you owe me. And that man o' yours owes me too. I got him taken on, got him made a ganger, and I can get him fired ... '

For a moment the truth of what he said stopped her struggling. What had she done? How on earth was she to get out of it? He took advantage of her immobility to finish undoing his trousers, then lowered himself onto her again, holding her wrists to the ground either side of her head. His erection was warm and moist on her bare skin. It disgusted her; she would die before she let him put that into her. If it meant she and Duncan were turned off, then so be it; there were other places to work. She leaned forward and bit his ear as hard as she could. He yelled and clapped his hand to the injury, releasing one of her hands. She punched out, felt her fist sink into his soft belly and heard his grunt of pain. 'Get off me, you filthy bastard! You sicken me.'

Before he could make any sort of rejoinder an explosion rocked the ground beneath them; it reverberated round the hills like thunder. It was like no explosion she had ever heard before, certainly not like those deliberately set with the proper charge to move a calculated amount of rock, to which she had become accustomed. To Sarah Jane this was the sound of her own doom. *'Duncan!'* she shrieked, though she did not know why.

The shockwaves diverted the startled Charlie Bender from his purpose sufficiently for her to be able to push him off and scramble to her feet. She had always been conscious of the danger of blasting, but the men, by the very nature of their work, were given to taking risks and laughing at their own fears. Duncan had told her not to worry, that they knew what they were about, and she had taken him at his word, but now a little voice inside her, a voice full of accusation, told her that this was different. She did not give another thought to the despicable little man behind her who was trying to button himself up, as she raced down the hill to the shanty village, now hidden from view by a great cloud of dust which hung in the air like fog. She could think only of Duncan and that not very coherently. What had blown up? Was he anywhere near? Charlie had said Duncan wasn't on the hill with the drilling rig, he was down at the tunnel.

Her flying feet took her past other woman who were converging on the tunnel from the huts. Twenty yards from it she stopped and gaped, unblinking, unbelieving. It was nothing but a heap of rubble, tons and tons of it; it reminded her of the work of a butty gang, only this was much, much bigger. She remembered her fear at the time and Duncan's laughter. 'We know what we're doing.' But this was unintentional, she was sure of it. And Charlie had sent him down there! Had he known what would happen?

Some of the men, cold sober now, had already begun to claw frantically at the débris with bare hands. She pushed her way through the crowd to where the men were digging. 'Where's Duncan McBryde? Where is my husband?'

They stopped to look at her and silently inclined their heads towards the great heap of earth and rock before turning back to their task.

She stared, her mouth open in a silent scream. He couldn't really be behind that lot; the men were mistaken. 'No!' she shouted, turning towards the drilling rig. 'He's up there, on the hill.'

One of the navvies took her arm. 'No, he went into the tunnel, alonga Randy Joe and another fella not half an hour since.'

'He can't have.' She did not want to accept it; her senses reeled.

The man shrugged and stooped to pick up a boulder which must have weighed a hundredweight. 'I ain't got time to argue.' He tossed the rock easily to one side and turned back for more. 'You can please y'self what you believe.'

She stood, unable to move, unable to take her eyes off the pile of rubble. It would take an army to shift that. But they had an army.

She looked about her as more men joined the digging. Could anyone be alive? Could there be space under all those boulders for a man to go on breathing? 'Dear God,' she prayed. 'Let Duncan come out, let him be unhurt.' With all the mental strength she could command, she willed him to appear through the small hole the men were making. It was only a few inches across but they were enlarging it, moving the rocks, one by one, with infinite care lest they displace others. She fell to her knees. 'Please God. I'll be good, I promise. I'll do anything . . .'

'Go home, missus,' the navvy said roughly. 'You'll only get in the way.'

Another took her arm to raise her to her feet. 'Go home, Mrs McBryde. We'll get them out.'

'Them?' she asked dully. 'Who else?'

'The old fella in the white hat. He followed Duncan McBryde when he went in after Randy Joe. They were all three in there . . .'

'James,' she said slowly. 'Dear God, not James too.' She turned from him to look about her. 'Where's Maggie?'

'I'm here.' She heard Maggie's voice from a long way off, though it was at her elbow. 'Come away, Sarah Jane, the men must have room to work.' She took Sarah Jane's arm. 'They'll fetch them out. It's miraculous what these men can shift when they have to, there's none better. I've seen worse falls and it's been all right.' A little self-deception was in order too. 'We'll go and wait in the hut.'

'No!' Sarah Jane cried, running among the men working on the débris. 'I must help get him out.' She began scrabbling at the tumbled earth and rock with her hands, throwing it frenziedly behind her.

One of the men grabbed her to safety just as another fall cascaded down from above them and covered the hole they had made. She stared in horror as she realised they would have to start again and it was her fault.

The man turned to Maggie. 'Get her out of here.'

Maggie, stony-faced, pulled at Sarah Jane's arm. 'Come on, lass, ye'll only be in the way. Leave them to it.' She wished the girl would pull herself together; carrying on like that only made things worse. 'We must trust in God and pray the lads will have the strength to get them out.'

'How can you be so good about it?' Sarah Jane was weeping now, scalding tears which stung her face. 'I'm not good, I'm hurt and angry and I feel like screaming.'

'Scream if you think it will help,' Maggie said, 'but you'll find it willna.'

They returned to The Haven and the two families sat around waiting, waiting, waiting in silence for hours and hours, while the work at the tunnel-mouth continued. Joseph, who had been one of the first on the scene, returned, filthy and exhausted, when the cuts on his hands became too painful for him to go on. He told them what had happened in a tired flat voice, but Sarah Jane could not take it in. 'They'd been arguing about whether to work or not,' he said, 'though they had been told it wasn't safe. One of the buggers fetched dynamite, took it into the tunnel and Duncan went after him. Then James ... '

'Could they be alive in there?' Daisy had to ask the question that filled everyone's mind because neither Maggie not Sarah Jane could bring themselves to voice it.

'Could be. Depends where the explosion was and how near they were. There might be a cavity, room to breathe. Until we're sure, we'll keep digging.' He gulped the tea Daisy had made, while she bandaged his hands, then he went back.

They harnessed horses to pull off the bigger boulders, but mostly they used their hands, and not one of them referred to the events leading up to the explosion or stopped to speculate on what would happen if the men could not be found. When it grew too dark to see, they brought torches and flares and went on digging.

Night merged into day and still the men worked, while Sarah Jane sat and cuddled her son on her lap, unable to believe it was happening. Duncan had so much vitality, so much to give. He was moulding his life the way he wanted it; he was doing it for her, for Jason and his family, for all navvies everywhere. Didn't God know how good he was, how unselfish, how much he cared for others? Didn't that count for anything? Didn't it counterbalance her own wickedness, her terrible guilt? Of course it did, she told herself. Duncan McBryde hadn't done with life yet. He would emerge and laugh his teasing laugh and she would say, 'Oh Duncan, what a scare you gave me.' But why were they taking so long about it? Why must her torment go on beyond the hours when you might expect to have nightmares? It was day, and day was meant for sunshine and daydreams.

In the middle of the morning a loud cheering shout carried on the still air to the hut where she sat with the McBrydes and Barnabys, all of them gaunt from worry and lack of sleep. They were up in an instant and out of the door towards the sound.

The throng of men was thick around the tunnel-mouth, all stripped to the waist, sweating and begrimed, their teeth white against cracked lips and blackened faces. They were crowding round someone who broke away from them and pushed his way through to the anxious women. It was James.

With a cry of 'Thank God,' Maggie threw herself into his arms, and for the first time, she cried, sobbing on his shoulder, noticing and yet not noticing, that he was covered in bruises and scratches and his coat was torn.

'Wish't my love,' he said, stroking her hair, as the men behind him went back to their digging. 'Wish't ye.'

She lifted her head to look into his face. 'Duncan?' Her voice was a whisper and Sarah Jane, standing just behind them, held her breath for his reply.

He did not answer, but slowly shook his head, now without its customary felt hat, and looked steadfastly into his wife's eyes, willing her to understand without the need for words. He couldn't tell her that he had seen their son blown to bits because a hot-headed navvy had been careless with a box of dynamite he had no business handling in the first place. Randy Joe had been intent on setting charges and Duncan, highly suspicious of the continuing presence of the water, had tried to prevent him. The two men had struggled, but James had been too far away to intervene. He did not know exactly how it happened but the next minute he had been blown off his feet as first the tunnel opened to the sky and then caved in on itself. When the tumult of tumbling rocks had died, he had found himself in a tiny space, its ceiling a large boulder which had become wedged. The air had been foul but he had kept alert to every sound, afraid that anyone digging from the top would dislodge his precarious roof. He had shouted to let them know he was there and thank God they had heard him. The experience was one that would give him nightmares for the rest of his life and he could not tell his wife about it.

'No hope?' she whispered.

'None.' His voice was barely audible, but Sarah Jane was near enough to hear it and the full meaning of what he said slowly penetrated her desperate prayers. The colour drained from her face, making her wide green eyes look huge and brilliant and her mouth a round red source of sound.

'No!' she screamed. 'No!' She looked from one to the other and then subsided into a crumpled heap on the ground, repeating Duncan's name over and over again, as if to conjure him up from wherever he had gone. They stood and watched, unable to help her, as she buried her face in her hands and sobbed out her despair. 'Duncan. Duncan.' Salt tears trickled through her fingers and fell onto the coarse material of her skirt. 'Come back to me. Come back. Don't leave me.' She looked up at James and Maggie, seeing them through a mist. 'Tell me it's a mistake. He can't be gone, he can't.' Her voice rose. 'Tell me! Tell me!'

They said nothing, for their own grief was too overwhelming. Undemonstrative, dour, strong-minded as they were, they could not comfort Sarah Jane. It was Daisy and Joseph who each took one of her arms and pulled her to her feet, then half-dragged her back to The Haven.

Someone thrust a glass of brandy into her hand but she didn't even have the sense to drink it. People came and went, some spoke to her but their voices were indistinct, their words meaningless, their faces a blur. She took Jason onto her lap and buried her face in his hair; the nightmare had been wrong, it was not Jason who had been taken from her but Duncan. Duncan. Duncan.

Immersed in grief, she did not know that Timothy had arrived on the site with Lord Chevington in a gig borrowed from Lord Hailey, and if she had, she would not have shown the slightest interest.

The part of the tunnel near the entrance, where the roof had been closest to the surface, was open to the sky, making a big boulder-filled pit. A small rivulet of spring water had found its way from the heart of the hill between the rocks and over the rubble and meandered down the hill. The men were still working, though they knew there could be no more survivors, and the urgency had gone, as if they were unsure that what they were doing had any relevance. Timothy expressed his sorrow that lives had been lost but he was equally sorry that work on the line had come to a sudden stop. He knew that if they couldn't open the tunnel up again, the undertaking would be a financial disaster; a lesser giant than the Chevington business empire might succumb to bankruptcy. In any case, he would lose what he had put into it himself and that was hardest of all to stomach.

How Lord Hailey must be laughing up his sleeve! He had rid himself of the company and left the Chevingtons to pick up the bill when it all, quite literally, collapsed. The pill was a bitter one to swallow because he had, only the previous evening, proposed to Caroline and been accepted.

'If the men had not been driven so hard, none of this would have happened,' his father said.

'Are you suggesting I'm to blame?'

'I'll blame no one until I've heard all the evidence, and seen your working figures.'

'I saw no reason to alter Lord Hailey's.'

Lord Chevington turned to look at his son. 'Then you perpetuated the problems he was having. I thought you knew better than that.'

'I brought in the drilling rig, which would have made all the difference. The men had only to be patient.'

'Patience does not fill hungry bellies, Timothy, and it is not necessary for us to make a profit at the expense of men's lives.'

'I will not be held responsible. You cannot shift it all onto my shoulders. Mr Bender ... '

'You knew he was useless. You should have dismissed him as soon as you took over.'

'Why? I had no reason to doubt his competence and ... '

'And he came cheap,' his father finished for him. 'And he has obviously decided it would be expedient to make himself scarce.' He paused and looked at his son. 'But this is no time for recrimination. Ask one of those fellows to fetch the Scotsman over. I want to know exactly what happened in that tunnel.'

James delivered his account in a flat, unemotional voice, as if he had learned it by rote and the words themselves had no meaning for him. Lord Chevington listened without interrupting, while Timothy stood by the window looking out on the wreck of his plans. His father thought him a failure; it left him with a sour taste in his mouth and a determination that one day he would continue the line to its end, and he didn't care how long it took or how many people were discommoded in the process.

'The men have put in a superhuman effort,' Geoffrey said when James had finished. 'And I am sure they would continue to do so as long as hope remained, but if you are sure ... '

'Certain, my lord.'

'Then I think we will abandon the rescue work and await the arrival of Mr Miller, who will be here in a day or two. I do not need to tell you that your son was a very brave man.' He paused to look at the man who faced him, big, broad-shouldered and tough, there was pain in his blue eyes and weariness in his smile. 'Is there anything I can do for you, Mr McBryde? Did either of the men have wives and children?'

'Randy Joe was single as far as I know. As for my son, he had no wife as you would describe one, but ... '

His Lordship smiled. 'A navvy wife? He had – what do you call it – "jumped the broom"?'

'Yes, my lord. She has not stepped outside her hut since it happened, and she will not speak.' He shrugged. 'But life must go on and she will pull herself together and get on with it, if only for the sake of her child.'

'There is a child?'

'A boy.' No need to explain that Jason was not Duncan's flesh and blood; he had still lost a beloved Da.

'Ah ... ' His Lordship's sigh was one of understanding. 'It is always the children who suffer most. Please convey my deepest sympathy. And if it should turn out your son was blameless, there will be some compensation.'

James watched the two men go back to the gig and ride away, then he returned to The Haven to recount the interview to the rest of the family.

After that first outburst of weeping, Sarah Jane had not cried again; she felt drained of all emotion, all love, all hate, all desire for revenge, for who was there to blame, except herself? All she felt, and felt acutely, was guilt. She moved dry-eyed about the hut, speaking mechanically when spoken to, but hardly knowing what she said, because the only words she wanted to say were, 'It was my fault. I used him, made him into something he did not want to be. If I hadn't taken presents from Charlie Bender, if I hadn't gone on the hill alone, if I had run down when Charlie first arrived, if I'd kept my temper, if ... if...' But she could not say them, not to anyone, because, now that Duncan was gone, there was no one who would understand.

No one, least of all Maggie and James, knew how to comfort her and they didn't try, but they insisted she accompany them to the memorial service held two days later in the little church in Hailey village. She didn't want to go; it was as if attending it meant that she had accepted Duncan's death, recognised she would never see him again, never be held in his arms, never again hear his soft voice calling her 'my love'. For five years, he had been her whole life; five years, that was all they had had. It was so little, so very, very little measured against a lifetime, the future she had to face without him.

After the service they returned to the site to find Jack Miller had arrived to begin the enquiry. Navvies, wives and children gathered about him when a table was brought from the contractor's hut and he climbed onto it to speak to them. 'First let me say how deeply sorry I am that this tragedy has occurred, and give you His Lordship's personal assurance that everything possible will be done to help the bereaved.'

He means Lord Chevington, thought Sarah Jane dully, unable to equate this ugly, dirty valley with its heaps of sleepers, rails and wagons, with Chevington House and the park which surrounded it. What did he know of bereavement – what did any of them know? Lost and bewildered, she could hardly attend to what the man was saying.

'We intend to make a thorough investigation into the cause of the accident . . . '

'We know the cause,' someone shouted from the back of the crowd. 'Men forced to work in pitch dark and danger on slave wages, so you and the bloody owners can grow rich. What we want to know is what you mean to do about it.'

The engineer held up his hand to silence the murmur of agreement that went round his audience. 'I am here to make a survey into the possibility of clearing the tunnel but I would be failing in my duty if I did not tell you that a preliminary inspection seems to rule out this particular section of the line in the foreseeable future. You would do well to look elsewhere for your livelihood. I believe they are building railways in Scotland . . . '

'There,' said Joseph to Sarah Jane. 'That's what I said. It's back tae the hame country for us.'

'What about our pay?' someone yelled.

'All wages will be paid up to the end of next week.' If the engineer imagined such generosity would impress them, he was mistaken. The murmuring began again; their silence was being bought and the bloody owners were afraid it would get out about the conditions under which they had been working. They roared their displeasure.

Jack Miller held up his hands and slowly the noise subsided. 'I ask anyone who can throw any light on the events leading up to the explosion to wait until I have spoken to them. I particularly want to see Mr Bender, so if anyone knows of his whereabouts, I'd be grateful for the information.'

'Why not ask Lady Muck?' There was a surprised silence and then everyone turned to see who had spoken. Alice was sitting on a canvas bundle on a donkey cart, with the reins held loosely in her lap. Now the centre of attention, she stood up in the cart. 'Ask Sarah Jane where Charlie was when her man blew up. She knows.' All eyes turned from the whore to Sarah Jane, who could only stare uncomprehendingly.

'I saw her comin' down the hill after the bang,' the woman went on. 'Charlie jus' behind her, doin' up his trews. I saw it with my own eyes.' She pointed with a grubby finger at Sarah Jane. 'You sent Duncan McBryde to his death, you and Charlie Bender, jus' so's you could carry on with yer fornicatin'.'

Her words, by their very stridency, at last penetrated Sarah Jane's consciousness, but she could make no sound. The fact that she had not welcomed Charlie's attentions and he had not succeeded in raping her was irrelevant; the accusation was no more than she deserved. She had been telling herself that ever since it happened. She became aware that everyone was looking at her. 'Where's Charlie Bender?' they asked in chorus. 'You're goin' to meet him later, goin' to share our wages with 'im, is that it?'

'No, no,' she cried, stung to reply at last. 'I don't know where he is, nor do I care. If he's run off with the wages, that's the owner's affair, seein' he's promised to make your money up.'

'All the same,' Jack Miller said, addressing Sarah Jane. 'If you know where Mr Bender is, then I should like to know.'

'I don't.'

Maggie took Sarah Jane's arm, pulling her round to face her. 'Sarah Jane, were you carrying on behind Duncan's back?'

Sarah Jane looked at her blankly and did not reply.

'Ye've only to say the whore's lying,' James said. 'And we'll forget all about it.'

'How can it ever be forgotten?' Sarah Jane cried, angry for the first time since the tragedy. 'True or false, the seed's been planted in your minds now and it'll take root whatever I say.'

'Ye don't deny it, then?' Daisy said. 'Ye were untrue to Duncan McBryde and after all he done for ye too, taking you on when you had nobody and looking after your bairn an' all. Why, ye should be beat out ...'

'Yes, let's beat her out.' The crowd had been roused to fury. If they couldn't get the better of the engineer and his masters, then they'd find someone else on whom to vent their frustration. 'Beat the whore off the works,' the women screamed, ignoring Jack Miller who was trying to restore order. 'Ma Bender, you're the wronged one, what do you say?'

Mrs Bender knew her husband better than anyone; he was a lecher, always had been, always would be, but he was her husband and she must stick by him. She knew he would find some way of letting her know where he was so that she could join him and take the men's wages to him, for she had them safe in a tin box under her bed. 'She needs thrashing, but ... '

The women did not wait for her to finish but dispersed to find pots and pans, shovels and tins, anything with which to make a noise; in a few minutes they would reassemble for the traditional ceremony. Sarah Jane had seen it inflicted on other women who had transgressed and it was humiliating and terrifying.

'Run, lass,' James urged her. 'I'll find Jason and bring him to ye. Run now, run.'

She dashed back to the hut and snatched up clothes for herself and Jason, heaping them onto a thin blanket from her bed. Her books would be too heavy to carry for long, but she put her receipt book on top of the pile and tied the blanket by its four corners. Then she fastened a cooking pot and a parcel of food to the outside and turned to look about her at the familiar surroundings, the bits of cheap furniture, the cracked mirror, the colourful rag rugs. The hut had not been a palace, but it had been home, hers and Duncan's, the only one she had really known since that day, oh so long ago, when she and Billie had taken that long road to Penny Drift. It was something she and Duncan had made together, had built with love and a sturdy self-sufficiency, had intended to last. And it would have too, if he had lived.

He would never have doubted her; he would never have found it necessary to ask her if she were true to him. He knew she was, as certainly as he knew she lived and breathed. Impatient with herself, she scrubbed at her eyes with the back of her hand, and, picking up the bundle, turned for the door.

They were waiting for her, shrieking obscenities and abuse, banging on the tinware they carried and labouring her bowed head and shoulders as she darted this way and that to avoid the blows. She knew there was no escape, she would have to endure the ignominy just to give them the satisfaction of having rendered rough justice. And in some strange way, she felt that if she bore it stoically, she might, somehow, absolve her own feelings of guilt. She welcomed punishment.

She was bruised and weak by the time she had passed between their ranks and run out into the open, but she did not turn round to see if any of them were following. A few started to do so, but gave up, to return to their fellows, to gossip and theorise on what had happened and to begin packing their own belongings. Sarah Jane sped on down the hill and did not stop until she came to the river bank, where a copse of trees gave her shelter.

James, with Jason perched on his shoulders, found her there half an hour later, crouched on the ground, crying and exhausted. 'Are ye all right?' he asked, knowing there was nothing so ferocious as a band of self-righteous women. 'No bones broken?'

She smiled wearily, drawing Jason into her arms as he set him down. 'No, I'm all right, a few bruises. I just need a moment, then I'll be on me way.'

'Where will ye go?'

She stood up. 'I don't know. Home, perhaps.' But where was home? It was the hut she had just left. 'Don't worry about me.'

He took her hand and put a bag of coins into it. 'Maggie sent this. It will last ye a wee while.'

'But you need it yourself . . . '

'No. I've still got my health and strength, I can work. Besides, it's rightly yours. The folks at the works made a collection and gave it to Maggie. If they hadna been so riled up, they'd have given it to ye.'

Sarah Jane smiled wanly. 'No, they wouldn't, they never liked me. An' if they gave it to Maggie . . . '

'Maggie wants you to have it,' he said. 'She said "Tell Sarah Jane I want her to have it for Duncan's sake. He would wish me to give it to her". Those were her words. Don't refuse it, Sarah Jane, ye'll need it.'

It didn't mean that Maggie had forgiven her, simply that she believed Duncan would have done so and Sarah Jane was only too aware of that. She reached up to kiss his cheek. 'Thank you, James, and thank Maggie for me.' She paused. 'What will you do now?'

'We're going back tae the Highlands. I'll leave word as we go, so that ye can follow if ye've a mind to.'

She was fairly sure his wife had not joined in that invitation. 'Thank you, but I don't think I will.'

He understood. 'Keep an eye out for the result of the enquiry and then go to Lord Chevington for the compensation he promised. He's a good man, Sarah Jane. He meant what he said – it wasn't just empty words.'

'I don't want anything from him! If it hadn't been for him and the men he employs, Duncan would be alive now. I'll not take his blood money.'

'Ye're not being fair, lass. Lord Chevington owned the line, but he hadna had it very long, ye ken that ... '

'I'm surprised at you, James McBryde,' she said, fiercely. 'You, of all people, to be making excuses for him.'

He smiled slowly. 'Hate and vengeance make uncomfortable bedfellows, Sarah Jane, and neither will bring Duncan back. Dinna spoil his memory with black thoughts.' He took her shoulders in his hands and dropped a kiss on her forehead. 'Good luck and God go with ye. Make a start as soon as ye can, just in case someone decides ye haven't had enough punishment.'

She looked up at him, realising how like him Duncan had been, and caught her breath in a sob. But there was no time for tears. She took Jason's hand, picked up her bundle and set off along the towpath, though she had no idea where she was going.

Chapter Thirteen

*T*hey walked slowly, Sarah Jane and her son, dawdling in the meadows, picking the yellow-eyed daisies and bright red poppies with their heady perfume, paddling in brooks, resting in the shade of a tree. She talked to Jason of their farm cottage, her parents and Billie, her brother. Somehow the tragedy of Duncan's death had re-awakened a memory of an earlier one and made her long for her childhood again, her father's slow smile and the comfort of her mother's arms. The intervening years were pushed from her mind – she didn't refer to them. It was a deliberate policy; the workhouse, Chevington and Jason's birth all led inexorably to Duncan and memories of him she put into the dark recesses of her mind and buried them there. Yet he was always there, walking along beside her, his presence felt but never acknowledged and she didn't move many miles from Hailey Common.

She had no sense of direction, even supposing she knew where she wanted to go, and they often found themselves back at the spot they had started from that morning. She would make camp, which meant lighting a fire, cooking a meal and spreading out the blanket before settling down for yet another night. She dreamed a lot, seeing again all the people she had ever known: Billie, still seven years old because her imagination didn't seem able to add the intervening years to his stature and childish features; Thomas Wistonby in his black clothes, wagging an admonitory finger at her; silly, giggly Tilly. And Duncan, of course. She dreamed of Duncan a lot and woke up in tears. And now and again, her sleeping brain conjured up the handsome young man who was Jason's father, but always he appeared to menace her and she woke up shaking. She would pull herself together and prepare for another day of tramping, telling Jason, 'Let's hurry or we'll not be there by dark.'

Quietly troubled by the absence of his Da, he didn't ask where 'there' was, trusting that his mother knew, but 'there' could be anywhere, an abandoned cottage, a hut beside the railway line, a hedgerow, a clearing in a wood; 'there' was wherever they happened to be when night fell.

And one evening, almost without realising where her feet were taking her, she walked back into the Hailey Common works. The site was deserted and new turf was springing up in the mud where a thousand stout boots had tramped; the huts, already falling into disrepair, stood silent and empty. She gazed for an agonising moment at the heep of rubble at the tunnel-mouth as if trying to see through the rock at what lay beyond, then shook herself, turned and picked her way between the deserted huts, discarded bits of metal and lumps of wood, to the door of her former home. She pushed it open, went in and sat on the creaking iron bedstead, tired of travelling to no purpose, but not sure, even now, why she was there or what she meant to do.

She woke in the early hours, though she could not tell what had disturbed her and, unable to go back to sleep, went to the door and sat on the step. The moon shone nearly as bright as day, casting deep shadows between the silent huts and over the twisted ironwork of the drill standing starkly outlined against the sky. 'Duncan,'she whispered, leaning her head against the doorpost. 'Duncan, what shall I do? Where shall I go? I'm lost without you.'

In her mind's eye, she saw lamps come on in blackened windows and pools of light at open doors. She heard the sound of voices; the echo of pick and shovel on rock; the jingle of harness and the rattle of wagons as they passed over the uneven temporary track; singing, laughter, Duncan's laughter and, very close at hand, his soft voice. 'Dinna grieve for me, Sarah Jane. While I live in your heart, I am nae dead. Ye must go forward, my love, go forward with courage and hope; dinna be afraid of the future. Take hold of life and shape it the way ye want it. I will be with ye always.'

Sitting with her back to her old home and her face to the moonlit hills, she began to feel more at peace with herself. Duncan had given her his love, the most precious of human gifts; he had given it unstintingly to make her the woman she was and she could not throw that gift back at him. He had been strong and resilient and she, too, must be strong. It was as if she had been forced through a long, dark tunnel in order to pass from one life to the next. Behind her was Duncan's love and that would never die, in front of her were new opportunities, new things to strive for, new heights to reach for. For Jason's sake, for her own, for Duncan's memory, she had to go forward because there was no going back. She stood up and went back to her bed.

The next morning was unusually warm for so late in the autumn and they breakfasted in the open air, sitting on a railway sleeper with their backs to the drilling rig and their faces to the opposite hill which rose gently to a ragged skyline. She had been sitting up there when Duncan met his death. The guilt had gone now; she knew she had done nothing to bring about the tragedy and as for her foolishness in accepting gifts from Charlie Bender, Duncan, who watched over her, had forgiven her, she knew.

'Look, Mam! Look!'

Sarah Jane saw the fox almost at the same time as Jason did, streaking along the site between the huts, nose forward, tail straight out behind like a rudder, intent on escape. They watched it dart across the stream and disappear among the boulders on the other side of the hill, and then the peace was shattered by a cacophony, made all the more intrusive because of the silence which had gone before: a hunting horn; excited, barking dogs – a score of them at least; horsemen in hunting pink, their faces almost as red as the coats they wore. They streamed past, halloo-ing after the terrified fox, followed by two stragglers who seemed more intent on each other than the pursuit of the animal. The girl, for she was not yet a woman, was dressed in an expensive green riding habit, whose well-fitting jacket set off her slim waist. Her face, beneath the matching hat with its tall crown and long backward-raking feather, had the translucence of porcelain. But it was not the girl who commanded Sarah Jane's attention, but her companion.

He reined in and stopped a few yards from her, sitting his horse, not speaking, simply staring at her. His companion, puzzled by his stillness, pulled up beside him.

'Darling, what is it?' she asked. 'Who is this ... this person?' When he did not reply, she turned to Sarah Jane. 'Who are you and what are you doing here? Don't you know you are trespassing?'

Sarah Jane made herself stand up, though her legs were shaking, and put her hand lightly on Jason's shoulder. 'I am Mrs McBryde,' she said, tilting up her chin. 'And that was my home.' She lifted her hand in the direction of The Haven and smiled at the girl's grimace of distaste.

'McBryde, did you say?' Timothy spoke at last. 'Wasn't that the name of ... '

197

'The ganger who died in the tunnel,' Sarah Jane finished for him. 'He was my husband.' She could say it now and say it with pride.

'Husband?' he echoed. She was ragged and ill-clothed, with unkempt hair and dark-rimmed, troubled eyes, but he saw only what his memory wanted him to see, a bank by a stream and a beautiful red-haired girl whose green eyes were alight with mischief, a naked girl with her arms about him and her soft lips on his. 'McBryde was your husband?' It was almost an accusation.

'Yes.' The chin tilted a little higher.

'Darling,' said the beauty beside him, impatient to be gone, to separate the man and the girl who looked at each other in a way that sent icy shivers of fear down her spine. 'We are being left behind.'

He ignored her and dragged his gaze from Sarah Jane to look at the sturdy, straight-backed child who stood beside her and who was gazing up at him with dark, penetrating eyes. Could it be? 'And the boy?'

Should she tell him? Should she say, 'He is your son?' It would be amusing to see the reaction such a statement might have, both on him and his companion, but the satisfaction of wiping that supercilious smile from the other girl's face was not enough to make her deny Duncan's place as Jason's beloved Da. 'Jason is my son and Duncan McBryde's,' she said, gripping Jason's shoulder so hard, he winced.

Timothy smiled; if anything was needed to convince him that this was Sarah Jane, it was the name of her child. No one but Sarah Jane, with her love of ancient myth, would have chosen that. 'Jason.' He paused, watching the life flicker briefly in her eyes, before the veil came down and clouded them again. 'I like it.'

'Oh, do come on,' Caroline said.

Timothy took no notice of her and continued to gaze at Sarah Jane. 'What are you doing here?'

'Visiting my husband's grave.' She pointed to the rubble. 'There.'

'Oh.' Two navvies were still entombed there, one of whom he had met – Sarah Jane's husband. But he hadn't known that until now. 'Do you intend to stay here?'

She shrugged with a pretence of indifference. 'Maybe, maybe not.'

He did not know why he asked. Did he still want her? He curled his nose up at the sight of her grubby clothes and tangled hair; he had been right, the navvies had degraded her. The old Sarah Jane would have made an admirable mistress, but this one ... 'There is nothing for you here, Mrs McBryde,' he said. 'Nothing at all.' Then he turned his horse and cantered after Caroline.

Sarah Jane watched him go and was surprised that she felt nothing but a dull ache as if a long-suffered pain had receded at last. It was the man and the horse of her nightmare but he had not taken Jason. Jason stood beside her, staring after him in childish curiosity. At the top of the hill man and mount stood outlined against the sky for a moment and then were gone.

Sarah Jane went back to the hut and stood before the mirror. She looked ages older than her twenty-one years; there was no gaiety in her eyes, no smile on her lips. Timothy Myson had not seen the girl he had loved that summer in Chevington – all he had seen was a common navvy's wife, a peasant in shabby clothes, someone to despise, someone to mock. Where was her pride? How could she have let herself get like this?

She filled a basin with water from the stream, now conveniently close, took it to the hut and, stripping off all her clothes, washed herself in the ice-cold water until she was clean and tingling all over. She rummaged in her bundle for fresh clothes and dressed herself, then took out the hairbrush and groomed her hair until it was dry and shining, its copper lights gleaming in the sun. 'Now I feel better,' she said aloud, and began the same operation on the protesting Jason. Her period of mourning, symbolised by self-neglect and aimless wandering, was over; she would rekindle her lost ambition, make a future for herself and her son, a good future. And if, by some whim of fate, she ever crossed paths with Timothy Myson again, he would not look down on her as he had just done; she would be his equal.

They set off almost at once, while the gossamer on the damp grass still shimmered in the morning sun, stepping out firmly, breaking the fairy-spun silk, leaving a trail which pointed southwards, back to the fens of her childhood, back to Billie. They should have been together from the start, sharing the hardships, taking the thick with the thin, the rough with the smooth. It was unlikely he was still at Chevington Union, but the workhouse was the only contact she had and to the workhouse she would go.

It took ten days to reach Chevington and for the last two it rained; green meadows became marshy bogs, easily fordable streams turned to rivers. Boots which had seen them happily through the dry days of summer, let in the water, but Sarah Jane plodded stubbornly on, stopping every now and again to encourage Jason who had become tired and fretful. 'We're nearly there, my darling,' she said.

He had heard that before, but this time his mother's step had some purpose in it. They marched, as if time itself marched beside them. It didn't make him feel any better and although his feet ached, she would not pick him up. 'You are too heavy now,' she said, whenever he held out his arms to her. 'We'll soon be at Chevington.' It was a name he had heard often in his young life; it seemed to have some importance, though he did not understand what it was, nor why they should hurry.

Sarah Jane paused at the familiar crossroads, half-afraid of her memories. Here her troubles had begun. Here she and Billie had come, hand in hand, to the refuge of the Union; from here she had fled to have her child and she had never been sorry for that. She had had five years of happiness, full of back-breaking toil though they had been, and she thanked God for them. Her only regret was that she had left Billie behind. Now she meant to remedy that, though she had no ready plan for what she would do if Billie had gone. They would have to move on, but not tonight, tonight they needed shelter from the rain.

She took a deep breath and walked resolutely forward until she stood, once more, before the door with its plain inscription *Penny Drift and Chevington Union 1837*, and the bellrope Billie couldn't reach when he was seven. She lifted Jason as she had once lifted Billie. 'Pull the rope, Jason. It has a bell on the other end of it.'

He laughed delightedly when he heard it peel. 'Is this Chevington House?' he asked.

'No.' Fancy him thinking that! But he couldn't be expected to know the difference, he had hardly been in a large building in his life. Huts were all he had known. Well, that would change, she would make sure it did. They would have a proper home made of bricks and mortar . . .

She heard bolts being drawn, hitched her son higher on her arm and straightened her back. The door was opened by a thin little urchin who looked so much like Billie that she could do nothing but stare at him with her stomach lurching. Her mind flew back to the first time she had seen that door opened and now nothing would induce her to step inside.

A hand appeared from somewhere in the gloom behind the boy and lifted him by his coat collar and a voice said, 'Thought you'd sneak out, did you, boy? Get back where you belong before I send you to the master for a thrashing.' He was set down and scuttled away to reveal the speaker, but Sarah Jane had recognised the voice and knew who it was. He had not changed except that he was plumper and balder, but he was definitely smarter. He wore a well-tailored frockcoat, a pristine white shirt and a blue silk cravat.

'Hello, Thomas.'

His eyes came to life as he recognised her. 'Why, bless me, if it isn't Sarah Jane.' He looked her up and down, saw the thick red hair, wet though it was, the even features, the big green eyes, the graceful bearing which had so attracted him before, saw the child in her arms and remembered. He remembered how much he had wanted her, how she had given him the will to live again, and the abortive plans he had made; she had run away and left him to rail at her ingratitude. He had been angry and bitter for weeks but, in the end, had realised that their marriage would never have worked, even if Timothy Myson had agreed to be generous. It would have been built on foundations so shaky, the edifice would have toppled at the least breeze; he was fooling himself if he thought otherwise. But, looking at her travel-stained clothes and the sleepy child, he knew he could never stop caring. 'Do you want admittance? Has it come to this? Oh, my dear child, I am so sorry.'

'No, I don't want to come in,' she said, hurriedly. 'I came to ask after my brother. Is Billie still here?'

'Is that all you have to say to me, Sarah Jane? After all this time? Have you no thought for me who only wanted to help and cherish you?'

'I'm sorry,' she said. 'But I did try to explain when I wrote ...'

'You wrote – when?'

'As soon as I could, soon after Jason was born.'

'I received no letter.'

'You mean you didn't know where I was, or who I was with?'

'I certainly did not. It grieved me, Sarah Jane, grieved me sorely that you thought so little of me that you could not even let me know you were well and that your baby had been born.'

'I'm sorry the letter didn't reach you, Thomas. I addressed it here, sure that it would find you.'

'If it hadn't been for Lady Chevington, I would not have stayed ...'

'Lady Chevington? What has she to do with it?'

'With you, nothing, except she felt you had let her down too, but thanks to her good offices, I am no longer dependent on my sister. I am paid for my services. I look after the accounting at the Union, the legal aspects, the placing of boys and girls who need work and a home.'

'And you found Billie a place?'

'No. Billie ran away – years ago now.'

'Do you know where he went?'

'Can't say I do.' He paused, realising how unhelpful, even resentful, he sounded. And she looked exhausted and wet to the skin. How far had she walked? He wanted to know, he wanted to know where she had been, everything she had done. 'We should talk,' he said. 'Where are you staying tonight? Do you want a bed here?'

She recoiled. 'No, no, I don't. I'll go to the Jolly Brewers.'

'I'll meet you there at six o'clock.'

He arrived punctually and made his way to the parlour where she sat alone in an alcove. She did not immediately see him and he stood a moment to watch her. She was the same girl he had known, and yet she was different; she was still beautiful, but it was the beauty of a mature and confident woman, not the child he had known. She wore a simple grey wool dress with red embroidery round the neck and she had swept her hair up from the long arch of her neck. Her face bore the marks of recent grief, but there was a kind of strength about her, a poise which would always make her stand out in a crowd, even when, as now, her clothes looked as though she had slept in them. Her back was ramrod straight and her chin was high.

She looked up and saw him. 'Thomas.'

He sat opposite her and ordered brandy for them both. As soon as they had been served, he began a barrage of questions about her life since he had last seen her. She replied promptly enough but then, impatient to know the answers to her own queries, she said, 'That's enough about me. Tell me what you know about Billie.'

'It's little enough.' He remembered going in search of the boy in the oakum shed where he worked to ask him if he had any idea where Sarah Jane might have gone. Billie, who could only have been about ten years old, had been wary of him and although he had admitted to hearing rumours about Sarah Jane having a baby, he knew nothing that would help. 'The boy kept his own counsel. He'd not tell anyone what he was planning ...'

'But if he ran away, didn't anyone go after him?'

'No. He was of an age to work, so why should they? But I did hear something ...'

'What?' She sat forward eagerly, reaching out to lay a hand on his arm; although it was brown and work-worn, the nails were clean and neatly shaped.

'I was in a tavern out Walton way one day and I heard a farmer saying he had found a young lad asleep in one of his empty cottages.'

'What makes you think it was my brother?'

'The description fitted and it was about the time he left.' He paused, wondering whether to tell her the rest. 'The farmer introduced him to a chimney sweep and he went off with him. The sweep was a Londoner and was setting off back there, so I'll wager Billie became a chimney boy.'

'But isn't it illegal to employ boys for climbing?'

'So it is, but that doesn't stop them. They just call them apprentices and deny they do anything more than fetch and carry.'

'Oh, that's dreadful. Poor Billie. I must go to London at once and find him.'

'A needle in a haystack, that's what he'd be. London's a big place and besides, he'd have grown too big for chimneys long ago.' He sipped his drink, watching the expression of disappointment deepen on her face, wishing he could do something for her. He beckoned to the waiter to refill their glasses. 'Why didn't you trust me? Why did you run away when you knew all I wanted was to love and cherish you? Didn't you think about me at all? I went back to the Union expecting to find you waiting for me. I had everything arranged, it was all so simple.'

'What was?'

'Finding the father of your child. It didn't take above a day and you'd have been looked after, I as good as had his promise ... '

'Whose promise?' she demanded.

'Lord Chevington's. The father of your child is his son.'

'His *son*?' She looked startled. 'He is Lord Chevington's *son*?' It was unbelievable.

'Lord Chevington does not acknowledge him publicly on account of the boy not being Lady Chevington's child, but father and son are very close.'

'Lord Chevington's puppy dog,' she mused. 'That's what the navvy called him.' Other things began to slot into place, his presence on the Chevington estate when they met, although as far as she knew he had never come to the house; at Ashley Green when the navvies rioted; at the Hailey Common line after the explosion. It had been no coincidence that he had been hunting at Hailey Common, but she had been too laden with grief to wonder at the time what he was doing there. She shook herself; what was the point of dwelling on the past? She had vowed to put it behind her. 'What difference does it make?'

'Puppy dog or no, he has money and influence. He enjoys all the benefits of being His Lordship's son . . .'

'Except legitimacy.' She remembered the odd remarks Paris had made to her about his father, things she had not understood at the time. *I am the nobody my father has made me*, and something about belonging. 'Where and to whom?' he had asked, though he had been talking more to himself than to her. 'He is bitter about that, you know,' she told Thomas, 'and I do not intend that Jason should ever feel like that. It is better for him to believe his father died. Besides, Timothy Myson has already seen him.'

'When?'

'A month ago at Hailey Common.'

'And didn't you ask him for help?'

'No. I want nothing from Timothy Myson. I certainly don't want his charity, nor will I have him looking down his nose at me. Never again will he make me feel inferior. This I have promised myself.'

'It's not charity, Sarah Jane. It is your right as a wronged woman . . .'

'Wronged? I have not been wronged, not in the way you mean. As you so rightly said at the time, it takes two to beget a child and I could have said no. The only wrong was the way the railway line was worked, the incompetence which took Duncan from me. That was the wrong, to make a widow of me, as it has many another navvy wife, for the sake of gain.'

'Navvy wife? Is that how you see yourself?' He smiled slowly. 'Remember how you wanted to be a lady? Have you forgotten that?'

'No, I haven't forgotten, but that was just a childish dream. And going cap in hand to Timothy Myson will not bring it about.'

'So, you are prepared to sink into the abyss and take your son with you.'

'Certainly not.' Her voice was sharp. 'I am not the ignorant girl you taught to read and write, Thomas, and I have still a long way to go, but it will be up not down, I promise you. There are things to be done, wrongs to be righted, the guilty to be punished, the innocent to be helped. I know I can't fulfil that silly dream but I can be a different kind of lady, one who is looked up to for what she has achieved.'

He was impressed. 'Such as?'

'For the things I do. Duncan was a good man, not only because he looked after me and Jason, but because of what he was – strong and dependable, caring and generous. He would have achieved a great deal if he had lived. We would have done it together. I want to carry on with his work.'

He smiled. 'Don't you want anything for yourself?'

'Of course. Do you think I like being poor? Do you think I like wearing this?' She picked up a handful of her worn grey skirt. 'And these.' She lifted her feet to reveal what had once been sturdy boots but were now paper-thin. 'I should like to wear shoes, Thomas.'

'How will you do it without help?'

'I'll do it, you'll see, and I'll do it under my own steam.'

He smiled at the railway connotation. 'But you need fuel to make steam, do you not? Money makes very good fuel. Only with that will you be in a position to look after your son properly, make a gentleman of him, and find Billie, and once having found him, to have something to offer him.' He paused, wondering whether to go on. 'Sarah Jane, Timothy Myson used you once, so why don't you make use of him now?'

'Make use of him?'

'The man has ambition, Sarah Jane, more than you have, and he won't want the encumbrance of an illegitimate child, especially as he is soon to be married. I fancy he'll go to great lengths to keep him hidden ...'

'Thomas!' she exclaimed, as the implication of what he was saying dawned on her. 'That's blackmail.'

'No more than he practises on his own father. It's not so much blackmail as a way of keeping everything sweet. Lady Chevington knows nothing of her husband's love-child and His Lordship would die rather than tell her. Timothy is well aware of that.' He patted her hand and smiled. 'Let me deal with him, you won't regret it.'

'No, Thomas.' Her voice was sharp. 'I won't go to Timothy Myson for anything, do you understand? Nothing. Jason is Duncan's child in all but the seed that begat him and that is how it will stay. I'll manage and I'll ask no favours from anyone.'

He reached out to cover her hand with his own. 'Sarah Jane, I—' He stopped suddenly; was he going to suggest they begin all over again? Foolish, foolish old man! 'Oh, I know you might have married me once, and maybe I'd have made you a good husband, maybe not. You were young and beautiful, still are, and I would not have been able to hold you for long, so perhaps it's for the best.' He sighed. 'I made you happy, just for a little while, as Timothy Myson made you happy, and Duncan McBryde, in their own ways.'

'Duncan?' she said quickly, pulling her hand away. 'Duncan was different. Duncan was ...' She floundered unable to tell him, not wanting to, because the terrible ache was still there.

'There will be others.'

'No. All I want is to find Billie. I failed him badly and things won't go right until I've made up for that ...'

'Superstitious nonsense! You will only double your problems if you do find him; I doubt he's learned a trade and can earn a decent living. Likely he's forgotten you.'

'Perhaps, but I mean to find out.' She was tired and the room was so stuffy she could hardly breathe. 'Thank you for your help, Thomas.' She stood up and held out her hand.

Reluctantly he rose and took it, raising it to his lips. He had loved her once, still did, but he could not keep her, he knew that. He had to let her go but he would not lose track of her as he had before. 'When you arrive in London, where will you stay?'

'I don't know. I'll find somewhere.'

'I have a friend who keeps a boarding house – it's not much of one, but it's clean and cheap.' If she went to lodgings he had recommended, then at least he would know where she was. He released her hand to take a pencil from his waistcoat pocket and tear the corner from a discarded newspaper which lay on the next table. 'Here, take this.' He wrote quickly. 'Tell Mrs Grainger I sent you.'

She took the scrap of paper from him and put it in her pocket. 'Thank you, Thomas. You are a good friend, as always.' She reached to kiss him gently on the cheek and then turned and left the room.

He followed, absent mindedly rubbing the spot where her lips had touched. 'If you change your mind about Myson ...'

'I won't. Goodnight, Thomas.'

He stood and watched her climb the stairs and then, sighing, returned to the Union.

Sarah Jane travelled to London in company with Big Bill and a group of navvies whom she met on the platform at Chevington Halt the following morning. They were on their way to find work in the capital, there being little to be had elsewhere and she looked on their meeting as a stroke of luck; she could look for work with them. They boarded the Parliamentary, the daily train which, by law, had to be run on every line for the benefit of the poorer members of the community, and after six uncomfortable hours, packed like cattle in an open-sided carriage, they arrived at the *Great Northern*'s new Maiden Lane terminus in one of London's notorious pea-soupers.

Behind them, as they left the station, they could hear engines and whistles and voices, and in front, as if from a great distance and yet very close, the clatter of hooves and rumbling of wheels and the shouts and curses of people bumping into each other. Afraid of getting lost in the fog, they found a hotel quite close to the terminus where Big Bill, pushing his way through to the desk, announced their intention of staying for the night, even if they had to curl up on the floor of the foyer to sleep.

'It will cost you threepence each.' The manager saw no harm in taking advantage of a not-infrequent situation which deposited crowds of stranded railway passengers on his doorstep with no alternative. It cost him nothing to let them sleep on the floor and threepence from each of them amounted to a fair sum, because there must have been twenty of them altogether. He would get his staff up early and make a good profit on the breakfasts they would all want after their supperless and probably sleepless night.

Sarah Jane, already exhausted by her long walk from Derbyshire to Chevington, could hardly keep her eyes open, but she was afraid of being robbed while she slept. The small bag of coins which was all that remained of the money James had given her, was all she had in the world and she did not want to risk losing it. When she paid over her threepence, she asked the manager to put her purse in his safe. Then, relieved of the need to be watchful, she found a corner behind a potted palm, curled up on the floor with Jason snuggly in her encircling arms, put her head on her bundle and pulled her old coat over them both, and was soon deep in slumber.

The navvies had gone when she woke. She and Jason were alone in the foyer, except for the hotel staff, who were busy clearing up the débris and sweeping the floor. She had no idea where the others had gone but it would not be difficult to find them; navvy sites always stuck out like sore thumbs. She stood up and stretched her cramped limbs, bundled up her belongings and taking Jason by the hand went to ask for the hotel manager.

'He's busy,' she was told by an officious-looking being who was supervising the cleaning.

'I am sure he is,' she said, standing up very straight and putting on her best ladylike voice. 'And I, too, have more than enough to do, so you would oblige me by telling him I wish to see him.'

'Very well,' he said, reluctantly. 'I'll ask him.' He left through a door behind the reception desk but soon returned. 'Mr Dawkins says to come back later.'

'I'll wait,' she said firmly, seating herself on a chair near a swing door which obviously led to the kitchen regions because every now and again a waiter came through with a loaded tray, or returned with stacked crockery. No one was going to deprive her of her savings if she could help it; she'd stay there all day if necessary.

And it began to look as if that was what she would have to do, as the morning wore on and the hotel became busier. Every time the doors swung open she had a glimpse of the kitchens. They reminded her of the workhouse kitchens except that they seemed to have a great deal more equipment and a greater variety of food; the tables were laden with joints of meat and vegetables. The staff were talking and arguing noisily as they passed from cupboard to table and from table to stove. She saw a chef, in a tall hat, bending to take a roasting pan from the oven and the smell reminded her she had had no breakfast. A woman was standing at the stove, stirring something in a pan on the top. The chef pushed her out of the way, nudging her arm and making the pan tip. She screamed as the boiling liquid ran over her hand. There was a hubbub of voices, then the door swung crazily as the waiter ran past Sarah Jane and across the foyer, calling, 'Mr Dawkins! Mr Dawkins!'

Sarah Jane stood up and pushed the swing door open. The kitchen was in an uproar. The chef had dropped the roasting tin, and roast lamb and gravy were spread all over the floor, the injured cook had fainted and the rest of the kitchen hands were crowded round her, while one of them tried slapping her face.

Sarah Jane turned to Jason. 'Stay here and wait for me.' She made her way across the kitchen, stepping over the spilt food. 'Give her air, for goodness sake,' she ordered, pushing everyone aside. 'And fetch me a bowl of cold water, and a clean cloth.'

They had no idea who she was but her air of quiet authority sent them scurrying to obey. She loosened the woman's clothing and, once the already-blistered arm had been immersed in water, deftly tore the teacloth she had been given into strips and soaked them in cold water, before placing them gently on the wound. 'Get her to hospital.'

The waiter returned with the manager. 'Who are you?' he demanded of Sarah Jane.

'Never mind who I am, this woman needs a doctor.'

The porter was sent scurrying away for a cab to transport the patient to hospital. Sarah Jane stood up and looked about her at the shambles. A saucepan was boiling over, a frying pan was creating blue smoke and a cat had come in and was making a meal of the spilt food. 'I never saw such slipshod working,' she said, rescuing a pan of gravy and stirring it vigorously. 'No wonder there are accidents.'

The manager began haranguing the staff. 'Get that mess cleared up. Throw away that burnt sauce and fetch some more chickens. Chef, see what you can do, our guests will be here in half an hour.' He took the saucepan from Sarah Jane. 'Now, madam, if you please, your name and business.'

'Mrs McBryde. I have been waiting all morning to see you.'

'Have we met?' Her face looked vaguely familiar but he could not place it. Was she one of his customers? He wished she had not seen the terrible state of the kitchen; it was not a good recommendation for the hotel.

'You put my purse in your safe last night.'

'So I did,' he said, relieved that she was no more than a casual traveller and a poor one at that. 'Come with me.' Sarah Jane followed him to his office and watched as he extracted a key from his waistcoat pocket and unlocked the safe. 'Do you wish to count it?'

'That won't be necessary.' She took the purse from him, deciding to seize the opportunity which presented itself. 'I need work . . .'

He shook his head. 'No, I'm sorry. There is nothing.'

'I am an excellent cook and you have just lost yours, have you not?'

That was true. He also had a luncheon party to cater for and had been hard-pressed before the accident, but now he would be lucky to get through the day without another mishap. 'What about the boy? What will you do with him if I take you on?'

'He stays with me,' she said firmly. 'He'll be no trouble.'

'Very well. Just for the day then, and only for your food.'

'Thank you.' It didn't really solve anything, it simply staved off hunger for another day, but she would take things one step at a time – food, then lodgings and a job, then the search for Billie, in that order.

At eight o'clock, when she was preparing to leave, exhausted after a day doing nothing more exciting than peeling potatoes and shredding cabbage under the watchful eye of the chef, she was told she could return the next day if she chose. 'Mrs Dove will not be back for at least a week,' Mr Dawkins told her. 'I can give you work until she returns.'

209

'And wages?' she queried.

'A shilling a day, payable at the end of the week, *if* you satisfy.'

She knew she was worth more than that, but she decided now was not the time to haggle. 'Very well.'

'Start at five-thirty, finish when the last guest has been served.'

Jason had fallen asleep on her bundle in the corner. She woke him up and picked up her belongings. 'Well, Jason, my son,' she said, taking his hand. 'Let's see if we can find those lodgings, shall we?'

It was only when she tried to locate the address Thomas had given her, that she realised how big London was, how many streets, alleys and courts it had, how many squares and parks, how many shops and markets. Thomas had been right; looking for Billie would be like looking for a needle in a haystack and it would take much longer than she had anticipated. Before she could even start, she needed the security of a proper job. Working for food was all very well, but lodgings had to be paid for with hard cash and she had little enough of that.

After asking her way several times, she found the four-storey tenement in Denmark Place. Her knock was answered by a dark-haired woman of about fifty, wearing a grey alpaca dress and white cap over dyed black hair.

'Mrs Grainger?'

'Yes.'

Sarah Jane thrust Thomas' letter into her hand. 'I need a room. I have an introduction.'

The woman read it, looked Sarah Jane and Jason up and down very thoroughly, then sniffed and said, 'This way.'

The room she led them to was high up at the back of the house. It was very small and furnished with two narrow beds, a washstand, a table, two chairs and a cupboard, but it was reasonably clean. It had a tiny grate, spilling cold ash. Sarah Jane looked round her, too tired to be critical. 'How much?' she asked.

'A shilling a night and that only because Mr Wistonby recommended you.'

Sarah Jane handed her seven shillings, which left her with less than two. 'Here's enough for a week. If we stay any longer, I'll give you more.'

As soon as Mrs Grainger had left them, Sarah Jane dropped her bundle on her bed and went to open the garret window. She found herself looking out on a sea of rooftops. That was all London seemed to be – wet streets and grey rooftops. Was Billie out there somewhere in that maze? How on earth was she going to find him?

Chapter Fourteen

Working at the hotel kept hunger at bay and paid the rent but, more than that, the chef's grudging praise when she nagged at him to allow her to create one or two special dishes with the aid of her receipt book, woke her sleeping ambition. She would make a name for herself as a cook. People would flock to the hotel to sample her dishes and when she had saved a little money, she would branch out on her own, have her own eating house. She set out to learn all she could. She found out about buying fresh produce, about equipment, about the routine needed to bring the dishes to the table at exactly the right moment, about how much things cost and how much profit was needed to cover overheads, simply by watching and listening. But, a month later, her hopes were dashed when the injured cook returned to work. 'Mrs Dove has always satisfied and I am not going to turn her off to make way for a tramp who turns up out of the blue without a character, however good she is,' Mr Dawkins said bluntly.

There was no changing his mind and Sarah Jane found herself on the street with ten shillings in her pocket and a paper parcel of leftovers, grudgingly given. Her natural optimism sustained her only as long as it took to realise that no one wanted a cook without references and certainly not one with the encumbrance of a child.

Day after day she tramped the streets and night after night she returned to their garret lodging, exhausted and dispirited. The only thing that kept her going was Jason; without the overriding need to provide for him, she would have given up. She stopped going to the better class hotels and turned to the cheaper boarding houses, who did not want cooks, but skivvies prepared to work for little more than their keep, but even those who were prepared to take her on, would not include Jason. Her tiny store of money dwindled until the day came when she spent the last of it on a little meat, fat and flour to make a pie. The rent was due the next day and if she could not pay it, Mrs Grainger would not think twice about turning them out.

So much for her grand ideas and ambitious plans. Thomas had told her what would happen and Thomas had been right. Perhaps she ought to write to him, humble herself and beg that he do something to help her, but that would mean admitting defeat and besides, his idea of helping her was to blackmail Timothy Myson. That she would not countenance. She would sell herself first. Matron had called her a whore and so had Charlie Bender, and Kate and Alice had mistaken her for one of their own kind. Even in the last few weeks, when she had been walking the streets looking for work, men had approached her. She had angrily shrugged them off, but it had set her thinking. Was there something about her, a look perhaps, something in the eyes, or the way she carried her body which made them take her for a tail? It was unconscious, if it was.

As soon as Jason was asleep, she stripped naked and stood before the cracked mirror in her room and surveyed her body critically. She was thinner than she should be because every scrap of food except what was necessary for her survival, went to Jason, but nevertheless what she saw satisfied her as she put her hands under her breasts to lift them and turned slowly to look at her rear; her figure was still good, she had long, shapely legs and her skin was smooth and free of blemishes. Her body was her only asset, she decided, and the sooner she came to terms with that the better. But for Duncan, she might have been forced to realise it sooner. Dear, devoted Duncan. 'Keep away from them or be tarred with the same brush,' he had said. He had saved her from that. What would he say if he could see her now, parading her naked body in front of a mirror and contemplating a step which, once taken, could never be retraced? She looked over at the sleeping Jason; he was neither cold nor hungry, but tomorrow ...

She washed in water fetched earlier from the pump in the yard, dressed and brushed her coppery hair until it hung about her shoulders in thick shining strands. Then, pulling a bright fringed shawl about her shoulders, she took a last look at her sleeping son and went out onto London's crowded streets, convinced that if she kept her mind on Jason, she could endure what she had to do. But when the time came, her courage failed her. She could not approach any of the men she saw walking alone, nor even adopt the stance she had seen other whores use to invite custom. And when one man did speak to her she angrily sent him on his way. As a whore, she was most certainly a failure and she felt nothing so much as relief. She turned to begging from the cheerful, noisy crowds coming out of Covent Garden theatre.

Begging was not something which came easily to Sarah Jane either; she was too proud and independent to ask for money she had not earned, and the exercise yielded no more than a few coppers. But she stayed until the last of the theatre-goers had dispersed in their lamplit carriages, then turned for home. What next, she asked herself. She could plead with Mrs Grainger to give her more time to find the rent, but even if the woman agreed, which was doubtful, did that put food into their mouths? Was the next step the workhouse? No, never! She would have to try again. But not now.

'Have a care, missh.' Engrossed in berating herself, she had been unaware of anyone else on the road until she bumped into him. He was well-dressed in evening tails and top hat, though obviously very drunk.

'I'm sorry,' she said, stepping into the road to pass him. 'I wasn't looking where I was going.'

'No' sho fas',' he muttered thickly, peering into her face. 'You're jush what I need.'

'Seems to me what you need is a cold bath and a strong cup of coffee.'

He fell against her, grabbing her shoulders to keep himself upright. 'You'll help a fellow in dish ... stress, won't you? You look the friendly sor'.'

'Let me go!' she shouted. 'What d'you take me for?'

'A lady of the night, ain't tha' so? A whore.' He lowered his face to hers. 'All I want ish a leetle comf ... fort.' The bittersweet smell of spirits on his breath almost choked her as he made a clumsy attempt to kiss her. Apart from the fact that he was too drunk to do the job properly, she realised with sudden insight that he was as new to the game as she was.

Was this what she could expect? It was revolting. 'I most certainly am not!' she snapped, wiping her mouth on the back of her hand. Not tonight, dear God, not tonight. Tomorrow perhaps. She needed more time.

'Oh, I shay, I sheem to have made a miss ... take.' He was concentrating very hard on what he was saying, blinking in the lamplight to try and focus eyes which insisted on showing him a double image. 'What can I sh ... say?' He made no move to leave her. 'But, you know, a lady sh ... shouldn't be out alone sh ... so late at night. I thought ...'

'I know what you thought.'

'Pleash let me make amends.' He was making an heroic effort to speak clearly. 'Allow me to escort you ...' He swayed from side to side, taking her in unwilling unison. 'If I had not ... taken a drop too much, I would have known you were a respectable woman.' He looked down into her face, but it was too dark to see anything except that she had the most lustrous eyes he had ever seen. 'A beautiful woman,' he added softly. He doffed his hat. 'Henry Carter, ma'am, at your sh ... service.' He replaced his hat. 'I am sh ... till a little tipsy and, to be honest, a little lost ...'

'Lost?'

'In more waysh than one. I do not know these sh ... treets.' He offered her his arm. 'In return for directions, I will eshcort you safe ... safely home.'

It seemed that fate had given her another chance and a better one than she deserved, for though he was drunk, he was clean and smart. She put a hand on his arm and laughed lightly. 'Very well, but I make no promises.' Would he know how inexperienced she was? Perhaps she ought to confess it to him and throw herself on his mercy. He might give her a shilling or two and let her off.

'How did you lose your way?' she asked, as they walked.

'I wash a little fuddled and mish ... ed my road.'

'Where were you going?'

He smiled. 'To be truthful, I don't know.' His speech was becoming less slurred. 'I suppose I would eventually have made my way home, but not until later, until I had walked my low sh ... pirits away. I am bereft. My heart has been broken. I thought ... ' He paused and smiled crookedly. 'I thought if I could find a woman, a clean woman ...'

She laughed. 'Like a small boy who has fallen and bruised his knee, you wanted a little comfort, is that so?'

'You think I am like a child?'

'All men are children.' She stopped outside the door of her lodgings and turned to face him. 'This is where I live.'

'Please don't leave me, I can't face going home yet. I need that comfort you spoke of.'

She took a deep breath. 'Then you'd better come in.'

'You haven't told me your name.'

'Sarah Jane McBryde.'

'Miss?'

'Mrs. I am a widow.'

He stepped into the hall behind her just as Mrs Grainger came down the stairs, candle in hand, hair in papers and a wrap flung hastily over her nightgown. 'Mrs McBryde, I'll have you know this is a respectable establishment,' she began, holding the candle aloft and peering at Henry. 'I do not allow men callers.'

'Madam.' Henry doffed his hat and though he was still not exactly steady on his feet, he was no longer rolling drunk. 'Mrs McBryde and I are childhood friends and we met again, quite by chance, tonight. Surely you do not condemn her for speaking to me?'

'At this time of night, and alone? I am not a fool.'

'Come, Henry,' Sarah Jane said, anxious to put an end to the interchange; if Mrs Grainger started asking questions about how and when they had met, either this evening or in their childhood, answering might be difficult. 'I will make you a cup of tea and we can chat over old times in the comfort of my room.' She pushed past her landlady and went upstairs, not caring whether he followed or not.

'For the child's sake, I'll give you until tomorrow to pack your bags,' Mrs Grainger called after her. 'I'll not have my home made into a whorehouse, not for you nor anyone.'

'Does she mean it?' he asked, as he followed her into the room at the top of the house.

'Oh, she means it.' She took off her shawl and lit a candle, before going to look at Jason. He slept peacefully, his hand flung out and his fair curls spread over the pillow. She tucked him up and turned to face her guest. He was in his early forties, perhaps a year or two younger, not much taller than she was, and rather portly, but she liked his face; his grey eyes were sad, belying the cheerful look of his rosy cheeks, full mouth and bushy side whiskers. 'Take your coat off and sit down. I'll make some tea.'

'I'm sorry, I shouldn't have followed you in but you see...' He paused. 'I wanted to talk to you, to apologise, to explain why I was so drunk.'

'I've seen worse.' She laughed, not wanting him to see how desperately worried she was. Where could they go? Who would take them in without money? The spectre of the hated workhouse loomed. She busied herself dispensing her precious tea. 'Tell me, why were you out on the streets looking for a woman?'

'I missed my way. I came out of the theatre, intending to walk to Piccadilly. I believe one can find ...' he paused, searching for a word '... diversions there.'

'You're too drunk for that,' she said bluntly. 'Money for old rope, it would be.'

He looked up at her from the only chair in the room, his surprise showing on his face. 'I thought you said ...'

'Talk first,' she said, wanting to put it off as long as possible.

He sipped the tea and then suddenly put the cup down, to cover his face with his hands. 'Oh, God! This is terrible!'

'Drink it, it will sober you.'

'I don't want to be sober.' He raised an anguished face to hers. 'Have you got a drop of something—'

'I'm afraid not. And you've had enough. What you need is food inside you to soak up all that spirit. When did you last eat?'

He shrugged. 'I've forgotten. Breakfast, I suppose.'

She went to the cupboard and fetched out the meat pie she had made that morning. It was the last food she had and her guest did not look exactly starving, but she had nothing else to offer him. She cut off a slice and put it on a plate. 'Here, eat this.'

He took it unthinkingly and bit into it. 'My ... my wife has left me,' he said.

'I'm sorry.'

'Without warning. Run away with some fellow she had met at a *soirée*. Left me a note.' He shut his eyes, but the tears squeezed themselves through and lay on his cheeks. 'I had no idea, no idea at all.'

'How can you *not* have known?' she asked. 'Women always betray themselves; she couldn't have been that clever.'

'Oh, I know I left her alone quite often. I have a business, you know, and need to work long hours, but she understood that, and she seemed content to busy herself with our home and our son. She went to lectures and concerts. They met ... Oh, why did I encourage her?'

'What is your business?' She didn't want to hear about his marital troubles.

'I have shops in Bond Street and Woburn Walk and Oxford Street, as well as some in less fashionable areas. They sell everything from hairpins to bedsteads, tea kettles to silver goblets, cambric to fine silks.' He had suddenly become animated and she realised that his shops were everything to him and she felt sorry for the wife who had been unable to compete. 'My father, the late George Carter, started the business with one shop, now I have six, all different, and yet all bear the hallmark of Carter quality. Most of my assistants live in and they live very well; I am a good employer and everything is found for them.' He had eaten every last crumb of the pie. 'I am a wealthy man. How could she do it to me? I went to the theatre because the ... the man performs there, or he did, until yesterday. An actor.' He shuddered. 'My wife has run off with an *actor* and I am totally broken ... an empty shell and I don't know what to do.'

He was pretty good at the histrionics himself, she thought. 'I can't tell you what to do. I do not even know what I am going to do myself. I suppose you must go back to your business and hope she will return, and I must tramp the streets for new lodgings and work to pay for them.' Her voice was sharp.

He was contrite. 'I am sorry. You have patiently listened to my troubles and given me tea and an excellent pie and said nothing about your own problems. I must make amends.' He reached in his tailpocket for his purse, but realising that he had rushed out with very little money and what he had, had been spent on drink, he put it back. 'I seem to be without funds.'

Her heart sank, though she smiled. 'Not even enough for breakfast and a cab?'

'No. Plenty at home, of course, believe me, and more in the bank, but in my pocket, not a farthing.'

'Then you'll have to walk, but you might as well wait until daylight. There'd be less chance of being set upon.'

'I've no money to steal.'

'No, but you've a fine gold watch and a ring on your finger, besides the clothes on your back.'

'Are you honest, Mrs McBryde?'

'Don't worry, I will not steal from you.' She paused, as an idea occurred to her which was so brilliant, it lit her face. He was a businessman and he had money and, according to Thomas, money made very good fuel. If she could only catch his imagination and fire him with her own enthusiasm, she might solve her immediate problem. She had to. She had needed a miracle and Henry Carter was her miracle; she would not let him go out of her life. 'Do you sell food?' she asked. 'Cooked food, I mean?'

'Oh no, I don't deal in comestibles. It is not the class of trade I want.'

'But everyone has to eat. You enjoyed that meat pie, didn't you?'

'It was excellent.'

She smiled. 'I made it. Now, admit it was the best you've ever tasted. The meat was succulent and the gravy mouthwatering and the pastry melted in your mouth.'

He laughed. 'I'll say one thing, Mrs McBryde – you are not plagued with false modesty.'

'You are a salesman, or you must have been once, so you know there is no point in hiding your goods if you want to sell them.'

'You want to sell pies?'

'Why not?'

'In my shops? Oh dear no, that would never do.'

'Not in *your* shops, in mine.' She was thinking as she went along, one idea following another in quick succession, until she was bright-eyed and breathless. She sat on the edge of Jason's bed and leaned towards him. 'I can make dozens of pies, all as good as that one you've just eaten. Given premises, I can make and sell pies all day and I'll wager I can make money at it. I know where to buy the best ingredients and how to haggle over the cost, and I know how much people are prepared to pay for good food. I mean good food, not hashed-up leftovers minced up and put into pastry to disguise the fact that they're fit only for pigs.' She had learned a lot at the station hotel, had drunk up every morsel of information, like a man dying of thirst. He need not know how recently she had acquired her knowledge; it was sufficient to put on an air of knowing what she was talking about.

She was carrying him along too fast, and he shook his head. 'Steady on, Mrs McBryde, are you asking me to finance you?'

'Yes, why not?' She paused, smiling. 'You need something to take your mind off your troubles and what could be better than a new venture, something so different it takes up all your energies and leaves you no time to brood. Think of the excitement of finding premises and equipping them, advertising, the first day of opening and people flocking to buy pies, because they are baked on the premises, fresh every day, and everywhere clean as a new pin. And you would be earning a percentage without ever having to set foot in the place, if you don't want to.'

'There are dozens of eating houses already.'

'Yes, fine places with damask tablecloths and real silver and waiters in white gloves. They're too expensive.'

'There are other places, cookshops and taverns.'

'And they're too cheap and dirty. Working people are not dirty from choice, you know, and they like good, clean food as well as the gentry. Think of all the workmen in London, the masons and bricklayers, the roadmenders, the painters, the railway-workers, who leave home at dawn each day and do not go back until night. They have to eat somewhere. We must find premises in an area close to where such work is going on – King's Cross, for instance. They're building a fine new railway terminus there.'

He sighed; this was a new angle and no mistake, but he was far too tired to play her game properly and, besides, he did not know the rules. What he needed was a little sleep, just a few minutes to clear his head, then he might be able to think of the riposte which was expected of him and carry the game through to its conclusion. He eyed the narrow bed longingly. 'I need to think . . .'

'Well, don't think for too long because I'll have to take my idea to someone else if you aren't interested.' She turned and cut another thick wedge of pie, leaving only a small piece for Jason's breakfast. 'Here, have another slice of pie while you're doing it. And I'll make more tea.'

'I could not possibly make a decision tonight,' he said, deciding to humour her; it must be what was expected of him. 'I need to know more about it, how much it will cost, the return on investment.'

'Of course.'

'But not tonight,' he said wearily. She was so vibrantly alive, he was afraid she was going to bombard him with facts and figures there and then and he could not take it, not in the state he was in. Tomorrow, he could put her off. 'I need to sleep.'

She nodded towards her bed. 'Sleep there.'

'And you?'

'Whatever you wish.' If that was what it took, so be it. She would grit her teeth and think of Jason.

He looked from her to the bed, wondering if she meant it. She laughed. 'I might as well be hung for a sheep as a lamb; it won't make any difference to how soon I'm thrown out.'

He finished eating, drank a cup of tea and lay down on her bed and, in the space of a minute, was snoring loudly, indifferent to whether she joined him or not. She continued to sit where she was, far too excited even to think of sleeping. He was not handsome and she guessed he was weak, but he was her knight in shining armour, her saviour, and she would not let him walk out of her life, until she had what she wanted. She would not cheat him, nothing was further from her mind, but she would use him. Survival was all about seizing opportunities; she had been doing it all her life. She had used Thomas to learn to read, and Timothy Myson to assuage her loneliness, and Duncan ... She had used Duncan, too, in the beginning, and been punished for it. There would never be anyone else like him, but if she meant to make a good future for Jason, and find Billie and help the navvies and their children, she had to make the most of any chances which came her way. And if it meant going to bed with this man whom providence had sent to her, then she would. But it would not be tonight and she was thankful for that.

Jason woke first, surprised to find his mother sitting on the edge of his bed, staring into the cold ashes of yesterday's fire. And there was a strange man lying on her bed with all his clothes on and snoring his head off. He reached out and touched her arm. 'Mam,' he whispered. 'Who's that?'

'A friend, Jason, just a friend who had nowhere to sleep. I think he is going to help us.'

She rose stiffly and gave him the last of the pie. While he ate, she washed and packed her few belongings. That done, she shook her guest. 'Wake up, Mr Carter, wake up.'

He grunted and opened one eye, then the other. It was broad day, the light was hurting his eyes and his head ached abominably. He blinked hard and sat up, groaning. 'God in heaven, where am I?'

'Don't you remember? You insisted on coming home with me.'

'Did I?' He looked round the poky little room and then at her, as if seeing her for the first time. 'How did I get here?'

She smiled. 'You were looking for a clean woman and you found me.'

'Oh. Did I ...? Did we ... ?'

She smiled. 'No, but we came to a business arrangement. Have you forgotten?'

He ran his fingers through his thin gingery hair and shook his head. 'I must have.'

She put a cup of tea into his hand. 'Drink this, it will refresh you. I am going down to settle with Mrs Grainger and then I'll be ready to leave. There's hot water in the kettle if you want to wash while I'm gone.'

'Leave? Where to?'

'Wherever you wish to take me.' To Jason she said, 'Stay there with Mr Carter, darling. I won't be long.' She went out, leaving man and boy looking at each other with equal curiosity.

What did she mean? Why the devil couldn't he remember? Where exactly was he? What business arrangement? Was she a whore or wasn't she? He looked at the boy, wondering what had happened to his father. 'How old are you, son?'

'I'll soon be six. I can read and write my name and count.'

'Can you, now? Shillings and pence?'

''Course. Four farthings make a penny and twelve pennies a shilling and twenty-one shillings a guinea and a guinea is an awful lot of money.'

'Who taught you that?'

'Me mam.' He was very proud of his mother. 'Me mam is a cook.'

Yes, he remembered it had something to do with cooking. 'Where has she been a cook?'

'At a big hotel.'

Henry could not remember her telling him that, but other things were slowly returning to his memory. Her landlady had turned her out, he recalled. Had that been his fault? Was she expecting him to give her a home? Had he agreed? He must have done or she would not be packed and ready to leave. His housekeeper? Did he need a housekeeper? His mistress? God, that was impossible! He looked at the boy and smiled uncertainly; whatever they had arranged, would have to be unarranged. 'How long have you been in London?'

'Oh, ages.' Time meant very little to Jason. 'We came on a train.'

'And before that?'

'Hailey Common and . . . and Chevington.' He added the last because his mother had gone on about it when they had been on the tramp.

Henry Carter knew that name and he supposed Sarah Jane had worked in the kitchens at Chevington House. It was a fair recommendation because His Lordship was known to keep a good table, and the information, coming from the child, must be the truth.

Sarah Jane returned. The effort of running up the stairs had made her breathless and her cheeks pink, and Henry became aware of her as a beautiful woman and not the common whore he had taken her for; she outshone her drab surroundings like a diamond in a sack of dust. She could almost make him forget . . . he shrugged the thought from him. 'Tell me, Mrs McBryde,' he said, standing up so that he did not have to look up at her; he had to assert himself, though his head throbbed. 'Just exactly what was our business arrangement? The details escape me.'

'Why, that you would back me in a cookshop venture, you to supply the money to start it and I to supply the expertise to run it.'

The relief was so great it put him off his guard. He smiled. 'How did you convince me?'

She laughed. 'By giving you a sample of my wares. You agreed the pie was best you had ever tasted.'

'Did I?' He must have been more drunk than he realised. 'And the apportionment of profits?'

She paused, not wanting to stretch his forgetfulness too far. 'We did not finalise that, sir.'

'But I definitely agreed? You're not pulling the wool over my eyes?'

Now was not the time for hesitation; she could not give him time to change his mind. She smiled. 'Of course you agreed.'

What had he let himself in for? He opened his mouth to tell her the whole idea was ridiculous, but her bright eyes and smiling lips had him mesmerised. He found he could not utter the words, could not turn his back on her. If he had raised her hopes, drunk or not, he could not dash them now. Later, when his head no longer throbbed and he could think of a way of doing it without upsetting her, he would tell her how impossible it was. Why was he so reluctant to upset her? He suddenly realised he was returning her smile with every appearance of cheerful acquiescence. 'Then are you ready?'

'As ready as I'll ever be.'

He turned to pick up the pitiful bundle she had collected together. 'Is this all you've got?'

'I like to travel light.' She took Jason by the hand to lead the way downstairs, trying to still the swift beating of her heart, to stifle the joyous cry, 'We're on our way! Jason, Billie, we're on our way!'

Neither of them had money for a cab and he would not demean himself by walking through the streets with her in broad daylight, so he borrowed from Mrs Grainger, leaving his watch as security. 'I am temporarily embarrassed,' he told the landlady, 'but as soon as I can get to my bank, I will send a servant to redeem my timepiece.' When the cash had changed hands, he sent Jason running to fetch a hansom.

Once inside he sat back and looked Sarah Jane up and down. Her worn grey skirt was clean but that was about all that could be said for it. He could not be seen to associate with anyone so poorly clad; he had to consider his reputation as a costumier. He sighed. This was going to turn out to be a hideously expensive undertaking. He must be mad. 'You must have decent clothes if you are to go into business,' he said. 'It's important to create the right impression, don't you agree?'

She was suddenly reminded of Timothy, stripping off his clothes by the river bank, telling her that clothes did not make a gentleman. What a long time ago that had been and how innocent and childishly happy she had been. She smiled. 'Oh, absolutely, but I shall consider the clothes part of the business arrangement and repay you.'

That, at least, was a relief. 'And we shall have to see my banker. I shall need his advice.'

The banker could be a stumbling block, she realised, and she would need all her poise, all her powers of persuasion to convince him that the idea was a good one. She smiled. 'I think the clothes first, don't you?'

'Yes.' He felt utterly helpless. If Ellen were at home, he could have asked her advice. He brought himself up short; he had never asked Ellen's opinion about anything to do with business, so why did he think he should start now? Because Mrs McBryde was a woman? He looked across at her. She was sitting there, beside her ragamuffin son, for all the world as if she were an aristocrat whom he could not afford to offend. He swore he would never touch another drop.

The cab drew up outside a shop in Bond Street. The cabbie let down the step and touched his cap, something which was new to Sarah Jane, but which she decided she could easily grow used to. She stepped down and looked up at the blue and gold facia. 'Carter & Son, Drapers and Milliners,' she read aloud. The window display was dazzling, with yards and yards of colourful silks and satins draped over rails, stands of beautiful hats trimmed with silk and feathers and, on the carpeted floor, delicate shoes and fine kid gloves.

A commissionaire held the door open for them; if he noticed his employer had not shaved and looked as though he had slept in his clothes, he did not show it. 'Good morning, Mr Carter.'

Henry sailed past, hardly sparing him a glance. Sarah Jane straightened her back, lifted her chin and, clutching Jason by the hand, followed.

He took her past the sales floors and up the stairs to his office, where he shouted to a clerk to fetch Mrs Golding. Sarah Jane stood just inside the door, while he paced up and down, his hands clasped behind him under his tails and his head sunk on his chest. She dare not give him time for regrets. 'You will be able to provide all the furniture and equipment at cost, won't you?' she said. 'We ought to put together some figures for your financial advisers. We must be able to demonstrate that the venture will be profitable.'

'It had better be,' he grunted. 'I am not in the habit of laying out good money without a rock solid return.'

'You shall have it. If I make a list of what I'll need, will you cost it out? Then we can discuss it before we go to the bank.'

'Later, later,' he said, then, in answer to a knock on the door, 'Come in.'

Sarah Jane turned to face the woman who entered. She was big and raw-boned and dressed in black. A tape measure hung round her neck. 'You wanted to see me, sir? If it's about Mrs Townsend's dinner gown ...'

'No, it isn't. I leave that sort of thing to you. I want you to take Mrs McBryde and fit her up with whatever she needs – a good afternoon gown, a coat and hat and gloves.' He looked down at Sarah Jane's worn boots. 'And a decent pair of shoes. In fact, everything she needs to be seen in respectable circles.' He saw the woman's dark eyes widen. 'This is a business arrangement and there is no need to prattle of it to anyone else.'

'I wouldn't dream of it, sir,' she said, with perfect truth. 'I would not last long in my profession, if I could not be discreet.'

He turned from her to address Sarah Jane. 'I am going home to Islington to shave and change. I shall return at noon. Be ready.'

And she was. Carter's had a selection of ready-to-wear gowns and she chose a light brown day gown, with rows of darker brown braid, with a deep cream lace collar and cream lace undersleeves, over which she wore a three-quarter-length coat in brown merino wool. The effect she wanted was to look quietly elegant. Her coppery hair, washed and dressed by a fashionable hairdresser who had an establishment just down the street, could not be subdued, but, she decided, she needed that little vanity to make her stand out. Bankers, men with shops to let, butchers, grocers, must notice her and want to please her. And she knew how to please them. Flattery and good food, you couldn't go wrong with those.

Henry was pleasantly surprised by the transformation. He was very elegant himself in a fawn frockcoat, with darker velvet lapels, though his visit to his home, without his wife there to greet him, had made him morose; he was not in the mood to pay compliments. He simply said, 'You'll do,' and bundled her into another cab, leaving Jason in the care of one of the assistants.

William Langford, manager of one of the most prestigious banks in the City, knew Henry well and was only too pleased to listen to his ideas, and though he might wonder why the lady had come with him, he treated Sarah Jane with courtesy, finding her a chair, so that she might listen but not take part in the conversation. She did interrupt once, which made him open his eyes in surprise while Henry quelled her with a look, making her fall silent in the middle of a sentence; women did not take part in business discussions, it said. Sarah Jane was immensely relieved when Mr Langford stood up and held out his hand. 'With you in control, Mr Carter, I am confident the venture will be a success.'

Henry thanked him and shook his hand, bemused by the speed with which events had overtaken him. Sarah Jane, getting to her feet, treated the banker to a dazzling smile before following her saviour from the room, leaving him almost as hypnotised as Henry.

The estate agent they visited next hid his elation that someone should want to look at premises near railways and sent them to a property close to where they were building the new terminus. It was here the big railway companies, like the *London and Birmingham* and the *Great Northern*, were extending their lines further into the city and converging in a tangle of lines. Here was a land laid to waste; buildings shored up with beams, market gardens overgrown, streets torn up, water-filled holes, and all in the name of progress. The navvies were busy, but the crock they shifted was more rubble than earth and they seemed out of place working in their traditional way while the traffic of a busy city clattered past them.

'You'll never keep the place clean,' Henry said, looking at the thick layer of dust on the floor of the shop.

'Yes, I will, and it has to be near the works. I doubt if the navvies are made to use tommy shops in London – it's not like the country where there is no alternative. They'll come in for my pies, and they'll pay for them. If not, I might be prepared to take their tommy tickets.'

'Tommy tickets? You didn't say anything about tommy tickets when we were talking to my banker, did you?'

She forebore to remind him that he had not allowed her to speak. 'You deal in credit, don't you?'

'Yes, but you can hardly compare my clients with ... with ... ' He pointed to the other side of the road where a gang of navvies was tearing up the cobblestones ... those.'

Sarah Jane wandered round, examining windows and doors, inspecting the drains and poking about in the kitchen, while the owner hovered anxiously. He wanted the place off his hands, before anyone heard the railways wanted it.

'How much do you want for the lease?' Henry asked.

'It isn't the lease we're after,' Sarah Jane said. 'We want the freehold.'

Henry shot her a disapproving look, excused himself and drew her out of earshot. 'Are you mad?' he hissed.

'I'll wager we can get it cheap,' she whispered. 'In its present vacant and dilapidated state, it will be worth very little in compensation from the railway companies.'

'All the more reason to keep our hands in our pockets.'

'All the more reason to buy,' she said. 'Railways consume land, you know. They begin by taking the minimum because, like everyone else, they have to watch finance. They have to be more careful than most because of the time it takes before the lines are in operation and bringing in revenue, but as the work progresses, they find they need space for locomotive sheds and shunting areas, repair shops and coal bunkers, and they want them as near the terminus as possible. Whoever owns the land must be bought out and compensated. If we make it into a thriving business, we'll be sitting on ... ' She was about to say 'a fortune', but realising it would not be a fortune to him, changed it to 'a good investment'. 'It won't break you to speculate a couple of hundred, will it?' She smiled. 'I'll wager you've gambled more than that before.'

He laughed. 'And lost.'

'You won't lose this one.'

He looked hard at her, trying to size her up, and failing. She was standing straight, arguing with him, like a man, and just as determined. Did she know what she was talking about? He was far from sure, but those huge green eyes had paralysed his senses. Besides, he still had a headache and he had spent so much energy worrying about his wife and imagining her in the arms of her lover, he was worn out. He capitulated, and once the sale had been agreed, gave Sarah Jane a letter of credit to take to his stores in order to furnish and equip the place, plus a few guineas in cash for incidentals. Then he went off on his own, determined to find his wife, leaving his new partner, who had agreed to hand over sixty per cent of the profits, to do almost as she pleased.

By evening, Sarah Jane was in a seventh heaven of delight at what she had accomplished, but quaking at the enormity of what she had taken on. It was almost twenty-four hours since she had first met Henry, twenty-four of the busiest and most productive hours of her life. She had seen the most important items of equipment and furniture installed and then fetched Jason, put him to bed and set about arranging everything to her liking.

When Henry arrived next day, he found her, dressed in her old clothes, already at work in the kitchen, her arms up to the elbows in flour and a saucepan of meat and gravy bubbling on her new stove. Jason sat on a stool in the corner of the room, giggling aloud as he read Edward Lear's *Book of Nonsense* which she had bought from a second-hand book stall.

'I've sent for a signwriter,' he said. 'He'll be here directly.'

'*Carter's*?' she queried, knowing the answer.

'Yes.'

'Could we not have in small letters underneath, *Proprietors, Carter & Winterday*?' It was not that she wanted to deny Duncan's name, far from it, but if Billie saw the nameboard, he might be curious enough to come in.

'Oh, very well.' He had not slept and his efforts to find his wife had been fruitless; he had no energy for arguing.

They were interrupted by the arrival of a messenger with a parcel. Sarah Jane wiped her hands and went to her newly acquired cash box, where there was just enough to pay him, then she tore open the parcel, extracted a large sheet of paper and handed it to Henry.

CARTER'S PIES it said in large capitals and underneath in smaller letters: *Quality meat pies and fruit pies, baked daily by cook of national renown on premises at King's Cross. Opening in the forenoon of February 6th. Free to first twenty customers. Half price for the remainder of the day. Come and try.*

'Free!' Henry nearly exploded. 'Twenty free and goodness knows how many at half price? You'll ruin us!'

'The best advertising we have is our merchandise,' she said calmly. 'We'll let the pies do the work for us.'

'And what about our profit? You can't make a profit on half price.'

'Oh, Henry, it's only for one day.' She pulled the rest of the brown paper from the parcel and picked up a handful of the leaflets. 'Jason, I want you to run over to the workmen and give everyone you see one of these. Give them to passers-by too. And when you have used them up, come back for more.'

The child took a bundle under his arm and ran from the shop. Sarah

Jane returned to her pastry. She had to appear outwardly calm and confident; Henry must not see how nervous she was, how afraid of failure. He could only be carried along while he believed she knew what she was doing, and she wished he would not stand there, watching her as if he were watching gold coins trickling down a drain. She smiled at him. 'This is only the beginning, Henry. We'll grow and I shall soon need help, and then we'll open another shop and then another. Wherever there are navvies and builders, there are customers.'

Half an hour later, a group of workmen crossed the road towards the shop, each anxious to be one of the first twenty. They crowded in, jostling each other and clamouring for pies, and Sarah Jane laughed. Enjoying herself hugely, she put pies into paper bags and handed them to her customers, leaving Henry to take their money. By eight o'clock that evening, they had sold two hundred pies, besides the twenty they had given away, and she was tired, but satisfied. Henry took off the long white apron he had been wearing and rolled down his sleeves. 'I could do with a drink,' he said, forgetting his vow never to touch another drop.

'I thought you might. There's a bottle upstairs. Come up and have a glass while I put Jason to bed.'

He followed her and made himself comfortable in one of the chairs she had purchased from his emporium, while she put her son to bed. 'I don't know how you can keep going all day and still look so bright and chirpy,' he said when she returned.

'I'm used to it.' She poured him a large glass of brandy. 'Did you find your wife?'

'No.'

'What are you going to do about it?' She looked down at him, twisting the stem of his glass in pudgy fingers; he did not look like a man who had sex on his mind and she had no intention of mentioning it if he didn't. One day, she supposed, he would demand his payment, just as Charlie Bender had done, but now there was no Duncan to be hurt about it.

'I don't know. I've been so busy today ... '

She laughed, determined to keep things on a business footing as long as possible. 'I'll wager you never expected to be serving in a pie shop, not even yesterday when we began this venture. It wasn't so bad, was it?'

'Let's just say it was an experience I shall never forget and never repeat. If you want help, hire someone.'

Sarah Jane smiled and sipped her drink. Things were going nicely to plan. The first of her priorities had been met, she had a job and a home, now all she had to do was find Billie. Later they would buy Henry out – his heart wasn't really in it – and become *McBryde & Winterday*.

Chapter Fifteen

*W*henever she could find the time, Sarah Jane pursued her enquiries for her brother. She sent for unnecessary chimney sweeps in order to question them, but none would admit to using climbing boys and most became very indignant when she suggested such a thing. In any case, it was a forlorn hope; Billie would have grown too big for climbing years before. The idea that he could be in a workhouse she dismissed; he would have been sent back to Chevington, his official 'place of settlement' if he had gone to one and, like her, she was sure he would not even have considered it. She took out several advertisements in newspapers and offered a reward for information leading to his whereabouts, but nothing came of them, and she began to wonder if he were in London at all.

She had no idea where to look next and by now was too firmly established on her chosen path to uproot herself. Billie might find her, she told herself, especially if her pie shops became famous. He would walk in one day and say, 'Here I am.' She often dreamed of it, planned what she would do for him, because now there was much she could do.

Her partnership with Henry Carter had been more successful than she had ever dared to hope. The profit they had made on the compulsory sale of the King's Cross shop had amply compensated for its loss and enabled them to acquire more shops and, more recently, an eating house in Oxford Street, which was a class above their other establishments and served all kinds of cooked food, besides pies. Here they did very good business serving the workers who were building the Great Exhibition hall in Hyde Park. She had moved into the apartment above this shop which was far superior to the one at King's Cross and allowed her to indulge her taste in good furnishings and to employ a live-in maid. Betsy had thin, gingery hair and a pasty complexion, but that was hardly to be wondered at; the girl had been recruited from among the scavenging urchins of Covent Garden, much to Henry's disgust.

Sarah Jane still worked from dawn until well into the evening hours and had little time for leisure. What she had, she spent in reading, particularly *The London Gazette* because that published all the proposals for new railway lines, and she wanted to keep herself up to date on what was happening in the world of the navvy. It was in this newspaper that she read the report of the enquiry into the Hailey Common disaster.

The enquiry had established the sequence of events which led up to the explosion, and while none of the navvies should have been in the tunnel at the time, it was found that Duncan McBryde's actions had been heroic rather than culpable. It was, the report concluded, a tragic accident and it had been decided to pay Mrs McBryde some compensation for her loss. The paper asked her, or anyone who knew her whereabouts, to contact the railway company. The report went on to give a summary of the latest survey of the site, the outcome of which was that the line was unlikely to be finished on the original route and choosing another at this late stage might prove too costly.

Sarah Jane was relieved; she didn't want Duncan's remains disturbed and hated the thought of boots tramping over his grave, shiny steel lines running over his bones. She wanted nothing to do with the compensation either. If she had read that report when living at Mrs Grainger's and at her wits' end trying to make ends meet, she might have been tempted but now she was glad the enquiry had taken so long. Still a little afraid of losing her son, though she knew it was illogical, she did not want the railway company to know where she was. She was not ready to meet Timothy Myson again; she could not yet call herself his equal, but one day she would. Before long she would be able to look him in the eye and that humiliating meeting among the ruins at Hailey Common would be expunged from her memory. It was also the reason why she had not written to Thomas Wistonby.

Apart from her business, Jason was her whole life, the reason for her endeavours, the source of her inspiration, the embodiment of her hopes and dreams. If he were to be taken from her, she would lie down and die; there would be no reason not to. He was growing into a fine boy; he had blond curls like Billie at the same age, and his dark eyes were a constant reminder of Timothy, but he had a character all his own – sturdy, sometimes wilful, always lovable. He attended a private school, where he was good at his lessons, and she was very proud of him. The only cloud on his horizon was his lack of a papa. His teachers had been told his father had died in an accident, and this inclined them to make allowances for his general disregard of the social graces and an inclination to fight with his fists for anything he wanted. Henry said she was too soft with him and spoiled him. But why shouldn't she, when she could afford to give him the best?

She still dressed very simply, but the clothes she wore were of the highest quality, made for her at *Carter's* by Mrs Golding's best seamstress. And her hair, more magnificent than ever, was dressed by a hairdresser who came to her apartment twice a week. She rode in cabs and tipped the drivers generously and occasionally went to the theatre with Henry, though the visit usually made him morose because it reminded him of his wife's lover. Not that he knew where either of them were; it seemed they had left the country and he had been forced to accept her desertion as irrevocable. Sarah Jane felt sorry for him, but she did not love him and she was glad that he had asked nothing from her except continuing profits; money was his god and she was glad to be able to give it to him.

'Just because you were right and we made a good profit on the King's Cross shop, does not mean you are right about everything,' he said, one evening towards the end of 1850, after she had shut the Oxford Street shop and they had gone up to her comfortable sitting room. He often came to supper with her there, being too fond of her cooking for his own good, and also glad of her company.

'Good?' she queried with a smile. 'I should say two hundred per cent was more than good. If we had only taken the tenancy, we would have been given notice by the landlord and he would have benefited from the compulsory purchase, not us, but as we had the freehold and a good business into the bargain, it was only a matter of holding out for the best price.' She still had a bewitching smile and, even more, knew how to use it to her advantage.

He conveyed a forkful of rump steak in oyster sauce to his mouth and did not answer. His behaviour on the night Ellen had left him had been so out of character, that he could not afterwards explain what had come over him. He had never been that drunk in his life before, and he had certainly never contemplated going to a whore. It was, he told himself, because of his extreme grief, his hatred of the man who had taken his wife and son, his loneliness. But even so there had been no need to compound his foolishness by going into that dreadful house in Denmark Place and allowing himself to be bullied into a partnership he had not sought and did not want. His shops, built on the solid

233

foundations his father had bequeathed him, did well; there was no need to speculate on something for which he was not suited. So, why did he continue to allow Sarah Jane to dictate to him?

He was not a philanthropist; he had not felt sorry for her in the beginning and he certainly did not feel sorry for her now. Oh, he admired her and if it had not been for her pushing, he would have sunk into the mire of self-pity long ago. Perhaps that was the answer; she kept his fighting spirit alive, if only to do battle with her. And battle they did, over everything – the sites they chose, the staff they employed, the butcher's bill, the prices they charged, and her latest idea, which had nothing to do with cookshops, but the starting of a school.

'There are plenty of ragged schools,' he said.

'Those! All they do is keep the children off the streets while their mothers are at work. The knowledge they impart could be written on a single sheet of paper. I mean to educate the children properly.'

She had a comfortable home and money in the bank, and Jason was learning a great deal more at school than she could ever teach him, and that made her more determined than ever to do something for the navvy children. She had made a success of her life, if material possessions measured success, but her single-minded quest for money and status had put her in danger of becoming cold and calculating. She needed to give something of herself, to redeem herself in her own eyes, and the school idea would go some way towards it.

She had a vision, not of a single classroom which was what she was arguing with Henry about, but of a chain of schools right across the country, schools she would call the *Duncan McBryde Memorial Schools*. They would be clean and bright, well-furnished and equipped and, most important of all, they would have the very best teachers. Out of the unpromising material of a navvy child might come a prime minister, a great soldier, a famous musician, a fine writer who would be able to put into words the hopes and aspirations of that rough, tough and close-knit band of men and women.

'You?' He felt his anger rising. 'You have more than enough to do cooking pies.'

She rang for Betsy to come and clear the plates and bring in the pudding. 'I have not cooked a pie, except for your supper, for months now.'

He rarely visited the shops during opening hours but if he had stopped to think, he must have known she could not supply three of them single-handedly. 'But you must supervise those who do.'

'Of course, but I have trained them well. I can be spared for an hour or two each day.'

'Schoolrooms were not part of our agreement.'

'Our agreement was that I would run the business and that I am doing, and doing well,' she said, serving him with a lemon-flavoured cream dessert whose sharpness contrasted well with the richness of the oyster sauce. 'Have you any complaints?'

He smiled; she was at it again, bullying him. 'No, my dear, no complaints now, but I may have in the future, if you neglect the shops.'

'Poof,' she said. 'I can run them on my head.'

'As I said before, modesty is not one of your virtues.'

'How else am I to get my own way? All I want is a room or two, near a navvy site.'

'I have no doubt you have already chosen somewhere.'

'Not exactly, though I know the area – somewhere between Chalk Farm and the Caledonian Road, preferably near where the *Great Northern* crosses the *London and Birmingham*. There are a lot of men working there and many of them have families.'

'But that's a slum.'

'If railways are obliged to buy the freehold of anything lying in their path, then it stands to reason they will choose to go through slums. The children there are no less in need of education than anywhere else, and it need not make a loss ...'

He sighed. 'Are you trying to persuade me there is a financial advantage?'

She laughed and refilled his empty wine glass; if he chose to think that, then so be it, her motives were her own. 'It is the only argument you have ever listened to. It is the only thing that keeps us together, isn't it?'

'Is it? I do not know.'

'What else is there? You are not in love with me, are you?'

He looked at her as if considering the question seriously. 'What is love? Something you give or throw away, or something extracted from you, which is it?' He sounded bitter.

'Something you give,' she said firmly. 'It is never thrown away and cannot be extracted if you are not willing. Neither can it be easily withdrawn.'

'That is a romanticism which is out of character coming from someone like you, Sarah Jane. It makes me feel uncomfortable.'

She laughed. 'Why? Have I ever asked you for love? Did you think I might?'

'No,' he said slowly. 'I don't think so.'

'Then what are we talking about?'

'Why we remain in partnership.'

'Do you want to dissolve it?' She hoped not; she still needed him to deal with prejudiced men who would not do business with a woman.

'No,' he said. 'I should miss you, if we parted. I should miss our daily battles.'

'Wouldn't you also miss that little bag of money I bring to Bond Street every week?'

'That too, but I am also aware that it could all disappear like a puff of smoke, if we are not careful.'

'You are always careful, Henry, but you are also clever and you would not allow me to sway you against your better judgement. Oh, I know you throw your hands up in horror whenever I suggest making some trifling outlay, but that is only to keep me in my place and show yourself my master. Now, admit it.'

Her flattery brought forth a grudging assent. 'So, tell me, what have I to gain by going along with this school idea?'

'Investment in property, rents and resale value. You may not think so now, but it will soon be seen as an advantage to live close to a railway line.'

'Pie in the sky.'

'No, it isn't. I'm prepared to put in what I've saved, if you make up the rest.'

'And how much have you saved?'

'About three thousand.' She was amazed how easily the figure tripped off her tongue, as if it were of no consequence and did not represent nearly two years of unremitting toil. 'Oh, I know it's not much compared with what you have, but if you only take the profits from the cookshop business, you must have made a like amount. Five thousand could buy a whole terrace of small houses. I'll take one for a school and you could have the rents for the rest. What do you say?'

'I'll have to sleep on it.'

She laughed. 'Like you did before? You're welcome, you know.'

He wiped his mouth on his napkin and stood up. 'No, my dear, I think my lonely bed at home would be wisest. We may have established I am not in love with you, but I am a man for all that. I could not answer for the consequences if I stayed. Besides, it would not look well if my driver is left dozing outside in my carriage all night.'

Sarah Jane knew that her neighbours had already noted that Henry's barouche stood outside until very late on many an evening, but she saw no reason to inform him of what his common sense should already have told him. 'Sleep on it, Henry, and tomorrow I'll come to your office for your decision.' She reached up to kiss his cheek. It was no more than a sisterly peck, but it illustrated their relationship and both understood it.

Before going to bed, she looked in at Jason. He slept the sleep of the innocent, his curly head tousled on the pillow, one arm flung out on the counterpane and the other clutching a toy train; he loved trains and anything to do with railways. She smiled and stooped to kiss his cheek before going to her own room. She had thought she was content, but talking to Henry about love had unsettled her.

Sometimes, in the early hours, when she stirred in a bed more comfortable than she had ever known, she was aware of an aching loneliness, the emptiness of a life without love, the longing for physical contact with someone whose need was as great as hers. Oh, she adored Jason; he was her reason for living, the impetus behind her every move, and without him, she would wither away, but that was not the same as having a man to love, of being loved and caressed, of having her body aroused to consummate passion. But perhaps passion was dead – perhaps she would never feel it again. The prospect of that depressed her. With Duncan, she had felt warm. Through the bitterest winter, when she did not even have a good coat, she had been warm in his love, and yet now, when she had a wardrobe full of clothes, a fire in every room and as many blankets as she needed on her bed, she felt cold. No one could replace Duncan in her heart, but she could not mourn him forever; he would not have wished her to but, apart from Henry, there was no one. Sometimes, like tonight when they had been talking of it, she was almost reduced to trying to seduce Henry, just to see if she could rouse him, but she was afraid it would not satisfy her craving and would certainly alter their relationship and that, she told herself sternly, would be foolish. But it was hardly flattering that he preferred his own bed. 'Stupid, weak woman,' she told herself, thumping her pillow. 'Go to sleep, you have work to do tomorrow.'

The next morning, she went down to the shop and supervised the beginning of the day's baking, then took a cab to the King's Cross shop which was opening for the last time before it was vacated and reduced to rubble. It made her a little sad, but she had no time for nostalgia. From there she went to their establishment at Covent Garden and set to rights an argument between the pastrycook and the butcher, after which she left for Bond Street.

When she arrived, Henry dismissed his clerk and taking her coat, invited her to sit down.

'Did you sleep well?' she asked, with that mischievous smile which always managed to captivate him.

'Thanks to you, no.'

'Oh dear. Perhaps you should have stayed with me, after all. I could have ...'

'... made me forget myself long enough to agree to your impossible plans,' he finished for her. 'When I am with you, I find myself agreeing to things which in my saner moments I would never contemplate.' He moved restlessly about the room. 'But not this time. I am advised that buying property so close to railways is not good business sense. The trains shake the foundations and render the buildings unsafe. We would find ourselves spending a fortune on repairs.'

'We can find somewhere far enough away for that not to happen.'

'If we do that, we will lose the advantage of buying cheaply.'

'You mean you are afraid to gamble.'

'Yes, when I am bound to lose.'

'I'll do it alone, then.'

'How? You are a woman – no one will do business with you.'

'I managed to persuade you.'

'That was different. You caught me in a weak moment.'

She laughed. 'And you have never regretted it.' She paused. 'Henry, I want to do this so much. I've had a great deal of good luck, meeting you and being able to put my talents to use, and I am very grateful to you, but I want more than that, I want to do something for those less fortunate.' She stood up and went to stand beside him, putting her gloved hand on his arm. 'Please take time to think about it again.'

He did not want to look into her eyes, because to do so would weaken him; he gazed steadfastly out of the window onto the busy street below him. Lady Hailey was being handed out of her carriage by the doorman. If, because of ill-considered speculation, his business went downhill and he lost customers like the Haileys, the Chevingtons and the Townsends, he would have nothing to live for; his shops had always been his life, but more so now that he was obliged to lead a bachelor existence.

'You will not make me change my mind, Sarah Jane. Now, let us talk of other things. Did you go to King's Cross?'

'Yes.' She knew it would be unwise to say anything more for the time being, so she sat down in the leather chair opposite his desk and put her mind to discussing the redeployment of the staff from the King's Cross shop.

If he would not help her, then she would have to find someone who would. In her contrary way, the fact that he had turned her down made her all the more determined to succeed. It was as if obstacles were put in her path in order to test her mettle, that the measure of her success was in direct proportion to the height of the mountain she had to climb. Until she had begun her enterprise with Henry, she had not been aware of the truth of that, but as each new challenge had been faced and met, she realised there was nothing she could not do if she put her unflagging energy into it.

They spoke of business matters for the next half hour and then she left him to go and see Mrs Golding about the winter coat she had ordered for Jason. The dressmaking department was fronted by a sitting area with comfortable chairs and low tables scattered with periodicals, potted plants and ornaments. Here, the clients were served with tea, while they discussed their requirements and looked at pictures and samples made up in cambric. Mrs Golding, holding a box containing rolls of ribbon and lace, was listening to a young lady customer who was evidently being hard to please. A length of heavy cream satin was draped across a chair, another of white silk was spread across a table and there were patterns heaped everywhere. An older woman, evidently the young lady's mother, was fingering an ermine tail. Sarah Jane paused in the doorway.

'I think the oyster satin,' the girl said. 'Let me look at it again.' She turned towards the bolt of cloth and in so doing, faced Sarah Jane.

The two young women stood for a moment looking at each other, both trying to remember where they had met before, and aware that it had some significance. It took Sarah Jane only a moment to recall the incident, but Caroline was still groping in her memory long after Sarah Jane had acknowledged her with a slight inclination of the head, spoken swiftly to Mrs Golding and left.

Sarah Jane was in no doubt that this young lady was the one who had called Timothy 'darling', and that she was about to become his bride. It amused her to think that, even though the girl had half-recognised her, she had not connected the self-assured, immaculately dressed woman, who spoke with such authority to the dressmaker, with the grubby navvy wife at Hailey Common. I wonder how long it will be before it comes to her in a blinding flash who I am, she thought, as she made her way back to her cab. And I wonder if she will mention it to Timothy.

The dinner party at Lord Chevington's London house was a small one. Besides Timothy, there was His Lordship, Lady Hailey and Caroline, and the occasion was the visit of Caroline and her mama to London to choose a wedding dress and trousseau. The engagement had been a protracted one because Lady Hailey had insisted on her elder daughter being married before the younger, and that wedding had only recently taken place, but now the date was fixed for Boxing Day and preparations were well in hand. Lord Hailey, who had not been well, had excused himself from what he considered the business of the ladies, and had remained at his country home.

'Oh, you will like it, Timothy,' Caroline enthused, speaking of the wedding gown. 'But of course you must not see it until the day. Oh, I can't wait! Papa has promised a banquet – five hundred guests . . .'

'Do we need so many?' Timothy demurred, because he guessed it was expected of all bridegrooms, but in truth, he was pleased. The thought that anyone who was anyone would be at his wedding strengthened his bid to be recognised as a gentleman of substance; Lord Hailey would not go to such expense for a mere nobody. 'I'd as soon it was a quiet affair.'

'Oh, but it is such an important day and we mustn't disappoint all our friends.' She contrived to put a hand on his thigh beneath the tablecloth and give it a squeeze. Ever since he had first seduced her on the moors above Hailey Common, she had used all kinds of pretext to be alone with him; her sexual appetite was insatiable, but she was always passive, lying immobile beneath him while he worked himself to a climax. She never gave of herself and he was never satisfied. And she was blissfully unaware of it.

He smiled easily. 'Have your grand wedding, my dear, and I will fall in with whatever plans you make.'

'I'm going to have the most heavenly outfit to travel in, pink with silk rosebuds round the skirt, and a matching bonnet with roses under the brim. And because it will be winter, I'm having a fur cape made, trimmed with ermine. *Carter's* are going to make everything; they have such a fine reputation, and everyone is so attentive. We spent nearly the whole morning at the Bond Street shop.'

'Did you, dear? How wearisome that must have been.'

'Not at all. I love choosing clothes, especially my wedding clothes.' She paused, racking her brains. 'Oh, I knew I had something to tell you that would amuse you. Do you remember the woman we saw at Hailey Common the day of the hunt? The one who was at the workings with the little boy after everyone had left. Well, I saw her today.'

'Woman?' queried Lord Chevington, when it appeared that Timothy was not going to reply. 'At Hailey Common?'

'Yes. What did she say her name was, Timothy?'

'Mrs McBryde,' he said flatly, offering no further information.

'The navvy's widow?' His Lordship queried.

'Yes, I believe so,' Caroline said.

'And you saw her today?'

She was puzzled; she had expected Timothy to take an interest, not His Lordship, and yet it was Lord Chevington who questioned her and Timothy who sat silently inspecting the contents of his wine glass, as if he could see pictures in the ruby liquid. 'Yes. At least I think it was her, though it was difficult to be sure.'

'Where did you see her?'

'At *Carter's*. And the astonishing thing is that she was dressed like a lady, very modish, and she spoke very refined. You'd never guess she was no more than a peasant ...'

'She spoke to you?' Timothy looked up from his contemplation at last.

'No. She spoke to Mrs Golding, said something about Jason's coat. That was one of the things which made me remember her, that funny name, and her hair. I have never seen such red hair in my life, positively vulgar, it is.'

Timothy allowed himself to dream a moment, to picture Sarah Jane as he had first known her, young, wild and free, for all she was a servant, and then as he had last seen her, with her child. Jason. Who had fathered that child? He smiled, remembering the protective way she had stood beside the boy with her hand on his shoulder, as if daring him to contradict her assertion that the child was the navvy's. He had no wish to do anything of the sort; she was part of the past and he wished she would not keep coming back into his life uninvited. She unsettled him when he needed to see the road ahead clearly.

'Do you know where she went after that?' His Lordship asked. 'You see, we have been trying to find her for months, to pay her the compensation we promised.'

'Compensation!' Caroline laughed. 'She did not look as though she needed that at all. I should say she was doing very nicely.'

'Did you see where she went?'

'No, I had no interest in her. If I had known you wanted to see her ...' She stopped, remembering Timothy's reaction when they had come upon her at the navvy site; it was rather like that now – preoccupied, as if there were no one else in the room. It made her shiver with apprehension.

'Would you like us to ask about her when we go back for a fitting?' Lady Hailey asked.

'Yes,' said Lord Chevington, and 'No,' said Timothy simultaneously.

'Why not?' His Lordship asked his son.

'Because if Caroline is correct, she would not want to be reminded of her impoverished days as a navvy wife. She was, if you remember, not legally married to the fellow and that would make her son a ...' He paused, not wanting to use the word in company and still only too aware of the fact that it applied to him too. 'He is a love-child.' That was better and it was true; he had loved Sarah Jane at the time, as far as he was able to indulge in that luxury. 'It seems that she has obviously found another man to support her.' The thought of Sarah Jane satisfying someone else's sexual hunger brought him up short. Who? That reprobate lawyer who had promised to bring her to the London office and never had, or someone with a little more substance, someone who could afford to dress her as a lady? Was she someone's mistress? Or even a high-class whore? Was his son being brought up by a whore? Why was he angry? Why was his heart thumping as if he had run a mile?

'Yes, perhaps you are right,' Geoffrey said. 'If she wants to, she can always come to us.'

Much to Timothy's relief the subject was dropped and they turned to discussing railways and the way they were all vying with each other to circle London and reach the docks. 'We can't afford to be left out of it,' Timothy said. If the Chevington lines were to have their share of the freight now being rushed from one end of the country to the other, then they must be able to load their wagons at the docks. It was not enough to pick up other companies' leavings en route. 'We need a junction with the *Great Eastern*.'

'And then what?' his father asked. 'We'd have to run to the docks on the same lines.'

'I believe the *Great Eastern* is somewhat strapped and would welcome an injection of capital in return for certain rights. We could run into their lines just north of the Caledonian Road.'

His Lordship smiled. 'And suppose their shareholders do not agree?'

'I've already spoken to some board members and they are open to negotiation. Besides ...' Timothy paused to sip his wine and then smiled slowly. 'For the last few weeks I have been busy buying up their shares. I am now a substantial shareholder myself.' His Lordship's expression of astonishment made him laugh and he added, 'Oh, do not worry, I have not invested Chevington money. This little enterprise is my own.'

'Oh, Timothy,' Caroline said. 'Isn't that risky?'

'Not at all,' he said, keeping the annoyance from his voice with an effort. Did she think he was a schoolboy who could do nothing without his guardian? 'I have been in the railway business long enough to know what I'm doing, believe me. Without speculation there is no gain. His Lordship will tell you that.' If he controlled the *East Fen*'s way to the docks, his father would have to negotiate with him for the rights to run on the lines from the Caledonian Road junction. To be able to dictate terms to his father was something he had long dreamed of, but if he had expected His Lordship to show any sort of agitation at the prospect he was mistaken.

Geoffrey smiled amiably and signalled to a servant to pour more wine. 'This is neither the time nor place to discuss business,' he said mildly. 'We will talk about it tomorrow.' He turned to Caroline. 'You were telling us about your shopping trip. What else did you buy at *Carter's?*'

Caroline set forth on a catalogue of her shopping but Timothy had ceased to listen. He looked at her in animated conversation with his father about nothing at all, but he did not see her. It was as if her face were overlaid with another; the golden head became the colour of an evening sunset, the blue eyes turned to green. It was unnerving, to say the least. Was he to be forever haunted by this phantom of his past? Perhaps if he met her as a women of means, a woman who did not need his pity or his money, perhaps then her spectre would go away and leave him to pursue the only goal he had in life – the acquisition of a title and land and the power that went with it.

While he had been forging a life for himself out of his bastardy, treading his chosen path without consideration for those who stood in his way, she had been at the back of his mind, forgotten, and yet not forgotten. Sitting in a brightly lit, overheated dining room, making polite conversation, he felt the sudden and urgent stirring of a passion in his loins which Caroline could never assuage.

Long after his bride-to-be and her mother had returned to their hotel, he was still thinking about those far-off days on the banks of a stream and his memories set his body on fire with anticipation. Before he married Caroline Hailey he would taste the pleasure of coupling with Sarah Jane once more. He would conquer his unruly desires by subduing her, making her want him as much as he wanted her, and then he would take her savagely; she would not be so proud then. Oh, the game would liven up many a dull day before the wedding. He could not sleep for thinking about it.

Carter's would not divulge the private address of a client, he knew that and, in any case, he would only draw attention to himself if he asked for her there and that was not a good idea. The next morning he sent for Thomas Wistonby, addressing his letter to Chevington Union and enclosing a guinea for the train fare. It was a long shot and he should not have been surprised when the lawyer arrived two days later and claimed no knowledge of Sarah Jane's whereabouts. He was irrationally disappointed just as he had been on that other occasion when neither lawyer nor Sarah Jane had turned up. 'But I thought you and she ...'

'That was a very long time ago, Mr Myson.' Thomas smiled. 'What she does with her life now is no concern of mine.'

'I want her found. She has been seen in *Carter's* in Bond Street. Apparently she is well-heeled enough to afford clothes from that establishment. Find her, but come and tell me before you speak to her. I don't want her running off again.'

'She may have married.'

'What difference does that make?'

'If she has found contentment should you not leave well alone? Her new husband might not understand ...'

Timothy looked hard at the lawyer, remembering that it was he who had taught Sarah Jane how to satisfy a man, how to make love; he had made her into the whore she was. 'Great Heavens, man, what do you think I am going to do to her? Run away with her? Rape her?'

'No,' Thomas said uncertainly.

'She has been awarded compensation for the loss of her husband, though the fact that she was ever married is debatable. All we want to do is to pay it to her.'

Thomas stood up to go. 'Very well, Mr Myson, but it might take a week or two and ...' He paused, spreading his empty hands. 'I have few resources.'

Timothy handed over five guineas, telling himself the man was a parasite and it was highly unlikely he had the smallest intention of looking for Sarah Jane or of divulging her whereabouts if he found her – not without more money. Just how much more of that was he prepared to lay out on a quest that was nothing more than curiosity to see how a servant girl had managed the metamorphosis from navvy wife to a woman who could afford to buy her clothes at *Carter's*? He smiled suddenly. How she had wanted to be a lady! Had she managed to achieve her ambition before he had accomplished his? He could almost hate her for that.

Thomas pocketed the money and left, but not to begin his quest. He did not need to; he knew perfectly well where Sarah Jane was, and he knew her circumstances down to the last farthing. What he did not know was how emotionally involved with Henry Carter she was, and until he did, he had no intention of imparting his knowledge to Timothy Myson.

He had confronted his sister about the missing letter the day after he had talked to Sarah Jane in the Jolly Brewers, and Elizabeth had admitted she had burned it. 'I did it for your sake,' she had said defensively. 'You were making a fool of yourself, pining for that green-eyed slut almost as much as you did for that simpering, extravagant wife you had. If I'd given it to you, you'd have gone off after her, wouldn't you?'

'And why not?'

'Why not indeed! I said at the time the girl was a whore and the letter proved it. No decent female would stoop to living with the navvies. Everyone knows they live like animals, preying on respectable girls, copulating like rabbits so that their shanty villages are overrun with little replicas of themselves. What would you have done – gone to live in squalor with them?'

'No, fetched her back.'

'Never! Not to this Union, brother! And I was right not to give it to you. You are better off without her, for hasn't Lady Chevington seen fit to notice you and find work for you? You should be grateful.'

He was grateful, but his gratitude was directed at Sarah Jane; it was Sarah Jane who had brought him out of his torpor and made him worthy of Lady Chevington's attention. It was Sarah Jane who had made him want to join the world again, and it was because of that he had been determined to keep his eye on her and protect her if he could.

As soon as he could get away from his work at the Union, he had gone to Denmark Place to see her, only to be told by Mrs Grainger that Sarah Jane had not only brought a man home one night but had gone off with him the next morning. She could tell him no more except the man had claimed to be a friend.

'Did she go with him willingly?'

'That she did. Cocky she was with it, too. He was well turned out, though he had no money on him, not a brass farthing. He had to borrow the price of a cab fare from me and left his gold hunter as security.'

'Did he return for it?'

'He sent a messenger for it that same day.' She had smiled. ' 'Twas a pity for it was worth a deal more than I lent him.'

Thomas had been concerned for Sarah Jane's welfare, but was unable to do anything about it then, because he had been obliged to go back to Chevington. He had returned a few weeks later, and taken a room at Mrs Grainger's with the intention of finding her.

The end of his search had come when he least expected it, late in the evening on a windy day in March when he had decided that the search was hopeless and he would have to give it up. He was walking to the Maiden Lane terminus to catch a *Northern Line* train back to Chevington, when a scrap of paper wrapped itself round his trouser leg and refused to be shaken off. He bent down to pluck it from his shoe and then noticed that it advertised the opening of a pie shop a month before. He had half an hour to spare and Elizabeth was unlikely to have saved any dinner for him, so he had gone the short distance out of his way, to sample the fare. Only when he glanced up at the blue and gold facia and saw the name Winterday, did he realise, with a growing feeling of excitement, that he might, just might, have reached the end of his quest.

Even then, he had not gone inside. The clean new shop with its smart facia seemed to indicate that she was doing well and perhaps would not welcome a reminder of the past.

Over the following months, he would return to the shop from time to time. He had watched and waited, had seen the business thrive, had seen Sarah Jane grow in poise and self-confidence, a vision of loveliness which tore at his heart, but he had never been close enough to see the emptiness in her eyes. He still lived at Chevington Union but he occasionally returned to Mrs Grainger's lodgings to reassure himself that all was well with her.

And now Timothy Myson had asked him to find her and he was in a dilemma. If the man was determined, he would find Sarah Jane whether he was helped or not. The time had come to go and see her.

Chapter Sixteen

Sarah Jane was delighted to see him, kissing him as one would a favourite uncle, with warm affection. She took his hat and coat and handed them to Betsy, bade him be seated and offered him refreshment.

He sat down and looked about the comfortably furnished room, watching her pouring wine, so poised, he could hardly believe she was the same girl he had known at Chevington Workhouse. She was wearing a wide-sleeved green silk crinoline with a pleated bodice and a row of tiny covered buttons down to the pointed waist. Her glorious red hair was coiled over her ears and caught up high at the back of her head. A small tendril had escaped at her neck, making him want to reach out and curl it round his finger.

'I've thought about you often,' she said, handing him a full glass. 'How are you? Still at Chevington Union?'

'Yes, I've nothing to complain of. No need to ask how you are, you look ravishing.'

She smiled. 'How did you find me?'

'You were hardly in hiding, my dear. Each new shop has the name Winterday written in larger and larger characters.'

'You know about the other shops?'

'I've known for months. And about Henry Carter.'

'He is my business partner.'

He looked at her with his head on one side, smiling. 'Nothing more?'

'No.'

'Why not?'

She shrugged and sipped her wine. 'We prefer it that way. And he is a married man.'

'But he comes here frequently and you spend time alone together.'

'Thomas, I hope you are not going to preach at me, because I would rather talk about other things. I have something I want to ask you.'

Because of Henry's refusal to participate in the schools project she had been obliged to scale down her plans. Instead of buying up a terrace of houses and relying on rents to recoup her investment, she would have to make do with a single building and finance it herself with her share of the profits from the shops. But she still needed help because it had not taken her long to discover that Henry had been right; no businessman would take her seriously. She had been at an immediate disadvantage, because she had to visit them in their mahogany-furnished, masculine offices, very different from the environment in which she had first won over Henry. They had been polite, of course, because she was obviously a lady of some substance; how little substance she never got around to telling them. But she would not be defeated; if no one would do business with a woman, then she would have to find another man, someone who understood about being poor and needing a little learning, someone who would take his lead from her. It was then she had thought of Thomas.

His name had come into her mind with a pang of guilt because he had asked her to keep in touch with him and she had not, but she knew he would help her if he could. It was not his money she wanted because she was fairly sure he had none, but he could act for her and negotiate the purchase of premises and see to the hundred and one legal details. She would pay him a fee, of course, and none of those supercilious so-called businessmen who had looked down on her from behind the armour of their desks need know they were dealing with someone from what they chose to call the frail sex.

'I'm all attention.' He leaned back in his chair and watched her. At first glance he thought she had changed almost beyond recognition. She had a quick way of moving as if she knew where she was going and could not wait to get there but, looking at her more closely, he realised that, under the veneer of respectability and prosperity, she was still the same girl, still Sarah Jane, still vulnerable, still a child at heart with a child's need to be nurtured and cherished, but she was also a woman, beautiful, generous, made to be loved. Who had that loving of her now, he wondered.

'Have something to eat first.' She did not wait for his reply, but went out to the kitchen and organised a meal, telling Betsy to serve it as soon as it was ready, then she returned and poured more wine for them both.

'I need your help,' she said slowly, handing him one of the glasses and sitting down opposite him with her own in her hand. 'In your professional capacity.'

'Oh.' What else had he expected? 'Don't you have lawyers to look after your legal affairs?'

'For the shops, yes. They are adequate for our day-to-day needs, but they are very stuffy and disinclined to take risks.' She laughed, tossing back her head and showing the long arch of her neck, encircled by a single rope of perfectly matched pearls. 'Sometimes I can persuade them to my way of thinking, but I'm afraid I failed this time.'

He chuckled, imagining her arguing with a room full of narrow-minded legal men. 'And you think I might be easier to manipulate?'

'I would not have to do any manipulating at all if men were not so bigoted,' she said. 'They think because I am a woman I don't know what I am talking about and insist on dealing with my "man of business". It infuriates me and then I find it difficult to be civil. I need an intermediary.'

The maid came to tell her the meal was ready and they went into the dining room where she told him of her plans for a navvy school while they ate. 'Henry thinks I'm crazy,' she said. 'And since he has washed his hands of the idea, I thought of you.'

'I expect he realises a school will not be as profitable as a pie shop.' Thomas smiled. 'And, like me, he would hate to see you lose all you have worked so hard for. Why not wait a little—'

'The navvies work hard, too, and their children need educating now, not in some distant future. Besides, even if I do lose my savings, I still have my business. It can be earned again.' She surprised herself with the calm way she contemplated that eventuality.

'Where do you want to have this school?'

'Near where they are building railways. The *London and Birmingham* and the *London and North Western* are desperate to take their lines to the docks but because they are forbidden to go south of King's Cross, they have been obliged to skirt round north London and join up with the *Great Eastern* and the *London and Blackwall*. The Islington to Bow section has already been opened but they are still working between Chalk Farm and the Caledonian Road and will be for some time. That is where I want my school.'

'How will you choose those who are to benefit from this education? Will you charge a fee?'

'Only to those who can afford it. Some of the navvies earn quite high wages and would willingly pay for a school if one were provided, while others are not so well off, and some of the children in very poor districts could not come at all, if they were charged. I must take all that into account.'

'You mean to teach them yourself?'

She laughed and filled the room with the sound of mischievous merriment, which made him remember Sarah Jane the child, sitting on a bed in the workhouse infirmary asking for reading lessons. 'You know I am not competent to do that. My education has hardly progressed from what you taught me, and though I shall always be grateful for that, I am only too aware how limited it is. I have realised it more and more since Jason has been going to school. He has outstripped me already.'

'You do yourself an injustice, my dear, but I see you will have to employ teachers if the standard is to be good.'

'I want it more than good, I want it high, very high. Some of the navvy children are quite clever.'

'Aren't you being a little over-ambitious?'

She laughed and served him with a plum pudding, almost black with fruit. It was too heavy for her taste, but Henry always liked it. 'You are the one who gave me my ambition in the first place, Thomas. And I have done very well because of it.'

'I grant you that.' He paused, wondering how to introduce the reason for his visit. 'There is a way to do it without using all your savings ...'

'Tell me.'

'You know the Chevington railway company has decided to award you compensation for Duncan McBryde's death?'

'Yes, I read it in *The Gazette*, but I told you before I would not go to the Chevingtons for anything.'

He picked up his wine glass and looked at her over its rim, trying to decide how badly she wanted her school. 'As it happens, I have been employed to find you so that the compensation can be paid. It is one of the reasons I came here tonight.'

'They know where I am?' A cold fear clutched at her heart and she found her hand shaking as she conveyed a fork to her mouth. She put it down, the food untasted. What, she asked herself, had she to be afraid of? They could not harm her, could they?

'No, I have told no one. It was Myson who asked me to find you. Gave me five guineas for the task, not realising I already knew where you were.'

She laughed, the moment of panic gone. 'Thomas, that was dishonest.'

251

'You would rather I told him what I know?'

'No. But why him? Why not Lord Chevington, if all they want to do is pay me compensation?'

'Timothy has a very large holding in the Chevington business and Hailey Common was almost entirely his responsibility. He is acting on behalf of the Company.' He wasn't at all sure that was true, but it would be unwise to tell her of his doubts. She had loved Timothy Myson once, of that he was sure, and perhaps that love was not entirely dead. He wished it were and not for selfish reasons.

'I would not ask Timothy Myson for help if he were the last man on earth and I was starving.' She laughed suddenly. 'I *was* nearly starving once ...'

'You can't forgive him for giving you your son, can you?'

She smiled; trust Thomas to put it like that. It made her seem unreasonable, almost as if she ought to be grateful. And in a funny sort of way, she was. The years had dulled her resentment and Duncan and his goodness had quelled any thoughts she might have had for revenge. Nowadays she had to make a conscious effort to rekindle either. 'He used me,' she said stubbornly. 'Used me and left me.'

'He was – is – forbidden to visit Chevington when Her Ladyship is at home and he would not have dared to go there once she had returned. And you put yourself out of his reach, didn't you? Sarah Jane, be fair.' He paused to allow his words to sink in. 'They won't eat you, Sarah Jane, and you would only be claiming what is yours by right.' He put his spoon down and sat back in his chair with the contented sigh of a man well fed. 'That was delicious, my dear, and I can see why your business has been so successful.'

'Thank you.'

She rang for Betsy to clear the plates and then poured him a glass of brandy. He took it and cupped both hands round the bowl. 'Supposing, instead of trying to do it alone, we could get His Lordship interested in the scheme? Supposing we could persuade him to patronise it, then you would be assured of success. His name alone ...'

'I told you before, I would make my own way, under my own steam.'

He reached across the table to take her hand, wanting to kiss the troubled look from her face, but knowing he could not touch her heart in the way Duncan had, or, come to that, Timothy Myson. 'And so you have, my dear, and wonderfully well, but even you have to admit you need assistance with this school idea, and not only from me. Even the best men of business use their friends to further their aims, so why should you be any, different?'

'Because I am not like that.'

He smiled, 'No? Who was it used Henry Carter when it suited her – and me?'

'That was different. I have not cheated either of you. Henry has made a good profit and I mean to pay you . . .'

'Who said anything about cheating anyone? Simply take the compensation and go on from there.'

She hesitated. It was in her power to create something good out of what had been cruel and corrupt. From Duncan's untimely death would emerge a brighter future for all those navvy children who swarmed about the sites with no education and no hope of getting one. And if it needed someone like Lord Chevington to help bring it about, then she could not really choose anyone better. And, she admonished herself, why should she be afraid of Timothy? He would not be interested in a one-time servant girl he had seduced long ago. He was soon to be married; neither she nor her son had any part in his life. 'Could you act for me?' she asked. 'If I gave you power of attorney?'

'Of course.'

'But only for the compensation and go only to Lord Chevington himself. Unless Timothy has told him, he is unlikely to know that Mrs McBryde is the same person as Sarah Jane Winterday.'

'Very well,' he agreed, wondering how he was going to deal with Timothy. 'I'll go and see His Lordship tomorrow. It's too late to do anything tonight.'

'Where are you staying?'

He looked at her quizzically; was she going to offer him a bed – her bed? The thought set his pulses racing, but her expression was innocuous and he perceived that such a thing was a long way from her mind. Their affair, if affair it had ever been, had been expunged from her memory. He sighed. 'I have lodgings with Mrs Grainger.'

'Oh Thomas, can't you do any better than that? I'll pay your fee in advance.'

He held up his hand. 'No, no, my dear. Mrs Grainger suits me very well. We have . . . an arrangement.'

She laughed. 'Oh, I see.'

'A fellow needs companionship, Sarah Jane, sometimes a little more than that . . .'

'Of course. I would not presume to criticise. But I shall pay you a retainer, because there will be other tasks for you in connection with the school. You'll agree to that, won't you? '

He inclined his head; she had come on, this little pupil of his, she had absorbed all he had taught her and much more besides and her natural wit and intelligence had done the rest. She was so vitally alive, so full of energy and ambition, that she made him almost breathless. He could understand how difficult it must be for Henry Carter to keep up with her. But she deserved her school and anything else it was in his power to help her obtain. He rose to leave, but at the door, stopped and turned back. 'Did you ever find your brother? '

'No. I tried everything. I don't think he is in London, if, indeed, he ever was. To be honest, I sometimes wonder if he is still alive.'

'Would you like me to find him for you while I'm in town?'

'Could you?'

He smiled and raised her hand to his lips. 'I can but try.'

She leaned across and kissed his cheek. 'Thank you, Thomas, you are a good friend.'

He left her, clattering down the stairs and out onto the street. Good friend. It was better than nothing.

The compensation the directors of the railway had set aside for Duncan McBryde's widow amounted to the princely sum of £300, which they had decided was more than generous, considering she was still a young woman and likely to remarry. Sarah Jane thought it was hardly worth the effort of applying for; her shops made more than that in a day. 'Mean buggers,' she said, when Thomas brought the document for her signature. 'It's an insult. Duncan was worth—' She stopped short. 'No, Duncan had no price.'

'You will also see,' he said, leaning over her as she sat at her davenport to read it, 'that it is an *ex gratia* payment: the directors accept no responsibility for what happened, and in taking the sum of three hundred pounds, you absolve them from any further claim.'

She laughed. 'I suppose it will pay for furniture and equipment, if nothing else.' She put her name to the bottom of the document and folded it. Then she crossed the room to pour wine for them both. 'Will you go and look at that property for me?'

'Of course.' He sprawled in a comfortable armchair, watching her move about the room, her taffeta skirts rustling. It always gave him great pleasure just to look at her. Afterwards he would go back to

Denmark Place and assuage the desires she aroused with Mrs Grainger, who would have no idea how her pleasure had been achieved.

'Get a surveyor onto it and if it's suitable, offer half the asking price.'

'Half, Sarah Jane?'

'We'll start at half and haggle from there.'

He who had taught her so much, was learning a thing or two himself and he grinned appreciatively. 'You are a hard nut, Sarah Jane, do you know that? I should hate to come up against you in business.'

She joined in his laughter, but he knew how serious she was and he would fight for all he was worth to help her get what she wanted.

The building she had chosen stood in its own small garden at the end of a side road near the new railway junction, but not in its path and not so close as to be in danger. Although the area was almost derelict while the navvies were working there, she was convinced it would return to life when the line was finished. Once the ground was cleared, new houses and shops would spring up and the dispossessed would return like migrating swallows.

As soon as the purchase had been completed, she set the builders to work and watched eagerly as the school began to take shape. She interviewed several potential teachers and chose two, a man and a woman who believed as passionately as she did in educating the masses; they would begin work as soon as the building was finished. She went among the navvies, making herself known to them and telling them about the school. There would be no shortage of pupils when it opened. Many of them had known Duncan McBryde and all had heard of the explosion; a school in his memory was something of which they approved.

Today, in spite of Henry's grumbles that she was neglecting the business – they had six shops now and still she could not keep pace with the demand for pies – she had taken a cab to inspect the almost-finished school, confident that it would be open for business in a month. They would have a grand opening just after Christmas; the children would be snugly indoors during the worst of the winter. Should she invite Lord Chevington to attend? She smiled to herself at the idea of a little showing off, but as so often when thinking of His Lordship, she thought of Timothy. Thomas had told her he had left London. Had he returned? And if he had, she asked herself as she left the cab and made her way up the school path, what difference did it make?

One of the first tasks of the stonemasons had been to set a stone slab into the wall above the door, on which was carved the words *Duncan McBryde Memorial School 1851.* She stood and looked at it for a moment, remembering the man Duncan had been, his love, his gentleness, his sacrifice. He had given his life for her and for the navvies, and she owed him a fitting memorial. It would be something to keep his memory alive long after she, who needed no memorial to remember him, had gone. She turned at last and went round to the back where the builders had installed modern privies in the outhouses, and where the overgrown garden had been put down to grass for a play area. She went in through the back door to inspect the kitchen with its new cooking range, black as ebony, reminding her of the range at Chevington House, and then on into the rest of the house where painters and decorators were putting the finishing touches to the rooms. She spoke encouragingly to the workmen and gave instructions about where the furniture was to be put when it arrived and then, happily satisfied, left the house by the front door.

Geoffrey, coming on foot from the railway workings, stopped when he saw her. It was not that he recognised her, it was simply that she stood out from her drab surroundings like gold in bare, grey rock and he was almost transfixed. Framed by a squat, smoke-begrimed brick house, its garden heaped with builders' rubble, she was breathtakingly beautiful; she carried herself with an easy grace which more than did justice to the expensive fur mantle she wore over a crinoline of heavy lemon silk whose bodice emphasised the neatness of her waist. Her matching yellow bonnet, ruched with the same material as the dress, was set on copper curls and framed a face whose expression was both pensive and mischievous – a combination which should have made it unforgettable. He must be getting old, he decided, if he could not remember where and when he had met her before, but he knew he had. He doffed his top hat and bade her good morning, hoping for inspiration.

'Good morning, my lord,' she said, smiling at his puzzled expression.

He glanced up at the house from which she had emerged and caught sight of the inscription above the door: *McBryde.* This was Mrs McBryde! The lawyer, and Caroline too, had said she had done well for herself, but this elegance was more than he had expected; it embodied self-confidence, a panache that left him almost tongue-tied. But he had never, to his knowledge, met the navvy's widow, so why was her face so familiar? He was about to confess his loss of memory, when she laughed and put up a hand to push a wisp of hair from her forehead. He had seen her do that before in his library at Chevington House. The elegant gown was suddenly changed in his mind's eye into the striped uniform of a servant and he found himself floundering, unable to disguise his astonishment.

'You are Mrs McBryde, the navvy's widow?'

'Yes, my lord.' Now she was face to face with him again, she was nervous; her throat was dry, her hands clammy and her heart was thumping like the driving rods of a steam engine. But there had been no shame in loving Duncan; the lack of marriage lines did not matter. She straightened her back and held her chin high.

'And the same girl who took a book from my library?' His smile conveyed the message that he remembered the incident with amusement.

'Yes.' She laughed and her green eyes sparkled like emeralds and held him spellbound. The child and the woman could not be separated and yet they were so different. It was unbelievable. But he should not be so surprised, for hadn't he thought all along that she would make something of herself – and hadn't he blamed Timothy for spoiling her chances? He could hardly credit that she had ever been a navvy wife, had lived and worked at Hailey Common in the dirt and squalor there. They had been within a whisker of meeting again after the explosion. Timothy had, on his own admission, met her afterwards and he had said nothing of the fact that Mrs McBryde and Sarah Jane Winterday were one and the same. Why not? He must have realised it, he surely could not have forgotten her. No man in his senses could forget he had once held her in his arms and made love to her.

'Please allow me to say how sorry I was about your husband,' he said, pulling himself together. 'He was a brave man to risk his life in the way he did. If we had known about the water in the tunnel ...'

'If you had had it surveyed properly, you would have done,' she said. 'No one troubled to trace the river up to its source.'

'Is that what the navvies said?'

She looked up at him, noticing how much Timothy resembled him, but the fine lines round his eyes gave them a humour Timothy's lacked and his mouth was softer, less intractable. His was a quiet face. 'Yes, and they were right, weren't they?'

'The survey was done before we took over the line, Mrs McBryde, and we saw no reason to doubt the original engineer's report. At least, not before we learned about the water in the tunnel and by then it was too late.'

'You didn't know about it?' She had blamed him as much as anyone; had she been wrong? Did it make a difference?

'Mr Bender was anxious because the work was behind schedule,' he continued. 'He didn't think the water was a serious problem, but he did stop the men working on that last day. If they had obeyed him ...'

'Are you suggesting they were at fault?'

'To a degree, they were.'

'But they were desperate! Most of them were in debt and couldn't go on much longer. All they wanted was to be able to make their piece rates. Randy Joe was a hothead and—' She stopped as her memory recreated that dust-filled, catastrophic summer's day. 'Duncan ...' She still could not say his name without gulping. 'Duncan went in to stop him. Surely you are not seriously suggesting he brought about his own death?'

'Not at all, or we would never have agreed to the compensation.' He smiled. 'Would you like to show me round your school?'

'If you wish.' She turned and retraced her steps. 'Did Mr Wistonby tell you about my plans?'

'Yes, but I should like to hear them from you.'

'Is that why you are here?'

'No, no,' he said hurriedly. 'I was in the vicinity, looking at the railway and felt like a walk before I returned to my office.' He followed her inside where the sound of hammering and scraping became a background to their conversation. 'Tell me about your life with the navvies.'

The invitation was heaven-sent and while she conducted him from room to room, she seized the opportunity to mount her favourite hobbyhorse. Without going into her reasons for joining them, she told him about the McBrydes and the Barnabys, about the poverty and hardships, the shanties and the hateful truck system. He listened with grave attention, while appearing to inspect the plastering and bright new paintwork.

'Truck is the cause of more trouble at the workings than any other half-dozen things put together,' she told him. He was not ignorant of it, she knew, but he only saw it from his own lofty viewpoint. 'Why do the owners exploit the navvies in that way?'

'You know as well as anyone the reasons why we have to give the men tommy tickets, Mrs McBryde.'

'It is hardest of all for the women and children,' she went on. 'They don't know what it's like to take a bath and wear clean clothes ...'

He took her elbow to steady her as she stepped over a bag of tools left on the floor. His touch sent a familiar tremor through her body to the pit of her stomach; he was a very desirable man. Shocked by her wayward thoughts, she brought herself back from the brink and went on: 'The greatest shortage when you're on a site miles from anywhere is clean water. What there is you need for drinking, so cleanliness goes by the board; the life is degrading enough without that and something should be done about the conditions ...'

He attributed her flushed cheeks to her strong feelings on the subject, but her high colour and bright eyes made her even more desirable. He would have liked to slip his hand from her elbow to encompass her waist ... 'What do you suggest?' he asked, refusing to let his thoughts wander along that road.

He was humouring her and she knew it, but she didn't care; she had never had such an opportunity and she meant to make the most of it. 'Ensure that the tommy shops are run for the benefit of the men,' she said. 'As it is, the contractors make more money out of truck than they do from laying the line; they live off the fat of the land themselves while the men who do the work go hungry and their children are barefoot and ragged, not even able to read and write.'

'Mr Wistonby has told me your views on that, but it's not only navvy children who lack learning. There are poor children in all walks of life who need an education, but if they want it badly enough they find some way to attain it, just as you did.'

She laughed and he became more than ever aware of how lovely she was, a loveliness that neither poverty nor affluence could alter. 'You think we should all go whoring to obtain an education? Because that's what it amounts to.'

'I was commending your enterprise,' His Lordship responded hurriedly. 'I did not know ...'

Serious again, she said, 'Oh, please do not misunderstand me, my lord. I am not, nor ever have been, a whore but all I can say is, "There, but for the grace of God ..."'

'Forgive me,' he said softly.

She smiled and turned her attention again to the subject of the navvy children, like a dog with a bone, unwilling to give it up. 'Are you afraid to teach the children of working people to read and write?'

259

'Not at all. I believe the time is not so far distant when education will be available to all. Be patient, it will happen.'

'Patience, my lord, is not one of my strong suits, and in the meantime children like Ned and the twins remain ignorant.'

'You told me they could already read and write.'

'Only because I taught them a little, but it is not enough. There should be a schoolroom on all the big sites, and it should be paid for from the profits the owners make from the railways.'

'But Mrs McBryde,' he said patiently, 'until the lines are in operation and bringing in revenue, the investment in building is dead money and there are no profits. Investors do not see the welfare of children as part of their commitment, and they would not agree to that kind of outlay.'

'Then they should,' she said firmly. 'Railway building has been going on a long time now and many, including yourself, are very rich by it.' She paused. 'There ought to be laws to control conditions on the sites.'

'You may be right, but I do not make the laws.'

'You can influence those who do, though. Speak to Mr Townsend, he's the one who takes your railway bills to Parliament, isn't he?'

Surprised by her knowledge and her ability to express herself articulately, he did not speak for a moment. Had Timothy realised that she was destined to be more than an ignorant servant when he had taken her to bed? She was an ambitious and determined woman who should not have been hampered by an unwanted child, before she had even become aware of herself as a woman, nor knew what she could achieve. Did Timothy know about this school? Geoffrey was suddenly reminded of why he was in the area.

Lord Hailey had been taken ill with a stroke while Caroline and her mother were in London, and an urgent message had been sent for them to return home at once. The Chevington private train had been put at their disposal and Timothy had accompanied them back to Hailey Manor. He had written a few days later to say that Lady Hailey and the girls were distraught and unable to cope with the helpless man, and he had been persuaded to stay on until Lord Hailey improved. He had asked his father if he would survey the site where he hoped the *East Fen* trains would join the confluence to the docks, and continue the negotiations with the *Great Eastern*. Seeing no reason why he should not do so, Geoffrey had complied. Until now he had not realised that Timothy's plans would mean a new line going slapbang through the school. 'You are a very strong-minded young woman, Mrs

McBryde,' he said. 'And I can understand why you applied for the compensation. But it wasn't only the money, was it? You wanted the railway to pay for the school.'

She smiled at his perspicacity, though he must know how little £300 could do. 'At least, my lord, it will furnish the first one.'

'You intend to have more than one?'

'Of course, right across the country. I started here, because there are so many navvies from so many different companies here and because it is near enough to my home and business for me to be able to supervise it myself.'

His eyes twinkled. 'You are not going to wait for me to do something about it, then?'

'I can make a start and hope you, and others like you, will follow my example.'

Could he? Should he? It would mean seeing her again, becoming closely involved. He was suddenly filled with pleasurable anticipation. 'I shall need more information – when, where, how much it will cost, how many children, how you are going to find them ...'

'I think, my lord, they will find me.'

He smiled, acknowledging the truth of that. 'I will give the idea serious consideration, if you could have your man of business prepare a proposal.'

'That, my lord, has already been done because I had hoped to interest financiers in a larger scheme than just one house.' She smiled easily. 'But I expect you can guess their reaction – I am a woman, a butterfly-brained female, full of foolish fancies about doing good. Doing good is laudable but it has no profit potential.' She sighed, leading him back to the entrance hall. 'What I suppose we need are philanthropists.'

'And you think I might be one?'

'My lord, I know you for a kind man and I cannot believe that the welfare of the navvies and their children is not a subject which concerns you.'

A kind man. It was almost damning with faint praise and made him feel uncomfortable. She meant him to feel that way; she intended to stir his conscience. No one had ever spoken to him like that before and with anyone else he would have been annoyed, but her words were accompanied by a smile so appealing, he found himself not only wanting, but anxious, to please her. And she was right – the welfare of the navvy children was something he cared about. 'I will certainly think about it,' he said.

'Thank you, my lord.' She moved towards the door. 'Mr Wistonby will call on you with my proposals. If you have any questions, I am sure he will supply you with the answers.'

She was the one who was bringing the interview to a close, and His Lordship found himself inexplicably wanting to detain her. 'I look forward to talking to you again. Perhaps we could have luncheon together?'

'Thank you, my lord,' she said, before walking to where her cab still waited. 'But Mr Wistonby will deal with everything from now on.'

She smiled slowly, withdrew her hand from his and pulled on her gloves, then she stepped into the cab and ordered the driver to take her back to the Oxford Street shop, leaving Lord Chevington staring after her.

As soon as the hansom had gone from sight, he turned and went back to his own carriage, left waiting in a side street near the *Great Eastern* site office. Somehow he had to arrange matters so that the new *East Fen* line avoided that little house with its oh-so-poignant inscription above the door. And it must be done before Timothy returned to London. He ordered his coachman to take him to his office where he knew Jack Miller was at work. He needed an ally.

Sundays, the only day Sarah Jane was free, were always devoted to Jason and they often went to Hyde Park which was no distance from their Oxford Street home. The Sunday after Sarah Jane had seen Lord Chevington at the school, it was snowing and she was half-inclined to use it as an excuse not to go out, but Jason, who was delighted at the prospect of throwing snowballs, dressed himself in warm coat, muffler, cap and gloves and danced around her, protesting, 'But Mam, we always go out on Sundays and the snow will be lovely. Do you think there will be hot chestnuts and muffin men and ... oh, do get ready.'

She gave in and went to change, choosing an outdoor gown of fine wool patterned in black, pink, green and orange over which she wore a black mantle with a deep fringe which echoed the colours of the dress. She topped it with a bonnet of soft velvet tied with wide green ribbons. Satisfied that she looked as fashionable as any lady she was likely to meet in the park, she picked up a fur muff and joined her impatient son.

They went on foot, mingling with the crowds who had come to see how far the Exhibition Hall was progressing. Covering sixteen acres between Knightsbridge Barracks and the Serpentine, it provided work for thousands of building labourers, who had been occupied, day and night, since September. Already towering above the wooden barricades built around it, the sections reminded Sarah Jane of a giant beehive, with all the worker bees buzzing round it, climbing its tall girders and popping in and out with pieces of machinery and equipment. Long before it was complete, it was already one of the sights of London.

'We'll be able to go inside when it's finished, won't we?' Jason asked. 'We've been learning all about it in our lessons.'

'I expect so,' his mother said, thinking of the extra business it would bring to the shops, and considering the idea of setting up a stall on the edge of the park when the exhibition opened in May.

'Let's go over there,' he said, racing ahead to where the snow was clean and untrodden. He stopped to pick up a handful of snow and hurl it at her, laughing delightedly when it found its mark. Sarah Jane, still young at heart, giggled and retaliated and they were soon in the thick of a snowball fight.

Catching sight of them on his way to Cumberland Terrace, Geoffrey stopped his carriage on the road and picked his way through their footmarks to join them as Jason, rosy-cheeked and bright-eyed, gathered up more snow to hurl at his mother, whose elegant clothes bore the proof of his accuracy.

'No, Jason, no more,' she cried, breathlessly. 'It's all gone down my neck and—' The snowball was already sailing through the air towards her. She ducked and then slipped and landed on her bottom on the ground, where she sat with her feet straight out in front of her and her crinoline tip-tilted, laughing delightedly. Geoffrey, who had been standing silently watching them from a few yards away, went to help her up.

Taken by surprise, she gasped. 'Lord Chevington!'

He smiled and retrieved her bonnet from the snow and handed it to her. 'Are you hurt?'

'Not at all, my lord.' She was once more composed. 'We were having a great battle, Jason and I.' She turned to draw her son to her side. 'This is Jason, my lord.' Then to Jason, 'Say good morning to Lord Chevington, darling.'

'Lord Chevington?' he queried excitedly. 'The railway lord?'

His Lordship smiled. 'Yes, for my sins, some call me that.' He was staring down at the boy, memorising every feature, every detail of his sturdy frame.

Jason returned his look with an uninhibited one of his own.

Anything to do with railways fascinated him; he had a sort of proprietorial interest in them, for hadn't his Da been a navvy ganger and hadn't he taught him all the secrets of navvying? And hadn't Da told him that Lord Chevington was one of the best? 'My father was a ganger,' he said proudly.

'I know. And a very brave one.'

Nothing could have been more surely calculated to win the boy over, and Sarah Jane knew it. She knew with a certainty that sent her heart into her shoes, that His Lordship would want to see the boy again, and Jason would never stop boasting about the fact that he had met the great man. And how could it be kept from Timothy?

Chapter Seventeen

*L*ondon was a very exciting place to be in 1851, and for Sarah Jane and her shops it was also a very busy time, as they tried to keep up with the demand for pies from the workers on the Exhibition site. Then, as wagonloads of exhibits began to arrive from all over the world, they brought more customers. There was little time for leisure and she rarely went out, and then only in the company of Henry. He was good to her in his fashion, and she owed him a lot, so they continued in the old way, arguing incessantly and making a great deal of money. She was glad of that because she needed it more than ever now that the school was open. It was already bursting at the seams and somehow or other, she would have to expand it. She had asked Thomas to make enquiries about adjoining properties, but she needed funds to pay for them.

Lord Chevington had studied her proposals and given her helpful advice and suggestions, but he was not yet ready to commit himself to anything more. She had to find the money herself and this could best be done by further business expansion. That meant getting round Henry.

'I think we need separate premises for cooking,' she told him one evening in February as they returned by hansom from a visit to Drury Lane to see the farewell performance of William MacReady in *Macbeth*. 'If we had a central bakehouse, the pies could be delivered to the shops daily and the staff there could concentrate on serving customers.'

'Once the Exhibition is over, demand will fall,' he said, showing his usual caution.

'Not if we have established ourselves as the best pie-makers in the kingdom, and we would be fools not to take advantage of the thousands of visitors who will be coming.'

'You can't compete with Schweppes.'

Sarah Jane knew that Schweppes had won the contract for the

catering in the Exhibition Hall. 'Not everyone will want to eat inside the hall, and besides, I have been talking to them about buying pies from us. We need a bakehouse – a factory – to be able to satisfy the demand if we sign a contract with them.'

Her reputation was growing so that she was able to do a certain amount of negotiating on her own account, but she still needed Henry for the final signing of any documents and though this annoyed her intensely, she swallowed her pride in order to get what she wanted.

'Sarah Jane, I am not contemplating expansion ...' The food shops were looking set to overtake his emporiums in turnover and importance, and something in him rebelled against that.

'In heaven's name, why not?'

'We will over-reach ourselves. Taking on a manufactory is a huge step; we would have to be certain of continued production for a very long time.'

'We would, don't you see? We won't be competing, but working with other businesses. We can provide readymade pies for retailers, and deliver them all round town.'

He sighed. 'Sarah Jane, you are bullying me again.'

The cab stopped outside her home. 'Come in and let's talk about it,' she said, as he helped her to alight.

Sighing heavily, he asked the driver to wait and followed her up to her sitting room, where he stood with his back to the fire and his hands clasped under his tails, almost as if he were warming his backside in his own home; it was where he was comfortable and pampered and for that reason as much as for any other, she knew he would give in to her.

'Knowing you, I expect you have all the figures for me,' he said.

'Yes.' She sat on the sofa sipping her own drink and looking up at him over the rim of her glass, her green eyes alight with enthusiasm. She was never happier than when making plans, producing new ideas, making them work and work profitably. She had no doubts about her own ability on that score; her doubts and misgivings lay in another direction altogether.

'And you've been scouting for premises?'

'I've looked at one or two, yes.'

He sighed. 'Let's hear about them.'

'Sit down then.' She went to the davenport and took out a sheaf of papers. Realising that by seating himself he was committing himself to studying her figures, he hesitated, but then shrugged his shoulders and sat down beside her. They spent the next hour discussing the idea and by the time he left, her enthusiasm had transmitted itself to him and he was as good as committed.

All Sarah Jane's projects were doing well except her search for Billie, and now Henry had agreed to further expansion she was convinced that nothing could stop her. She became busier than ever, working over sixteen hours a day, blissfully unaware of the cloud building up on the horizon.

The business seemed to grow in direct proportion to the growth of the Crystal Palace, as it was coming to be called, so that by the time the building was completed and ready for the grand opening on May Day, she was exhausted, but satisfied that whatever happened afterwards, *Carter & Winterday* would continue to grow.

Ten days before the ceremony, when she was enjoying a rare evening at home, with nothing more important to do than read *The Art of Dining*, Betsy appeared in the doorway, looking flustered. 'There's a gentleman to see you, ma'am.'

Sarah Jane looked up at the girl. 'Tell him to return in the morning and see me in the shop.'

'I told him that, ma'am, but he won't go away.'

'Who is he? Did he give you his card?'

'He said to give you this – it would tell you more than a calling card.' She stretched out a hand, on the palm of which was balanced a little black box.

Sarah Jane sat and stared at it for several seconds, then slowly took it and opened it with shaking fingers, though she knew perfectly well what it contained. 'Tell him ...' she began.

She did not finish because Timothy had pushed his way past the maid and stood in the middle of the room. He was dressed in immaculate evening dress, as if he had just come from some function and stopped by on the way home. She sprang to her feet and they faced each other silently, unmoving, for fully a minute, until she became aware that Betsy was still standing by the door, eaten with curiosity. She dismissed her without taking her eyes off Timothy. He was everything she remembered, tall, handsome, easy in his manner, smiling like an overgrown schoolboy, except that schoolboys did not have the power to stir her insides the way he did. His eyes, dark as coal, were Jason's eyes and those she could not help but love. It was a moment she had both longed for and dreaded and she could not speak.

'Why did you sell it?' he asked at last, nodding towards the apple in her hand.

'Our hut burned down. We needed the money.' Her voice was toneless with the effort of trying to control the conflicting emotions which chased each other from heart to brain and back again; love, hate, despair, revenge, fear and a desperate feeling of loneliness, and the knowledge that this was a battle she was going to have to fight singlehandedly.

He smiled. 'Well, that disaster is unlikely to strike again. Keep it this time, won't you?'

'How did you find me?' she demanded.

'I followed a certain legal gentleman who was more than usually careless.' He knew from what Caroline had said that Sarah Jane had done well for herself and he had been prepared for a change – but this! This was something altogether different. The contrast between the woman he faced now, dressed in a softly falling peignoir in dark blue organdy, and the girl in the dirty cotton skirt and peasant blouse at Hailey Common was startling. If he hadn't known differently he could have sworn she was a gentlewoman, born and bred; the way she held herself, the creaminess of her skin, her well-modulated voice as she dismissed the maid, were all evidence of more than just material changes. Even in rags she had been graceful but now she was destroying his peace of mind. 'I paid him to find you and successful though he was, he did not think fit to come and tell me of it.'

'Perhaps because I asked him not to.'

'Why?' he asked softly, suppressing an urge to pull the combs out of her wonderful hair and watch it cascade to her shoulders in a shining copper torrent. 'Why didn't you want to see me?'

'We have nothing to say to each other.' She was determined to stay cool and not let him see that she was shaking like an aspen in the wind. 'Please leave.'

'Leave, my dear Sarah Jane? You surely do not mean to dismiss me in that offhand way without even asking why I have come, or even offering me refreshment?'

'I am sorry if I appear inhospitable but I would rather you went away and forgot you ever met me.'

'Forget you? I could not do that, even if I wanted to.' His voice was like the gentlest of caresses, and it made it even harder to fight him. 'If I couldn't put you out of my mind all those years when I had nothing to feed my memory on but one delightful summer, how do you suppose I can forget you now, after I have found you again and you are all I remembered and more besides? To the end of my days,

Sarah Jane, you will still be my Aphrodite.' He took a step towards her, holding out his hands. She backed away and, finding a chair against her knees, sat down quickly. He seemed to take that as an invitation to be seated himself and sat on the sofa opposite her, leaning forward, so that she could not avoid looking at him. 'Sarah Jane,' he murmured, watching her eyes. They gave her away, they always had. 'How could you think I would ever forget you?'

'What do you want?' She felt suddenly weary, tired of fighting. 'Why have you come?'

'Do I need a reason to visit the mother of my son?' He paused, smiling easily, but when she did not answer, went on, 'He *is* my child, isn't he?'

'He is mine. You have forfeited your right to have anything to do with him.'

'Now, I know you do not mean that.' He reached out to touch her but she flinched away as if his hand were redhot. 'Did you think I *wanted* to leave you that summer?'

'You did, though, didn't you – and without a word of warning.'

'I had no choice, not then. Later, when Mr Wistonby said he would bring you to me, I was looking forward to seeing you and explaining why I left, but it was you who ran away, wasn't it?'

'Ran away?' She gave a brittle laugh. 'Do you know what the alternative was? An impoverished existence in the workhouse, and I was determined my child would not have that. And it's of no consequence now because I have made a good life for myself.'

He dragged his gaze from her to look round the comfortable room with its upholstered chairs and sofa, its little tables, its overflowing bookcase, its davenport and ornaments, and smiled. 'You have, indeed, but that has nothing to do with how I feel now. I want to make up for what happened in the past.' He had come coldbloodedly to conquer and instead of that he found himself shaking with a desire he could not control. He had forgotten telling his father she had bewitched him, but he remembered it now. He was held enthralled, like a fly in a spider's web. Was she aware of it? 'Why did you think I searched for you?'

'Perhaps you had a guilty conscience.'

'About the child? That was only part of it.'

'No, I meant about the navvies, about Duncan's death ...' Did he know she had accepted the compensation?

'This is nothing to do with that. This is something between you and me, something unfinished.'

269

'It is finished, finished and done with.' Why was she bandying words with him? Why hadn't she flung him out when he first arrived? 'When I was expecting Jason, I might have been glad of your support, but not now. Not long ago we were living in the dirt and filth of a navvy encampment and when Duncan died I might have sunk even further, but I didn't. I clawed my way up. I did it without help and shall continue to do so; I haven't done climbing yet. Jason wants for nothing, nor will he – ever.' She paused, but he made no move to go and she went on: 'I believe you are betrothed to marry. Go back to your bride, Mr Myson, and leave us in peace.'

'I cannot, and besides, there is to be no wedding for a year. Lord Hailey has been ill since Christmas and died two weeks ago. The family is in mourning. In any case, it was to be a marriage of convenience, a business arrangement.' He sat back and filled his senses with the glory of her. 'You see, that's what my father thinks of me. I am just someone to be manipulated, as he manipulates everyone, you included.' His smile was twisted with bitterness; it spoiled his handsome features. 'We are two of a kind, you and I. We have both had to fight for what we have and we have learned to harden our hearts to anything that comes between us and our goal. But with you I can be different, with you there is always warmth. I need to thaw a little now and again if I am not to become totally frozen.' He stopped and smiled suddenly. 'You understand what I'm saying, Sarah Jane?'

'Oh, I understand all right,' she snapped. 'You are looking for an undemanding mistress.'

He laughed and reached out to touch a tendril of hair that had fallen from its pins and curled over her cheek, making her shiver. 'If it were only a mistress I wanted, I could find one. You underrate yourself, my darling.'

She felt confused and weak; he had hit on the word warmth, just as she had, and the reasons he had given for wanting it were uncannily like her own. But she would not weaken. She would not. 'I am sure Miss Hailey would not approve of your visit here,' she said, drawing away from him and standing up so that she could look down on him. 'And as for what she would say if she learned you had a son . . .'

He gave her a twisted smile. 'A bastard son, Sarah Jane, just as I am a bastard son. You didn't know that, did you?'

'Yes, I knew it.' She was tired and distressed and her control was cracking. 'It is hardly important.'

He reached up to grab her hand and pull her down beside him. 'Not important! I'll tell you how important it is, shall I? It means that I can never take my place as a true Chevington, I cannot go to Chevington House, I cannot claim my father and he cannot, or will not, claim me. I do not know and have never known the mother who bore me. I don't even know her name.' He laughed harshly. 'My father invented my name. Did you know that?'

'No.' She spoke softly because she suddenly found herself feeling sorry for the child he had been. She shook herself, knowing she must not falter. 'But my son *does* have a name: it is McBryde. Duncan McBryde was his father.'

'Stepfather, Sarah Jane,' he corrected her, suddenly perceiving that the way to Sarah Jane was through Jason. 'But Jason deserves better than that.'

'Better than what?' she demanded. She was angry now and that was good; it made it easier to fight him.

He realised his mistake and his voice softened. 'Better than struggling all his life as McBryde had to do, and as I have had to do.'

'How can you do anything about that? You are ...' She paused. 'You are what you are.'

'... a bastard, but a rich bastard – and one day I shall inherit all the Chevington wealth, you see. There is a lot I can do for Jason.'

'No!'

'What are you afraid of?'

'Nothing.' She could not tell him that her fears gave her nightmares. 'Mr Myson, I have had a long day and I am tired. Please leave me.'

He did not believe she was truly anxious for him to be gone; she was putting on a show of reluctance in order to teach him a lesson. He remembered how he had won her that first time; he had let her dress and asked for nothing but a little conversation. For all his impatience, he would have to do the same again. He meant to have her and the more she resisted, the more determined he became. He stood up. 'Very well. But I shall come back.'

He took her hand and put the palm to his lips, then with a smile of irritating self-confidence, picked up his hat and gloves and left her. She heard him call out to Betsy that he would let himself out and then she heard him go downstairs and a moment later the street door banged shut behind him. She lay back on the sofa and closed her eyes.

She could do with a drink, but her legs would not support her if she stood up to get one. She put her hands over her face, trying to stop the tears which trickled between her fingers. How could she stop him returning? How could she keep him away from Jason? All the time they were talking, she had been picturing him in the river at Chevington, naked, muscular, every inch a man, carrying her in his arms, holding his wet shiny body close to hers, his erection hard against her thigh, laughing in joyous abandonment, a man to give oneself to in wholehearted lovemaking. Tonight, she had felt the stirring of that long-forgotten passion and found herself wanting to throw herself at him, to tear the clothes from his back and rekindle that summer's joy. How could her body betray her so when she ought to hate him? It would be easier if he were completely rotten, but she suspected that somewhere, buried beneath the bitterness, was a man it would be easy to love again. Too easy.

She dropped her hands and opened her eyes. The golden apple lay in her lap, glinting at her in a kind of defiance. She flung it from her and it landed in the hearth with a crash just as Betsy came in to see if there was anything she wanted. 'Pour me a brandy,' she told her, bending to pick it up. She put it in its box and laid it on the table beside her. If she had not sold it, if ... if ... But she knew it would have made no difference; her fate had been sealed on the day she accepted it.

Now what was she going to do? Leave? Take Jason and whatever she could carry and run away? She swallowed her drink and hurried to Jason's room. He was fast asleep. A smile played round his lips and one arm was flung round a toy railway engine which Lord Chevington had given him when he called a few days before. Gently she eased it away and stood it on the table beside his bed before creeping from the room. Not tonight. She would not rouse him tonight.

She went to her own bed, though she knew she would not sleep. What would they say at Jason's school when he did not turn up? Was she prepared to sacrifice his schooling? What would Henry do, if she abandoned him? Did he deserve that? And Lord Chevington, what would he think of someone so weak, so unsure of herself that she threw away her long-cherished hopes and ambitions at the first hurdle? She could almost hear Thomas scolding her, as she crept between the sheets. 'You knew when you agreed to claim the compensation that you might have to meet Timothy again. You wanted it badly enough to take the risk, so you must go on taking it.' She wished she could talk to Thomas but, as far as she was aware, he was not in town. She had to confront her fears, to defy them, for what were they? They had no more substance than a puff of wind.

She dozed at last and her nightmare returned, more frightening than ever before. There was a violent storm but Jason, sitting behind the man on the horse, was laughing and not wet at all; the storm did not touch him. It was that which frightened her most of all. Desperately she ran after them, falling down the black hole and reaching out for the helping hand, but there was only emptiness and darkness. She woke with a start to find that dawn was coming up over the chimney pots of Oxford Street and another day had begun.

Slowly she climbed out of bed and went to the washstand. The mirror above it told its own story; she looked deathly pale and there were dark rings round her eyes. It was not the face she wanted to present to the world. She washed and dressed in a brown taffeta day gown and carefully applied a dusting of pearl powder, then straightened her back and walked purposefully through to the dining room, where Jason was playing on the floor in his nightshirt, trundling the engine up and down the carpet to the accompaniment of train noises. 'How would you like to come with me today?' she asked, suddenly aware that she could not bear him out of her sight.

He looked up, beaming. 'You mean it?'

She went to help him dress. 'Yes. You can come with me to the shops and to see Uncle Henry and then we'll go to the new school, shall we?'

She did not know why she wanted Jason to see the navvy children. Perhaps it was to remind him of his Da, to make him realise how lucky he had been in having Duncan for a father, or to show him how far they had come since those days. And perhaps because she was so proud of her school and had no one else with whom to share her achievement.

It was late afternoon before they left Henry and took a hansom to Caledonian Road, and by then the children had left for the evening. They wandered round the empty classrooms and Jason said, 'Can we go and see the navvies?'

'Why not?'

He walked beside his mother towards the excavations, chattering excitedly, but she wasn't really listening. During the day, the nightmare had diminished and with it the fear that Timothy Myson was a threat. He had just been playing a game with her, expecting her to fall on his neck and begin all over again, for no other reason than he liked to demonstrate his power over her. And she had very nearly succumbed! Sarah Jane cursed herself for allowing him to see her weakness. He would not come back; he would not persist in the face of determined opposition, not when he could get all he wanted from a high-class brothel.

She suddenly became aware that Jason had left her side. She looked round at the clutter of equipment, wagons and busy men but she could not see him. Panic rose in her throat, making it almost impossible to breathe. 'Jason!' It was all she could do to make a sound and her voice did not carry. 'Jason! Where are you?'

Then she caught sight of him, standing a little way off, clutching his toy engine, watching a horse pulling a truck full of spoil up a half-finished embankment. At the same moment, she saw his danger. The boy who was running the tip had pulled the horse to one side too soon and the wagon had overturned on the slope. Several tons of rubble fell out of it and began to tumble down the hill towards Jason in a rumbling cloud of dust. '*Jason!*' she shrieked, beginning to run and knowing she could never reach him in time. 'Jason! Look out!' He seemed transfixed, as if he did not know which way to run. In the midst of her terror she heard the sound of hooves and the next moment Jason had been swept up by a man on a great black horse. She screamed and fell, down into the black abyss of her nightmare ...

When she came out of her faint she was lying on the bare earth in the centre of a little knot of navvies. 'Jason,' she said, trying to sit up. 'Where is he?'

'He is safe.' It was Timothy who answered. He put his arm round her. 'There's no harm done. Come and sit down in the office until you recover.'

She struggled in his arms. 'No! Bring him back to me, do you hear?'

'Mr Myson saved the boy,' said one of the navvies. 'You should be glad o' that, missus, not yellin' at 'im.'

She felt weak and stupid. She looked blankly about her as Timothy helped her to her feet. Jason was sitting on top of a stack of sleepers, unhurt and apparently unconcerned. Beside him, Timothy's horse stood patiently waiting. 'I'm not hurt, Mama, and I still have my engine.' He held it up to show her. 'It's got a dint in the side.'

Sarah Jane uttered a cry that was more like a whimper and ran to fold him in her arms. 'Oh Jason, I thought I'd lost you.'

'What in heaven's name are you doing here?' Timothy demanded, his voice harsh with censure. 'Why did you bring the boy here?'

'Why not?' She was defiant now. 'He must not forget his roots.'

'His roots are not with the navvies, Sarah Jane, and you know it. How did you get here? Have you a carriage?'

'No, a cab. I told the driver to wait.'

'Then let us take you back to it.' He left her side to speak to one of the men. 'We'll talk again later. If someone would be kind enough to look after my horse . . .'

Sarah Jane was too dazed to pay much attention to the arrangements being made to convey her and Jason home. That her nightmare had finally come to pass, she did not doubt, but she had completely misinterpreted it. She smiled weakly as they made their way to the hansom waiting outside the school.

Timothy put Jason on to the seat and then handed her up. Turning to give instructions to the driver, his eye caught sight of the inscription above the door of the school. Who had sited that there, right on the projected line of the new junction? Shrugging, he climbed in beside her.

At the door of her apartment she turned to him, trying to hide the fact that she was still trembling. 'Thank you for your help, Mr Myson.'

'I am dismissed, then?' His voice was soft, silky as a caress. 'Am I not to be allowed to make sure you are completely recovered?'

'I am, thank you.'

'And do I not deserve a reward and an explanation?'

'What reward?' She felt weak, as if she had run a great distance.

'The pleasure of your company for half an hour.' He looked down at Jason, who stood beside him clutching his engine. 'You would like me to stay to tea, wouldn't you?'

Jason looked from Timothy to his mother, feeling the tension in the air but not understanding it. 'Please, Mama. Mr Myson has been on Lord Chevington's engine, this very one. It draws His Lordship's private train.'

She had been in a world of her own and, unaware of any conversation in the carriage, had not noticed that Timothy had taken the opportunity to ingratiate himself with Jason. She, who could deny her son nothing, gave in with an almost imperceptible nod of her head and Timothy handed his hat and gloves to Betsy and followed her into her sitting room. She took off her own coat and hat and helped Jason off with his, while she ordered tea and cakes to be brought, then turned to invite Timothy to be seated, but he was already on the floor beside Jason, knocking the dint out of the train with one of the fire irons.

She stood for a moment watching them, the dark head and the fair one, and she was struck by a likeness she had never noticed before. Their eyes, with their finely arched brows, were almost identical and the determined set of Timothy's jaw found an echo in Jason's. Even their movements, the way they shrugged their shoulders or spread their hands, were alike. Apart from the blond curls, so like Billie's, there seemed to be little of the Winterday in him. Timothy, having completed the repairs, sent the train rolling across the floor where it crashed into a chair leg. Jason giggled with delight.

'Come for your tea, Jason,' Sarah Jane said, as Betsy brought in the tea tray and set it on the table.

'Oh, Mama!'

'We must do as we're told,' Timothy said, getting to his feet and sitting opposite Sarah Jane, where he could look at her without having to screw his head round. 'Or I shan't be asked to come again.'

'Will you play with me after tea?' the boy asked.

'No!' Sarah Jane said quickly, making Timothy look at her with a hint of amusement in his dark eyes. 'No, it's late.' She put a sandwich on a plate and handed it to him. 'Be a good boy and eat that. I don't think you know how fortunate you are to have tea in the drawing room with grown-ups. Most little—' She stopped because she had been going to say 'boys' but remembering the navvies and realising that was patently untrue, she changed her mind. '. . . young gentlemen have it in the nursery.'

'Nursery!' he scoffed. 'I'm too big for a nursery. I go to school.'

'And children should be seen and not heard,' Sarah Jane said.

He looked at his mother with a questioning look, as if asking her what she was talking about; he had always had his tea with her and he had always been able to say what he wanted. His gaze went from Sarah Jane to Timothy but Mr Myson was smiling at him, so he couldn't have done anything very bad. He liked Mr Myson, if only because he knew about trains, and Lord Chevington's trains in particular. He bit into his sandwich.

They were like a family group, Sarah Jane thought, mother, father, child. If only . . . She stopped her thoughts from going along that road and turned to pay attention to what Timothy was saying to the boy.

'And what is the name of this excellent school you attend?' Was it sarcasm? Sarah Jane did not know.

'Miss Dean's Academy, sir.'

'And what do you learn?' he asked, unaccountably relieved it was not the Duncan McBryde School.

'Reading, writing, arithmetic, the scriptures ...'

'Latin? Greek?'

'Not yet, sir. Maybe next year, if I'm able.'

'And do they teach you any sport?'

'No, sir.'

'No riding?'

'No, sir.'

'Would you like a pony?' Timothy asked Jason. He had been right to think Jason was the kingpin of Sarah Jane's existence; her love of him was her weakest point. 'And riding lessons?'

'A pony?' Jason's eyes were alight. 'A *real* pony?'

'Of course, a real one. All young gentlemen should learn to ride at an early age.'

'When you are old enough, I shall buy you a pony,' Sarah Jane said, speaking to Jason but looking at Timothy. How dare he! How dare he come back from the past and assume he had a place in their lives! 'Now, I am sure we have kept Mr Myson long enough and it's time for you to go to bed.'

Timothy ruffled the boy's hair and was rewarded with a beaming smile; it was as if the two of them were conspiring against her and she felt as if she had been turned out in the cold. 'Would you like me to read to you a little while?' To get her alone he had to stay until Jason had gone to bed and the sooner that happened the better. He smiled. 'Your mother will allow that, won't she?'

'Tell me a story about the railways.' It was always railways he wanted to hear about, how they were built, the engines and rolling stock, the engineers, like Stephenson, Bruno and Cato, and the entrepreneurs like George Hudson, whose empire had crashed two years before, leaving investors facing losses of eighty million pounds. But most of all he wanted to hear about the Chevington lines. He looked at Sarah Jane. 'Please, Mama?'

Too weary to answer, she nodded and watched them leave the room together. The trauma of the afternoon had drained her energy, but it was not only that – it was Timothy's effect on her. She told herself over and over again that he had used her for his own pleasure, casually, thoughtlessly, selfishly, and she hated him for it, but she knew that was a lie. She had no right to hate; she had not been an unwilling partner. She had taken from him, not only the pleasure of the moment which was undeniable, but the great and lasting joy of their son and that was something for which she never ceased to be grateful. Did that account for her ambivalence, her indecisiveness, her stupid weakness where Timothy was concerned? She rang for Betsy to clear away the tea plates, then went to the sideboard and poured herself a brandy to help summon up the courage to send him away.

The story finished, he returned to the sitting room and noticed the glass in her hand. 'A little early for that, my dear, isn't it?'

'I have had a bad shock today and I need it.' She tipped the remaining liquid down her throat and stood up. 'Now, if you don't mind, I'm tired.'

'I have yet to be given an explanation of your strange behaviour,' he said, taking the glass from her hand and going to refill it, pouring himself a drink at the same time. 'It was hardly the reaction of a grateful mother.'

'I know, I am sorry.'

'What were you afraid of?'

'Nothing.'

He laughed. 'Did you suppose I was lying in wait for you?'

'Yes. No. Oh, I don't know.' She sank back onto the sofa.

'How could I possibly have known you would be there?' He sat down beside her, took her glass from her hand and set it on a side table. 'But it seems I should have done. That school . . .'

'It is a school for navvy children,' she said. 'I started it in memory of Duncan.'

'You did?' He was surprised. 'But that is no reason to take Jason to the site. He could have been killed.'

He was surprised how angry that made him feel; his son should never be anywhere near a navvy site. He wanted him kept away from all navvies.

She shuddered. 'Yes, and I am truly grateful. I know you saved his life, but—'

'I think you had better tell me what it was all about.'

She picked up her glass again, took a mouthful of brandy and told him about her nightmare, so relieved to get it off her chest that she did not notice the gleam in his eye – or the little smile of triumph that played around his mouth. 'I'm sorry,' she said. She had eaten no food and the brandy was befuddling her. 'I lived with it so long.'

'It's over now,' he said. 'You won't have that nightmare again.' He moved closer to her, taking her hand. She did not withdraw it. 'Is that why you sent me away last night?' He smiled, telling himself to stay calm for just a few more minutes and then he would have his reward. Already he felt himself stiffening. 'You won't send me away now, will you?'

The tension between them was strung out on a wire, so taut, her every muscle and sinew was stretched beyond her ability to control it. She expected something to snap at any minute with a sudden 'ping', leaving her dangling helplessly. 'What do you want?' she whispered, afraid of her own beating heart, afraid of her treacherous body, afraid of his gentleness, his smile, afraid, most of all, of her own craving.

'You,' he said, without a second's hesitation. 'And the love I never had, and never could have, from anyone else.' He lifted her hand to his lips and kissed the palm, running his open mouth slowly up from her fingers to the insides of her elbows, making her shiver with desire.

She sat, trying to hold herself aloof, trying to ignore his warm breath on her cheek, as he lifted his head to whisper in her ear. She tried to shut out what he was saying, tried instead to pay attention to the voice of reason, which told her she was putting her head in a noose, knowing that even while she listened to his soft voice murmuring endearments, she was growing weaker.

'Sweet Aphrodite,' he whispered. 'Do you remember, that first day by the river?'

How could she forget? It was her awakening, the blossoming of her sexuality, the beginning of Sarah Jane, the woman; she could not deny it. 'Yes. And you would not tell me your name, nor where you lived.' She found herself smiling at the memory. 'You said you lived in the clouds. I should have known then that you would have no more substance than a mist. Even when I knew Jason was coming, you still seemed unreal.' She paused. 'But it was all a long time ago and best forgotten.'

'Too long,' he said softly, taking her shoulders in his hands. 'And impossible to forget. You enchanted me right from the start with your funny practical ways, all mixed up with your reading and your dreaming, your use of words few skivvies know, spoken in accents that could only have come from the fen farm where you began. It was as if you were two people and not one.'

'I think we are all two people,' she said. 'Even you.'

'Me most especially,' he said morosely. 'Me most of all. But I liked being Paris, it gave me a better identity than being Timothy Myson, made me part of your dream life. That's why I gave you the apple, my tribute to your beauty.' He paused, taking her chin in his hand and forcing her to look into his eyes. His voice was soft as summer rain on a parched landscape. 'Don't try to fight it, Sarah Jane, because it is written in the stars, as immutable as night follows day.'

She was trembling and in that trembling there was excitement and passion, fear of beginning something she could not control, of losing herself in another's will, of past and future, joy and despair. Joy because he had remembered what their love had been to them and despair because she ought not to like what he was doing to her with his soft persuasive tongue, which had stopped speaking and was licking round her ear and down into the crevice between her breasts. But it was too late. Her nipples, her belly, her warm, damp thighs cried out for fulfilment. She took his head in both her hands and lifted it to look into his dark eyes, searching them for reassurance, for hope, for sincerity, and, because she wanted it so desperately, she imagined she saw it there.

'I have been so afraid . . .'

'Afraid of me?'

The tears were bright on her lashes. 'Perhaps, but mostly of myself. I have felt so cold and alone . . .'

'You are not alone now.' He picked her up in his arms and carried her into the bedroom, kicking the door shut behind him. 'You need never be alone again.' He laid her on her bed and began undressing her, slowly and carefully, murmuring endearments, kissing her over and over again. She tried, but oh, so feebly, to push him away, but it was only a token resistance. He removed his own clothes and lay down beside her, holding her close against him, pressing his body against hers from breast to thigh, so that she was aware of the strength of him, the hardness of him, the passion in him. Her emotions, bottled up for so long, overflowed into tears and then into an overwhelming desire which swept through her whole body and could not be denied. She flung her arms round him, clawing at the hair on the nape of his neck, sliding her hands down his spine to his buttocks, clinging to him fiercely, until they were both completely lost to everything but the satisfying of a long-suffered hunger.

Chapter Eighteen

*I*t was not until after he had left, that Sarah Jane stopped to think about what had happened and why it had happened, and she was appalled at her spinelessness. For years she had been trying to persuade herself that Timothy Myson was an uncaring seducer, the man responsible for Duncan's death, and now he had inveigled his way back into her life, made her weak and compliant, taken her strength and her resolve with nothing more than soft words and passionate kisses. How cheaply she had surrendered them! For the second time in as many days she was tempted to take Jason and lose herself again, but she knew she could not do that. All they needed was here – her home, her business, the comfort she had come to take for granted – and she could not, would not, ask Jason to make sacrifices because of her stupidity. She must not let Timothy Myson complicate her life with passions she thought she had taught herself to do without; it must not happen again.

'I'll come again tomorrow,' he had said, as he dressed in the half-light before dawn.

'No.' Even then the first stirrings of shame and guilt had been making themselves felt, though she had not spoken with any conviction. She was still too warm and satisfied, like a cat curled up by the fire, selfishly purring.

'No?' He had turned to face her, buttoning his trousers.

'I don't want you to.'

She had watched his reflection in the mirror as he wound his silk cravat round his collar and tied it in a flamboyant bow. He had smiled. 'You want me, just as much as I want you. You have just demonstrated it most ably and there is nothing on earth or in heaven or hell will alter that.'

'Get out!' She had grabbed a candlestick, the nearest thing to hand and flung it at him. 'Get out!'

He had ducked and laughed and blown her a kiss as he picked up his coat and left with it over his arm. 'I will be back, my love, be sure of that.'

But he did not come. Her emotions in the days that followed veered from relief to disappointment, from anger at his arrogant assumption that she would be waiting, to hurt feelings when the days passed and he stayed away. She tried convincing herself that he had come to her out of the ether, summoned by her own unspoken yearnings, and to the ether he had returned; Paris was a myth, not a real person at all. But oh, how she ached for him!

Then, two days before the end of April, late on a sunny spring afternoon, denying all her theories, he appeared on her doorstep and Betsy, charmed by his smile and forgetting her instructions to the contrary, let him in. He was carrying a huge bouquet of red roses and a model of an ancient galleon, perfect in every detail, right down to the fifty tiny oars, the brown sail and the name *Argo* painted along each side of its bow.

'I've brought a gift for Jason,' he said, giving Sarah Jane the roses and handing Betsy his hat.

'Why?' She was wary as a frightened rabbit.

'Why not? I missed his birthday. In fact, I have missed seven birthdays, haven't I?' This last was addressed to Jason who stood just behind his mother.

'You didn't know me on my other birthdays,' the boy said, chuckling with delight.

'No I didn't, more's the pity.' He turned to Sarah Jane. 'Are you going to ask me to sit down?'

She was a grown woman, an independent woman with a prosperous business, she held the livelihoods of more than fifty people in her hands, she could command and expect to be obeyed – so why did he make her feel so shaky, so unsure of herself? Why could he make her forget everything, except the fact that he had come back to her and she wanted to throw herself into his arms? 'The boat is your Trojan Horse, is it?' she said levelly, giving the flowers to Betsy to put into water.

'It got me in, didn't it?' He laughed and handed it to the boy, who stood and held it at arm's length, his eyes bright with wonder.

'It's lovely!' Jason said. 'Will it sail?'

'I sincerely hope so. A boat that won't sail is not much use, is it? Shall we go and try it?'

'Oh, yes.' He turned to his mother. 'Mama?'

'No,' she said, in an effort to be firm with herself, if not with him. 'It's getting late ...'

'Oh Mama, please.' He turned to Timothy. 'Mr Myson, you ask her. She'll do it for you.'

Timothy smiled. 'Well, Sarah Jane? We could walk to the Serpentine.'

She hesitated. At least if they were outdoors in a crowded thoroughfare, he would not be able to touch her and if he did not touch her, she might manage to keep cool and aloof. Jason took her silence for consent and hurried to find his jacket and cap, and five minutes later she found herself walking to the park, with Jason skipping along ahead of her carrying his boat and Timothy beside her, chatting about the forthcoming opening of the Exhibition, unaware of, or simply ignoring, her lack of response.

They spent an hour sailing the boat and then, in spite of her protests that it was unnecessary, Timothy escorted them home. Sarah Jane was tense, acutely conscious of his presence beside her, his hand lightly under her elbow, his stride matched to hers and she knew that she would not be able to deny him, that night or any other. Her body would not obey her head, which told her to send him away, that he was betrothed to someone else and she wanted nothing to do with him; her swiftly beating heart and trembling limbs told a different story.

She hesitated on the doorstep; if she was going to send him away, now was the time to do it. He stepped back to look at the shopfront. The facia was newly painted, and the window shining, but what he found so distasteful was the huge imitation pie, sitting in the middle of the window on a plate whose border was decorated with the words *Carter & Winterday, Pies of Renown.* 'Are we going to stand on the step all night, Sarah Jane?' he asked.

'You do not have to stand there at all,' she snapped, unlocking the side door. 'Goodbye, Mr Myson.'

Before she could shut the door in his face, he had pushed past her into the narrow hallway. 'Sarah Jane, why this coolness? You were not cool the other night, were you? You were on fire for me then.'

She looked anxiously towards Jason, wondering if he had understood, but he was dashing up the stairs to their living quarters. 'That was different.'

'How was it different?'

She turned on him suddenly. 'You want everything, don't you?

You want your position in society and you want to come to me whenever society bores you and expect me to fall into your arms. Well, I won't. Forget about the other night, it never happened. I have forgotten it already.'

'Liar!' he said.

Without answering she turned from him and followed Jason upstairs, unwilling to admit he was right. She could not forget it, could not forget the warmth of his body, the strength of his passion and her own uninhibited response. In silence she took off her bonnet and coat and ordered Betsy to bring tea and cakes into the drawing room. Jason had taken off his cap and coat and was sitting cross-legged on the hearthrug playing with his boat, moving the tiny oars and sails. Timothy smiled. 'Contented little chap, isn't he?'

'Yes, he is, and I don't want you spoiling that.'

'Spoiling it?' he queried, flinging up the tails of his coat to sit in one of the armchairs. 'I have no wish to do that, but I do want to talk to you about his future.'

'I am perfectly capable of looking after my son's future,' she said.

'But he could do so much better.' He stopped speaking as the maid came into the room with the tea tray and set it down on the table by the window. He dismissed the girl with a wave of his hand. 'For a start you could employ a more presentable parlourmaid. In fact, you ought to have a proper establishment. I don't want my son growing up above a pie shop. I'll find you somewhere more suitable.'

She ignored his presumption in giving her maid orders; it was hardly worth arguing about because she was determined he would not be admitted again and she must convince him of it. 'Suitable for what, Mr Myson?'

'Suitable for my ...'

'... mistress?' She finished for him.

'No, I was going to say for the mother of my son.' He paused. 'Sarah Jane, why don't you sit down and talk about it? I could send him to a good school and then to University, give him everything a gentleman's son should have. What is so dreadful about wanting the best for my – our – son?'

'Nothing. I will give him the best.'

'However well you do in business, I doubt if you can provide half the advantages I can. All I am asking is to see you as often as possible and to be allowed to be a father to my son.'

She looked down at Jason, playing happily at her feet; he did not appear to be listening and in fact was talking to the little oarsmen in his boat. 'Just as your father is to you, hiding you from his wife and pretending you are his ward? No, Timothy, better he should believe the father he loved died in a navvy tunnel.'

'Look at him,' he said. 'Does he look like a navvy's son? Will he take to being a labourer when he grows up? Will he enjoy rolling up his sleeves and working in your kitchens? Will he serve customers, bowing and scraping and saying "Yes, sir" all the time? Or will he expect more than that? Will he expect to be looked up to as a man of means, a gentleman?' He laughed, making Jason look up in surprise. 'Don't you remember how you wanted to be a lady? It's no difference from that.'

'I was only an ignorant child then.'

'Oh, no you weren't. You were all woman.' He wanted to pull her into the bedroom and strip off all her clothes, sink himself into her, knowing she would satisfy him as no other woman could. He was almost bursting his elegant trousers at the thought. 'You still are.' He smiled. 'Very nearly a lady, but not quite, eh? No lady would throw candlesticks about.'

'I am who I am and you will not alter that.'

'I don't want to alter you. I want you just as you are.'

'And what about Miss Hailey? Don't you love her? Her children will be your heirs. Look to your own problems, Timothy, and leave me to bring up my son in my own way. You are not my keeper and I will not surrender the independence I have worked so hard for, especially to be your paramour.'

A thought came to him like a bolt of lightning and stopped him in his tracks. Had he overestimated her capacity for love and underestimated her cunning? 'Are you trying to make me choose between you with my son and Caroline without him? Is it marriage you want?'

She laughed suddenly, a strange brittle laugh that made Jason go to her and kneel against her with his head in her skirt. She stopped to put her hand on his hair. 'It's all right, darling, Mr Myson made a little joke. Now, sit up to the table and eat your tea.' He did as he was bid and she turned back to Timothy, calmer than she had been all day. 'It was the last thought in my mind,' she said, in a voice so low that Jason could not hear. 'Don't you understand, you vain, conceited man, that I am trying, without causing a scene and upsetting Jason, to get rid of you?'

285

He realised he had gone too far; antagonising her would not achieve what he most desired. And what he most wanted was to install her in a little house where he could come and go as he pleased, where she would be dependent on him and he could control her. It had become more than a whim; her resistance had made it a necessity. He smiled and reached out to cover her hand with his own. She withdrew it and moved further away from him. Ignoring this evidence of her determination, he spoke softly. 'Why are we fighting, my darling Aphrodite? We should be making love, not war. All I wanted, all I ever want, is to be with you and if I sometimes use unfair tactics, then it is a measure of my great need of you. Don't you understand that?'

'No, I don't.' She was weary with arguing, tired of denying her own traitorous body which, even while she rejected him, wanted his arms round her, his kisses on her neck, the feel of him between her thighs. They were hardly the feelings a decent, respectable woman could admit to; did that mean she was not decent and respectable? But it was not love, it was unbridled passion and that was what was wrong about it. 'Go away, Timothy. Go away and leave me in peace.' Her voice was as cool as she could make it. 'You are not welcome.'

'Jason welcomes me.' He stood up and went to the table to lean over Jason and pick up a piece of cake. He popped it into his mouth and then in a voice of mock despair, said, 'Your mother wants to send me away without my tea, Jason, and I do so enjoy her cakes.'

'Leave the boy out of this,' she snapped.

'How can we?' He returned to her side and his voice was soft as silk and just as sensuous. 'He is part of us, part of you and me.' He took her hand. 'We made him together, that summer on the banks of the stream at Chevington. You do not really want to forget that, do you?'

She refused to answer. She loved Jason, no mother could love a son more, but was it unnatural to want a man's love too? She could only cease to love Timothy if she could hate him; there was nothing in between. Hate him, she commanded herself, humble him, crush him before he destroys you. But how could she hate him? She understood his black twisted thoughts better than anyone, and because she could understand, she could forgive. She could forgive his longing for recognition, his inability to express or admit his need for love, even his conceit because it was a shield against his bastardy; she could forgive him and pity him, but did she love him? Had she ever really loved him? Once perhaps ... but now? Oh God, how was she ever going to keep this up?

'Timothy, I—' She looked up as the door was opened and Betsy stood aside to let Thomas into the room. 'Mr Wistonby, ma'am.'

Timothy dropped her hand and muttered a curse as Thomas moved across the room to take Sarah Jane's hand and raise it to his lips, before acknowledging Timothy with a slight inclination of the head. If he was surprised to see him there, he gave no sign of it. 'Good evening, Mr Myson.'

Timothy's face darkened, but he did not reply. Of all the bad luck to have that blackguard arrive just when he was making progress! What the lawyer's motives were he had no idea, but he did know that he had tricked him with long and involved stories of not being able to find Sarah Jane when he knew where she was all along. Not that there was anything to be done about it because you could hardly go to law for five guineas and besides, His Lordship knew nothing of it and it was better that he did not.

Thomas looked from Timothy, who appeared decidedly annoyed, to Sarah Jane with her bright eyes and heightened colour, and wondered just how far things had gone between them. 'I have some news for you, Mrs McBryde, but if it isn't convenient . . .'

'Of course it's convenient,' she said quickly. 'You are always welcome. Mr Myson was kind enough to take us to sail Jason's new boat, but we mustn't keep him any longer.' She turned to Jason. 'Say thank you to Mr Myson and then you must go to bed.'

'Aren't I going to have a story tonight?' The boy looked from Timothy to his mother.

'Not tonight, Jason,' she said firmly.

Timothy ruffled the boy's curls. He was as bright as a button and every inch the young gentleman – a Chevington, in fact. It was a pity he would be burdened with the stigma of bastardy just as he himself had been, except, of course, that Sarah Jane maintained Jason was a McBryde. His son, a navvy brat – he didn't like that idea at all, any more than he liked the idea of Sarah Jane and Thomas Wistonby in each other's arms. He did not know what she saw in him; the man was old enough to be her father. He had a good mind to throw everything up and marry her just to punish that interfering old lawyer. It was a mad idea, unthinkable, brought about by his frustration, nothing more. Breaking off his engagement to Caroline would lay him open to a suit for breach of promise, and though he could afford the damages, he could not afford to jeopardise his inheritance. He had to marry Caroline, and he had to make Sarah Jane understand it and accept it,

287

because he would not give her up. Patience, he told himself, that was all he needed. Patience, and the boy on his side. He told Jason, 'I'll come another time, shall I?' and smiled at Sarah Jane, so sure of himself she wanted to throw something at him.

'I'm extremely busy,' she said lamely.

'Then I shall be patient.' He lifted her hand to his lips, aware that it was shaking. '*Au revoir*, my dear Mrs McBryde.' Then he left the room, picked up his hat from the table in the hall and hurried down the stairs, leaving Sarah Jane staring after him.

'What was all that about?' Thomas demanded.

'What?' She dragged herself back to pay attention.

'You and Timothy Myson. When did he turn up?'

'I'll tell you all about it after Jason has gone to bed.'

Half an hour later, ensconced in her best armchair with a glass of port in his hand, Thomas brought up the subject again. 'Am I right in assuming you were relieved to see me just now, Sarah Jane?'

'Yes, infinitely.' She poured herself a drink and sat down opposite him.

'Has he ...?'

'Yes.' She paused and took a mouthful of brandy before going on. 'And the worst of it is, it didn't seem to occur to him that I might not welcome him with open arms.'

He laughed. 'Which is what you did, I don't doubt. You were never much good at hiding your feelings, Sarah Jane, and what you feel, you do.'

'Am I as transparent as all that?'

'Only to those who love you, as I do.'

She was sidetracked enough to ask in surprise, 'Do you?'

'Of course. I always have. But do go on.'

'Ever since he came here, over a week ago now, I have been torn between wishing he were with me and relief that he was not. I hate myself for it and I hate myself even more for agreeing to walk to the park with him, simply because he brought Jason a gift. I can't deny Jason anything, you know that, and I suspect Timothy knows it too. I am on a seesaw, up one minute, down the next.'

'You are not normally ambivalent, my dear. You usually know exactly what you want, and most of the time you get it.'

She smiled ruefully. 'The trouble is that what I want is not right or just but it doesn't stop me wanting it.'

He got up to refill their glasses. 'And what do you want from me,

Sarah Jane?' he asked, with his back to her. 'I am not a priest to hear your confession and it is unfair of you to treat me like one.' He turned and handed her a brimming glass. 'It hurts me to think of you in the arms of another man and if I were entirely selfish, I should say be done with him, be done with all men. Keep what you have, your home, your business, your good works, and forget about love. But I cannot condemn you to that.'

'It is not love. I do not love him and he doesn't love me.'

'Perhaps not, but perhaps he does. He may not even know it himself, and he would certainly try to hide it under a veneer of cynicism.' He looked at her over the rim of his glass. He had to act the devil's advocate, to make her analyse her own feelings, to come to terms with the fact that Timothy existed. 'He bought you the golden apple, didn't he? Any ordinary lover would have given you a necklace or a diamond pin, but Timothy had that bauble made specially for you.'

'How do you know that?' Such a possibility had never occurred to her. The apple's intrinsic worth had never been important but now it took on a value which had nothing to do with gold. Paris had taken trouble over the gift, made it personal to her alone and she found herself remembering her joy when he gave it to her. Had anything changed at all?

'I make it my business to know about everything that concerns you,' he went on. 'And what about that boat? Only Timothy would have thought of the *Argo*, something especially for Jason.'

'Why are you defending him?'

'Because I am a lawyer, I suppose,' he told her thoughtfully, 'and I look at facts, not feelings.'

'But this is all about feelings, Thomas. What he feels, what I feel.'

'Feelings or passions?' he asked mildly.

'What's the difference? It doesn't make me feel any less guilty.'

'Why do you feel guilty?' His voice was gentle. 'Because of Caroline Hailey – or because of Duncan McBryde?'

She hesitated. Duncan. Did she feel she was betraying his memory? Was that the trouble? While she had Duncan, whose steadfastness had been the mainstay of her life, it had been easy to see Timothy as selfish and arrogant, one of the hated owners. Because she lived among the navvies and knew how they struggled, she had seen him as the enemy. But nothing was ever as clear-cut as that; few people were ever all black, or all white. And talking to Lord Chevington had given her an insight into the other side of the argument; it was another reason for her equivocation. 'Both, I suppose.'

'Duncan is dead, Sarah Jane. Accept the fact that you will never meet his like again and thank God for those happy years, but you cannot spend the remainder of your life without love. You are too warm-hearted and passionate for that.'

'Sometimes, when I think of the way Jason has taken to him and I see them together, so easy in each other's company, I think that's how it should be – father and son and me together in a proper family. But I am not such a fool as to think that's a possibility.'

'You are as good as he is, any day. After all, what is he but the bastard son of a wealthy baron? Without Lord Chevington he is a nobody.'

'And that is precisely the reason he would not consider marrying me. He needs His Lordship and he is betrothed to Miss Hailey and he would never risk the scandal of being sued for breach of promise.'

'Did he not tell you it would be a marriage of convenience?' Thomas paused, watching her face carefully, trying to divine what was going on behind those troubled green eyes.

'Isn't that what they all say? And whose convenience? Timothy Myson's, no one else's.'

'Oh, I think Miss Hailey will find the money very convenient,' he said, ironically. 'And so will her impecunious papa.'

'He has died.'

'Then she will need it all the more. Lord Hailey will have left his family in sorry straits.'

'I am not an adulteress, Thomas.'

'Then, my dear, you have your answer.' He sat down beside her and raised his glass to her. 'Send him about his business.'

'Yes.' She sighed and took a sip of her drink.

'My advice is to do whatever makes you happy,' he went on. 'But do beware of making an enemy of your son's father. He could be dangerous when crossed. Now, can we forget about Timothy Myson and turn to Billie Winterday?'

'You have news of him?' Her expression, so sombre a moment before, lightened and she leaned forward eagerly. 'Do you know where my brother is?'

'No, I am afraid not, but I know where he has *been*.'

'Where?'

'I'm sorry to say, in prison.'

'Why? What did he do?'

'According to the records, quite a number of things, but he was caught red-handed breaking into an umbrella shop with a no-good friend of his and sentenced to two years in Newgate.'

'Newgate! Oh Thomas, that's dreadful. Poor Billie.' She knew from her own experience how hard life was in the city if you had no work and no means of making a living, and if he had not had the luck she had been blessed with, she could not find it in her heart to condemn him. 'How did you find out?'

'By asking, my dear, using an introduction Lord Chevington gave me, which meant I was able to talk to police chiefs, prison governors, people like that.'

'Are you sure it was my brother?'

'Yes, there is no doubt.'

'Poor Billie,' she said again. 'If only I'd been able to find him sooner. When is he due out?'

'He finished his sentence, though where he went when he was released, no one knows.'

'Then we must find him – and find him quickly. Employ some help, Thomas. I will gladly pay.'

'I will do what I can, that goes without saying.'

She reached out and put a smooth, well-manicured hand over his and smiled. 'Thank you, Thomas. And will you thank His Lordship for me, too? I am most grateful.'

He stood up to take his leave. 'He gave me three tickets for the opening day of the Exhibition so that I could take you and Jason. Would you like that?'

'Yes, very much, but we are so busy ...'

'Nonsense. You have excellent staff, I know that. You work too hard, my dear. All work and no play ...'

She rang for Betsy to bring his hat. 'I enjoy my work and we've done very well out of it, so I've no complaints.' She reached up to kiss his cheek. 'But I don't know what I should do without you.'

'I'll call for you at nine o'clock. We ought to take our places early.' He took his hat from the maid and made his way down the stairs to the street door.

As soon as Thomas had gone, Sarah Jane turned back into her drawing room, fetched the shop ledgers from a cupboard and sat at the table working on them until it was time to go to bed. Working was easier than thinking, and she wanted to put off the moment when she would have to lie in her empty bed and try to sleep.

The wanton side to her nature told her that there was no need for her to sleep alone, not every night – that she could enjoy being Timothy's mistress for as long as they both wanted it. It would hurt no one, not even Caroline Hailey, who need know nothing of it. But the other side of her, the side that knew right from wrong, the side which could reason, argued that affairs with men in public life always caused scandal in the end; and not only would Caroline Hailey get to know of it, but if her name were linked publicly with Timothy's, it would hurt Jason and her business. Thomas had said, 'You have your answer,' and he was right.

When Henry arrived next day to collect the ledgers, Sarah Jane was busy making sure everything would run smoothly and that they would have enough pies baked and delivered to meet the orders they had received for the opening of the Exhibition on the following day. If all went well, orders would continue to flood in so long as the Exhibition lasted and by the time it finished in October, they would have established their reliability and the quality of their products, and could continue to go from strength to strength. Already she was planning a second bakehouse, perhaps in a different part of London, or even outside it. She finished giving instructions to the shop manager and went upstairs with Henry to collect the ledgers and the previous day's takings.

Jason, who was getting ready for school, greeted him enthusiastically and insisted on showing him his new boat.

Henry smiled. 'Who gave you that?'

'Mr Myson. We took it out and sailed it in the park. But when we got back Mr Wistonby came, so Mr Myson would not tell me a bedtime story like he did before, but he said he would come again if Mama would let him.'

'Jason, you will be late,' Sarah Jane said, knowing that she was going to be quizzed by Henry and already feeling defensive. 'And Uncle Henry does not want to hear your chatter. Don't you know little boys should be seen and not heard? Now, away with you.'

He went obediently but the damage had been done. She tried to avoid Henry's eyes as she fetched the accounts books and the heavy bag containing money for the bank. 'Mr Wistonby is taking us to see the procession tomorrow and we have tickets to go inside after the opening,' she explained, handing the bag and ledgers to him. 'This is for the Oxford Street shop. I'm going over to the manufactory later today, to interview more staff and I've left instructions for Mr Perkins to bring you the takings from the Covent Garden shop tomorrow evening. He is very trustworthy and I think I'll promote him ...' She was running on breathlessly, trying to make him respond to what she was saying, but instead of rising to the bait and questioning the need for more staff or how she could promote a man who was already a shop manager, Henry put down the things she had given him and moved over to his favourite place with his back to the fireplace where he could survey the room in his proprietorial manner and wait until she had run out of steam.

'It's got to stop, Sarah Jane,' he said, when she paused for breath.

'What has to stop?'

'This immoral life you lead.'

'Immoral, Henry?' It was spoken pleasantly but there was an undercurrent of anger she could not disguise.

'Yes. If it isn't that disreputable Wistonby, it's that rakish ward of Lord Chevington's.'

'Mr Wistonby is my legal adviser and he is not disreputable,' she said, ignoring his reference to Timothy.

He laughed grimly. 'Legal adviser! Oh Sarah Jane, the man is besotted by you, it is patently obvious in the way he looks at you.'

'He is a very old and very dear friend. And it is none of your business; you would have nothing to do with my school idea and I had to have help from someone. If you don't like it, you have no one to blame but yourself.'

'And what about Mr Myson? When I was told he had been here the whole of one night, I refused to believe it, but Jason has more or less confirmed it.'

'He is also an old friend,' she said, wondering who the informer was. 'And if I choose to invite him to stay that is my business.' She should be placating him, explaining that Timothy had only stayed once and it would never happen again. Instead she was taking a savage joy in defying him.

'Sarah Jane, the man is betrothed and would have been married by now if the lady had not been in mourning.'

'How do you know that?'

'Lady Hailey has ordered mourning clothes for all the family. If it gets out that Mr Myson has been entertained here by you, we will both be ruined. I beg of you to think carefully. Put an end to the affair. Take a holiday, then when you come back, we can go on as before and I will never mention it again.'

293

'How can I take a holiday? Do be practical, Henry, we are too busy.'

'We can hire a manager.'

'Do you suppose I'll leave my business for strangers to ruin? I didn't work my fingers to the bone to throw it all away.'

'That's just my point, Sarah Jane. You *are* throwing it away – and for what? A night or two of dubious pleasure.'

She laughed and it was a cracked, humourless sound. 'Oh, there's nothing dubious about it, I assure you.'

'Now you are being vulgar.'

'And you are being prudish. It seems to me that there is one set of values for men and another for women. Everyone feels sorry for you because your wife has left you and, of course, it is natural and understandable that you need to seek solace, but for me to admit the need for a man's companionship, for physical love, is vulgar and something to be ashamed of!'

He was completely taken aback by her outspokenness, and for a moment wrestled with a way to answer her. If he had known her views before, he might not have been so careful of her. There had been many times when she could have assuaged his sexual hunger but he had been afraid she might have expected a commitment from him and that he could not give. 'A woman's fulfilment comes with looking after home and family, Sarah Jane. Think of Jason, if you will not think of me. The child will be ostracised – he will never be accepted in society.'

Remembering her earlier ambition to be a lady and knowing now how impossible that had been, she laughed. 'His mother is a pie-maker and his father was a navvy. Are they good credentials for society?'

'I should have known better than to appeal to your good sense,' he said with a heavy sigh, as if he were talking to a recalcitrant child. 'I should have done something about it months ago when Lord Chevington came ...'

'Lord Chevington? What has he to do with it?'

'His Lordship is also one of your callers, is he not? I'll wager they don't all arrive together.'

His assumption that Timothy and His Lordship visited her for the same reason took her breath away. She walked over to the window and looked down on the busy street with its carriages, pedestrians, hawkers and beggars to give herself time to answer. 'I was paid compensation for the death of my husband and I used the money on my school project. Lord Chevington has been a great help to me and there is a lot to discuss.'

'When a married man visits a lady at home without benefit of chaperon, what do you expect people to think?'

'That's preposterous. You visit me.'

'We are business partners.'

She laughed suddenly. 'And do you think London Society, as you call it, can tell the difference? If it's acceptable for you to come here on business, so it is for His Lordship.'

'And what about his ward? Are you going to explain that away by saying it was business?'

'Henry, I do not have to answer to you for what I do in my own time in my own home,' she said wearily. 'We will speak of it no more.'

'If you want to continue in partnership with me,' he said, so calmly that it stopped her in her tracks, 'you will put an end to your association with Mr Myson and see Lord Chevington only at his office.' He smiled slowly, infuriating her still further. 'And the premises are half mine.'

'I will not be dictated to.'

'Think on it, Sarah Jane,' he said quietly, picking up his hat and gloves, the ledgers and the money bag. 'I really do have your interests at heart.'

When he had gone, she sank into a chair and covered her face with her hands. She was still seething, but her anger did little to delay the onset of the heart-searching. What a fool she was! She had, with Thomas' help, come to the same conclusion as Henry, so why had she stood there and defied him, put her business and her home in jeopardy, making him think badly of her? There was a little devil in her which liked to shock; it had been there all her life, but most of the time she had managed to suppress it, so why let it surface now, when she had so much to lose?

Lord Chevington had been good to her, recommending architects and builders and even helping in her search for Billie; he would be sadly disappointed in her if she threw it all away for a love affair which could have no happy ending, and with his own son, too. She was surprised how much his approval or disapproval mattered to her. He had always been kind to her, not looking down on her as a nobody, but talking to her as an equal, listening to her ideas and putting forward one or two of his own, and she was grateful. But it was more than gratitude; she liked and respected him, and Henry's accusations had shocked her.

On the other hand, the school was heavily subsidised with her personal profits from the shops. How could she manage without them if Henry carried out his threat and she lost her business? She couldn't survive and besides, apart from Jason, the shops, once only the means to an end, had become her whole life. She had a tightrope to walk, but if she wanted to survive, she had to walk it, right to the end.

The opening day of the Exhibition had been declared a public holiday, except for those unfortunates who had to cater for the needs of the vast crowds who came by train, carriage, omnibus and on foot. Sarah Jane's staff, left behind in the shops, had been compensated for the loss of their holiday with tickets for the following week.

'Mama, Mr Wistonby is coming up the stairs.' Jason had been up and about almost as long as she had, fidgeting and impatient to be off. To give him something to do, she had told him to watch for Thomas.

She smiled at his eagerness, gave Thomas a perfunctory greeting and then went into her bedroom to change from the printed gingham she had been wearing for work into a green and cream striped silk dress decorated around the hem and down the long pointed bodice jacket with green velvet ribbon. She topped it with a waist-length green satin mantle and did up the row of buttons down its front before setting a matching bonnet on her red hair, then giving herself a quick appraising look in the mirror, joined Thomas and Jason who were waiting impatiently for her.

As they walked, she told Thomas about Henry's ultimatum.

'Why don't you buy him out?' he suggested.

'I can't. I used all my savings, as well as the compensation, on the school. Besides, I still need him.'

'I can do whatever it is you need him for, surely?'

She smiled. 'Yes, Thomas, of course, but it doesn't matter because in my heart I know he is right. I don't know what came into me, arguing with him like that, but I suspect it was nothing but pride. I cannot afford pride, nor can I afford a scandal.' She smiled and tucked her hand into the crook of his arm. She was a woman of means, if not a lady; she had made a niche for herself on the fringe of society and she was realist enough to know that being on the fringe was better than being nowhere at all. 'If Henry were to dissolve our partnership . . .'

He laughed aloud. 'Now why should he do that? He has as much to lose as you have. You are meeting trouble halfway, Sarah Jane, and that is a foolish waste of energy, so stop worrying and let us enjoy our day.'

She smiled and squeezed his arm affectionately as they hurried along to join the sightseers who had begun arriving before dawn to take their places in the park, on both sides of the Serpentine and along the route of the royal procession. It was colourful and noisy with flags flying, cannon booming and the colourful uniforms of the soldiers.

Sarah Jane and Thomas fought their way into the cheering throng and were near the front as the royal carriages came into view. Thomas put Jason on his shoulder, so that he could see, while the roar of the multitude rose about them. But Sarah Jane did not see the procession pass because her whole attention was rivetted on the ranks of soldiers who lined the route. One of them, on the opposite side of the road, standing stiffly to attention, reminded her of Billie. She could not say what it was – perhaps his stance, or the way his hair curled about his ears below his shako, or possibly his blue eyes and that rather wooden expression. Billie had looked like that the last time she had seen him, in Matron's sitting room, the day she left the Union.

'Billie!' she screamed above the tumult of music and cheering. She pulled on Thomas' arm. 'Look – there's Billie – on the other side of the road. I know it's him! Oh Thomas, we must go to him.'

The procession passed and the crowds surged forward, intent on following the royal carriages as far as they could, and Sarah Jane and Thomas were carried, unwillingly, along with them. By the time they had fought their way back to the same spot and crossed the road, Billie had been marched away. 'I'm sure it was him,' she said, almost crying with disappointment. 'Oh, why couldn't he have been on this side of the road? To be so near and then lose him again. Where do you think they went?'

'Back to barracks, I expect.'

'Which barracks?'

'I have no idea, but it shouldn't be difficult to find out.'

'Oh Thomas, do you really think so?' She was alight with eagerness. 'Are we really going to be reunited at last? Will he be pleased to see me, do you think?'

'Of course he will.' He smiled. 'Tomorrow I'll begin making enquiries but now let's go and see what this Crystal Palace has to offer.'

They spent hours in the Exhibition, but Sarah Jane hardly noticed the marvellous things on display, the furniture, sculptures, jewellery, pottery, odd inventions and new machinery. At any other time, she would have been as enthusiastic about it as everyone else, but her mind was on Billie and, tinged with her disappointment was the knowledge that he had not returned to crime, that he was serving his Queen and country, and she could be proud of him. And this time, Thomas would find him and they would meet again. Already she was making plans.

Chapter Nineteen

*T*imothy had missed the opening of the Great Exhibition to spend a stifling week in the country with Caroline and her mother, but the time had not been wasted because he had been able to meet Jack Miller at Hailey Common. The engineer had informed him that the tunnel could be reopened and the line continued. When the junction was made with the *Great Eastern* at Caledonian Road, and the Hailey Common line was finished, Timothy would be the major shareholder in a line extending all the way from the London docks to the Midlands, and no one – not even his own father – would be able to hold a candle to him. He had returned to London in a cheerful frame of mind to set the wheels in motion, only to discover that the line to the junction had been changed in his absence.

'Do you mean to say you moved the whole line because of that pitiful little school?' he demanded, standing over His Lordship's desk and jabbing a finger at the plans. 'We must sweep it away.'

'We can't do that, the school belongs to Mrs McBryde! Upwards of a hundred children attend it every day.'

'Who owns the freehold?'

'She does.'

'Good God! I thought it was only rented. Does she know she is on the route of *my* line?'

'Not unless she reads *The Gazette* in some detail.'

'On its own it is worth very little, but as part of the scheme ...' Timothy stopped to contemplate what this meant to him and the thought that Sarah Jane could frustrate him in yet another way made him furious. 'You could have bought the site from her.'

'I saw no reason to and she wanted it so badly.'

Timothy looked up sharply to meet his father's gaze. Had Sarah Jane bewitched him, too? 'She wanted it?' He was aware that his voice had risen and he paused to modulate it. 'What about what *I* wanted? You knew how important this project was to me. You knew I had invested all I had in it.'

'All, Timothy?'

'Yes, after what has been set aside to reopen the Hailey Common site.'

'That was foolish of you.'

'I did not know that you would go soft in the head, did I, Father? I asked you to carry on with my plans, not to alter them out of all recognition.' He was so angry, he was hardly aware of what he was saying. 'And for what? That troublemaking whore . . .'

'Can you mean Mrs McBryde?'

'You know I do.'

'Those are hardly the words of a gentleman about a lady.'

'Lady!' Timothy laughed harshly. 'She is no lady. She is nothing but a trumped-up skivvy, a navvy's doxy . . .'

'And the mother of your son.' The words were said quietly but they stopped the young man in full flood.

'How did you know that?'

'I met her at the school and realised who she was. She showed me round, told me of her plans . . .'

'And on the strength of that, you changed the whole course of my life.'

'You are being melodramatic, Timothy. How can it affect the course of your life?' He pointed to the drawing on the desk. 'The new route . . .'

'. . . will cost too much and take too long. A detour would mean purchasing whole streets of good buildings and compensating businesses whose owners thought themselves well clear of danger. I cannot afford it.' Timothy picked up the plans, screwed them into a rough ball and flung them in the fireplace. 'We must buy that damn school off her before she finds out what trouble she can cause.'

Geoffrey gazed at the crumpled paper as if mesmerised by it. 'I hope you do not mean to go and see her. It would upset her.'

'Upset her! Oh, that's rich!' Timothy threw back his head and laughed, though there was more panic than humour in it. His father obviously did not know he had been seeing Sarah Jane and that was just as well. He had gone to her as a diversion from the cloying affections of Caroline Hailey, not realising what the consequences would be. He should have known, should have remembered how it had been all those years ago; Sarah Jane had cast a spell on him that first day on the banks of the stream, which would bind him to her for the rest of his life – and whoever or whatever came between them could never alter that. It was not love, he told himself, he had schooled himself to be immune to that most destructive of emotions, but it was more than a passing fancy which he could get out of his system with one night in bed with her. She made him feel strong and powerful, but because the strength and power came from deep within her, it also weakened him. The paradox disturbed him, frightened him a little; it smacked of witchcraft. He wanted to squeeze it out of her, like squeezing the stone from a ripe plum, leaving only the soft flesh to be enjoyed. And now, with his plans balked by her, he was more determined than ever. He wanted to hurt her. 'But you are right, we must not upset her.' His voice was full of sarcasm. 'We'll make the offer through an intermediary.'

'She is no fool, Timothy.'

'Neither am I.' He yelled for the office clerk and sent him scurrying to fetch their legal adviser.

Sarah Jane's reaction to the letter was one of curiosity rather than interest; she certainly had no intention of taking it seriously. She wanted to buy, not sell, and Thomas had been given instructions to make offers for the other houses in the row so that she could extend the school. She was unprepared for disappointment.

'They were sold to the railway only last week,' Thomas told her when he came to Oxford Street to report on his progress.

'Railway? But that is half a mile away!' It was the end of a long day and they had just finished an evening meal and were relaxing over a glass of wine in her sitting room. School affairs always had to be relegated to the evening in deference to Henry, who expected her whole attention on the catering business during daylight hours.

'I'm told this is a new one, intended to join up with the *Great Eastern*.'

'Whose railway? Which company?'

'*Railways Incorporated*. I gather it is a consortium.'

'*Railways Incorporated*. Never heard of them.'

'Newly formed, I think, specifically for this project.'

'That accounts for this,' she said, picking up the letter from the mantelshelf and handing it to him. 'I received it today by special messenger – an offer for the school building from a firm of solicitors. It doesn't mention the name of their clients.'

'That's not unusual.' Thomas scanned it quickly, then looked up at her. 'It's not a bad offer.'

'You're not suggesting I should accept it?'

'Why not? If you don't, they'll get a compulsory purchase order and you may find that less generous.'

'I am in the market to buy, not sell, you know that.'

'Sarah Jane, I think we can rule that out now. At least on that site.'

For the first time in months, she found herself thwarted and she did not like that feeling at all. 'I'll fight,' she said angrily. 'I'll fight every inch.'

'But, my dear, you don't know who or what you are up against.'

She dashed over to a cupboard where she stored back copies of *The Gazette*. 'It's here somewhere,' she said, throwing newspapers all over the floor. She opened several and discarded them along with the rest. 'Ah, here it is.'

'What?'

'A bill for a new line.' She brought the paper back to her chair to read. '... presented by Mr John Townsend on behalf of *Railways Incorporated*.' She read on. 'The directors ... Sir John Davey, Mr Robert Clarke, Mr Timothy Myson ... I might have guessed!'

'Perhaps the bill was refused.'

'They would not have bought all those properties in that case, nor want mine. Now what do we do?'

'Do as you did before, hold out for as much compensation as possible and move elsewhere.'

'But I don't want to move. The school is well-established now. We've worked hard to get everything just right and it is so handy for the navvy children.'

'You'll have to in the end.' He was infuriatingly calm.

'What I find so baffling,' she said slowly, 'is that Lord Chevington said nothing. He must have known about it and yet he encouraged me to carry on.' She set the paper aside to look across the hearth at Thomas, comfortably sprawling in an armchair. It was funny how the men in her life made themselves at home in her apartment. Thomas did it and Henry and even Lord Chevington, when he came. As for Timothy ... No, she did not want to think of the man; she had banished him. 'I am disappointed in His Lordship, Thomas. Very.'

'They are all the same, these so-called gentry, and especially if they get a toe in the business world. They think they can ride roughshod ...'

'Well, they will not ride roughshod over me. I refuse to budge.' She gave a cracked laugh. 'You may take that as my instruction to you as my man of business.'

He held his glass up to her. 'Then here's to a battle royal.'

'Timothy is punishing me,' she said. 'He wants to hurt me – because I sent him away, I suppose. But that is so childish. After all, I am not the only woman in London. He could find what he wants in a brothel.'

Thomas laughed. 'Could he, my dear? Do you really imagine he thinks of you in those terms?'

She smiled, but there was a weariness in her that he had not seen before. Wrestling with herself was more draining than fighting Henry and coping with all the day-to-day problems of a thriving business. 'It's of no consequence now,' she said. 'I have finished with him entirely. He knows that.'

But Timothy knew nothing of the sort. As far as he was concerned, the fight had only just begun. He was prepared to use any means at his disposal, not only to inherit the Chevington name and wealth, not only to further his own ambition to overtop his father as a business magnate – which meant buying the land for the new line – but also, to win Sarah Jane. He did not believe she did not want him; he knew she did. She had betrayed her lusty desire for him once and if that lawyer fellow had not turned up the last time, she would have done so again. Her refusal to see him since then was a pretence, her way of demanding more than he was prepared to give.

Just how much was he prepared to give? Money and the things money could buy, certainly, his time and loving attention whenever they both felt the need, and the assuaging of her hunger for sexual fulfilment, along with his own. He knew that was there, she had admitted as much. But he would not, could not, give up his marriage for her, nor his chance to become a true member of the society his father took so much for granted. He wanted the best of both worlds and he would have it. And this business of the school made it even more important. He wanted Sarah Jane in the palm of his hand where he could manipulate her.

He chose a Sunday for his next move, knowing Sarah Jane liked to take Jason in the park on the only day she was free of work. He rode out on his own big bay, leading a small piebald pony.

The child spotted him first. 'Look!' he cried, tugging on his mother's arm. 'There's Mr Myson! And he's brought a little horse!'

Sarah Jane had been so busy catering for the thousands of people who came to buy her pies, she had left the business of the school to Thomas, knowing that a compulsory purchase would take weeks to enact. It gave her time to organise a petition among the navvies and to assemble a case for allowing the school to remain *in situ*. It was a very long shot and she knew she would have to sell in the end, but she had no intention of making it easy for her protagonists. That one of these was Timothy, she was only too well aware, but she had given herself no time to brood over it. When he was absent it was easy to think of him as an unwanted tormentor. But now he was coming towards her, smiling and confident of his welcome, and already his magnetism was drawing her to him, making her knees buckle and her heart beat at twice its usual rate. She stood and watched him approach, gripping her parasol as if her life depended on the strength in its slim handle.

'Is this another Trojan horse, Mr Myson?' she asked, as he dismounted. 'Because if it is . . .'

He laughed, doffing his top hat. 'I didn't think such a thing was necessary now.'

'You assume too much, sir.'

'In what way? That I need no longer trick my way in to see you, or by buying Jason the pony I promised him?' He turned to Jason with an impish smile. 'Good-day to you, young shaver. Are you ready for your first lesson?'

'Oh yes, please.' Jason's voice was a squeak of excitement. 'Is he mine?'

'The pony? Yes, of course he's yours.'

'Mr Myson.' Sarah Jane hoped the formal address would help her to convince him. 'I cannot possibly accept such a present.'

'I'm not giving it to you, Mrs McBryde, I'm giving it to Jason.' He smiled at the boy and received a beam of delight in return. 'All young gentlemen should learn to ride and he wants to, don't you, my boy?'

'Oh yes, please.'

'Timothy,' she said evenly. 'It is unfair of you to give Jason such a gift without asking me first. If I think he should have a pony, then I'll buy him one myself.'

'Oh Mama, do stop talking,' Jason said, tugging at her sleeve. 'I want to mount.'

'So you shall, son, so you shall.' Timothy hoisted the boy into the saddle. 'Now take the reins in your hands so, and sit still while I speak to your mother.'

She didn't like the way he addressed Jason as 'son', but she dare not protest for fear of arousing the boy's curiosity. He was so obviously over the moon with his new acquisition, she did not have the heart to make him dismount and accompany her home. And Timothy knew it!

He turned from Jason to smile at her. 'Where's the harm, Sarah Jane? I'll take him up and down where it's quiet and then bring him home to you safe and sound, and don't say "another day" because the animal is saddled and needs a little exercise.'

'Please, Mama,' Jason begged. 'I won't fall off. I'll be quite safe with Mr Myson.'

'Very well,' she said, knowing she was making a rod for her own back. 'Half an hour. I'll sit on that bench over there and wait for you.'

She watched as Timothy remounted the bay and, taking the rein of the piebald, led Jason along a quiet path between the trees. The boy was unafraid and sat his mount well. From the back, they looked so alike, the set of their shoulders, the way they held their heads. Jason was a Chevington. Ought she to deny him that? She smiled wryly; she would not be the one to deny him, it would be Timothy himself.

Did he realise she was aware that he was a director of the company which had made the offer for the school? Did he know she was strenuously resisting it – and if he did, was the pony meant to be more than something to lure her into his bed? A bribe, perhaps? It was paltry, if it was. She smiled to herself. If he did not know, then he was in for a rude awakening. Suddenly she felt quite cheerful.

Half an hour later, the pair returned and she stood up to help her son dismount. 'Oh, must we go home?' he pleaded, reluctant to surrender the reins. 'I want to go on.'

'Not this evening, Jason. You mustn't be too tired for school tomorrow.'

'Where are you going to take him?' The look of adoration on his face as he looked up at Timothy frightened her. What would the child say when she managed to banish his beloved Mr Myson from their lives? Would he, in his childish way, hate her for it? He would certainly not understand.

'Patch will have to stay in my stables. You can't take a horse upstairs, can you?' Timothy grinned at Sarah Jane. 'Unless, of course, you were thinking of moving into a house with a garden and a stable ...'

'As a matter of fact, I am,' she said.

'Good.' He lifted a hand and clicked his fingers over his shoulder. A groom materialised as if from nowhere and took the reins of both horses. 'Take them back to the stables, Fletcher,' Timothy instructed.

'And get your boy to give Patch a ride; the young gentleman is not up to exercising him properly yet.' The man touched his cap and walked the animals away, leaving Timothy to offer Sarah Jane his arm.

She should have known he would contrive something of the sort, she thought as she took Jason's hand. She should have known he would not be content with taking the child for a ride and then leaving them. 'Say goodbye to Mr Myson, Jason,' she said, in an effort to dismiss him without creating a scene.

'Come now, Sarah Jane, you will allow me to escort you home, surely?' The pony had been a good idea because Jason, who was allowed everything he wanted, would not now give it up, and Sarah Jane would surrender herself eventually, but being in a public place was inhibiting. He could not touch her and his whole body cried out for physical contact. She still wanted him, he could see it in her eyes, and all he had to do was to make her admit it, or better still, demonstrate it. 'I want to talk to you.'

'What about?'

'Not here, not with so many eyes on us.'

'I prefer that,' she said.

'I shall kiss you in front of everyone, then.'

She laughed. 'I doubt it. You are too well-known and someone would be sure to tell Miss Hailey. You wouldn't want that, would you?'

'No,' he admitted, falling into step beside her, as she hurried out of the park and crossed the road to Oxford Street, holding Jason by the hand. The reason he would not kiss her in public was also her reason for not doing anything to stop him accompanying her, but what she would do when they arrived at the shop, she had no idea. It was too much to hope that Thomas would save the day a second time.

'We've said all there is to say,' she told him quietly. 'I want you out of my life, Mr Myson. I can't think why you persist in pursuing me.'

'Can't you? Oh my dear, how can you say that? We need each other, don't deny it.'

'I do deny it.' She hurried on, pulling on Jason's hand until he cried out for her to slow down. 'I do not need your help to bring up my son. I have managed perfectly well until now.'

'I was not talking about that kind of need, and you know it. But since you mention business, why do you let that fellow Wistonby dictate to you? He cheated me and, given the chance, he will cheat you.' If he could wrench her away from the lawyer, it would be easier,

306

not only to take her to bed, which was his immediate aim, but to influence her decisions about the school – before she realised how important it was to him. 'There are thousands of good lawyers, so why him? He will give you bad advice and ruin you, take my word.'

'What makes you think he has given me any advice at all? I make my own decisions.'

'About everything? About selling that school of yours? Was it his advice that you should site it there?'

'No, it was mine.' They had arrived at the shop and she stopped to take the key from her reticule although she was reluctant to unlock the door while he stayed. 'And there, Mr Myson, it will remain.'

'No, Mrs McBryde, there it will *not* remain.' He was scornful. 'Do you think railway builders are fools? They will not spend thousands on an unnecessary detour, particularly when all that stands in their way is one small building. It can soon be acquired and demolished.'

There was something about the way he spoke which reminded her of His Lordship telling her what she already knew – that money invested in building railways was dead money until they were in use and bringing in revenue, and she realised quite suddenly that not only was it important for Timothy to have the school, but he had to have it quickly; time was not on his side. She had been feeling weak, a victim of his magnetism, but now, all at once, she knew her own strength. 'You have applied for compulsory purchase, I take it?' she said amiably. 'Will that be granted soon enough, do you think?'

'Me? Who said anything about me?'

She laughed. 'Did you think I didn't know you were behind the offer to buy the school?'

'If I were,' he said, taking the key from her hand and opening the door, 'it is purely business and has nothing to do with you and me. Let the lawyers take care of it.'

'The school is not for sale,' she repeated, as Jason ran ahead of her up the stairs. 'And neither am I.'

He blocked the doorway so that she could not shut the door. 'No? What about Henry Carter? What about the lawyer? Are they your lovers? How many lovers do you have – besides me, that is? How much do you sell yourself for? You think I'll pay the going price of a railway line?'

Two high spots of colour flamed on her cheeks and her eyes sparkled with rage, making her more vibrantly alive than ever. She could hardly speak for the fury which enveloped her. It was like a shield, protecting her from him. 'How dare you!'

'You are even more beautiful when you are angry, do you know that? But of course you do; it's part of your stock in trade, isn't it?'

'Goodbye, Mr Myson,' she said, clenching her fists in her skirts to stop herself lashing out at him. 'I wish you and your bride every happiness.'

'Oh, so that's it – my marriage. You are jealous of Miss Hailey.'

'Rubbish!'

'Admit it. Admit that what you really want is this.' He took her face in both hands and brought his mouth down onto hers, crushing her lips, forcing his tongue between her teeth, taking her breath away and making her legs buckle. She felt the old familar stirring in the pit of her stomach and, even while he kissed her, hated herself for it. He lifted his head at last and, still holding her face in his hands, looked down into her eyes, with a smile of triumph. 'I'm right, aren't I?'

She flung her arms up and forced his hands away. The fury had gone, leaving her cold as ice. 'If you ever do that again,' she said slowly, 'I shall make sure the whole world knows of it. Do you understand?'

'Have a care before you threaten me,' he said, wiping his mouth with the back of his hand. 'Just think what you have to lose.'

Her answer was to push him out into the street and slam the door. She stood leaning on it for a moment, trying unsuccessfully to regain her composure before running up the stairs to the sanctuary of her bedroom where she flung herself onto the bed. It was open warfare now. Thomas had told her to beware of making an enemy of her son's father, but that was exactly what she had done. In order not to love him, she had made herself his enemy, but she felt no relief. In fact she felt miserable. She could still taste his mouth, could still feel his hands on her face, his body hard against hers, and was still quivering with the desire he had aroused. He had been right; she did want him. If it were not for Jason, in the next room, she would have given vent to her misery in one long howl of torment.

But what good did it do to cry? Weeping solved nothing; she had learned that long ago. She sat up and caught sight of herself in the mirror. Her hair was falling from its pins but that was the only outward sign of the tumult inside her. She forced herself to smile at her reflection, though it did not reach her eyes. Was she or was she not a sensible, independent woman with a cool business head? Was it sensible to long for something she could not have? Was it sensible to hope for something that could only bring her more heartache? She stood up, shook out her skirt and went back to the sitting room. The practical thing would be to work on the shop ledgers and put all thoughts of Timothy Myson out of her head.

Timothy would soon be involved in wedding plans, deciding what to wear, where to go for a honeymoon and making a new home, and she and Jason would be forgotten. Poor Jason! She would have to make it up to him when he found himself deserted. First thing in the morning, she would set about finding a small house with a stable so that she could buy him a pony. And because houses and ponies cost money, she had better set to work on those ledgers and find ways of expanding her business yet again. Henry would argue, but arguing with Henry was far more satisfying than fighting Timothy.

The smell in the sickroom caught at Geoffrey's throat and made breathing difficult; the windows were tight shut and the blinds drawn. Constance lay in the middle of the four-poster, surrounded by doctors, nurses and maids, all of whom moved aside so that he could sit on the edge of the bed and take his wife's hand. He was unable to believe this could be happening. Typhus was a disease of the common people, not one to be found in a respectable household. Damn that Union! She had gone on one of her regular visits and taken tea with Matron as she usually did. How was she to know the young girl who served her was carrying the disease?

'Geoffrey?'

'Yes, my love?'

'Forgive me ...' Her voice was hardly audible and he had to bend over and put his ear against her lips. 'I could not give you what you most wanted.'

'You gave me all I could ask of you,' he said softly. 'You gave me your love, though I didn't deserve it. I am the one who needs forgiveness.'

'You have been punished enough, my darling.' She smiled, a faint upturning movement of her lips, nothing more. 'Timothy ...'

'Timothy?' he repeated, completely taken aback. 'You mean my ward?'

'Your *son*, Geoffrey.' She paused, her eyes burning like twin lights in a face devoid of colour. 'Let him come home. Let him come home to Chevington and be the son you have always wanted him to be.'

He sat and stared at her, wondering if he had heard right, but her words, though weak, had been clear enough. He dabbed at her brow with a damp cloth handed to him by the nurse and smiled, though he felt like weeping. 'How long have you known?'

She gripped his hand, drawing him down to her. 'Right from the beginning, Geoffrey. You couldn't fool me for an instant. I love you, you see. I have always loved you. Besides, I have seen him occasionally and he is so like you ...' She stopped to fight for breath, then went on, growing weaker. 'I should have told you before but I ...' Her voice faded to a thread of a whisper. 'Bring him home, give him your name and find a nice wife for him. The Chevington line must continue.' Tears glistened on her lashes. 'That's what you want, isn't it?'

All those years of deceit, all those years of feeling guilty, all those years of trying to placate Timothy, all to keep a secret which was no secret at all. 'Yes, my darling, if that is what you wish me to do.' His voice choked on the words. 'But you know, you are going to get better, and we can talk about it again then. Do not trouble yourself now.' He bent to raise her hand to his lips and then, looking at her face with brimming eyes, realised she had not heard him. 'Oh, my darling,' he murmured, slipping from the bed and sinking onto his knees beside it. He still held her hand, unwilling to relinquish it. Slowly he rubbed it against his cheek, unable to speak, knowing it was now too late to say what was in his heart, what had always been in his heart, his love for her. She had never known how strong that was and yet she had been a loving and loyal wife and it would be a churlish man who could have asked for more.

Behind him he heard the maid begin to sob loudly and one of the doctors give a little cough. After several minutes, he rose slowly to his feet and stood gazing down at his wife, still and peaceful now, then he folded her arms across her breast, closed her eyes and strode from the room. In a daze, he walked along the gallery, past the gilt-framed pictures of earlier Chevingtons, down the wide staircase, across the hall past the library and out through the front door.

He walked for hours until he found himself, without knowing how he got there, standing outside the gamekeeper's cottage, deserted ever since its original occupant had died and the new man had been given a more modern dwelling. His mind had been so full of Constance and their life together, he had been unaware of where his steps were taking him. His father had arranged the marriage, as had so often happened a generation before, and he had accepted it, having no strong views one way or another. The inheritance had been all that mattered – that and the continuation of the Chevington line. Constance brought a good dowry and she was the daughter of an earl; her breeding was impeccable and though only seventeen, she had wanted the match, and both families were enthusiastic about it. 'The wedding of the year', the world had called it.

He had been well-content with his bride, although she had been lamentably ignorant of what to expect in the marriage bed. He was very young himself and his previous sexual experience had been found in the beds of servants and whores; it was all part of his growing up and he had no idea how to arouse her so that she was not only compliant – she had been that because she had been told it was her duty – but to make her enjoy it. It had taken months, even years to accomplish that, and those early weeks had been very difficult.

He remembered her tearful rejection of him on the night before he met Rachel. And his anger. He had had no right to be angry with her and he had had no right to take out his frustration on a simple gypsy girl.

He pushed open the door of the cottage, breaking the cobwebs which festooned it. He did not notice the cobwebs, nor the bare dusty floor and rubbish piled up in a corner, the broken chair and musty-smelling mattress, from which the mice scurried. He saw it as it was when Rachel had brought Timothy there, wrapped in a grubby shawl. The place had been clean then and simply furnished, with cotton curtains billowing in a light breeze and making patterns of light and dark across her face as she stood looking up at him with defiance in her dark eyes. The gamekeeper and his wife had been paid to stay away for an hour or two, though he had an idea they were not far away. 'I ain't goin' to take 'im to the poorhouse,' she had said. 'Though me folks says I mus'. I don' wan' that for 'im. You 'ave 'im, 'e's yours.'

'Me?' He had been astounded. 'What can I do with him?'

'You got money, ain't yer? An' you got more'n one house. You take care on 'im, or I'll 'ave to take 'im to the poorhouse and if they was to ask me who 'is father is, why, I should 'ave to tell them, shouldn't I?'

He could not have risked that. His coupling with the young gypsy had released his frustration, like a dam bursting; afterwards he had been able to woo his wife gradually and gently so that she had become less fearful and tense. Nine months later, the gypsy all but forgotten, their marriage had been a happy one. 'Are you sure he's mine?'

He remembered her cracked laugh; he could still hear it echoing through the gloom, twenty-seven years later.

311

"Course 'e's yours! Spittin' image, 'e is. See.' She had held out the bundle towards him, pulling the shawl away to reveal a tiny screwed-up face and a tuft of dark hair. He could see no family likeness, but it must have been there even then. 'Go on,' she had said. 'Take 'im. 'e won't bite, seein's he ain't got no teeth yet.'

He had taken the bundle awkwardly. 'Why can't you keep him?'

"Cos o' this feller I'm to marry. Jack won't 'ave no bastard, specially one that ain't one of our own kind.'

The child had opened dark eyes and blinked up at him, bringing a lump to his throat. 'What's his name?'

'Ain't got one. Call 'im what you like.'

'I don't know how you can bear to part with him.'

'I 'ave to, don' you see?' She had reached out to touch the child for the last time and suddenly the tears spilled down her face like a river bursting its banks. 'Look arter 'im for me. Give him a home ... and ...' She had moved away, sobbing her heart out, leaving him standing in the middle of the room holding the baby, mesmerised into immobility. At the door she stopped to look back. 'Love him, love him if yer can, for 'e won't find life easy.'

Oh, how true that had been! Timothy was his own worst enemy; it was almost as if he had nurtured his bastardy, sought refuge behind it, so that the unkind world could not reach him. The house in Islington had been well-staffed, even though few could put up with the boy's tantrums for long, but it had not been what you could call a real home and Geoffrey had been only too aware of that. He had tried to make it up to him, with the result that Timothy had been impossibly spoiled as a child and now, in adulthood, he did not see why he could not continue to have everything he wanted. It was the prohibitions he found so irksome, never to come to Chevington House, never to address him as 'Father' in public, knowing that he depended so heavily on a guardian whom society praised for bringing up the child of a dead friend in such a generous fashion and to whom he should be forever grateful. To Timothy it was not generosity, it was his right as a son. And Constance had known all along! Why had she never told him so? Why not even a hint? It would have made all the difference.

Geoffrey turned and left the cottage, shutting the creaking door carefully behind him, as if enclosing the ghosts that haunted it. Poor Constance. She was gone now and he had to face a future without her, a future in which Timothy would feature even more strongly and, God forgive him, he was not at all sure that was what he wanted. A year ago, even yesterday, he would have said it was his dearest wish, but now he was not so certain. What was so desirable because it was unattainable suddenly took on a different face when it could be had for no more than a nod and the flourish of a signature. He sighed heavily and went back to the house to make the funeral arrangements.

There were crowds of people at the service held in the little church on the estate. They came from London and all round Chevington, friends, relatives, tenants and employees, the Master and Matron of the workhouse and representatives from the various charities on whose committees Her Ladyship had served. They came to offer their condolences and respect, and some came out of curiosity to see if Timothy would dare to be there. And, of course, he was. Afterwards, when most of the congregation had gone their separate ways and the grave-diggers had begun their task of piling earth on the brass-bound oak coffin, Geoffrey and Timothy walked back to the house through the park, sending the empty carriage round by the road.

'She knew you were my son all along,' Geoffrey said after several minutes of silence. 'She told me on her deathbed.'

'She knew?' Timothy's surprise was no less than Geoffrey's had been. 'Why did she say nothing?'

'I fancy she was punishing me. That and a little pride, I suppose. I don't blame her.'

'And in punishing you, she punished me.' He was so near to getting what he wanted, yet he sensed his father still holding back. 'All those years wasted ...'

They emerged from the trees and began to walk across the grass towards the house, which stood on its hill with the morning sun shining on its mellow brick. At the west end stood the folly, built onto the house but not part of it. It was so ivy-covered as to appear completely green, a living, growing monument to whoever had raised it. In Timothy's eyes it was ugly and spoiled the lines of the building; one day, when he could do as he liked, he would have it demolished. One day soon he would take his place among the gentry and, in the fullness of time, his antecedents would be forgotten. He was a Chevington, the only Chevington besides His Lordship. Except Jason, of course, but there was no question of him inheriting anything. Caroline would give him heirs aplenty ...' He stopped his rambling thoughts to pay attention to his father.

'Of course, there is no longer a ban on your visiting the house. Come whenever you wish.'

'Then you will acknowledge me as your son?'

'I will think about it. It is too soon to make decisions like that.' He didn't know why he did not give the boy the assurance he needed; it wasn't as if it was not something he had himself wanted for years. But he was in no mood to be pressed. 'Give me a little time.'

'Do you want the Chevington name to die out for want of an heir?'

Geoffrey disliked the implication that he was past begetting a child and managed a wry smile. 'I might marry again and still have legitimate sons. Don't make false assumptions, Timothy.'

'You can't mean that! Your wife is hardly cold in her grave.'

'No, that is why I say it is too soon. Leave it, Timothy. Trust me to do what is best for both of us.'

Timothy opened his mouth to argue, but the set look on his father's face made him realise that it would be unwise. He bit his lip and walked on in silence, though his insides were churning with anger and resentment and hope stillborn.

'Have you heard from Mrs McBryde's lawyer about the school?' his father asked, to change the subject.

'No,' he said, wondering what had made his father's mind switch so suddenly from his inheritance to the unconnected topic of Sarah Jane.

'She will not give in easily.'

Timothy did not need to be reminded of that. Sarah Jane's angry words still echoed in his head. It was no longer a pursuit for sexual gratification, it was a battle of wills. He would have the land and destroy the school, and he would have Sarah Jane and his marriage. He smiled. 'I know, but she will sell in the end and when the Hailey line is reopened, we will have the biggest railway consortium in the country.'

'Can you maintain your interest in both projects without overstretching yourself?'

'Yes of course, as long as there are no unforeseen hitches. We should never have left it this long; the Hailey line is too important to abandon.'

'But isn't the water still there?'

'We can avoid it. The first tunnel was dug deep to keep the gradient down, but with the new locomotives that's no longer necessary. We can afford to go a little higher, above the water level.'

'What about the bodies?

'If we find them, we will exhume them.'

'Then do it with respect. And be sure the navvies understand why it is necessary. Write to James McBryde, invite him down. And inform Mrs McBryde ...'

'Why?' Sarah Jane again. Wherever he went, whatever he tried to do, she was there, blocking his way. Would he ever be free of her? 'She was never really married to the navvy, was she?'

'It is only common courtesy. We paid the compensation to her and by that token acknowledged that she was. She might want to take possession of the body and make proper funeral arrangements.' He was dog-tired with sitting up with Constance and making funeral arrangements of his own and now it was all over, all he wanted was a little peace.

'Very well, I'll tell her.'

Geoffrey looked up sharply. 'Have you been seeing her again?'

'Why shouldn't I? She is my son's mother.'

'Leave her alone, Timothy. You are betrothed to Caroline. You cannot, in honour, break that off.'

'Why should I want to? And if I did, I would not marry Sarah Jane.'

'You are not being fair to her. She is too good—'

'Too good!' Timothy's anger rose to the surface like a volcano erupting; the composure he always adopted when speaking to his father vanished in the heat. 'Too good for me, that's what you mean, isn't it? A skivvy, a navvy's whore, is too good for me because I am not your son, not your heir, but your bastard. All this time I have been thinking that it was Her Ladyship preventing you from acknowledging me, but it isn't, is it? You can't bear the thought of a gypsy's son living in your house!

'Timothy, I did not mean—' But his son had already left him, striding away towards the house. Poor, poor Sarah Jane, Geoffrey thought, following more slowly. Timothy was bound to take his anger and hurt out on her. He prayed she was strong enough to withstand it.

Chapter Twenty

*T*he news of Lady Chevington's death, published in *The Times*, saddened Sarah Jane who had always thought of her as the pinnacle of ladylike behaviour. Constance was the person on whom she had modelled her own dress and manners when being a lady was all she wanted from life. She wrote a letter of condolence to His Lordship, wondering as she did so if Her Ladyship's passing would make any difference to Timothy. It might make him feel more secure and if that were so, he might leave her alone and settle down to married life with Caroline. He would not risk making their affair public; he had as much to lose as she had. Neither did he care for his son; he was simply using Jason in the same way as he used everyone else, to get what he wanted. He would soon tire of that and then she would have to make it up to Jason and learn to get on with her life all over again. It must, she told herself firmly, be as if he had never reappeared, never reawakened her passions, never made her aware of what might have been.

But there were times when she could not rid herself of her longing for the man who tormented her, times when her body cried out to be held in his arms, to feel his stroking fingers on her breasts and belly and thighs, to be roused to ecstasy, to feed her hunger on his. She was disgusted with herself for her weakness and ashamed that she allowed it to influence her moods, making her snappy and irritable.

She was even more ashamed when she thought of the school, because thinking of that reminded her of Duncan and all they had been to each other. Timothy would destroy that if he could. Timothy destroyed everything. She would not allow it. She had the trump card; she had the school and he could not build his line without the land on which it stood. She would fight him to the end. Thomas said her stubbornness would be her undoing, but he continued to act on her wishes with unwavering loyalty. Letters had been passing to and fro between lawyers, and new offers made, but she had stuck to her guns, wondering what Timothy would do next.

She was totally unprepared for it when it came. Less than a week after Lady Chevington's funeral, she came home one afternoon, rather later than usual, to find Betsy alone, sitting at the kitchen table with a pot of tea in front of her, poring over a penny dreadful she had bought in the market.

'Where is Jason?' Sarah Jane asked. His school was only half a mile away and he had been going back and forth by himself ever since his classmates had teased him for needing an escort. Sometimes he was a few minutes late because he stopped to play or watch the traffic, and then he poured scorn on his mother's fears when she scolded him. 'Has he had his tea?'

Betsy, who had not heard her arrive, scrambled to her feet. 'Yes, ma'am. He had it before he left.'

'Left?' Sarah Jane repeated.

'Yes, ma'am. Mr Myson said you knew about it and it was all right.'

Sarah Jane's heart plummeted to her shoes. 'I knew about what?' she demanded, trying to quell the feeling of panic which was rising in her throat and threatening to engulf her. 'I would have told you if I had been expecting Mr Myson to come for him. Surely you knew that?'

'He said it would be all right,' Betsy repeated.

'He probably took him to the park to ride his pony.'

'No, ma'am. Mr Myson said he was taking Master Jason on a little holiday. He asked me to pack his clothes . . .'

'Pack?' Sarah Jane repeated, not wanting to believe what she was hearing. 'You packed his clothes and let him go?'

'Yes, ma'am,' Betsy said, backing away because it looked very much as if her employer were about to strike her. She had had some beatings in her time, but never from Mrs McBryde.

'You imbecile!' She clenched her hands on the folds of her skirt to stop herself hitting out at the girl.

'I didn't know Jason wasn't to go. You never told me I shouldn't . . .' Betsy's last words were muffled as she flung her apron over her head and gave way to noisy sobs which had less to do with Jason's disappearance than her conviction that she was about to lose a comfortable job.

'Stop crying, Betsy. I'm not blaming you.' Sarah Jane forced herself to speak calmly. Timothy could be very persuasive when he chose and, to all outward appearances, he was a family friend; it was unfair to castigate the poor maid. 'Just tell me where they were going.'

'He didn't say, ma'am, only that they must make haste.'

'And what about Jason? Was he upset?'

'No, he was tickled to death to be going. That's why I thought it would be all right.'

Timothy would think it a great jest to frighten her out of her wits, Sarah Jane decided, for hadn't she put the idea into his head with her talk of nightmares? But why take the child's clothes? She rounded on the girl. 'How long have they been gone?'

'I don't know. An hour or two, maybe more. I didn't notice the time.'

They would be at Timothy's London home. He wouldn't take the boy far, just far enough to worry her, to upset her enough to make her give him what he wanted, though now she was not sure what that was. She ran back into the street. Why were there no cabs when you wanted them? Why were the crowds getting in her way? Jason, oh my son, what a fool I've been. What will he do to you, who trusted him so completely? She found a hansom at last, clambered in and ordered the driver to take her to Kensington.

It was growing dark by the time she had located Timothy's address, with the help of the cab-driver, and then the servant who came to the door was insistent that Mr Myson was not at home. 'Why not go to his place of business?' he suggested.

Despairing, she returned to the cab and ordered the driver to take her to Euston Road. It was late; would anyone still be there when she arrived? 'As fast as you can,' she said. 'I'll double your fare.' She sat in the swaying vehicle, heard the horse being whipped up and the shouts of the driver clearing his way, yet they hardly seemed to be moving. Where had Timothy taken Jason? To Chevington? She didn't think so; it was too soon after Her Ladyship's death and His Lordship, who had remained there after the funeral, would never condone kidnapping. And kidnappers usually demanded a ransom. What ransom would she be expected to pay? Not money, she was sure. Did Timothy think that she would agree to be his mistress and live where he wanted her to and do exactly as he said, in exchange for her son? It was too ridiculous an idea to be considered. Or was it the school? Could her refusal to sell be at the root of it? Was he that desperate to have it? He was behaving like a spoilt child, causing trouble because he couldn't have his own way. If Jason hadn't been involved it would have been laughable.

The chief clerk, who always took the opportunity to leave early when His Lordship and Mr Myson were out of town, was just going home when she arrived. 'Why, Mrs McBryde, what is wrong?' he asked, looking at her in alarm. 'Has there been an accident?'

'Do you know where Mr Myson is?' she asked, realising that it must indeed look as if she had been involved in a mishap of some sort. 'I must know, it's very urgent.'

'I think he has gone to Hailey Common, Mrs McBryde.'

'Hailey Common?' She stood on the threshold of the office, neither in nor out, while he faced her with the keys in his hand, waiting for her to leave so that he could lock up. Why would Timothy take Jason to Hailey? Would he be mad enough to introduce the boy to Caroline? Was he doing what he maintained his father should have done for him all those years ago? Surely he would never take the risk.

'He returned from Chevington today specifically to hear the debate on the new Hailey Common bill and as soon as the vote had been taken, he came back here and said they would be resuming work on the tunnel in a few days' time. I am sure he would want to be there when they start.'

The tunnel. Even in her concern for Jason, her mind flew back over the years to the day she had lost the only man she had truly loved. Timothy counted for nothing against that, even without today's perfidy. She pulled herself together. 'Did he have my son with him?'

The man looked puzzled. 'He didn't bring a child here, Mrs McBryde.' He paused. 'Though there is a letter for you. I was instructed to post it tomorrow.'

'Tomorrow?' she repeated. 'Did he suppose I would wait a whole day for news of my son?'

'It is not about your son, Mrs McBryde, but about your husband. I'll fetch it for you.' He turned and went back into the office to take a letter from a drawer. 'I wrote it at his dictation this morning, but he asked me to delay sending it. I thought it was because he wanted to tell you about it in person.' He watched her as she tore it open. 'Do you mind if I lock up now?' he asked. 'My wife is expecting me for supper.'

Engrossed in reading, she moved out of his way without speaking, then slowly put the letter in her pocket and walked back to her cab. 'Oxford Street,' she said dully.

She had been invited in polite, but cold, terms to witness the exhumation of Duncan's body and though the letter did not say so, she knew with dreadful certainty that if they did not find it, they would build the railway over it. She sat in the cab, staring straight ahead at the driver's back, but all she saw was Duncan's face. He was smiling at her, in the tender way he had when he was teasing her, bringing back memories she had been trying for years to smother because they hurt so much. Duncan carrying Jason through the meadows, singing to him; Duncan sitting on the roof of their hut, hammering in nails; Duncan wielding a pick, soothing a horse; Duncan's strength, Duncan's love. In her memory he was alive and she shrank from the idea of looking at him in death. Timothy would know that, wouldn't he? Could he be jealous of a dead man? Was that what it was all about?

But why take Jason there? The child was full of curiosity about railway building; would Timothy take a macabre delight in telling him all about the tragedy? Jason would be very upset if he had to look at the gruesome remains of the navvy he had called Da. Would Timothy tell him that Duncan McBryde was not his father at all? She could have sworn he had some affection for the boy, so why subject him to that? Mad as he was – and he must be mad – there was a kind of wild logic about it. He wanted to make sure she went to Hailey Common and there he would gloat over her while she witnessed the exhumation. The fight over the school dwindled to insignificance in the face of this new villainy.

'This where you want to go, missus?' The cabbie's voice broke in on her reverie. The vehicle had stopped outside the shop. She shook herself, got out and went up to her apartment where she stood in the drawing room, looking about her in a kind of daze. Although there was evidence of Jason's occupation – a small toy abandoned in the corner, a picture book, a pair of shoes thrown carelessly down – without him it was empty and hollow. The thick carpet, comfortable chairs, the glow of the lamplight, were meaningless. Her control suddenly snapped and she sank onto a sofa and sobbed, giving herself up to the self-indulgence of a misery that those who had caused it would never be allowed to see. She wept until all her pent-up emotion had drained from her, leaving her empty and very calm. Then she rang for Betsy, who had heard the weeping but dare not enter until she was summoned by the bell. 'Have you found him?' Her homely face was full of concern.

Sarah Jane shook her head.

'Oh, ma'am,' Betsy began to cry. 'It's all my fault. I shouldn't have let him . . .'

Sarah Jane smiled wearily. 'You couldn't have stopped him, Betsy. If it's anyone's fault it's mine for not foreseeing it.'

'You aren't going to dismiss me?' The relief in her voice was almost comical.

'No, of course not.'

'Do you want me to serve supper?' the maid asked. 'You haven't had a bite to eat.'

'Supper?' Sarah Jane repeated vaguely. 'No. I'm going out again.' She began pulling papers out of the davenport, flinging them behind her. 'There's a *Bradshaw* here somewhere.' She seized the timetable and flicked through its pages, looking for a train to take her to Derby or somewhere near enough for her to be able to take a coach or hire a vehicle to complete the journey to Hailey Common.

'Do you mean to go tonight?' Betsy asked in surprise. 'Shouldn't you wait 'til morning?'

'Wait – when my son is heaven knows where and probably frightened to death? Now, pack a few clothes for me ...' She stopped. There was hardly a thing in her wardrobe suitable for a tramp across the moors. 'No, I'll do it myself. You can take a week's holiday.'

'Oh ma'am, a whole week?' The girl's eyes lit up. 'You really mean it?'

'Yes.' Sarah Jane didn't know why she mentioned a week, except that she could hardly go to Hailey Common and back in less. She opened her purse and gave the girl a week's wages and as soon as she had gone, packed clean underwear and a few toiletries into a carpet bag, dressed in the plainest skirt she owned, topped it with a cream blouse and a fringed shawl, then sat down to write a letter to Henry saying she would, after all, take the holiday he suggested. She would leave the letter down in the shop – someone would make sure he had it. Looking up from writing her name at the bottom, her eye was caught by the golden apple, standing as it had done ever since Timothy had brought it back to her, on a shelf above her desk; she had been a fool ever to have accepted it a second time. She picked it up and put it in her bag. If Timothy needed convincing that she meant what she said, returning the apple to him should do it.

By the time the cab arrived, her preparations were complete. She tied a fine silk scarf over her hat and hurried out to the waiting hansom. She was driven away just five minutes before Thomas arrived to tell her that he had located Billie.

The train was the last one going north that night and was unusually crowded, but she found a first-class seat and sat down, trying to control her impatience to be off. She barely noticed the band of navvies, with their shovels carried over their shoulders and their bundles tied over the handles, who were boarding the same train until the sound of her name made her look up. One of the men had put his head in the open carriage window. 'Sarah Jane! Well, I'll be blessed!'

'Big Bill!'

'Where are you off to?'

'Hailey Common.'

'Hailey Common, now there's a thing!' His gaze moved from her face to appraise her clothes. 'Dressed like that? Grown a mite high and mighty, ain't yer? First class yer travel nowadays, do yer?'

'Why shouldn't I, if I can afford it?'

He grinned. 'Lady Muck.'

In spite of her anxiety over Jason, she managed to smile. 'If you like. But I'd still be a navvy's wife if it hadn't been for ...' She stopped, unable to go on.

'Prove it, then. Come and join us, we're goin' to Hailey Common too. We'll hitch up an' make room for yer.' He grinned. 'Though 'twould be easier if yer didn't have them 'oops in yer skirts.'

She laughed suddenly. It was good to be among friends and she would have allies when it came to facing up to Timothy. She stood up. 'I'll be happy to join you.'

He opened the door and reached up to put his big hands round her slim waist and lift her down. They were an incongruous couple, for he wore filthy moleskin trousers and an old blue frockcoat, and she appeared to be a gentlewoman, but she set off down the platform arm in arm with him, ignoring the stares and tut-tutting of the other passengers in the carriage.

He took her to a third-class compartment where his companions had found seats for themselves. They made room for her and a moment later the doors were banged shut, the whistle blew and the train jolted into motion.

'Well, me lovely,' Big Bill said, after introducing her to the rest of the navvies who shared the carriage. 'Why are yer goin' back to that godforsaken place? Thought you'd 'ad enough of it.'

'They are going to reopen the tunnel.'

'We know that. That's why we're goin'. There's good wages offered.'

'They've invited me to be there when they fetch out the bodies,' she said.

'If they can find them,' Bill said morosely. 'It was a mighty powerful explosion.'

'I would much rather they left the dead in peace,' she went on slowly, as an outrageous idea invaded her mind and took hold. Big Bill had always been a troublemaker, perhaps he could be persuaded to make some on her behalf.

'I c'n understand that, me lovely, but the line 'as to be built.'

'Does it? Does it have to be built just there?' she queried, looking from one to the other. If Timothy had not taken Jason from her, she might have gone to Hailey and then attended a new interment – sad, yes, but in a mood of quiet acceptance. But now, now she had nothing in her heart but vengeance. She was going to fetch her son back and Timothy would pay for abducting him, for all the torment he had put her through, for thinking he could use Jason to break her. He had destroyed in one cruel move any love or affection she had ever had for him. 'That tunnel is Duncan's grave, his and Randy Joe's. I hate the idea of it being disturbed.' She turned to the other men, who were watching her intently. 'Would you work on it knowing there were men buried beneath you?'

They looked from one to the other, then at Big Bill. 'No one said anything to us about bodies.'

He shrugged. 'The owners promised to fetch them out and bury them agin, proper. And they've offered good wages.'

'You mean you can be bought?' she said, knowing just how to rouse him.

'No, by heaven!' he said. 'And you ain't goin' up there just to see a body, are yer?'

'No.' She paused, then took a deep breath and set the avalanche in motion. 'I want to stop the tunnel being opened. I don't want the work to start again. I want the owners made to change their minds. And I need help.'

He looked at her in surprise. 'You mean you want the men to go up there and be taken on and then refuse to work in the tunnel, is that it?'

Was that really what she had meant? 'Yes.'

One of the men whistled. 'I ain't so sure that's a good idea. I'm going there to work, not cause trouble ...'

'I'll pay you. I'll make up whatever you lose and pay your train fare there and wherever you want to go afterwards.'

'Why?' Big Bill demanded.

323

'I told you. I don't want Duncan's remains disturbed and I don't want the line built over him.' Her heart had turned to steel; not even mentioning Duncan could soften it.

'Thought you'd got over 'im,' Bill said. 'Thought you'd done very well fer yerself, too much the grand lady to want yer past life dragged up.'

'That's not true or I wouldn't be here now. If I didn't care, I wouldn't worry about the navvies at all, and I wouldn't have started the school for your children, would I?' She shouldn't have brought that up, but anything was fair now.

'What's that to me?' Big Bill said. 'I ain't got no kids.'

'But I 'ave,' one of the other men put in after a moment's silence while they looked from one to the other. 'An' the lady's done a lot for our little 'uns.'

'I ain't said we won't 'elp 'er, 'ave I?' Bill retorted. 'But if we does, we do it the way I sez.'

'How?' Sarah Jane asked. She had never expected agreement so quickly and was beginning to feel nervous. 'What will you do?'

He grinned. 'Do? Why, I'm goin' to stop them reopening the tunnel – that's what you want, ain't it?' He needed a cause to shake the men out of their apathy, something to stir their passions, to make them look beyond next payday and Sarah Jane had thrown it straight into his lap. It hardly mattered that it was irrelevant to legitimate union matters of pay and working conditions; if he could rouse them enough, they would follow him. 'I'll show them bloody lords I'm a force to be reckoned with, that what I sez counts for somethin' and the men will follow me. What good's their money and titles, if they can't get the men to work for them? They need us, they can't get rich without us. We're the ones who matter in this life – us, the working men.'

'Steady on,' said one of the others.

'It's a monstrous thing to tamper with graves,' he went on, ignoring the caution. 'There were prayers said over that ground, that makes it consecrated and the men were to be left in peace, that's what they said. "Their last resting place" – those were the very words. You can't go in with dynamite and shovel and forget they are there. Their ghosts will haunt whoever goes in ...'

'Ghosts,' Sarah Jane repeated, as the first shiver of apprehension at what she had started began to bother her.

'Aye,' he said firmly. 'The ghosts of Randy Joe and Duncan McBryde will haunt the men who disturb them.'

'I don't believe that,' she said.

'No? But others might, the women 'specially, and that's a help, for we'll have 'em with us instead of agin us as they usually are.'

It was too late to turn back now, too late to change her mind; she had committed, not only herself, but a whole band of navvies, to the task of bringing Timothy Myson to his knees. Poverty and hardship had never defeated her spirit as Timothy had almost managed to do; the navvies had never degraded her as he wanted to. And she had almost let him! And not one of the navvies would have stooped to using her son to punish her. Timothy Myson deserved whatever humiliation she could heap upon him.

Anxious as she was to reach her destination and be reunited with her son, she had to stay with her new allies, who kept leaving the train so that Bill could address groups of navvies they saw on the way. Most preferred to remain where they were, but some downed tools and joined him, so that by the time they reached Ashley Green, the little band numbered about fifty, all vociferous militant men. The Hailey Common tunnel was not to be reopened, but another started to take the longer route through the valley, and provide work and wages for at least twice the number of men originally estimated. Sarah Jane heard all the arguments and, even knowing that Bill was using her for his own ends, and that her own cause was hardly based on logic, she found herself carried along with them.

They marched over the hill to Hailey Common, singing as they went, and Sarah Jane, who had discarded her hoops and neat town shoes for the more serviceable boots she had been accustomed to wearing among the navvies, was easily able to keep up with them. As they topped the rise, she could see a group of men at the tunnel-mouth, slowly moving the rubble, picking up large boulders in their arms and dumping them into a waiting wagon. She stopped in her tracks as soon as she saw them; the sight of the navvies, the huts and the deserted drilling rig was so familiar, she was transported back into the past and half-expected Duncan to come strolling up alongside her, chatting to her in his low Scottish brogue, making her feel secure and contented and loved. 'Oh, Duncan,' she whispered. 'Oh, Duncan.' But he was not there, and she had to force herself back to the present and hurry after the men, who had gone on past her.

Her intention, as soon as they reached the site, had been to find Timothy and issue her ultimatum. 'Give me back my son or I will see that the tunnel is never reopened. I will see you ruined.' But when she went over to the contractor's hut, once occupied by Charlie Bender, there was only Smithers, waiting to enrol the recruits.

'Mrs McBryde?' He looked at her as if he were not sure it really was her.

'Yes. I must speak to Mr Myson.'

'I have no idea where he is – in London, perhaps. I haven't seen him for at least a fortnight.'

This was an unexpected blow. Where was he? And, more importantly, where had he taken Jason? She found it difficult to accept that she had made the journey for nothing. 'But you *are* expecting him?'

He shrugged. 'He didn't say. He comes and goes.'

She turned away and walked slowly back to where Big Bill was addressing the navvies. She had been so sure she would find Timothy and Jason here, she had not considered what she would do if they were not. Where else would they be? Chevington? But if that were so, what had Timothy said to persuade His Lordship to take Jason in? She refused to believe he was as unfeeling as his son. She must go to Chevington at once. Would that also be a wildgoose chase? Could she have been wrong all along, and Timothy had never taken Jason from London? Oh, if only she could think straight! And Big Bill was not helping her to do that.

'What d'you think you're at?' He was shouting at those who were already at work on the rubble. 'You are desecrating a grave.'

''Tain't a grave, 'tis a blocked tunnel,' one of them said, tossing aside a boulder.

'Aye, and very soon you'll find bones, maybe with flesh and blood on them and the clothes they was working in.'

Sarah Jane shuddered, but his words hardened her resolve. She did not want the tunnel opened, did not want Duncan's remains exposed to the light and the curious gaze of strangers.

'We've work to do,' the man retorted. 'It's what we're paid for.'

'To look for bodies?'

'No, to shift muck.'

'What will you do, if you find bodies?'

'Stop, o' course.'

'Why not stop now? The next thing will be pumping engines to get rid o' the water. What if yer haven't found the bodies before that? What if they come up in one o' yer buckets?'

They shrugged and turned back to their task, but Bill did not intend to fail so early. He grabbed Sarah Jane's arm and pulled her forward. 'This here's Duncan McBryde's woman. She should have her say and she don' want 'im fetched out, and you can't build a railway on top of 'im.'

'The contractor said he'd be buried in a proper graveyard.'

'If you can find him.'

'Leave him in peace,' begged Sarah Jane. 'For pity's sake, go away all of you and leave him to lie in peace.' She needed tranquillity too, but the doubts which had begun to torment her soon after they left London had returned a thousandfold. What had she done? She should have remembered Big Bill's fanaticism, she should have known that once he had taken over she would have no control of events. She was being swept along on the tide of anger and resentment Big Bill had created.

The men turned from Bill to look at her. She was dusty from travel with her lovely hair windblown tumbling about her shoulders, and her eyes brilliant with tears. She looked wild and full of an unseen power. The men were wary of her, afraid almost. Bill saw it and smiled. 'She'll put a curse on any who disturb those rocks and don' you make no mistake, she can do it. You'll never know another minute's happiness.'

Her protests went unheard as a disbelieving voice called out, ''Tis foolish to believe such nonsense. There ain't such things, except in the minds of simple people.'

'Who says we're simple, eh? Who says it?' another demanded. 'I could tell you some tales would make yer hair stand on end.'

'Go tell 'em to your granny then, for I'll not believe it.'

'You callin' me a liar?'

While they argued, they were not working, and Big Bill stood by, grinning triumphantly. 'Would any of yer go alone into that tunnel after dark?' he yelled. 'I'll give the man what does it ten pounds of me own money.'

They murmured and muttered, their voices a low rumble, growing louder as each man tried to make his views heard. Big Bill's group stood facing the other until, one by one, they moved over to join him, leaving only a handful prepared to work on the tunnel.

Smithers, coming over to see why they had stopped work, found a hundred men facing a dozen and knew that the twelve would soon capitulate. He suspended operations for the day and left them, going back to the wooden office beside the temporary track, which ended

327

abruptly just short of where the tunnel had once begun. If the men he had taken on would not work, then they must be dismissed and others sent for who had fewer scruples – men who could be paid to forget their fear of ghosts and curses. He sent a message up the line that there were generous wages to be had for excavating the Hailey Common tunnel.

His reply was a band of Irish navvies who arrived with admirable promptitude late the following afternoon, accompanied by a priest brought along to exorcise the tunnel once access had been gained. By then the earlier arrivals, knowing that a confrontation was imminent and that their most likely protagonists would be Irish, had gone on a randy and worked themselves up with bad beer and cheap brandy until they seethed like a bubbling cauldron.

The ground around the tunnel-mouth became a swarming mass of men; they no longer remembered why they had stopped work and started drinking; all they knew was that the Irish were prepared to work the tunnel and they were not, that a Catholic priest was presuming to say words over a Protestant ghost, and this they would not tolerate. They armed themselves; they took up shovels and picks, lumps of wood and broken bottles, then they ranged themselves raggedly before the mouth of the tunnel, while the Irish navvies advanced, prepared to fight for their right to work.

Sarah Jane stood and watched them with horror. What dreadful thing had she done? These men were fighting because her son had been taken from her. They had never heard of Jason, his name meant nothing to them; their struggle was false, Big Bill's motives were false, just as hers were, hers most of all. It was nothing to do with Duncan and she had besmirched his memory. But it was too late to turn the tide of hate and anger; the first blows had already been struck and the battle begun.

'Stop!' she screamed, trying to separate two of the struggling men. 'Stop! For God's sake, stop! You'll kill each other!' They pushed her aside and laid into each other, asking and giving no quarter, battering arms, shoulders, heads and legs with whatever weapons they carried, shouting and cursing. The confrontation had developed a religious fervour and not even Big Bill could control it.

Smithers, who had been trying to make himself heard, gave up and went back to his hut. He wrote an urgent letter to Lord Chevington and then locked himself in.

*

328

His Lordship was in the library studying the new plan of the London junction which was spread out on the desk in front of him, when Timothy arrived with Jason. He had been finding it difficult to put his grief to one side and concentrate on work, and even harder to banish feelings of guilt which had been with him ever since his visit to the gamekeeper's cottage. He had been eating and sleeping badly and the fine lines round his eyes had deepened, and though he told himself a dozen times a day to pull himself together, he could not. He would suddenly find tears filling his eyes and whatever he was going to do or say, was completely forgotten. For twenty-seven years Constance had been there when he wanted her and now he was bereft. Even if the conversation had been of no consequence, her chatter had been part of her endearing nature, but he was trying very hard to live with the loneliness, of not having someone to talk to, especially since he had quarrelled with Timothy. He should have known how his son would react to any delay over his inheritance and approached the matter more tactfully. Especially, he should not have mentioned Sarah Jane.

When Timothy was shown in, he was surprised and pleased to see him. 'Timothy, I wasn't expecting you.'

'I came to make my peace, Father. I apologise for my outburst the other day. It was unforgivable.'

'Then I am doubly pleased to see you.' He looked down at the boy, standing shyly behind his mentor. 'Jason?'

Timothy smiled. 'He is learning to ride and I thought it would be nice for him to ride in the grounds. It will make a change from jostling with the crowds in Hyde Park. You don't mind, do you?'

'Not at all, as long as his mother agreed.'

'Of course she agreed,' Timothy lied without hesitation. 'She wanted to be at Hailey Common when the tunnel is reopened so that she could arrange for her husband's interment, and she didn't want to take Jason. She thought it might upset him.'

Geoffrey found it difficult to believe that Sarah Jane would part with her son, even for a few days. You had only to see them together for a short while to realise how deeply she felt. He admired her for it, admired the way she had worked and fought for everything she had, and he could see no reason why she should think sending Jason to Chevington would be a good idea. He stifled his doubts because it was easier than thinking ill of his son.

'Good,' he said. Then, ruffling Jason's hair, 'How are you, young shaver?'

Jason, always at ease with him, smiled. 'I am well, sir.'

'I am glad to hear it.' Geoffrey smiled and tugged the bellrope by the chimney and when Wilkins appeared, as if by magic, he ordered rooms to be prepared. 'And give Master Jason some dinner in the kitchen. I imagine it is way past his bedtime. Is there anyone who can look after him?'

Wilkins remembered the red-headed skivvy he had dismissed and though His Lordship had said nothing, he knew he was supposed to forget that and serve her son as if he were a young gentleman. Gentleman, indeed! Whatever was His Lordship thinking of? Sometimes he wondered if the loss of his wife had unhinged him. But Wilkins was a loyal servant and not by the tiniest flicker of his eyelids did he show what he felt. 'Hannah, my lord. She has younger brothers and sisters and she is used to young people. I will tell her to make herself responsible for him.'

Timothy put his hand on Jason's shoulder. 'I'll see you later, Jason. Go with Wilkins to have supper and then off to bed with you. There will be someone there to help you. Tomorrow we'll go riding, shall we?'

'Yes please, sir. And will Mama be here tomorrow?'

Geoffrey looked at Timothy but he did not speak until the boy had followed Wilkins from the room. 'He is expecting his mother?'

'Sarah Jane told him that, to make him feel better about coming.'

'He does not know you are his father, does he?'

'I mean to tell him.'

'Why, Timothy? You will upset him terribly, if you do. Put yourself in the child's shoes. Remember how you felt.'

'How do you know how I felt, Father? I never spoke of it.'

'Oh, I knew. How could a father who loves his child not be aware of the turbulence he is causing with such a piece of news? And I loved you, still love you, more than perhaps you realise. Don't make the mistakes I made, Timothy.' He felt decidedly unsure and confused; Timothy was so plausible. He suspected that, given enough provocation, his son was quite capable of behaving irrationally, perhaps even hurting the people he most loved. Geoffrey didn't want either Jason or Sarah Jane hurt; he was surprised how strongly he felt about it, but until he could speak to Sarah Jane himself, he would say no more. He smiled and changed the subject. 'The Hailey Common Bill has gone through, then?'

'Yes. I've got Smithers up there waiting to start. He's already begun recruiting.'

330

'Have you instructed him what to say to the men about the bodies?'

'Yes. I'm sure there will be no problems on that score.'

'Don't you think you ought to be up there?'

'There is no point until some headway is made. Smithers can handle it.'

'Hm.' His Lordship did not sound altogether convinced. 'Well, since you're here, come and look at these new drawings. I think there must be some mistake – the line has been drawn right through the Duncan McBryde school.'

'It's no mistake.' Timothy suppressed his impatience with difficulty; they had been over all that before and nothing had changed. He could not afford the route his father had proposed and that was the end of it. 'Those were my instructions.'

'I did not realise Sarah Jane had agreed to sell.' Geoffrey remembered the last time he had seen her; they had met at the school when the builders were there. She had been marvellous, bullying the workmen, in the nicest possible way, because they had not quite finished and should have been gone and already she was full of plans for expansion, bubbling over with enthusiasm. 'I find it difficult to believe she would give up so easily.'

Timothy was surprised by his father's use of Sarah Jane's Christian name; did he know her better than he pretended? Was that why he had changed the plans? He felt a sudden turmoil in his gut which he would not recognise. 'I made her an offer she couldn't refuse.'

Apparently satisfied, Geoffrey rolled up the plans. 'Let's go and have supper. Tomorrow we can enjoy Jason's company. It will liven us all up to hear his bright chatter and see him running about the place.'

Jason did liven them up. His spirits, a little low because of the absence of his mother, soared with each new discovery, the flowers in the woods, rabbit burrows, the icehouse in the kitchen garden, the cellars with their dusty bottles of wine, the pictures on the walls and the books in the library. He did not stop talking or asking questions from the moment he climbed out of bed, until he was packed off to amuse himself for an hour or two after luncheon while the men talked business in the library.

It was only when he did not appear for his tea and everyone set out to look for him that Geoffrey came to realise just how much the boy meant to him, that he had transferred some of the affection which had been Timothy's alone, to his son's son. 'Where is the young shaver,' he muttered, as he looked in unused rooms and then out in the grounds and through the shrubbery, carpeted now with the russet and gold leaves of autumn. 'Jason, Jason, show yourself!' he called. 'I know you're hiding ...'

Timothy was not so sure. In spite of his careful explanation to the boy about taking him on a little holiday of which his mother had approved, he wondered if he might have tried to return to London on his own. He set off down the drive and along the village street towards the station but no one he asked had seen the boy and he returned to the house more worried than he cared to admit. He was met by his father who told him that Wilkins had tracked him down. His fears had been groundless; Jason was quite content to remain at Chevington because he had been told his mother would join them there very soon and he had no reason to disbelieve it.

'Where was he?' Timothy asked his father.

'In the tower.'

'In the tower? How did he get in there? I thought it was always locked.'

'He climbed in through the little window at the side, it's easy enough to get a grip on the ivy, but once in, he couldn't get out again. It was fortunate Wilkins heard him shouting.'

'We must forbid him to go to it again.'

'I don't know what I'd do if anything happened to him,' His Lordship said. 'Nor what Sarah Jane would do. I don't think I could face her wrath.'

Again that use of Sarah Jane's Christian name. Timothy shrugged it off; she had been his father's servant, after all, and that was probably how he thought of her. He smiled. 'Nor I. He must not be allowed to put himself in danger like that again.'

Jason took his scolding manfully and promised never to go to the tower again and the rest of the afternoon passed pleasantly with a ride through the grounds, ending in a canter out across the park and back to the stables.

Breathlessly, all three returned to the house for hot chocolate and cake, and it was then they found a letter from Hailey Common sent by the worried Smithers. Lord Chevington read it through quickly and handed it to Timothy. 'It seems my doubts were justified,' he said. 'The navvies are rioting. We must go there at once.'

Chapter Twenty-One

*T*he battle raged on and on for two days as new men arrived looking for work and joined one side or the other. An enterprising brewer had made matters worse by bringing up a dray laden with full barrels and now the men were drunk as well as angry. Abandoning any effort to restore order himself, which he knew from experience would be a useless exercise, Smithers had sent for the militia and now awaited their arrival. He hoped Lord Chevington was also on the way because if anyone could calm the men and make them see reason, he could. In the meantime, he watched events from the hut where he had taken residence and, surprisingly, the men left him alone there. It was the big navvy who was causing all the trouble, the one they called Big Bill, and Mrs McBryde. He did not understand her. By all accounts she had done well for herself, so why should she choose to return here, of all places?

Sarah Jane hardly understood herself. Over and over she asked herself why she had been so unthinking, so short-sighted, so irresponsible as to give Big Bill the opportunity for which he had long been waiting. She had let him use her, and use Duncan too, and that was worst of all; she had encouraged him to use Duncan's death to bend a mob of men to his will and further his own ends. It left an unbearable heaviness in her heart and a sour taste in her mouth. She would not have stayed if she had not been convinced that Timothy would arrive with Jason before long, and because she was present, she was involved – Bill saw to that.

Sporadic fights broke out. Nearby, two men rolled in the dust, grappling with each other in demented fury. 'Stop!' she screamed. 'Stop it! Stop it, before you kill each other.'

They did not hear her. One, sitting on the chest of his opponent, crashed an iron-hard fist into his face. 'That'll teach the bugger,' he said triumphantly, getting to his feet. Then to Sarah Jane, 'Get on home, woman. This is no place for you.'

No place for me, she thought, and yet I started it. The navvies had sheltered her and befriended her and none would have harmed her, and yet she had done this to them. She felt numb with shock and helplessness and guilt. She had to do something, anything to help ease the torment inside her and she could think of nothing beyond nursing the injured. No one paid her any attention as she stopped to take off all her petticoats and sat on the ground to tear them into strips, then she ran to the stream which had continued to flow down the hillside ever since the explosion had brought it to the surface, soaked some of the material in it and returned to the injured navvy. Kneeling on the ground beside him, she bathed his face.

He's probably got a wife and children, Sarah Jane thought, and all he wants is a chance to work. That's what they all wanted. It wasn't their fight, it was hers, and hers alone. She got to her feet and moved in among them, stopping every now and again to bandage a head, an arm or a leg, to comfort, to soothe, to offer a cup of water, and to everyone she said, 'Please stop fighting. It doesn't matter about the bodies, they are already at peace. No one will haunt you.'

But they either did not hear or would not listen. In despair she desisted and walked up the hill away from the mêlée and sat on the rough ground. The site, scattered with all the paraphernalia of railway building, was like an open wound in the green hills; it ought to be healed. Could that best be done by leaving nature to cover the scars or by finishing the line, clearing away the huts, the drilling rig and all the débris to leave nothing but the gleaming railway disappearing into the tunnel. Duncan's grave. She looked up at the skyline: etched against it was the ironwork of the rig on which Duncan had been working. She had been so proud of him when he was made head of that gang. 'The bottom rung of the ladder,' he had said, the start of the fulfilment of their ambition. Only it was her ambition and not his and he had died for it. And today, more men might die for it. If only she could put the clock back. If only . . .

Fires had been started here and there, though whether by accident or design she did not know. Thunder rumbled in the distance and clouds gathered overhead. It would rain soon and put the fires out; would it also snuff out the anger of the men? Would it make them stop fighting and disperse? How would it all end? And where was Jason? She should not be here, she should be with her son. She got to her feet and went back down the slope.

*

'It is plain to see why we need this line,' Geoffrey said. 'Taking to horse for the best part of twenty miles is quite ridiculous in this day and age ...' he stopped suddenly as they breasted the hill and could see the works. 'My God! It's a battlefield!'

The Chevington train had been in London when Smithers' letter arrived, but they dare not wait for it to be fetched. While Timothy had explained to Jason that he and Lord Chevington had to leave for a few days and he would be well looked after in their absence by Wilkins and Hannah, Geoffrey had sent a groom to Chevington Halt to hold the public train. At King's Cross they had picked up their private train and continued their journey through the night, arriving at Ashley Green the following morning. Here they had hired riding horses to take them to Hailey Common. Now they rode down into the mêlée, where the shouting and struggling bodies set their horses rearing and made it impossible to stop and speak to the men, though that had been Geoffrey's intention.

'Let's get out of this!' Timothy said, making for the hut where Smithers was waiting for them.

'Are you hurt, m'lord? Mr Myson?' the contractor asked, as they dismounted at the door.

'No.' Geoffrey dusted down his coat and straightened his cravat before following the contractor and Timothy into the hut. 'But those men are at fever pitch. How did it all begin? Who, or what, set it off?'

Smithers' forehead was creased with worry. 'It's all on account of the bodies still being in the tunnel, my lord. They are saying it's haunted.'

'But that's nonsense!' Geoffrey exclaimed. 'Didn't you explain we would find the remains and give them a decent burial?'

'Yes I did, but they wouldn't listen. They've had plenty of time to get drunk, too, so there's no reasoning with them. They're led by a giant of a fellow by the name of Big Bill and—' He paused, unsure of himself. 'Mrs McBryde.'

'Sarah Jane!' Timothy and Geoffrey spoke together.

'As I understand it, my lord, she came on the train from London with him and that's when it started. The men I already had here were content until they arrived.'

'Why?' Geoffrey asked, though he was not addressing Smithers, but his son. 'Why should she want to cause trouble?'

'I don't know,' Timothy said. 'All I wanted from her, she was willing to give, I swear it.'

'Are you sure?' his father asked, then with sudden insight! 'You took Jason from her, you abducted him without a by-your-leave. Has she any idea where he is?'

'How could she do this to me?' Timothy asked, ignoring his father's question.

'What's worse, you have involved me in your diabolical schemes and that I will not forgive.' Geoffrey looked at his son, whose face was set in an obdurate expression which he knew from past experience could preface an outburst of anger. And there was enough anger here at present without adding to it. He moderated his voice. 'Why, Timothy? Why?'

'She had to be taught a lesson,' his son said stubbornly. 'She knows I'll not harm the boy.'

'She's been badly hurt and now she's fighting back,' Geoffrey said. 'And I can't find it in me to blame her. If you take my advice, you'll abandon this attempt to reopen the tunnel and try to make your peace with her.'

'I won't abandon it. It's too important. And no woman is going to dictate to me how I go about my business. I'm surprised at you for suggesting it, Father. The men must be made to see reason.'

'Then this could get even bloodier,' His Lordship said heavily.

'I have already alerted the military,' Smithers said. 'A show of strength and a reading of the Riot Act should calm them down.'

'I dislike using troops. I would rather try talking to them.'

'They are beyond talking to, my lord.'

'Where is Mrs McBryde now?' Timothy asked, going to the window to peer out. The navvies were milling about apparently without direction, shouting obscenities, battering each other and inflicting terrible injuries. It was impossible to distinguish one side from the other and there was no sign of Sarah Jane. Yet he knew she was out there somewhere and deep inside his gut, so deep he had no idea it was there, he felt the first faint stirrings of a conscience.

Smithers shrugged. 'I don't know, sir. In the vicinity somewhere, I imagine.'

Timothy began pacing the floor of the tiny room, imagining Sarah Jane's lovely body mangled, her beautiful face trampled on, and he had a sudden picture of Jason waiting patiently for the return of his mother. 'I'm going to find her,' he announced suddenly and ran from the hut, ignoring his father's cry of warning. He sped across the muddy turf to the area around the tunnel-mouth where the fighting was at its

336

thickest. She was there, struggling like a wildcat, vainly trying to separate two men, her long hair down about her shoulders, her once-pristine skirt muddied and torn. 'Sarah Jane!' he yelled.

She turned and saw him. Leaving the men, she pushed her way towards him. 'Where's Jason?' she shrieked. 'What have you done with my son?' She stopped within a couple of feet of him. 'If you've brought him to this—'

'Here? Among this scum?' His panic cooled rapidly as he stood and surveyed her from head to toe. Was this wild termagant with the blazing green eyes the girl to whom he had once given his adolescent love, or even the mature and graceful woman whose bed he had shared so recently? Which was the real Sarah Jane? Come to that, where was the real Timothy Myson? He had come into the crush to find and protect her, to ... he stopped his thoughts abruptly. What else? To retract? To say he was sorry? Never! 'Jason is at Chevington House,' he said smoothly. 'Where else would he be?'

'You stole him! You have no right—'

'Oh but I have, my dear Sarah Jane. Look at you! You're half-dressed and filthy, not to mention half-crazed. Do you think that makes you a fit mother for a gentleman's son?'

'Gen'leman!' she scoffed, wanting to pierce the steel-like armour he had built round himself and reverting to the flat vowels and broad accents of her childhood. 'Who's the gen'leman? It certainly ain't you. You forget you was born on the wrong side o' the blanket y'self; you've no rights.'

The truth of what she said fuelled his anger. 'No?' His voice was icy calm. 'It would be easy to prove you are an unfit mother. It was bad enough in London, but now you have really put the cat among the pigeons, surrounding yourself with this ... this rabble, and inciting a riot. That's a criminal offence, didn't you know that? You could be sent to prison and what would become of Jason then? Do you think I want my son brought up by a convicted felon?'

Sarah Jane stared at him with her mouth open in disbelief. Never in her worst nightmares had she imagined this. 'You couldn't ... You wouldn't ...'

'Try me.'

'Jason is my son. And Duncan McBryde's.'

The crowd about them had fallen silent to listen. 'And you'll swear to that?' Timothy's voice was full of controlled venom. 'Even if you perjure yourself, there are others who know the truth – my father, for instance. Do you think you could get him to lie? And the old lawyer, though he mightn't be so trustworthy. And what about your friends, the navvies? Will James McBryde and his wife damn their eternal souls by lying on oath?'

She gave a bitter laugh that did not sound at all like the refined Sarah Jane who had led the life of a lady in London. 'They might swear Jason ain't Duncan's, but that still don' make him yourn. You'll never take 'im from me.'

'We'll see.'

'Nor I won't climb into bed with you neither.' They were both so angry they were unaware of the silent crowd about them, drinking it all in. And Sarah Jane didn't care who heard her, she didn't care if the world knew. 'You're nothing to me, nothing at all. Oh, I might have loved you once but not any more, do you hear? You're mad, mad as a March hare if you think you'll make me do your bidding with threats.'

'I don't threaten what I can't do.' He paused, suddenly aware of the silence around them, and turned to the men. 'Do you know what you are fighting for? Do you know why this ... this trollop set you against me? It has nothing to do with the bodies in the tunnel; she doesn't care an unripe fig for them or for you. She is using you to get at me.'

'They began to murmur among themselves and Big Bill, seeing the initiative slipping away from him, decided to take a hand. 'And you are using her. And it won't work 'cos we've got right on our side.'

Timothy turned from him to Sarah Jane. 'Call them off. Tell them the truth.'

'What truth? That you took my son to make me come to heel? Do you think that will stop them?'

'I don't know what the pair o' you are up to,' Big Bill said, 'but it ain't got anythin' to do with this 'ere dispute. We know we can't make our sets goin' through that rock ...' He jerked his head towards the mouth of the tunnel. 'We tried it afore, remember? It cost men's lives. If you want to build yer railway through these 'ills, you'll start it further down the valley where the goin's easier.'

'It's not for you to dictate to your betters where they build,' Timothy said, forgetting Sarah Jane for the moment. 'You'll excavate where you're told to.'

'Oh no we don't. If you want a fight, then you've got one, right 'ere and now.' He turned to the men. 'Ain't that right, mates?'

There was a rumble of assent from his own supporters but it was not unanimous, for many of the Irish navvies were still prepared to work. The ensuing argument threatened to break out into more violence, and already some scuffles had begun.

'Why should two dead men have the last word?' demanded a belligerent little Irishman who had wriggled through to the front. 'They don't have to worry no more about filling their bellies. We need the work, they don't.'

'And yer'll 'ave it if yer listens to me,' Bill shouted. 'More'n yer wants, I'll be bound. But not 'ere where Duncan McBryde and Randy Joe lie. It's runnin' with fisherman's daughter. I've been in there, I've seen it.'

'We can avoid the water.' Timothy turned from the big navvy to the men who stood behind him. 'You are being offered work to complete that tunnel, well-paid work, and there's nothing more to it than that.'

'Work to make profits for you, ain't that it?' Bill put in before they had time to think of a reply. 'Men's lives don' mean nothing to the likes of you. How many more will be killed before you're satisfied? How many more will have their last resting place in that tunnel?'

'You are fools led by fools,' Timothy shouted, too angry now to be conciliatory. 'Why sacrifice good wages for a couple of dead bodies? What is there to find? Bones, that's all.' He smiled, looking at Sarah Jane, his anger making his dark eyes shine like coals; there was something almost satanic about them. 'But for the squeamish among you, those who believe in ghosts and curses ...' there was contempt in his voice '... for those we have given an undertaking to respect the dead.'

'What if you can't find them?' someone shouted. 'Will you build the line on top of them?'

'We will make every effort to locate them.'

'That ain't good enough. They were blown to bits, so it can't be done.'

Sarah Jane, stupefied by Timothy's cruel words, had lost track of what was happening; she was incapable of doing anything to help herself or the men. Meaningless thoughts chased each other round her confused brain, as she was pushed this way and that in the crowd. What was she doing here? Why was she so far from Jason? Her son was all that mattered to her. 'Let me through!' she cried. 'I must go to Jason.'

'Oh no you don't, me beauty.' Big Bill grabbed her arm, almost pulling her off her feet. 'You started it, you'll stop here and see it through.'

'But I must find my son.' She turned to Timothy. 'Take me to him.'

'Certainly not. Jason is better where he is, he doesn't need to be reminded that his mother is a whore.'

'How dare you!'

'I dare. Now, go to the hut before these men decide they've had enough of your mischief-making and set about you themselves.'

'I won't!'

'Then on your own head be it. God knows why I risked my neck to come and find you. You're not worth the trouble—' He stopped, suddenly aware that the tumult had died and the men had become silent. It was as if some giant hand had been raised, a signal given which everyone knew and understood. But it was not a hand that had silenced the men, but the cry, 'Shut up and listen! Can't you hear it? It's the bloody militia!'

Faintly in the distance came the sound of a drum and then, coming over the brow of the hill, they saw the red jackets and white breeches of soldiers. The navvies stood and looked slowly from one to another and then turned a united front towards their common enemy as they marched firmly towards the works and halted.

Lord Chevington and Smithers came out of the hut to stand beside Timothy, who had left Sarah Jane and begun haranguing the men again.

'Leave it, Timothy,' His Lordship said. 'For God's sake, tell them we are not proceeding.'

'No! I will not let this rabble beat me, now or ever.' He turned to the men. 'I will give you one last chance to come to your senses and begin work. If you persist, you give me no choice but to ask the troops to intervene. You can see they are armed.' He nodded towards the young officer in charge of the soldiers, who ordered them to load their rifles and take aim.

Convinced they were about to fire, Sarah Jane forced herself out of the crowd and began to run across the open ground towards the uniformed men, her hair streaming out behind her and her arms outstretched as if to protect the navvies behind her. 'Don't!' she screamed, looking straight into the barrels of the rifles. 'Don't fire!'

She knew Timothy had started to run after her, but she did not stop and the row of rifles remained poised – all but one. It wavered ever so slightly as if its weight were more than its handler could manage.

'Take aim, that man there!' the lieutenant shouted, as the young soldier dropped his arm and the long barrel pointed at the ground at his feet. 'Wait for the order.' The gun was lifted again but the young soldier was white-faced and shaking.

Sarah Jane knew him; she had recognised him simply by the expression on his face. She had seen it before, on the day they had gone to the workhouse. She saw, in the wide brilliance of his eyes, the frightened plea of the seven-year-old Billie held in Granny Hewitt's grasp, and experienced again her own inability to help him. She had to reach the officer, to explain, to stop him ...

The shot shocked her into immobility. The row of soldiers hadn't moved; they were still pointing their weapons at the navvies. All except Billie. He had thrown down his smoking rifle and was running away like a terrified rabbit, tearing off up the hill towards the old drilling rig. She shrieked 'Billie!' once and then again in a hopeless whisper, as the officer ordered the men to go after him.

Behind her the silence deepened, forcing itself to her attention. Slowly she turned her back on the soldiers and faced the navvies. Smithers was helping Lord Chevington carry Timothy back to the hut, while the suddenly sober navvies stood and watched them go. She ran back, forcing her way through the handful of people grouped about the door. 'Let me in,' she cried. 'In God's name, let me in.'

Fleetingly she noticed that the back room of the hut was just as it had been in Charlie Bender's time; the furniture was still in place, the dusty curtains still at the windows and the crockery still on the dresser. They put Timothy on the bed. The front of the young man's shirt was stained with a crimson splash which grew larger as they watched.

'Is it bad?' she asked, going to stand beside him. 'Is he ...'

Timothy stirred and opened his eyes. 'No, my dear,' he said with a twisted smile. 'Nothing so dramatic.'

His strained voice brought her back to reality. She looked about her, picked up a small knife from the clutter on the table and began cutting away his shirt to get at the wound. The bullet was deep in his shoulder and he was losing a lot of blood; she did not know if she had the skill and strength to do what she knew had to be done, but it never occurred to her not to try. 'A bowl of hot water,' she commanded. 'And clean rags, lots of them.'

'I've sent for a doctor,' Geoffrey said, dully.

'He'll take hours to get here and Timothy will bleed to death while

341

we wait.' She turned back to probe the extent of the injury with sensitive hands, glad that Timothy had lost his senses and was unaware of what she was doing. 'I must do what I can. If there's a bullet in him, it'll have to come out.'

'But it's a job for a surgeon.'

'I know, but we haven't one, so you'll just have to make do with me.' She looked up as Smithers returned with water and bandages. 'Is this the sharpest knife you've got?'

'I'll have it honed.' He took it from her and disappeared. She sat back on her haunches and looked at Timothy's white face, and knew she had to save him if she were ever to live with herself again. Whatever he had done, she could not bear to have his death on her conscience, and that was where it would lie if he died as the result of this day's work.

Lord Chevington moved to the head of the bed to give her more room. He no longer protested, but stood silently watching her, trying to see in her the power to work a miracle. She had every reason to hate Timothy. Might she let him die? She turned to smile at him, a pale ghost of a smile, as if she had read his thoughts. 'Trust me.'

'Can I?'

'Yes.'

The lieutenant pushed open the door and stood on the threshold. 'He's got away,' he said. 'He must have found somewhere to hide.'

'Who?' Geoffrey asked.

'The one who did this.' He nodded towards the bed.

Sarah Jane, without looking up, said dully, 'Let him go.'

'Let him go, ma'am? I can't do that.'

'Why not? He was young and afraid. You had him standing at the ready too long, aiming a rifle at men who could be his brothers, it was no wonder he was so unnerved he didn't know what he was doing.'

'It was not our intention to open fire on the men, ma'am, only to threaten. He fired without a command to do so and must be punished. It's the way of the army.'

'And I suppose it's the army's way to hunt him down like an animal.' Looking up, past him, she saw Smithers returning. 'Let him go. What's done is done. Now, if you please, we've work to do. Unless,' she added as an afterthought, 'you've a surgeon in your party?'

'No, we are only a small troop.'

Smithers pushed past him to bring Sarah Jane the now-sharp knife and she busied herself scalding it in hot water. She did not notice the officer leave. Billie had recognised her, she was sure of it, and it was because she had been in his line of fire that he had lowered his gun. It wasn't his fault Timothy had been shot, for all he held the weapon that did it. If anyone was to blame, she was. She must make them see that when they brought him back. She bent to her task.

Geoffrey, resigned to whatever was going to happen, good or bad, pulled himself together and handed her whatever she asked for, mopped up the blood which was everywhere, and the sweat on Timothy's brow, and marvelled at Sarah Jane's coolness. She was an extraordinary woman; he had thought so before, he was convinced of it now. Timothy was bandaged and sleeping by the time the doctor arrived on a sweat-streaked horse, hours later.

He stood and looked down at Sarah Jane's handiwork, felt Timothy's wrist and forehead, poked experimentally at the bandage and said, 'He'll do.'

'You mean he'll live?' queried His Lordship, almost in disbelief.

'I mean that whatever was necessary has been done, and competently too. I'll leave something for the pain and, with good nursing, he should pull through.'

Geoffrey let out a long breath of relief. 'Thank God.'

'God had a little help.' The doctor smiled. 'The patient must on no account be moved for several days. Can you make him comfortable here until I send a nurse?'

'He doesn't need a nurse,' Sarah Jane said. 'He's got me.'

'Did you do this?' He pointed to the bandage.

She nodded, thinking, 'Yes, all of it, not just the doctoring. I put the wound there in the first place. I'll work till I drop before I'll let anyone else nurse him.' It was not love which drove her, but guilt – the love had gone and could never be rekindled.

'It's an excellent piece of work, especially in these conditions.' He stood up and closed his bag with a snap. 'I'll return tomorrow.'

'There are casualties among the navvies too,' Sarah Jane said. 'Can you do something for them?'

The doctor glanced at Lord Chevington, who nodded his agreement. 'Very well.' He clamped his top hat on his head and turned to leave, adding, 'Keep this patient quiet and don't let him thrash himself about when he comes round.'

He had hardly gone from the door before the space was filled by a tall, broad-shouldered man wearing a new big-brimmed white hat.

Sarah Jane, who had been gazing at Timothy, her churning thoughts at odds with her physical exhaustion, saw his shadow fall across the room and turned to look at him. 'James ...'

'Aye and it's too late I am, I see.' His warm Scottish burr made her taut nerves relax suddenly and for the first time since the accident, tears stung her eyes.

Smithers, who had been sitting on the edge of the table, silently staring down at his boots, looked up at the stranger. 'Are you James McBryde?'

'Aye, I am that. What can I do?'

The contractor's tone suddenly became businesslike; someone had to remember the job in hand, make a move to restore order. 'Will you talk to the men, explain about the tunnel, tell them you are agreeable to the removal of your son's remains?'

'Aye, I'll do that.'

'Then you had best take charge. Do whatever you have to do. Send away those who don't want to work, figure out an agreement with the gangers, offer them a fair wage and honest tommy.'

'I'll do what I can.' James turned to Sarah Jane and took both her hands in his own, surveying her from head to foot. ''Tis good to see you again, lass. How have ye fared?'

'Well.' She paused. 'James, The Haven is still watertight. You can sleep there, if you like.'

'What about you?'

'I'll stay here.' She turned her head towards the sleeping Timothy.

'Very well. We'll talk tomorrow, shall we?'

She knew she would be in for an uncomfortable cross-examination, but she didn't resent that. 'Yes, we'll talk tomorrow.'

It was a long, long night and Sarah Jane, watching by the light of a single candle, saw Timothy burn in a restless fever, heard him groan and mutter in delirium, staunched a new flow of blood and prayed. She prayed for his recovery, for her own absolvement and for the innocent Billie, while Geoffrey slept fitfully on a chair a few yards away. Smithers, being assured there was nothing he could do, had taken himself off to share the Haven with James.

By the time dawn lightened the sky above the hills and she extinguished the last inch of guttering candle, Timothy was sleeping peacefully. She stretched her cramped limbs and went outside, breathing in the early morning air, fresh after overnight rain. She stood with her back to the hut and looked about her. It was like old times; men and horses were moving about, there were trucks and shovels and piles of sleepers, and smoke curled from a dozen chimneys. The site was returning to life. A little way off, set apart, she was surprised to see that the soldiers had camped. Why had they stayed? Surely they were not still expecting trouble, or searching for Billie? Would they really punish him? Poor Billie. It was not his fault. Would they let her speak for him, get him off?

Lord Chevington emerged from the hut and stood beside her in brooding silence for a minute, then he said, 'Thank you, Sarah Jane. I believe you have saved Timothy's life.'

'It's too soon to say that,' she said. 'And I put it in peril in the first place. I'll never forgive myself for that, not if I live to be a hundred.'

'But it was the young soldier ...'

'He was my brother.'

He turned towards her in surprise. 'Your brother? The one that Mr Wistonby has been seeking?'

'Yes. When I left the Union I promised him that one day we would be together again.' She managed a wry smile. 'It was a foolish promise but one I always meant to keep. That was one of the reasons I had to make a good life – for him and for Jason.' Her voice faltered. 'And I failed them both, miserably.'

'You have failed no one, my dear,' he said softly. 'And I am sorry I doubted you. When I realised how skilful you were ...'

'Skilful at taking bullets out of people, you mean?' She gave a laugh hollow with fatigue. 'I had never done it before, but if I had admitted that, you would not have let me do it, would you?' She smiled at the expression of horror which crossed his face. 'Oh, I have bound up a few wounds, but never surgery.'

'But you looked so competent.'

'I knew what had to be done and I did it, that's all there is to it.'

'It took courage.'

'I didn't mean any of this.' She spread her hands to encompass the works.

'I'm sure you didn't.'

'Do you think I stirred up some evil, some dreadful thing in me that contaminates all I touch, everything I hold dear? Billie, Duncan, Timothy, even Jason ...'

'Nonsense. You are just tired, and small wonder. You need to rest.'

'I can't, Timothy needs me. I will stay until he is on the mend, but after that ...'

345

'I believe he loves you, in his own rather twisted way, and he loves Jason.'

'No. If he did, he would not have taken Jason from me.' She turned to him, her eyes bright with tears. 'He said some dreadful things about me being an unfit mother. It isn't true, is it? I won't ruin my son's life, too. This rottenness in me won't spread to him, will it?'

Her misery wrung his heart. 'Oh, Sarah Jane, don't cry.' He put his arm about her shoulder to comfort her. 'There is no rottenness in you, not one iota. You are a force for good. Why, you even manage to bring out the good in Timothy, and that is something I have always failed to do.' He lifted his other hand to turn her face towards him, so that he could look into her eyes, and found himself wanting to kiss the tears away. 'Sarah Jane, you have work to do and too much to give to waste yourself in bitterness and self-reproach. And as for Jason, he is a great credit to you. I think I know why Timothy brought him to Chevington and it wasn't so much to hurt you, as to punish me.'

'I don't understand.'

'I can't say I do entirely, but be assured, I was never party to his abduction.'

'No, I didn't think you were.' She paused. 'Is he well? Is he missing me? How did Timothy persuade him to go?'

'He is quite well and he trusts Timothy, as you must know.' He paused and wiped a glistening tear from her cheek with a gentle finger. 'Timothy would never hurt the boy.'

'But he can hurt me. I was distraught. Can you imagine what it's like for a mother to lose her son?'

'I think I can,' he said, thinking of Rachel, Timothy's mother. 'But you haven't lost him. Jason is expecting you to join him on his little holiday.'

'At Chevington?'

'Why not?'

She could see any number of reasons why a one-time skivvy could not be a guest in His Lordship's home. He was just being kind to her as he always was, and it was comfortable in his arms, comfortable and secure, too much so; it would be easy to learn to lean on him. She turned to go back into the hut. 'Timothy will wake soon and he must be watched in case he tries to move.'

'Then I'll watch him. You go and rest for a while.' He put a hand on her arm and added, 'I'll send for you if there is any change, I promise you.'

Her eyes were already heavy with the need to sleep; she smiled her thanks and left him to go to the Haven. He returned to the hut, ducking his head under the low doorway.

His son was awake, lying on his back on the narrow bed, gazing with fever-bright eyes at the rough wooden beams which supported the roof. Geoffrey pulled a small stool out from under the table to sit beside him. 'So, you are back with us again, eh?'

'What happened?' Timothy's voice was no more than a whisper.

'An accident. You've had a bullet taken from your shoulder and unless you lie very still indeed, you'll start to bleed again.'

'Sarah Jane?'

'She was your surgeon. She's been up with you all night, now she's gone to rest.'

Timothy grimaced as a small movement sent pain shooting through him. 'Don't hold it ... against her.' He tried to smile. 'She didn't mean ...'

'I know, I have spoken to her.' Geoffrey paused. 'Why did you do it, Timothy? Why did you take Jason from her?'

'To get her to sell that damned school. And to prove that I could.' He tried to laugh but it turned to a grimace of pain. 'You know what we've done, you and I? We've created a dynasty of bastards. Will Jason carry on the good work when he grows to manhood, do you think?'

Geoffrey looked startled. 'Timothy, there is no cause to talk like that.'

'Your lady wife knew all about me. Would she have accepted me if you had told her of my existence right at the beginning? Could I have been a proper son in the eyes of the world?'

'What is the good of asking ourselves questions like that? It's all in the past.'

'And if I had been, would I have been a different person? Would I have met Sarah Jane? Would Jason have been born? Your conscience must be burdened not only with me, but with him too.'

'Perhaps it is a little. Perhaps that's why, in the beginning, I suggested you should marry Sarah Jane.'

He looked sharply at his father. 'You make very free with her given name.'

'I have known her a long time, Timothy. She was part of my household.'

'Which was one of the reasons marriage was always out of the question.'

347

'I see that now. It would have been a disaster.' His reasons for thinking that were not the same as Timothy's; his consideration was for Sarah Jane and her happiness. Marriage to Timothy would have been condemning her to a life of misery. 'The doctor has left something to ease the pain,' he said. 'I'll give you a dose and then you must sleep.' He picked up a bottle of dark liquid and poured some into a spoon. 'Now, take this and rest.'

Timothy swallowed it and pulled a face. 'The tunnel? The work?'

His Lordship smiled. 'Listen,' he said. 'Can't you hear the rumble of wagons, the jingle of harness and the cries of the boys? McBryde is there, taking charge, and all is well.'

Timothy gave a little smile of satisfaction and fell asleep.

Chapter Twenty-Two

*T*imothy mended quickly and was soon pestering everyone who came to the hut with questions about how the work was progressing. There was no need for him to concern himself, Smithers and James had everything under control and there was no more trouble. The men had moved tons of rubble but still there was more, and Sarah Jane began to wonder if they would ever find themselves back in that ill-fated tunnel. She was half-hopeful, half-fearful, unable to leave, reluctant to stay, and so she went about her self-appointed nursing tasks in a kind of hypnotic trance.

Billie had not been found either, although the troops had searched every inch of the workings; he seemed to have disappeared into thin air. Sarah Jane spent some time talking to his comrades but learned little except that he was a good soldier, kept himself clean and sober and always obeyed orders. He'd often said enlisting was the best day's work he'd ever done, so they told her, and no one could explain why he had fired that shot. Sarah Jane noticed one of the men in particular. His name was Harker. He was rather old for a soldier and his uniform jacket was fastened across his portly stomach with buttons that threatened to pop off at the least exertion. His blue eyes, beneath bushy eyebrows, were kindly and regarded her as if he would like to confide in her but was unsure whether to risk it. She suspected he knew more than he was saying but she could never manage to talk to him alone.

The second evening after the shooting she saw him from the window of the hut. He was moving up the hillside towards the rig, carrying a spade and a small bundle. If it had not been for his furtive manner she would have assumed he was going to find the privacy to answer a call of nature and turned away, but he dodged from rock to rock and kept glancing back to where his comrades were camped and she became curious. Timothy called from the bed and reluctantly she went to make him more comfortable, and by the time she returned to the window, Rifleman Harker was almost back to the camp, still carrying the spade but now without the bundle.

'I need some fresh air,' she said. 'I'll not be long.'

Without waiting for Timothy's reply, she hurried to meet the soldier. 'Good evening,' she said.

He smiled. 'Evenin', ma'am.'

She hesitated, undecided whether to go on. 'The man who fired the shot ...'

'Billie, you mean?'

'Yes. He is my brother.'

'I know. He told me.'

'Then you've seen him since it happened?' The weariness lifted from her face and for a moment it was bright with hope.

'Yes. He fell into a shaft.' He raised his hand to the hill. 'That's why they couldn't find 'im.' He paused. 'You wouldn't let on, would you?'

'Of course not.' Her gaze shifted from him to the twisted metal of the rig and her mouth lifted in a wry smile. The shaft, Duncan's work, had served a purpose after all. 'Has he been hiding there all this time?' Her voice was cultured, he noticed, her words carefully enunciated, not a bit like Billie's broad vowels. But for the filthy clothes, you could take her for a lady.

'Yes, ma'am.'

'I would like to talk to him. I want him to know I don't blame him – no one does, not even Mr Myson. It could all have been sorted out, he needn't have run away.'

'He was shook up at seein' you, ma'am, and 'e didn't stop to think. 'e knew 'e'd done wrong.'

'If they find him, how will they punish him?'

'A floggin', ma'am, an' Billie'll do anythin' afore 'e'd take the lash. He told me once that he'd had more'n one beating in the Union, run away from that and ended up with a sweep and that were worse, near killed 'im it did. I tried to get 'im to come back, but 'e wouldn't, so I got 'im some clothes from one o' the navvies, so 'e could get away.'

'He's gone?' She didn't want to believe it. To be so close and still not be reunited; it was almost as if it were a kind of punishment for promising to look after him and failing so miserably. 'Where has he gone?'

He shrugged. 'He 'as to make a new life for 'isself.'

'If you see him again,' she said slowly, 'will you tell him from me, not to feel badly about anything. Tell him Mr Myson is going to get well. Tell him I am thinking of him and wish him luck and happiness. Tell him ...' She paused. 'Tell him I'm sorry ... so very sorry.'

'If I ever see 'im I will, but I shan't if 'e's got 'is 'ead screwed on. He'll be looking to get clean away.'

'I was on my way to that hut over there.' She nodded towards the Haven. 'Would you like to come with me so that I can write down an address where he can contact me if he needs to?'

He thought it a waste of time but didn't want to hurt her by saying so, and fell into step beside her. He waited while she found paper and pencil and wrote down her Oxford Street address, then he put the paper carefully in his pocket and returned to his comrades. She watched him go with little hope that her message would ever reach her brother.

The following morning, the troops gave up the search and packed up to return to barracks. It meant Billie would be posted as a deserter. Choked by regrets and a feeling of complete helplessness to do anything about anything, Sarah Jane watched them form up and march away, over the hill back to Ashley Green where they would entrain for London, then she turned and walked slowly back to the contractor's hut.

Timothy was more than usually irritable. He had tried to dress himself, but the effort had been too much for him and now he sat on the edge of the bed, staring at the cluttered room, angry at his own weakness. 'Where've you been? You said you wouldn't be long.'

'I've been looking after the injured navvies. Many of them need their bandages changing. You're not the only wounded one, you know.' Her voice was tart, hiding the lump in her throat. 'And it won't help if you disobey the doctor and try to get up.'

'I want to see what's going on.'

'There is nothing new. The men are working hard, very carefully, one stone at a time, but there's more crock in that tunnel than anyone realised.'

'How much did they shift yesterday?'

'About forty sets, I think, maybe more.'

'I want to go and see for myself.'

'Do you want to kill yourself?'

'Rubbish! It won't kill me. I'm fit enough to walk about and the fresh air will do me good.'

'Tomorrow then, if all goes well, you can sit outside for a while,' she conceded.

But she was forestalled. She returned to the hut next day after taking James a pot of hot thick soup for his midday break to find a carriage drawn up at the door and Caroline sitting beside Timothy's bed on the little stool she used when changing his bandages. The girl was holding his hand against her pale cheek, while her blonde ringlets fell forward across her face. She was in half-mourning and her voluminous mauve crinoline was spread about her, so clean and bright, it made the room seem filthy, although Sarah Jane had spent hours scrubbing it. She looked down at her own plain wool dress and heavy boots. In London, in *Carter's* of Bond Street, she might have been able to compete, but here and now, they were poles apart. She put one tanned hand up to her freckled face and wished herself anywhere but where she was.

'Ah, here's my nurse,' Timothy said cheerfully. 'This is Mrs McBryde, Caroline.'

She was infuriated by his patronising tone, put on for Caroline's benefit, though she doubted if the girl was deceived. 'I'll come back when your visitor has gone,' she said and turned to leave.

'Oh, but I'm not going,' Caroline said, eyeing her up and down with curled lip. 'Not without Mr Myson.'

'Miss Hailey has offered to take me home to convalesce,' Timothy said. 'It's wonderfully civil of her.'

'Dr Cross said—'

Caroline stood up and turned her blue eyes on Sarah Jane. 'I have spoken to Dr Cross,' she said, deliberately pretending she had not recognised her. 'He says it is perfectly in order for me to take Mr Myson home so long as we drive carefully and don't jolt him. It is only three or four miles.'

'But ...'

'If you are concerned about losing your job, I am sure Mr Myson will recompense you. I'll take care of the patient from now on.' Her voice conveyed the impression she considered she was talking to a servant.

Sarah Jane turned angrily to Timothy. 'So my usefulness is done, is it? I am dismissed?'

Timothy smiled easily. 'Mrs McBryde, you have been a good nurse, but I am heartily sick of these four walls. Besides, I need a bath and a change of clothes. Stay here with my ... His Lordship. I'll come back as soon as I can ride, a few days no more, then we'll talk.'

'And pray, what shall we talk about?' The old fiery Sarah Jane reasserted herself. 'The price of a nurse or the cost of silk, a servant's wages or maybe the future of my son?'

'Be silent, ma'am,' Caroline commanded before Timothy could speak. 'You are being impertinent. Now, be so good as to find Mr Myson's clothes so that I can help him to dress.'

'You will do no such thing,' Sarah Jane told her, and Timothy laughed aloud; he was enjoying the confrontation, actually enjoying it, and she became angrier than ever. 'Please go to your coach,' she added. 'Ti ... Mr Myson will join you when he is ready. If he needs help I'll give it.'

'Go on, Caroline,' Timothy said softly.

Sarah Jane watched her leave before turning back to Timothy, who was still chuckling. 'You relished that, didn't you?' she said. 'You think it's funny that she humiliates me, dismisses me with a wave of the hand as if she were royalty and I were dirt.'

'I'm sorry, Sarah Jane,' he said, serious again. 'But you were so angry.'

'And with good cause. Dr Cross said you were not to be moved, that if you start to bleed again, it could be very dangerous. And that one out there has no more idea of nursing than I have of flying.'

'Dr Cross is an old fusspot and I'm bored.'

'Then on your own head be it.' She fetched his overnight bag from the cupboard in the corner, took out his clothes, newly cleaned and pressed, and flung them at him. 'And you can dress yourself.'

'Sarah Jane.' He leaned forward and grasped her wrist, pulling her down to sit on the bed beside him. 'You saved my life and exhausted yourself looking after me, so if you feel guilty about my injuries, you need do so no longer.'

'Guilty? Why should I feel guilty? It's you should feel remorse, not me.' She made no move to help him as he clambered painfully out of bed and began to dress. 'I will never forgive you for kidnapping Jason. Never!'

'I took him for a little holiday, how can that be called kidnapping?'

'Without my knowledge or consent, of course it was. And you threatened me with the law. What have I ever done to deserve that?'

'You ask me that? I'll tell you, shall I?' Exhausted and breathless he sank back onto the bed, with his shirt unbuttoned. 'You have destroyed me.'

'Don't be so melodramatic. How can a little randy by a handful of navvies destroy you? And you will get a compulsory purchase on the school, even I know that.'

'All I've worked for,' he said, more to himself than to her. 'All the sacrifices I've made ...'

'Sacrifices! What sacrifices have you ever made? You have always had exactly what you wanted and be damned to anyone who stood in your way!'

He turned to look at her, a faint smile playing round his lips. 'Just as you have done, my dear Sarah Jane, just as you have done. But you had nothing to lose, while I had everything.' He began slowly doing up the buttons of his shirt.

'What, in heaven's name, are you talking about?'

'I am talking about my inheritance.'

'Chevington?'

'Among other things, but that most of all. Her Ladyship is dead.'

'Yes, I know, and I'm deeply sorry for His Lordship.'

'She knew I was his son, she knew it all along. What do you think of that, my sweet Sarah Jane?'

'I am not surprised – she was nobody's fool. But what is that to me?'

'She kept silent, all those years, not a word, until she was on her deathbed and then she told His Lordship to recognise me and make me his heir.'

'Congratulations,' she said tartly. 'You've got what you most wanted.'

'No, I haven't.' He smiled wryly, struggling to put his legs into his trousers. 'My father is eaten up with guilt because of what he did to my mother – not that he would have married her, even if he had been free.' He grinned lopsidedly and sat on the bed to pull on one of his riding boots, but bending over was a painful business and it fell from his hand to clatter on the floor beside its fellow. 'Because of that, he thinks I should feel guilty, too. He suggested I ought to do the right thing by you and marry you.' He took her shoulders in his hands and even weak from his injury, his grip made her wince. 'If you had your sights set on that, you can forget it.'

She was so astounded that she could only stare at him with her mouth open. What had made Lord Chevington suggest marriage, of all things?

'You may well gape like a fish out of water,' he went on. 'Isn't that what you wanted all along?'

Had she wanted it? Had she really hoped against all hope, that Timothy would ask her to marry him? Had that been her secret dream, one she had not even admitted to herself? If it had, it was gone now; it had shattered the day he had taken her son from her. The last flicker of feeling for him had died; there was nothing there now and she was free of him. 'No, it certainly is not,' she said. 'I would not marry you if you were the last man on earth. I can't think what made you think I would.'

He laughed humourlessly. 'Come now, Sarah Jane, admit it. That's what you've been angling for all along, hoping that by holding yourself aloof and denying me your favours, even refusing to sell the school, you would push me into a proposal.'

'Your conceit is beyond belief!' She sprang to her feet and faced him, her breast heaving, making him wish he had the strength to take her then and there, to make her body deny the words she was uttering. 'All I want from you is a promise to leave me and my son in peace to live our lives in our own way.'

'Jason.' He paused, as if considering it. 'And if I refuse to give him up? I could keep him, you know.'

A brief spark of fear made her heart beat in her throat, but then she realised he was bluffing. She smiled. 'And what do you suppose little Miss Hailey will say to that? No, you have more to lose than I have and I would caution you to think of that before you threaten me again.' She bent and put his boots on for him, her annoyance making her less than gentle. That done, she went to a corner where her own bag had been thrown down and, taking out the golden apple, pushed it in with his nightshirt and toiletries, then she took his bag out to the carriage, flung it in beside Caroline and returned to the hut. He was still sitting where she had left him.

'I suggest you join Miss Hailey,' she said. 'She is becoming decidedly impatient.'

He stood up shakily. 'Sarah Jane.' His voice was soft as he reached out to touch her shoulder. 'I do not want to hurt you, I never wanted that.'

Angrily she shrugged him off. He gave a melodramatic sigh and slowly made his way out to the waiting carriage.

She was still sitting on the empty bed, staring at the floor, when Lord Chevington returned. He had been down to the tunnel where the navvies were very near a breakthrough, and had hurried back to the hut to tell his son. 'Where is Timothy?'

She lifted her head slowly to answer him. 'He's gone home with Miss Hailey. She brought a coach for him.'

'Did Dr Cross agree?'

'She said he had so long as they drove carefully.' He sat down beside her and took her hand. 'It's for the best, Sarah Jane,' he said softly and when she did not reply, added, 'He is my son, but he is not worth your anguish.'

She turned to look into his eyes. 'But I was wrong to do what I did. I was hurt and angry and because of that so many other people were hurt – the navvies, Billie, Timothy . . .'

'Perhaps we should all have behaved differently,' he said. 'I, too, have regrets, but it is too late for that now. We must live with the consequences of what we do.' His voice was almost wistful. 'I should never have told Timothy he was my son.'

She understood him perfectly. 'You loved her very much, didn't you?'

He looked surprised. 'Who?'

'Lady Chevington, your wife.'

'Yes, of course, very much.'

'I'm sorry,' she said softly. 'I know how you feel because I loved Duncan like that. It was so sure, so abiding, I didn't ever think of it ending, and when it did, there was nothing left but an appalling emptiness.'

'Yes.' His voice was hardly audible. 'And guilt.'

'That too, but it passes. Everything passes, and you learn to live again, to remember the joy and be glad of it. I made a new life for myself and for Jason. I should not have let anything deflect me from that.' She paused. 'You know, sitting here with you, so close to the place where Duncan lies, I can clearly see my mistake. I mistook passion for love. What we had, Timothy and I, was passion. And passion dies. My love for Duncan will never die. He made me into a woman. He took care of Jason and me when we had no one and I was devastated when he died – and some say that was my fault, too.' She looked up into his face and smiled. 'I should never have let Timothy back into my life but he can be very charming when he chooses and I was weak.'

'What are you going to do now?'

'Fetch my son home. Get back to work. See if I can do anything to help Billie. The soldiers have given up searching for him but if I could find him, I could help him.'

'And the navvies?'

'I don't belong among them now and James will look after Duncan when they find him. I still have my memories and that is all I need.'

'You are a remarkably strong woman,' he said. 'And I admire you for it. But I also admire your compassion, your capacity for love. Don't lose that, Sarah Jane, or we will all be the poorer.'

She smiled, pleased by the compliment, and went to tell James of her decision. She was halfway across the open ground, when she was halted by a young lad running past her towards the hut she had just left, shouting, 'They've found one of them!' She turned towards the entrance to the tunnel, where the burrowing navvies had moved aside to let two of their number through carrying a bundle in a canvas sheet. It was closely wrapped, smaller than a man, not even the shape of a man; it could have been anything, a pile of rocks even, but she knew it was a body, or parts of one. What she didn't know was whether it was Duncan or Randy Joe. She took a few tentative steps forward as James came to her side. 'Stay there, Sarah Jane. I'll come and tell you. You needn't see ...'

He walked past her towards the men who had laid the bundle on the ground, while the silent navvies doffed their headgear and stood with heads bowed. She watched as James stood looking down at the covered bundle for several seconds before drawing a deep breath and stooping to turn back one corner of the canvas. His head was bowed and she could not see his face. Slowly he straightened up and nodded.

She had been holding her breath, but now she let it out in a long cry of anguish and sank to her knees. 'Duncan. Oh, Duncan.' Her hands reached out and she fell forwards with her face to the damp earth, earth which for three long years had imprisoned the body of the man who, above all others, had taught her the true meaning of love.

It was Geoffrey who helped her to her feet and back to the hut. He sat beside her on the narrow bed and held her in his arms, saying nothing, because he knew her tears for Duncan had been shed long ago, and today she wept for herself. Her shaking shoulders under his hand and her tear-streaked face buried in his neck, brought back his own intense grief and, for several minutes, they clung to each other and wept together, united in their sorrow.

Randy Joe's remains were found later the same day and the follow-ing morning both bodies were interred in the graveyard of the little church in the valley, witnessed by almost every navvy on the site, some of whom had been at that earlier service when all hope of a rescue had been abandoned. She had been half mad with grief then, but out of that grief had come a determination to rebuild her life. She could not have done it without Duncan, who had been with her every step of the way. But now she must let him go. 'Goodbye, my love,' she whispered, as she dropped a handful of wild flowers on the lid of the coffin as it was lowered into the grave. 'May you rest in peace.'

Lord Chevington would not give her time to brood. As soon as they returned to the site he insisted that she travel back to London with him in his private train and, conscious of her grubby clothes and lack of petticoats, she accepted, glad of the privacy it would afford her. They rode back over the hill to Ashley Green on the hired horses which had brought His Lordship and Timothy to Hailey, where the train had been kept in a siding for their return. It was almost a little town now; everything was spanking new, from the fine railway station and rows of brick-built houses to the paved main street and newly planted shrubs. Would Hailey Common come to be like that, she wondered as they boarded the train. Would the scars there be similarly healed?

For several miles Lord Chevington remained silent, sitting with his long-fingered hands idle in his lap and his chin dropped onto his cravat, deep in thoughts she could not share. Not wishing to intrude, she settled down to watch the countryside roll past the window, land she had covered on foot when she first joined the navvies, so many years before. Her life in London seemed an age away, but no more distant than the navvies she had left behind; she felt locked in time, doomed to travel forever between the two worlds.

She thought His Lordship had fallen asleep, but after a while he started to talk, haltingly at first, but then more easily, as he found in her a ready listener. He was anxious to return to his office and the conduct of his business. Smithers and James McBryde could be trusted to oversee the rail connection from Hailey Common to Ashley Green. 'That little drama will go down in the history books as a minor hitch in a great enterprise,' he said. 'It will soon be forgotten, except by you and me, for whom it has some significance.'

'What will you do now?' she asked. 'More railways?'

'I might involve myself with this idea of an underground railway in London,' he said. 'Oh, I know the big railway companies have not been enthusiastic and the City Corporation has withdrawn its support for the idea, but it will come, it will have to. Unless some way is found to travel easily from one terminus to the next, London's traffic will come to a halt.' He smiled at her. 'On the other hand, I might find other fish to fry – industry, commerce, politics. Railway-building has to come to an end some time. It can't go on forever.'

'What about the junction with the *Great Eastern* in Caledonian Road?'

'That was Timothy's own project. Whether it goes ahead or not is up to him.' He paused, watching her face with its expressive green eyes, unsure of how to proceed. 'I did try to persuade him to make a detour to avoid the school, but it would have been disastrously expensive.'

'So he was angry with both of us over it?'

'Yes.' He smiled a trifle wanly. 'I am tired of fighting him, Sarah Jane. It seems as though I have been doing it all his life and even now I cannot give him all he wants.'

'He asks too much,' she said. 'He asks too much of everyone, but if it helps you, I will give in over the school. I had planned to move from over the shop and buy a house; it would not be too difficult to have classrooms under the same roof.'

'You don't intend to give up the idea then?'

'Certainly not! I mean to have a whole string of navvy schools, but I've no doubt I'll have a fight on my hands. The contractors don't like anything they think might interfere with their profits.'

He smiled. 'Are you surprised?'

'This won't cost them anything except a small site and building materials – wood, nails, things they already have in plenty on the sites.'

He laughed. 'But education makes people think, and they are not keen on thinking navvies. They don't want more men like Big Bill to upset the status quo.'

'If he makes the owners sit up and take notice, then so much the better.'

'You will need help.'

She looked back at him, hope brightening her eyes. 'Would you? More than you have already, I mean.'

He smiled; she was nothing if not tenacious. 'I'll talk to my sister-in-law, Mrs Townsend, shall I? She does a great deal of good work among the poor and knows all the right people. Her help would be invaluable in forming a working committee.'

'Is that how it's done?'

'Usually. Several heads are better than one.'

She was dubious. She could not see herself working with a lot of upper-class do-gooders, who seemed to spend their time arguing about minutiae. 'Would it work?'

'It would be up to you to make it work, wouldn't it?' He reached across to touch her hand. It was done unthinkingly, a gesture of support. 'Amelia is very easy to get along with, but she is like you in many ways – tenacious and unused to taking no for an answer. You will deal well together.'

'And you, my lord?'

'I will not desert you, do not fear that. I have more than a passing interest in your success.'

She was not at all sure what to make of that but decided not to comment. Instead she said, 'I'd like the next school to be at Hailey Common because if James stays there, Joseph Barnaby and the rest will join him, then Celia and the boys will be the first to benefit.'

He laughed and his earlier sombre expression vanished. 'I am to be the first to pay up, am I? You will make a poor man of me yet.'

'Poor man!' she scoffed. 'You haven't the smallest notion of what poverty is like, nor ever will have.'

'I see it every day in my journeys.'

'Seeing it, my lord, is not living it. I doubt you would survive.'

'The will to survive is a very strong human emotion,' he said, leaning forward and looking into her eyes. They held him with a gaze that was frank and fearless.

'It is indeed. That's why poor men bow to cruel masters, why they fight and steal, and why women sell their bodies, when they have nothing else to dispose of. It is why I am sitting here now, talking so calmly to you because my will to survive is inseparable from my determination to give my son everything he needs. For him I caused a riot and I am afraid ...'

'You are afraid of me?' He crossed the carriage to sit beside her. 'Surely not?'

'Not of you, my lord.' She paused. 'Of Timothy. You know, he threatened to take Jason from me permanently. He said I was an unfit mother and he is furious enough with me to try and prove it.'

'He won't do that.' He smiled wryly. 'He has only one real passion and that is to become my heir; everything he has ever done since he learned the truth about himself has been with that aim. Except for his fatherhood – that was about the only unpremeditated move he has ever made.' He noticed her faint smile. 'If I make him my heir ...'

'Do you really want to do that?'

He patted her hand. 'It is what I always wanted.'

She sensed his reservations. 'But if you were to marry again and have children ...'

He chuckled. 'Who would have an old dog like me? No, my dear, I think Timothy is all the progeny I'm likely to have and if I make him my heir, he will marry Miss Hailey and leave you in peace.' He stopped suddenly. 'That *is* what you want, isn't it?'

'Yes, but I can't expect you to do something as important and irrevocable as that for Jason and me, if you really do not want to.'

There was an aura about her which was more than a beautiful face and a natural grace, nor had it anything to do with the way she had educated herself and clawed her way out of the mire; it had been there from the beginning. He felt a sudden desire to take her in his arms and kiss her, and a stirring in his loins which had nothing to do with compassion. He wanted to make love to her. To hide his confusion, he stood up and put his head out of the window. There was no fool like an old fool, he told himself. The cool air sobered him and when he turned back to her, his voice was level. 'No one will take Jason from you, I give you my word.' He sat down again opposite her and smiled. 'I hope fervently that we shall ...' He groped for words ' ... remain friends whatever happens, because I do not want to be parted from him either. I shall miss him when you take him home.' He could not tell her he would miss her, too. 'You know, there hasn't been a child at Chevington House since I left my petticoats behind and when Timothy brought him, I realised what had been lacking all through those years – the laughter of a child, the sunshine a young boy brings to a home. I suddenly understood how Constance had felt about not having a child. It had nothing to do with producing an heir.'

'You will always be welcome to visit us, my lord.' A memory of Henry's ultimatum flashed through her mind, but was dismissed. She would not have him dictate whom she might, or might not, entertain.

'You intend to go back to your business?'

'Of course. The only reason I joined those navvies going to Hailey was for revenge.' She grimaced. 'Vengeance is a totally destructive emotion, my lord. Mine nearly killed Timothy. Will he ever forgive me for that riot? Will you?'

'You were forgiven long ago. But, my dear, do you think you can go back to London and resume your life as if nothing has happened? There will be publicity, you know.'

'I can live it down.' She grinned, thinking of Henry and his threats. 'Oh, Henry will grumble, he always does, but he is motivated by profit and he knows I can make him a profit.'

'But if he does turn difficult, what will happen to Jason? Will you have the heart and stomach to start all over again?'

She answered without hesitation. 'I'll just have to, won't I?'

'No, you can come to me.'

She looked at him in surprise, wondering what had prompted the offer. 'That is kind of you, my lord, but I'm sure I can manage Henry.'

He stood up as the train chugged into the terminus. 'I have to go to my office first before I carry on to Chevington. If you wish, I'll send my carriage round when I'm ready to leave.'

She laughed, throwing back her head to reveal the long arch of her slender neck. 'Perhaps it would be a little indiscreet, my lord, for us to arrive at Chevington together.'

He chuckled at the image her words had conveyed as he stepped down onto the platform and turned to help her. 'What care I for that? I am supposed to be eccentric, didn't you know?'

'But not wildly so, my lord.' Her green eyes held more merriment than he had seen in them for months. 'I will travel down independently and take a room at the Chevington Arms. It would be best.'

'Very well.' Undeterred by her dishevelled appearance, he tucked her hand under his arm, to walk the length of the station to the cab-stand. 'And if you should find yourself delayed by pressing business, rest assured that Jason is being well cared for.'

She looked up into his face and again he felt an odd tug on his heart that told him she had taken hold there. 'You mean you would like to keep him a little longer?'

'Yes.' He beckoned to a cab-driver.

'I'm sorry, my lord, but I can't wait to have him back. We've never been apart before, not even for a single night and if it had not been for Timothy needing a nurse, I would have come back days ago.'

'I understand.' He lifted her hand to his lips and watched as she was driven away in the hansom. He turned to call another cab to take him to his office but then changed his mind; business could wait, returning to Jason was more important. He turned on his heel and went back into the station.

'Mr Wistonby called, ma'am,' Betsy said, as she moved about Sarah Jane's bedroom, preparing a bath and laying out her clothes. She picked up Sarah Jane's discarded dress and looked at it with distaste. 'Where did you find this dreadful thing, ma'am? Is it one of yours?'

Sarah Jane smiled. 'Yes, but you may dispose of it now. Did Mr Wistonby leave a message?'

'No, ma'am. I told him I was expecting you today and he said he would come back this evening.'

Sarah Jane realised with a jolt that it was exactly a week since she had left, which was why Betsy had been on hand to greet her; it seemed an age ago, a different existence, as indeed it was, and now she must put it behind her and make a new beginning.

'In that case, I'll delay supper until he comes, then he can join me.'

She bathed and dressed and sat down to wait for Thomas, filling the time dealing with her correspondence. Besides bills and receipts which needed to be entered in the ledgers, there was an offer from the railway company for one of the smaller shops which lay in the path of a proposed line, and she would need to talk to the company lawyers about that, and to look for another site if her expansion plans were to continue. And there was an increased offer for the school which she decided she would accept. It meant an upheaval for the children, but it had to happen in the end and she might as well face it. His Lordship had not been so wide of the mark when he spoke of pressing business, though she had no intention of allowing it to delay her departure for Chevington beyond the following morning. When Thomas arrived, she rose to greet him with a smile.

'You look ravishing, as always,' he said, standing back to appraise her. She wore a hooped gown in a warm honey-coloured silk with a tiny waist and long wide sleeves edged with lace. Her glorious red hair was piled up on her head in a neat coronet; her complexion was rosy and her green eyes sparkled in the light from the lamp. 'But what have you been up to?'

'I took a little trip.'

Seating himself in an armchair, he looked up at her with amused affection. 'And is all this talk about leading the navvies in a riot totally without foundation?'

'Where did you hear that?'

'I read it in the papers. Henry is furious and you will have a job to live it down.'

'I know.' She turned as Betsy came into the room carrying a heavy tray loaded with cold chicken, bread and pickles, a bottle of wine, cutlery and glasses. 'Leave it on the table, Betsy. I'll serve it.'

The girl left and Sarah Jane set about heaping Thomas's plate with food while she gave him an account of what had happened. 'When Timothy took Jason, I was so upset and angry, I couldn't think straight. I kept asking myself why. You know, Thomas, I believe he is a little unhinged. He doesn't really want Jason, he just wanted to bring me to heel.'

He chuckled. 'And got more than he bargained for, by the sound of it.'

'It wasn't planned, Thomas. When I met the navvies it seemed a heaven-sent opportunity to make a little trouble for him, that was all. I didn't foresee ...' She paused. 'It was all my fault and I'll never forgive myself.'

'You are too hard on yourself. How were you to know what that man, Bill, would do? Or the soldiers, either.'

'I know the navvies, I should have guessed what the consequences would be. And when I realised the young soldier was Billie, I could have cried with frustration and disappointment, because it had all got out of hand and I was powerless to help him. He ran away and they searched for two days, but they couldn't find him. I was glad. It wasn't his fault Timothy was hit and they said he would be flogged if he was caught.' She shuddered. 'Barbarity, that's what it is.'

'No more than what the navvies were doing to each other,' he said mildly, picking up his knife and fork.

'Perhaps, but that was done in the heat of the moment and it doesn't make me feel any better.'

'The evening you left I came to tell you I had found Billie.'

'You found him? Oh Thomas, I wish I had known.'

'I doubt it would have changed anything. I traced him from regimental records and went to his barracks. His commanding officer told me he had been sent to Derbyshire but we could go and see him when he returned. All gone by the board now, of course. He'll have gone into hiding, taken on a new identity, might even be planning to leave the country.' He saw the look of disappointment in her lovely eyes; he couldn't bear it. 'You don't want to give up, do you?'

'No. Try and find him, Thomas, please.'

'For you, I will try anything, though what to do when he is found, I don't know. We can't harbour a deserter.'

'You will think of something, Thomas, you always do. We must help him if we can.'

'What are you going to do about Timothy?'

'That's all over. I feel nothing for him at all now. Nothing.' She stopped to sip her wine. 'I said at the beginning the price of his help would be too high and I was right. I should have remembered that, instead of ...'

'... falling in love with him?' When she did not answer he reached across and put his hand over hers. 'When you came back to the Union after Duncan's death, you seemed so lost and unhappy and I thought ...'

'That Timothy would make me happy again?'

'Something like that. I knew you would have a tremendous struggle to support yourself and Jason, and if things went wrong it would have been my fault. I was the one who moulded you, fostered your ambition, awakened the woman in you. Giving you back to Timothy was a kind of penance for me. When I realised you were making a good life for yourself, it was too late – he had discovered where you were. I am sorry, Sarah Jane.'

'Don't be. My life hasn't been at all bad. I met Duncan and though we had so little time together, it was filled with joy, even in the hard times, and Jason has been my greatest happiness. As for my ambition, without it I would not have survived.' She smiled slowly. 'And I am a survivor, Thomas, make no mistake about that. And I have found an ally in Lord Chevington.'

'And you can trust him?'

'Oh, absolutely.'

He looked at her with his head on one side. 'You are blushing, Sarah Jane.'

'Nonsense! It's the sun, I've been living more or less out of doors for a week.'

'Are you going to see him again?'

'His Lordship? Yes, I expect so. I must deal with the business matters that have cropped up in my absence and calm Henry down, but tomorrow afternoon, at the latest, I go to Chevington to fetch Jason. Thank goodness Timothy is stuck at Hailey Manor and won't be able to stop me.'

Chapter Twenty-Three

Jason, bored with no company except that of servants, dashed from the house when he heard carriage-wheels on the drive. 'I'm so glad you're back,' he said, looking past Geoffrey towards the gig from which he had just alighted. 'Where is Mr Myson?'

Geoffrey ruffled the boy's curls. 'I'm afraid he has had an accident, but he will come when he is better.'

'And Mama?'

'I left her in London, but she will be here very soon.' If he noticed the look of disappointment on the boy's face, he did not comment, but took his hand and led him indoors, while the servants dealt with his bag and led the horse away. 'Now, tell me what you have been doing while I've been gone.'

'Nothing much.'

Geoffrey smiled and sat on one of the chairs in the hall, drawing the boy between his knees. 'Nothing much? Surely you found things to do?'

'One of the grooms took me out on the pony but he wouldn't let go of the rein and all we did was walk round and round. I wanted to trot.'

Geoffrey smiled. 'I expect he was afraid that if you took a tumble he would be blamed. What else have you done?'

'I went into the library. What a lot of books you've got! But I didn't feel like reading. I wanted to play hide and seek, there are so many lovely places to hide here, but no one wanted to play with me.'

'They have their work to do, Jason.' He smiled. 'But I'm here now, so let's take a walk, shall we?'

Jason took his grandfather's hand and dragged him round the house and gardens, talking non-stop, until both were exhausted, then they sat on the terrace until Hannah came to take Jason away for his tea. His Lordship stayed on with half-closed eyes, relaxing in the serenity of the old house and well-tended gardens, thinking about the future.

He would be lonely without Constance and once Timothy was married, he might not see so much of him, but there would be Jason; he would keep in touch with him, watch him grow to a man, help him if Sarah Jane would agree to it. He allowed himself to dream a little, to imagine Sarah Jane at Chevington House, saw her in his mind's eye, about the house and garden, enhancing its beauty with her own, and he realised with a start that it was of Sarah Jane he had been thinking all along.

He admired her courage, the way she had made a success of her life. In his book success was measured not so much by what you achieved, as by what you overcame, and she had overcome the most daunting obstacles. She was so vibrant and alive, unbeatable and yet vulnerable, independent yet warm and soft, and utterly desirable. He could so easily succumb. He shook himself; the idea was unthinkable, impractical and besides, he was nearly fifty, too old for love affairs, too out of practice – he would only make a fool of himself. And he would make an enemy of his son, not to mention alienating Sarah Jane, who would run a mile if he even hinted at such a thing. He was half-asleep, imagining what he would do if he were young again, when he heard footsteps on the path beneath the terrace.

'I'll murder the little beggar one of these days.' The voice was a girl's, undoubtedly one of the indoor servants, though His Lordship could not tell which. 'He let the cat into the chicken run last week and sent them squawkin' all over the yard. I got no eggs for days.'

'And he near overturned the beehive,' a man's voice said. 'He'd ha' bin stung to death if I hadn't pulled him away in time. Got stung m'self in the process, too. But was he sorry? Not he. I'd like to thrash the breeches off him, that'd teach him a lesson he wouldn't forget in a hurry.'

'And you'd be given your marching orders from His Lordship,' the girl retorted.

'Why is he here anyway? Whose child is he?'

'Mr Myson's o' course, that's plain as a pikestaff, but as to his mother, Wilkins taps 'is nose and says no one knows, but I reckon 'e does. He can't stand the sight o' him. I've seen him cuff the boy about the ears more'n once and lock him in the tower for a punishment. He knows he can't get out o' there by hisself.'

They were silent for a minute, but Geoffrey was certain they had not moved away; the fellow was probably kissing her or something of the sort. 'He needs a father's hand on his backside, good and hard.'

There was the sound of a slap and then a giggle, before the girl said, 'I reckon the poor boy is missin' his mother, that's why he's naughty. I've 'eard 'im cryin' in his room o' nights. He's no more'n a babe, after all.'

'Perhaps now His Lordship's back he'll mind his ways.' They moved on and Lord Chevington, cramped from sitting still, went indoors to change for supper. It was the first he had heard of Jason's pranks and although he was prepared to dismiss them as childish mischief, he realised the boy would have to be disciplined, if he were not to become a danger to himself and others. But if he were so dreadfully unhappy ... He must make it up to him, spend some time with him until Sarah Jane arrived.

They went riding the next morning and played cricket on the lawn and by the middle of the afternoon, Geoffrey was glad to leave the boy to his own devices and relax in the quiet of the library with a good cigar. It was here that Timothy, angry and in great pain, found him.

In spite of the coach-driver's care, Timothy had suffered a great deal of agony on his way to Hailey Manor and he had to be carried into the house and taken straight up to his bedroom where Caroline, defying her mother who protested at the impropriety of it, had fussed round him, flitting about the room, twittering like a bird, making him want to scream. All he wanted was to be left alone. He was beginning to wish he had never left the hut, and more than that, he wished he had not left Sarah Jane. And in anger, too. It was strange how her anger affected him. It roused his sexual desire, raw and untrammelled by thoughts of courtship or wooing or persuasion; it made him want to take her violently, to douse her anger with his passion. And when he could not, he wanted to shout at her, to hurl insults, anything to ease his need of her.

She had every right to be angry, but it was her own fault for telling him about her nightmare. It was that which had given him the idea, that and his father being so pompous. What had he got to be pompous about? He wasn't above a romp in the hay either; wasn't that how he, Timothy so-called Myson, had come into the world? He hadn't asked to be born and neither had Jason. His son. He couldn't keep him. Caroline wasn't another Lady Chevington; he'd never get away with what his father had done, even if Sarah Jane allowed it. Caroline. She was sitting on his bed now, talking fifteen to the dozen and he hadn't heard a word she'd said.

'Go away.' he said.

'Go away, Timothy? But I am going to look after you.'

'I want to sleep.'

'Of course. I won't disturb you.' She got up to pick up his bag from the chair where one of the servants had put it. 'I'll just put your things away before I go.' She opened the bag. 'Would you like a clean nightshirt? What's this? Oh, it's lovely!' She turned towards him with the golden apple in her hand. 'Oh Timothy, what a beautiful gift. But why hide it among your clothes?'

He scrambled painfully out of bed and snatched it from her just as she touched the spring which opened it. 'Leave it alone, do you hear?'

She looked startled. 'Why Timothy darling, whatever is the matter? It was a surprise gift for me, was it not?'

He sank back onto the bed, clutching it to him with both hands as if she had contaminated it. He stared at her. She was stupid and vain and possessive and he didn't like her one bit. What was he doing here with her when he could be with Sarah Jane? Sarah Jane, warm, generous, fiery, beautiful Sarah Jane. His Aphrodite. What had he done to her? Could he go back? Could he go back to those happy days by the river, or even to a few weeks ago when he had held her in his arms and known she loved him still. Could he go back to the Hailey Common works and find her still there, still nursing the wounded navvies with that cool hand of hers, still cooking stews for James McBryde and talking to the soldiers about her brother? Had they found Duncan McBryde? He envied him, even in death, because Sarah Jane held his memory so dear. She wouldn't remember him like that. She would remember him as the man who had kidnapped her son, the man who had hurt her for no other reason than his own conceited sense of power, and not just power over her, but over his father, too. He groaned and dropped back onto the pillows.

'Oh, Timothy.' Caroline's thin voice broke into his tortured thoughts. 'The journey has exhausted you.'

'What? Oh, yes. Go away and leave me to sleep.'

He did not hear her go. God, his wound was sore; if only Sarah Jane would come and make it better. Where was she? He opened his eyes. He was still clutching the apple. When had she put that in his bag? Why? Oh, he knew why all right. It was meant to tell him she had finished with him and this time she meant it; he had driven her too far. Where was she now? Had she returned to London? To Chevington? Yes, that's what she would do, go to Chevington and fetch her son. Would she go with his father? He was suddenly beset by a picture of the two of them cosily sharing a railway carriage and settling his future between them. His future. His inheritance. His father had said something about marrying again. Sarah Jane? No, that was unthinkable.

But he could not stop thinking about it, could not help remembering little things, like his father calling her by her given name so naturally. *I have known her a long time.* Did he mean he had known her in the Biblical sense? God, had he been blind? Sarah Jane belonged to him, Timothy Myson, no one else. There was no time to lose; he had to go to Chevington.

He sat up, suddenly aware that his cheeks were wet with tears. 'The witch!' he muttered aloud, massaging the golden apple in his hand as if to gather strength from it. 'I was right. She *has* destroyed me.'

He got out of bed and began slowly and painfully to dress, telling himself that it was his inheritance that he was concerned about, nothing else, but he could no longer deceive himself. He would do anything, give up everything he had striven for, to have Sarah Jane. He could not live without her.

His face was ashen and his breathing laboured by the time he had finished dressing and gone downstairs to find Caroline. She was in the drawing room sketching a rose in a vase. She had jumped to her feet, dropping the pad. 'Timothy, what are you doing out of bed?'

'I'm going back to London. Everything depends on it.'

'Whatever do you mean? What depends on it? You must have a fever or something.'

He could not bear her fussing round him. Nor could he tell her that he had finally and irrevocably seen the truth, that in one blinding flash of insight, when she had taken that apple from his bag – his gift to Aphrodite – and turned towards him with it in her hand, his whole life had been revealed as a barren sham, hollow from start to finish. His time and energy had been wasted on craving for something which was not worth half of what he could have had. Love. Sarah Jane's love. It had been his for the asking, way back in those halcyon days when they were both hardly more than children. He had thrown it away and for what? For something that could never be his, a place in society, a name. Myson, Chevington – what difference did it make if he could not have Sarah Jane? Was it too late to tell her so?

His desperation and impatience had sustained him through an interminable journey and by the time he arrived at Chevington House, he was fainting with pain and exhaustion. Being told by the butler who answered the door to him that His Lordship was working in the library, he stumbled along the hall and threw open the door.

'Timothy!' Geoffrey rose quickly to help him to a seat. 'What in heaven's name possessed you to travel in this condition?' He did not wait for an answer but pulled the bellrope and poured brandy into a glass. 'Here, drink this, then my man will help you to bed.'

Timothy drained the glass. 'Sarah Jane.'

'What about her?'

'Where is she? What have you done with her?'

'Done with her? I've done nothing with her. As far as I know, she is in London.'

'She's here, isn't she? You're hiding her from me.'

'My dear boy, I don't understand. Why should I hide her?'

'She has bewitched you too, hasn't she? You have taken her from me ... '

'Timothy, you are overwrought. I suggest you go to bed and—' He stopped speaking abruptly. Someone was shouting. 'Fire! Fire! The tower's alight.'

'*Jason!*' It was Geoffrey's first thought. He was already running to the door, but Timothy, for all his exhaustion, beat him to it. Dashing past the servant who had raised the alarm, he ran down the steps from the front door and round the side of the house, followed by his father.

They arrived at the blazing tower just in time to see Wilkins unlock the heavy door and disappear inside. The fire flared up with a roar as the blast of air from the open door made an efficient chimney of it. Shielding his face with his arms, Timothy bent to follow, only to be engulfed, like the butler, by the flames.

Geoffrey stopped a few yards behind him, unable to go on. He heard, as if in a nightmare, the two men shouting to each other, saw Wilkins carry Timothy out and lay him on the grass, but he could not go to his son; his legs would not obey him. There was an intolerable pain in his chest and he could not breathe. He took a step forward, stumbled and fell to the ground, unnoticed by anyone because they were concerned only with the fire. Wilkins, convinced that Jason was inside, turned to go back into the tower, but before he could get near, there was a great roar followed by the sound of crashing beams and falling masonry. Sparks flew like fireworks and, before anyone could do a thing to stop it, the house itself caught fire.

*

Sarah Jane walked briskly along the narrow lane which led from Chevington Halt to a gate in the side wall of the estate. Henry had been at his most bombastic and it had taken her much longer than she'd anticipated to calm him down. 'Send Mr Wistonby to fetch the boy,' he had suggested, when she said she was leaving again immediately. 'He is perfectly capable of bringing him back to London. You have had your holiday, it's time to return to work and put this whole sorry business behind you. Not that it will be easy to live down what you've done. I just thank providence that the business is *Carter & Winterday* and not *Carter & McBryde*.'

'I have dealt with all the urgent matters and given instructions to the staff,' argued Sarah Jane. 'Another day will make no difference. I shall be back at work the day after tomorrow. This is something I have to do myself, you must see that.'

'No, I don't,' he said stubbornly. 'What would have happened to my business if I had behaved as you are doing every time something went wrong at home?'

'You might still have your wife and son.' Then, realising how cruel that remark had been, she laid a hand on his arm and added, 'I'm sorry, Henry, that was uncalled for. Please forgive me.'

He shrugged as if it were of no importance. 'You always did have a caustic tongue.'

'Forthright, Henry, not caustic, not intentionally anyway. And it changes nothing. I mean to go.'

He had still been scolding with a mixture of threats and wheedling, when she left him. He could say what he liked, nothing on earth would prevent her from going to Chevington and if he chose to dissolve their partnership, then so be it; she had told Lord Chevington she could start again, and though she hoped it wouldn't come to that, she might have to. Poor Jason. He had done nothing to deserve being flung into poverty again.

A sound, borne on the wind, made her look up towards the house, just as a sheet of flame burst, almost like a rocket, a hundred feet into the air above the trees which screened it from view. She began to run. In front of the burning house, she found people rushing back and forth with utensils, bowls, jugs, anything which could hold water; she noticed the rusty old water wagon and the inefficient pump which had been stored, unused, in the stables for years, heard the noise, felt the heat, smelled the acrid smoke which caught in her throat as she ran, and could think of nothing, no one, but her son.

'Where's Jason?' she cried, running from one to the other, but the only answer was a shrug. She stopped to look about her and saw Lord Chevington lying near the path a short distance from the inferno of smoke and flames which had once been the tower, and next to him sat Wilkins, almost unrecognisable he was so badly burned about the face and hands. She ran to them and squatted on the grass beside Geoffrey, taking His Lordship's hand and automatically feeling for his pulse. 'Where is Jason?' she demanded of the butler.

Numb with shock, he hardly seemed to notice his pain, as he nodded towards the tower.

'In there?' she shrieked. 'He's in there?' She got up and ran towards it but the intense heat drove her back. She stood and stared at the flames, unaware that she was screaming at the full extent of her lungs.

'We tried to find him.' the butler croaked beside her. 'We crawled all over the floor. Couldn't find him ... so much smoke ... beaten back.' He turned to look down at Lord Chevington, who had not stirred since he had fallen. 'He needs help.'

Until Jason was found she could not put her mind to anything else. 'He's not burned at all,' she said almost callously.

'No, he collapsed when he saw us go into the tower.' She had assumed it was Lord Chevington who had gone with Wilkins to rescue Jason. 'You mean it wasn't His Lordship who ...'

'No, it was Mr Timothy,' he said, then added bluntly, 'And he's dead.'

'Dead?' she repeated.

'He came back this afternoon, nigh on dying already. He followed me in – 'twas a mad thing to do. I had to bring him out.'

'And left my son to perish. ' Her anger was so calm, it frightened him more than her screaming had done.

'No, I'll swear the boy weren't there. Someone must have let him out before the fire started.'

'Then where is he?' She looked wildly about her, searching for her son among the milling throng who had left the tower to burn in order to save the house. They were trying to get the fire engine to work and dashing back and forth with buckets of water. There were some youngsters helping the adults but no sign of Jason. 'Oh God, where is he?'

Then she saw him, kneeling beside Timothy's body a little way from the tower; silent tears coursed down his cheeks. Physically he appeared unscathed. She ran and hugged him to her, crying with relief. 'Oh, Jason, Jason, I thought ... Thank God! Oh, thank God!'

'He won't move,' he said. 'He won't talk to me.' He looked up at his mother. 'Mama, why won't he answer me?'

She took her eyes from her son to look at Timothy. His body hardly seemed burned at all and she supposed he must have collapsed and been brought out before the fire had really taken hold. She was glad of that; she could not bear to think of his handsome features being spoiled, not even in death. Later she might mourn, but not now; now there was too much to do. 'I'll tell you later, my darling,' she said, disengaging his hand from the dead man's. 'Now you must be good because I must see what I can do to help.' She picked him up and took him to the summerhouse, calling to one of the servants to stay with him and not let him out of her sight for a single minute, then with another quick hug and a kiss, she went back to the chaos.

The firefighters, inadequate as they were, had been partially success-ful and they had managed to confine the fire to the west wing, and now it was all but out. The part nearest the tower was no more than a shell. Hot, blackened timbers stuck out through glassless, frameless windows; the ivy on the wall hung scorched and dying, wisps of smoke drifted on the air and everywhere was the stench of burning.

Lord Chevington was still lying on the grass and although conscious, was in great pain and unable to move. She spoke to him briefly, but was not even sure he had heard her. Some of the servants were still milling about, still fetching buckets of water, others, realising the fire was out, stood and gazed up at the house as if mesmerised. Someone had to take charge and there was no one else. She directed two of the men to carry His Lordship to his bed, which was luckily in an undamaged part of the house, and dispatched another to fetch the local doctor, who would surely have seen the fire from a great way off and guessed his services would be required. She attended skilfully to Wilkins' burns and then had Timothy's body brought in and taken up to one of the bedrooms, ready for the doctor. That done, she fetched her son and gave him some supper before putting him to bed and sitting on the edge of the bed to talk to him.

'Jason,' she said, taking his hand. 'Tell me what happened.'

'Wilkins locked me in the tower.'

'Wilkins? *Locked* you in there?' She was horrified. That was what the butler had meant about someone letting him out. No wonder he had been the first to go in looking for him. 'Why did he do such a monstrous thing?'

'He didn't know I could get out by myself.'

'Why did he do it?' she repeated, forcing herself to speak calmly. 'Why?'

'I . . .' The boy hesitated. 'I kicked him.'

'Jason! That was wicked.'

'He called me names. He said I was a whore's brat and if he had his way I wouldn't be allowed in the house.'

'He said that to you? You're not making it up?'

'He said it to Cook. He said Lord Chevington must be out of his head.'

She decided not to pursue that line, knowing enough of the ways of the servants' hall to imagine how the conversation had gone. 'How did the fire start?'

'I found a piece of glass on the floor. Do you know, Mama, it was so pretty, it made a rainbow when the sun shone on it through the window. I turned it about to see all the colours and then the dead leaves started to burn. There were lots of leaves, all heaped up. Then there were flames everywhere and I climbed out. I was frightened, so I ran and hid.'

'Did you know Mr Myson had come home?'

'No I didn't, not 'til I saw him.' He paused. 'Mama, is he quite dead?'

She nodded; there was no point in pretending otherwise. 'Yes, Jason, I am afraid he is.'

'He was my papa, wasn't he?'

'Who told you that?' she asked sharply. 'Did he?'

'I heard the servants talking.'

'Duncan,' she began, then stopped. How could she explain to a seven-year-old boy that the man he had thought of as his father, was no such thing?

'*He* was my Da,' Jason said simply.

She nodded, unable to speak for the tears which suddenly engulfed her. To Jason, there was no conflict; Da and Papa were two quite separate beings. But both had been lost to him. Poor child, what a life she had given him! She hugged him to her and kissed the top of his blond head, where her tears had dropped. 'Oh Jason, I'm truly, truly sorry.'

He knelt up in the bed and flung his arms around her neck, rubbing his soft curls against her tear-wet face. 'Don't cry, Mama, don't cry. It wasn't your fault, was it?'

Gently she removed his hands and held them in her own, trying to smile. 'No, my darling, it was nobody's fault. Now you must go to sleep.'

'And you won't go away again?'

'No, I won't go away. I shall be here when you wake up in the morning.' She tucked the bedclothes round him and kissed him, then she left to go to Lord Chevington's sickroom.

'Are you the housekeeper?' Dr Gosport, a little man with iron-grey hair and a small pointed beard, snapped his bag shut and picked up his hat.

Sarah Jane hesitated. Lord Chevington had never had a servant with that title while his wife was alive and she had discovered that he had not appointed one since, because Cook seemed to have assumed the role. There was no one to take the doctor's instructions. 'Temporarily, yes,' she said.

'His Lordship has had a heart attack,' he said, moving away from his patient and speaking softly. 'But, thank God, only a minor one. With careful nursing, good plain food – nothing rich, you understand – and absolute rest and quiet, no excitement, no upsets of any kind, he will recover. I will send you a reliable nurse tomorrow. Can you manage for today?'

'Yes, of course, as long as is necessary.' She glanced past him to the big four-poster bed. His Lordship's face was grey against the white of the lace-edged pillow and his hair, always so neat, was tousled. He had seemed such a big, strong man when he was dressed and on his feet, but now he looked small and vulnerable and she wanted to go and comfort him, just as she had comforted Jason. She accompanied the doctor to the door and added, in a whisper, 'You know that Mr Myson . . .'

'Yes, I have issued a certificate. His Lordship will not be well enough to attend to the funeral arrangements.'

'I will see to them.'

'Lord Chevington has something else on his mind,' he went on. 'He keeps repeating a name, which sounds like "Jason". Do you know what is bothering him?'

'Jason is my son. His Lordship thought he was trapped in the tower. Luckily he got out when the fire started.'

'Then I suggest you put His Lordship's mind at rest at once, so that he can begin his recovery. I will call again tomorrow and give the nurse her instructions.'

It was on Sarah Jane's mind to say that he did not need a nurse, that she was not only capable but ready to fill the role, but she realised that there was so much else to be done and she could not be everywhere at once. She inclined her head. 'I will expect you.'

She watched him go and then went to Geoffrey whose head was thrashing from side to side, as if he were in the throes of a bad dream. 'Jason . . .'

She bent over and touched his shoulder lightly. 'Jason is safe, my lord, not hurt at all.'

Her soft voice made him open his eyes. 'Sarah Jane.'

'Yes, it's Sarah Jane. Now, you are not to worry about a thing. The doctor says you must rest and I mean to see that you do.'

He took her hand and his grip was surprisingly strong. 'He's not hurt?'

'Not a scratch. He climbed out of the tower when the fire first started.'

'Thank God!' His face mirrored his relief and he lay back and watched her as she fetched a chair to sit beside him. She was pale and her green eyes looked tired, but she was calm, a restful sort of person to have at his bedside. 'Timothy . . .'

She wondered if he knew what had happened to his son, and waited for him to continue.

'He is at rest now, isn't he? There will be no more battling with his own confused emotions, no more striving after a position he could never attain. He will be buried as my son and I want that on his stone. Do you understand?'

Relieved she did not have to tell him Timothy had died, she took his hand in her own. 'Yes, I understand.' She paused. 'You know, you won't be well enough to go to the funeral.'

'You go in my place.' He paused. 'And, Sarah Jane, you had better send for Miss Hailey.'

She had forgotten all about Caroline and did not relish another confrontation with her, but His Lordship was right; Caroline must be told. 'Of course.'

'He came back for you, you know.'

'Who did?'

'Timothy. He loved you – left her to come to you. Thought you were here.' He smiled weakly as his medication began to take effect. 'Had some idea I had brought you here . . . '

'You mustn't talk any more,' she said. 'Please try to rest.'

'He'd never have married her, you know.' His eyes flickered once or twice and then closed.

Unsure whether he had fallen asleep or not, she sat on watching him. He had lost more than anyone in this terrible affair and yet he had not reproached her once. From what she had heard, Timothy had not hesitated before dashing into the fire to save Jason and, weak as he was, he would have succumbed to the heat and smoke almost immediately. Had he really come back for her? What had gone on in that tortured brain of his to make him throw away all his carefully laid schemes and risk the reopening of his wound to return to Chevington? Love for her, His Lordship had said. Would it have made any difference if he had been able to tell her so? The realist in her doubted that, but perhaps she could remember him with sorrow and compassion for the unhappy young man he had been, and perhaps with the love she owed to the father of her son. Jason was alive and well, neither physically and, so far as she could tell, mentally scarred by the events of this dreadful day and she must see to it that he never had cause to think of Timothy with anything but love and gratitude. But how could she make it up to the man who had at last fallen asleep with his hand in hers?

She smiled to herself. Who would have thought, all those years ago, when she stood in his library expecting a tirade and receiving only kindness, that she would one day sit by his bed and feel so sorry for him? But it was not altogether pity, it was more than that. It was love for his gentleness, gratitude for his forgiveness, concern for his welfare. Just because he was titled and wealthy and a gentleman in the very best sense of the word, did not make him any less vulnerable to hurt. She found herself wanting to protect him.

He was breathing more easily now and she gently disengaged her hand and went back to the bustling activity of a household trying to restore order from chaos. There was only one way to drive away wild thoughts and self-recrimination and that was to work, to work so hard she had no time to brood, to labour until she was so exhausted sleep came unbidden when she lay down at night.

Her situation in the household was a strange one and she was unsure of her position; she was neither family nor servant, but Lord Chevington preferred her ministrations to those of the nurse who arrived the following day and whom he called 'that dragon', and because of that the servants deferred to her. Most of those had been taken on since she left, or did not remember her. Tilly had gone to live with her widowed sister in Norwich and only the cook and the badly scarred Wilkins knew who she was and they thought it prudent to remain silent. While Lord Chevington wanted her and needed her, she would stay; her business could run itself for a while and Henry would just have to manage.

The next afternoon, with the funeral arrangements well in hand, she set about supervising the cleaning of the undamaged east wing of the building, replacing the soft furnishings and arranging for the restoration of those pieces of furniture which warranted it. The west wing would have to be made safe, but otherwise it could be left; it was not needed for living accommodation. Wind and weather would soften the blackened outline, so that, in years to come, no one would be able to tell how it had come to be like that.

By the time Caroline and her mother arrived, two days later, the east wing was almost habitable again, and rooms had been prepared for them at the end of the house furthest from the damage. Sarah Jane, who had been dreading their arrival, watched from Geoffrey's sickroom window as they were handed down from their carriage. Both were dressed in unrelieved black and heavily veiled, but mourning did not mean they needed less luggage; several boxes and bags were unloaded from a second carriage which also brought their personal maids. It was no good putting it off. Sarah Jane, acting as hostess in the absence of anyone else, went down to the hall to greet them.

'Good afternoon, Lady Hailey, Miss Hailey,' she said, controlling her shaking hands by clenching them in the folds of her skirt. 'May I offer my condolences.'

If Caroline was surprised to see her, she hid it well. Fishing in her purse for a scrap of lace and dabbing under her veil at eyes swollen with weeping, she acknowledged Sarah Jane with an imperceptible movement of her head.

'Who are you?' Lady Hailey demanded, eyeing the simple gown of black bombazine Sarah Jane had found among some clothes in a boxroom; it had probably been Lady Chevington's and was certainly not a servant's dress.

Sarah Jane relaxed a little; there were obviously some things Caroline had not confided to her mother. 'I am Mrs McBryde, a family friend. I arrived soon after the accident and stayed on to help.' She paused, but as no other questions seemed forthcoming, she smiled, determined to be friendly. 'Rooms have been prepared for you in the east wing away from the noise of the workmen. If you would like to go up, I'll have tea sent to you. We can go over the funeral arrangements when you have rested.'

'Thank you.' It was Lady Hailey who replied.

Sarah Jane watched the two women make their way up the grand staircase behind the servants who carried their luggage and were, in turn, followed by their maids. She had no idea what the true relationship between Timothy and Caroline had been, but she guessed it had been more than Timothy had told her and, in truth, the girl was really the one who had lost most. She pitied her, and once she had discovered that fact, it was easier to be sympathetic.

All the same, it was going to be a difficult time and, for two pins, she would take Jason and leave, but that would be defeatist and what could she tell His Lordship? He was making a remarkable recovery, and much of that was due to Jason, who spent part of each day sitting on his bed. At first the doctor had forbidden it, but when it became obvious that the boy's bright chatter was beneficial, he had relented. She could not take Jason away under the circumstances.

'Do you really wish me to go to the funeral?' she asked, when she went to fetch her son from his room later that day. 'Won't I be an embarrassment?'

'Sarah Jane, you are all the family Timothy had, you and Jason. You must see him put to rest.' He was looking better every day, she thought, though still weak.

She smoothed the covers where Jason had been sprawling. 'Miss Hailey has arrived with her mother.'

'Oh, I see.' He smiled. 'But you are strong enough to stand up to them, aren't you?'

'Yes, but I do not want to be the cause of any more distress.'

He reached out and took her hand. 'Sarah Jane, they will be gone as soon as the funeral is over, but I shall still need you.'

'Will you, my lord?'

'Yes, and do you not think that after all that has happened, we could dispense with the formalities? I've been calling you Sarah Jane for some time now and we've been through a lot together, you and I. Could you not manage to put your tongue round Geoffrey?'

She smiled. 'If you wish.'

'I do. And when is that fussy old Gosport coming again? '

'This evening, I believe.'

'I shall tell him I mean to go to the funeral myself.' Sarah Jane did not know what persuasion was used, but Dr Gosport agreed that His

Lordship could go to the funeral, provided he went in a wheelchair with the nurse in attendance and retired to bed immediately it was over.

The morning of the funeral was cool and cloudy, threatening rain, and Sarah Jane was doubtful of the wisdom of allowing Geoffrey to attend, but he would not change his mind and the little cortège set off at noon, just as the sun came out and drove away the rainclouds. Lord Chevington with his nurse, Lady Hailey and Caroline went in the leading carriage, followed by Sarah Jane, Jason and Mr and Mrs Townsend in another. Some of the servants and a few villagers, knowing the rumours surrounding Timothy's birth and filled with curiosity, had already taken their places in the church when they arrived.

The service was a short one and Timothy was referred to as the much loved son of Lord Chevington, which caused a few raised eyebrows and angered Caroline, who wished fervently that she had not come. She felt sick, as she had been every morning of late, and she was quite sure that everyone could see right through her and knew that she already carried Timothy's child. What was she going to do? What would Mama say when she at last found the courage to tell her? How could she face the world? And it was all the fault of that conniving, red-headed harlot, who seemed to have taken over the running of Chevington House and its owner, and whose son was where her child should be.

Unaware of Caroline's simmering thoughts, Sarah Jane stood just behind her, dressed in a very simple gown of black bombazine which she had had sent down from London.

She kept her back straight and her gaze fixed on the stained-glass window above the altar, where the sun, flickering through the branches of a tree just outside, played on the coloured glass and made it look as though the figures were moving. She was determined not to weep because Geoffrey was dry-eyed and if he could control his anguish, then she must not let him down and besides, tears from her would be considered an impertinence.

But she had loved Timothy that summer long ago and, in some ways, it had been a love that endured, simply because it had produced Jason and Jason was a living reminder of it. But now Timothy was at rest, she could not deceive herself into believing it had been anything more than a short-lived passion, either then or later, when he had come to her in London. Then she had needed someone to assuage an

381

almost unbearable loneliness. Loneliness was something she was going to have to learn to bear, because she would not make the same mistake again. As soon as Geoffrey was well enough, she must go back to work, back to the shops, the bakehouses, the schools; she must fill her life with those. And Jason. She put her hand on his shoulder and smiled down at him. He looked up, pale-faced but smiling too, and slipped his hand trustingly into hers.

Chapter Twenty-Four

Sometime during the next morning Lady Hailey and her daughter left, but Sarah Jane was not aware of their departure; they did not think it necessary to seek her out to say goodbye, but Amelia Townsend came looking for her and found her supervising the removal of the water-damaged carpet in one of the smaller parlours. Her ready smile and friendly eyes reminded Sarah Jane of Lady Chevington, though Amelia was shorter and plumper than her sister had been. 'Good morning, Mrs McBryde. I was told I might find you here.'

Sarah Jane wiped her hands on the huge white apron which covered her mourning dress, and smiled back. 'Good morning, Mrs Townsend. Did you sleep well?'

'As well as could be expected under the circumstances. I came to thank you for all you have done for Geoffrey.'

'There is no need to thank me. I was here and there was no one else.'

Amelia looked around the smoke-stained room. 'Is there somewhere more comfortable for us to talk?'

Sarah Jane led the way to the drawing room and they sat together on one of the sofas. Outside the sounds of hammering and falling masonry told them that what was left of the tower was coming down.

'His Lordship has told me a great deal about you,' Amelia said. 'Do you mind?'

'Not at all. And I am glad you came, it was so lonely for him at the funeral. I don't think anyone quite knew how he felt about Timothy.'

'No, I don't think we did,' she said softly. 'You see, my sister ... But then I do not have to tell you about that, do I?'

'No, I understand.'

'Geoffrey has been talking to me about your ideas for navvy schools.'

'He spoke to you about them?' With all the things he must have on his mind he had remembered his promise to her. 'I am afraid I have been nagging him.'

Amelia smiled. 'Your nagging must have worked, he is keen to go ahead. He is not well enough to take an active part at the moment, but you and I can make a start, don't you think? Tell me exactly what you have in mind, then we can get down to practicalities, forming a committee, raising funds, finding premises, that sort of thing.'

They talked for two hours, at the end of which Amelia was as enthusiastic as Sarah Jane and they had formed a friendship which would last a lifetime. There was no snobbery about Amelia; as far as she was concerned, people were people and her friends ranged from earls and cabinet ministers to costermongers, whores and pickpockets. Sarah Jane found herself talking without embarrassment about Duncan and Timothy, Jason and Billie and her business. 'I have been so lucky,' she said. 'I want to do something for those less fortunate, but it's not just that. I believe everyone has a right to an education; it should be government-funded, not left to charity.'

'We have to leave politics to the men,' Amelia said, with a smile. 'Not that I don't think we women might not do just as good a job, but the time is not yet right. One day, perhaps, women will be able to vote and sit in Parliament. One day we might even have a woman prime minister.'

'The men would never allow that!'

'We must sow the seed now if our granddaughters are to reap the harvest, and in the meantime we must keep beavering away. And I have a feeling you are very good at beavering, isn't that so?'

Sarah Jane felt flattered. 'That's a nice way of putting it. Henry calls it bullying.'

'He will be missing your bullying, I don't doubt.'

'Yes, I must go back as soon as His Lordship is well enough to be left.'

'How will you judge that time? He will not willingly let you go. He has become very dependent on you.'

That became evident as the days and weeks passed; Geoffrey relied on Sarah Jane's advice for the smallest things, like what cravat to wear and what he should and should not eat, when to rest and when to get up. It was not that he did not have a mind of his own, because he could be obdurate when he chose, but it was easier to ask her and it kept her close to him. She could not bring herself to talk of leaving.

Thomas came frequently to bring her correspondence and keep her up to date with what was happening to her business. 'I went round to the Oxford Street shop while I was in town,' he said, one day when he found her sitting at His Lordship's desk in the library working on the household accounts. 'Henry was having an argument with the cook about the beef she had ordered, saying she didn't need to buy such good quality ...'

'I've told him and told him,' Sarah Jane said. 'You can't make a silk purse out of a sow's ear and you can't make a good pie with stringy meat. If he starts countermanding my instructions, we'll lose our reputation and once it's lost, we'll never get it back.'

'Then I suggest you do something about it.'

'I don't want to leave while His Lordship needs me.'

Thomas looked at her speculatively. 'Are you sure that's your reason? It couldn't be that *you* need *him*?'

'Of course. He is a great help to me with his advice about the schools and the navvies.'

'I didn't mean that, and you know it!'

'What else is there?' She did not like the way he was looking at her, smiling in his knowing fashion, hinting almost. 'If you think ...'

'Calm down,' he said quickly. 'I am only putting into words what others are thinking and saying, Henry especially.'

'You do not need to tell me, I am aware of it.'

'What are you going to do about it, then?'

'Leave.'

'When?'

'When I'm ready. I won't be pushed.' Geoffrey had said he wanted her to stay, but as what? His servant? That would be an untenable position and besides, she valued her independence too much ever to be a servant again. Thomas was right – she must go back. Geoffrey was almost fully recovered; there really was no reason why she should stay, except ... She shook herself angrily. Chevington was not her home and His Lordship was no more than a friend who had needed help and now needed it no longer. That was all there was to it; the gossips could believe what they liked. But Thomas had helped her to make up her mind and the arrival of Henry's letter the following morning precipitated her decision.

'*I am most concerned that the press has discovered who you are and made you the subject of their gossip,*' he had written. '*I do believe people come into the shops to buy pies in the hope that they might catch sight of the notorious Mrs McBryde, the woman who led a rabble and confronted an army and whose amours range from coarse navvies to peers of the*

385

realm.' She smiled at the hyperbole, so typical of him, but she didn't like the idea of Geoffrey being on his list. '*No one has said so but I am sure I am included among your conquests, and I do not like it. In fact, I will not endure it. Enclosed with this letter you will find an offer from my legal advisers for your half of the business. It is very generous and I advise you to accept. I intend to find a new partner.*'

Thomas had warned her to expect something of the sort, but now it had come, she was shocked, not because of the gossip, nor even his high-handed tone, but by his cool dismissal of her part in building up the business and his assumption that she did not want to carry on with it and would not object to handing it all over to someone else. He didn't like running the shops and bakehouses and it was not part of her agreement with him that he should; they were hers, she had given them birth and she felt possessive about them and proud of what she had achieved. She couldn't just hand them over to someone else, as if they were one of her pies. She let her mind drift back to the night she had met Henry. His unaccustomed drunkenness had been a stroke of good fortune if ever there was one, and she had built a little business empire out of it. She did not want to lose it. Quite apart from the money, she enjoyed working, pitting her wits against the establishment and making bankers and businessmen take notice of her. And she enjoyed the position it afforded her.

'Have you heard any of this gossip?' she asked Thomas when he joined her at the breakfast table.

'Henry is exaggerating, as usual,' he said mildly.

'But neither Henry nor Geoffrey should have to put up with gossip because of something I've done. And Jason – how will it affect him?'

'It will all die down as soon as you get back to work.'

'But what about this?' she asked, picking up Henry's letter. 'If I accept Henry's offer, I should have to use the money to start something else because I must make a living.'

'The pie shops were your idea. You are the one who has the reputation as a cook, not Henry. I suppose you could start up in competition with him. It would serve him right.'

Sarah Jane chuckled. 'He's thought of that. There is a clause in the agreement to exclude me from doing that.'

'Then go back and fight him over it, isn't that what you always do?'

'But every time I put up a fight about something, I hurt other people, people who rely on me, people who love me.'

'Poppycock!' Thomas snorted. 'You are a force for good, don't you know that? Without you, their lives – all our lives – would have been the poorer. You gave me back my will to live a decent kind of life, made me feel a man again and you did the same for Henry. Duncan, and even Timothy, were the better for having known you. You brought out the best in all of us. We will hear no more of this nonsense.'

She did not know if she believed him, but it was comforting to be told. 'What do you suggest I do, then?'

'Buy him out.'

'I haven't the money. The expenses of the school were heavier than I anticipated, and now I have to find new premises for that and a new home and Jason will soon have to go to a better school. Besides, I know Henry; he wouldn't want to sell his half and if he did, the price would be astronomical. We have seven shops now and two bakehouses; there are delivery vans and horses and stables and any number of peripheral assets. I could not afford it.'

'What are you going to do, then?'

Sarah Jane smiled. 'Go back to London and see if I can calm him down.' She wondered how she was going to break the news to Geoffrey. He was certainly growing stronger and though he still needed his afternoon rest, he dressed every day, was able to ride very gently, to shoot and fish, taking Jason with him as often as not; he would make some excuse to keep her, though she suspected it was only because he liked Jason's company.

'He makes me feel young again,' he said, when Sarah Jane scolded him the following day for doing too much. He had just come back from a canter with Jason and had sunk onto a cast-iron railway bench inscribed with the name *Chevington Halt*, which had been surplus to requirements at the station and had been brought to stand on the terrace of Chevington House; it made an excellent garden seat. 'He's given me a new lease of life.'

'I'm glad to hear it,' she said. 'But you're not fit to turn cartwheels yet.'

Jason giggled at the image of His Lordship turning cartwheels, making Sarah Jane frown at him. 'Go and change out of those muddy boots, Jason. I want to talk to Lord Chevington.'

'Dear Sarah Jane,' he said, when the boy had gone. 'What should I do without you?' He took her hand and drew her down beside him. 'No one else would have taken care of me like you have. No one else would have worked so hard to make this old house a home again. Without you I would have died and Chevington House would have remained a ruin.'

'You are exaggerating. I was here and there was no one else.'

'No one else,' he repeated softly. 'That's what my foolish son should have realised. Perhaps he did, that last day ...'

'Do not speak of it.'

'No one thought about your grief, did they? All of us were depending on you for everything and no one gave a thought for your needs.'

'I had what I needed – plenty of work.'

'Is that all? Did you not also need comfort and understanding?'

'You understand me, you always have.'

'But I was ill, and you soldiered on alone.'

'Thomas helped. He is a good friend and a very caring man.'

'There was a time when I thought you would marry him.'

She smiled. 'I very nearly did once, but for all the wrong reasons.'

'And what were they?'

'Security, I suppose, because I wanted to escape from my own folly. If I had I would never have met Duncan.'

'Do you still miss him?'

'I shall always do that, but the pain of it has eased. We cannot alter what is meant for us.'

'And now?'

'Now?' She was puzzled.

'Would you marry Thomas now?'

'No.'

'And Henry Carter?'

She could not understand why he was quizzing her. The last thing she had on her mind was marriage to either man. 'He is my business partner, though now he wants to buy me out.'

'Why?'

She shrugged. 'I suppose he feels neglected. I must go back to London.'

He looked startled. 'Don't you like it here? Have I been taking you too much for granted? Oh, how stupid of me!'

'You're not stupid, you are the kindest, most considerate man I know, but I have a business to run, people depending on me ... '

'Give it up,' he said, taking her hand. 'Accept Mr Carter's offer. Stay here with me.'

Suddenly she realised why she had been delaying her departure; she could have left a month before if she had been determined enough. Only now, when it looked as though it was coming to an end, did she acknowledge how much the last few weeks had meant to her. For the first time since that dreadful explosion at Hailey Common, she had been happy and there had been no nagging doubts about whether what she was doing was right. It had been so right, she had not even thought about it until Henry's letter arrived and shaken her from her complacency. The revelation shocked her into silence for a full minute, before she said, 'I can't, Geoffrey. I've been away too long as it is, and Henry has every right to be peeved. Besides, Jason is missing so much schooling.'

'He can have a tutor here, or go to a good boarding school. It's not a problem.'

'It's not only that.'

'You aren't worried about money, are you? Let me take care of that.'

She busied herself plumping up his cushions, trying to cover her confusion. 'No, it has nothing to do with money, or only very little. I can't expect you to understand, I hardly do myself. It's all to do with me, what I am, what I was and what I have become, what I want from life, not only for me, but for my son and his sons and, more importantly, his daughters, if he should have them. It's about opportunities and education and Duncan and Thomas and Timothy, how they have shaped and influenced me – you even ...'

'Me?'

'You had enough faith in me to lend me books.' She smiled. 'I'm not making much sense, am I?'

'Perfect sense, my dear,' he said. 'Your success is important to you, your achievements, what you have been able to do.'

'And what I can still do.' She felt easier now that her heart had resumed its regular beat. 'Do you know what Thomas once told me? He said you need fuel to get things done and money makes very good fuel. It's how we use it that matters.' She paused, because his attention seemed to have wandered and yet his eyes were still regarding her searchingly. 'There is still so much I want to do.'

He took both her hands in his own. 'You know, Sarah Jane, it has taken tragedy and illness to make me realise that there is more to life than dashing here and there making money, not having time to stop and look around at the goodness and the evil of this world and doing something about it. It is as if I had been looking through smoked glass, with hazy images, blurred outlines, nothing clear-cut.'

'Nothing ever is.'

'One thing is.' He lifted both her hands to his lips in turn. 'You are the most important thing in my life now and if you say you need to work, then I will accept that.'

He was going to let her go, after all. Had she been hoping he would try to detain her? Would she never learn? At least his acquiescence would make it easier for her. 'Thank you, Geoffrey.' How easy it was to call him by his given name now.

'You remember when we were coming back from Hailey Common in the train, I said I hadn't made up my mind what I was going to do next?'

'Yes.'

'If Henry is proving difficult, then I'll buy him out. I'll be your partner. Then you won't have to give up your business to stay with me.'

Her thoughts were tumbling about so much she could think of nothing coherent to say, except, 'My lord, it is hardly fitting.'

'My, we are formal again.' He laughed suddenly. 'You think I might regret something said out of gratitude because you neglected your business to nurse me?'

'Perhaps.'

'This has nothing to do with gratitude, Sarah Jane. It is something far stronger than that. My heart may be weak but I am still its master, or at least you are. And I am certainly not out of my mind.' He paused, looking at her tenderly. 'And as for it being fitting, I'm too old to worry about that, and I don't care a fig what people think and say about me. Or what they say about you, because I know you.'

'You have heard the rumours?'

'Rumours – what are they, but sour grapes?' He paused, searching her face. 'What I feel for you has nothing to do with rumour or Timothy or Henry Carter or anyone else. Oh my darling Sarah Jane, don't you see my need for you, my hunger, in my eyes? And I am not talking about housekeeping and nursing, I am talking about you, you as a woman, you, Sarah Jane, my love.'

She stiffened. Had she heard him aright? He was no better than Timothy, who thought he could bribe her with gifts into becoming his mistress. That was the reason for all those questions about Thomas. Upset and hurt, she pulled her hands from his and stood up. 'I've a great deal to do if I'm to catch the morning train,' she said, controlling her voice with care. 'I'll send your valet to help you up to your room.'

'Sarah Jane, you haven't answered me!'

But she did not turn back. She dare not, because she was crying. Didn't he know her better than that? Didn't he know that one of the reasons she had quarrelled with Timothy was that she would not be his mistress? She had thought Geoffrey was different, that he respected her. She had been telling herself for weeks now that she must go back to London and she had been putting it off. Why? Because His Lordship needed her? Because Jason was happy here? Because she loved Chevington House? She had been fooling herself if she believed any of that. It came to her like a flash of summer lightning; it was not just that she loved the place, *she also loved the man.* She loved him, not in the way she had loved Duncan, nor in the tempestuous fashion she had loved Timothy, but for himself, because of qualities he alone possessed, his kindness and consideration, his gentleness, his understanding of her, his humility and the way he treated her as an equal; the tranquillity he gave her, the feeling of being safe with him, because he would never hurt her. Until today.

The shock of recognising the strength of her own feelings at the same moment as she realised that he didn't see her in the same light, was more than she could bear. She went up to her room, fetched her carpet bag out of a cupboard and began piling her clothes on the bed. Then she sat down and began to laugh hysterically. She had sent home for gowns, mantles, gloves, shoes and underwear while she had been at Chevington and there was no way they could be accommodated in the carpet bag she had been carrying when she arrived. She would have to borrow a trunk and ask for a conveyance to the station. So much for her independence! What a predicament to get herself in; she still had to ask favours. And what would His Lordship demand in payment? A little kiss? Her imagination painted it, felt it, savoured it, and her laughter gave way to tears of anguish.

But it was no good crying over something she should have foreseen. She scrubbed at her eyes and went down to the butler's pantry to ask Wilkins to have a trunk lifted down from the attic and a carriage brought to the back door. She would go, as she had arrived, all those years ago, through the kitchen. As soon as she had packed, she went to Jason's room and collected together his belongings.

'But, Mama, why do we have to go?' He liked Lord Chevington and he wished he could stay here for ever. 'I like it here.'

'So do I, Jason, but the shops won't run themselves, you know, and besides, you are getting all behind with your schooling.'

Lord Chevington had taught him a lot about all sorts of things and it was much better than school any day, but his mother would not listen.

'I'm sorry, Jason, but we must go,' she said when he protested. 'Now, go and say goodbye to His Lordship and thank him for having you.'

She did not go with him; she could not face Geoffrey in case her eyes gave her away.

She hadn't returned a moment too soon, she told herself. The head cook at the bakehouse, chosen for her high standards, was threatening to resign over the matter of the meat, the manager at the Oxford Street shop was at loggerheads with his counterpart at Covent Garden – both thought they should be in charge in her absence – and Henry had given Betsy notice in view of the fact that without her mistress she had nothing to do. She reassured Betsy, settled the cook, scolded both the men and set off for Bond Street, in what Henry always called 'high dudgeon', relishing the prospect of a battle. It would take her mind off Geoffrey and Chevington and what she had left behind. She had been a fool to let herself become ensnared, but the net had been of her own making. It was a mixture of guilt and gratitude which had made her want to do what she could to help after the fire, and she had not stopped to think of her own wayward heart or what Geoffrey would think of her. Instead of being annoyed by the scandal, he had compounded it by asking her to stay. Had he thought that would please her? Housekeeper-cum-mistress. 'Fool! Idiot!' she berated herself.

Henry was in his office dictating a letter when she arrived. He sent the clerk away and waited for the door to shut before he spoke. 'Well, Sarah Jane?'

She went straight into the attack. 'Henry, why did you countermand my instructions to the cook? She knows where to buy her meat and how much to pay for it. We'll lose our reputation if we lower our standards, you should know that.'

'Reputation! You are a fine one to talk of reputation. Gadding all over the countryside with a crowd of rioting navvies. And not content with that, you inveigle your way into Lord Chevington's home. God knows how you did that, but his reputation won't stand another scandal.'

'Another?'

'Well, there was all that business of his ward turning out to be his son. Why couldn't you keep out of it? Now I'll have a devil of a job not to be tarred with the same brush.'

'What do you mean by that?'

'One of the men in your life.'

'But Henry, you *are* one of the men in my life, aren't you? You are my business partner. And I did not think you had ever regretted that.'

'I didn't until you chose to behave like a hoyden. Didn't you receive my letter?'

'Oh, I received it all right, but I have no intention of doing anything about it. I am grateful for the start you gave me, but if it hadn't been you it would have been someone else.' She paused, smiling at the memory of their first meeting. Would there have been anyone else? 'I built the business, I worked hard to make it what it is and I have plans for its future – and they *don't* include selling out to you!'

'You expect me to sit back and let you ruin me?'

'You are in no danger of being ruined but if you want to dissolve the partnership, I will agree.'

He sighed with relief. 'I knew you would see sense, though Mr Wistonby assured me you wouldn't sell.'

'Thomas was right. How much do you want for your share?'

'Me?' His surprise was comical. '*You* want to buy *me* out?'

'It seems the most sensible solution, doesn't it? You have never really had your heart in it. Now, name your price.'

She was mad, she told herself, as she took a cab back to Oxford Street. How could she possibly afford it? Where could she go for funds? Lord Chevington? No, definitely not. She would have to try the merchant bankers again. They had refused her over the school, but that had been a charitable project and this was business. The company had expanded and thrived and all she was asking for now was venture capital. All she had to do was persuade them that their money would be safe in her hands.

It soon became apparent that her notoriety had gone before her and instead of being easier, it was even more difficult to obtain an interview and those who did agree to see her, did so from curiosity alone. Her carefully prepared proposals were dismissed with a wave of the hand while they entertained her with cups of tea and thinly veiled references to the newspaper articles. She reacted by behaving outrageously, crossing her legs and asking for a cigar, and using language she would not have used even on a navvy site. They had laughed, but she had made them feel uncomfortable. It was the only satisfaction she had; no money was forthcoming.

In the end, Thomas persuaded one banker to see her and then the transaction was concluded with unbelievable speed. They celebrated with champagne and a meal at Rules, and the next day she set about putting her plans into action. She cancelled the purchase of the house because it now seemed an unnecessary extravagance, and consoled Jason over the loss of the pony with the promise of hiring both mount and riding-master at least once a week. By the end of the following day the ache in her heart had been smothered by exhaustion and a feeling that, if she put her mind to it, she could conquer the world. She was unprepared for a visitor, least of all Geoffrey.

Jason had gone to bed and she was sitting alone in her small drawing room wearing a very simple gown of emerald taffeta, when Betsy showed him in.

He looked rather tired, but he was smiling. 'You aren't going to throw me out, are you?'

'No, of course not.' She stood up to greet him, with a heart that was beating almost in her throat, and hands that shook. 'Come and sit down. When did you arrive in London? Are you sure you were well enough to travel?'

As soon as Betsy had left, he took her hands in his and drew her down onto the sofa. 'Why did you run away?'

'I didn't run away. I had to come back, I didn't want to lose my business.'

'And have you?'

'No, I've bought Henry out. I had to borrow heavily, but that doesn't matter.'

'I offered, Sarah Jane.'

'I know you did, but I couldn't take it from you.'

'I understand.'

Expecting an argument, she looked at him in surprise. 'You do?'

'Of course. Did you think I wasn't listening when you explained how you felt about it all? I respect you, as well as love you, Sarah Jane. And I didn't come here tonight to talk about *Carter & Winterday.*' He grinned. 'I suppose it's just *Winterday* now?'

'Yes.'

'I came to talk about us. You and me.' He paused, stroking the back of her hand with his thumb and making her want to throw

394

herself into his arms. How could she be a self-sufficient businesswoman if she couldn't control her own emotions? 'I listened to you, but you weren't listening to me, were you? Didn't you understand any of what I was saying the day you left?'

She lifted her eyes to his; there was defiance in them and pride, but also hurt and a misery which tore at his gut. 'I understood, all right. You said you would buy Henry out and become my partner, and in return . . . '

'I don't remember saying anything about what I wanted in return.'

'You didn't have to.'

'I was blind and thoughtless.' He had been so anxious to emphasise that he didn't want to deprive her of her independence, he had forgotten the most important thing of all. He realised how clumsy he had been as soon as she had left him, but he had to let her go; he had to give her space to be herself, to save her business and her pride. But he soon acknowledged he could not live without her. 'Sarah Jane, please listen now.' He took her shoulders in his hands and turned her to face him. 'You mean far more to me than you seem to understand. Without you I am nothing, nothing at all, an empty shell which should have crumbled to dust along with Chevington House. And there have been times, especially in the last couple of weeks, when I wished I had.'

'Oh no, you mustn't say that!'

'You are the breath of my life, the sight in my eyes, the voice in my head, my joy.' He lifted her chin with his finger so that she could not avoid his eyes. 'Didn't you understand, my love, that I was trying, in my clumsy way, to propose to you.'

'Propose? To me?'

'Yes, propose.' He raised her hand to his lips. 'So, my darling Sarah Jane, will you make an old man very happy and marry him?'

'You are not old.'

It was hardly the answer he had been expecting and he laughed. 'Forty-nine, but with you at my side, I will grow older much, much more slowly.' He paused, searching her face. 'There is only one thing I need from you.' He felt her muscles tense under his hands. 'And don't mount your high horse again until you have heard what it is.'

'What is it?' She was still in a daze over a declaration of love which had taken her breath away. No one had ever said anything so beautiful to her before and it made her want to cry.

'Your love. Can you find it in your heart to love me?'

'Oh, I do!' How true that was, she had only lately discovered – and how very near she had been to spoiling it.

'Then what about my proposal? Will you marry me?'

'It's not possible.'

'Why not?'

'The gossip . . . '

'Poof! I'm too old to worry about that, and too rich, and if I want to be unconventional then so I shall. I don't take kindly to being dictated to by a society which is mostly humbug and too full of its own importance. Like you, I value my independence. Now, what other obstacles are you going to put in the way of our happiness?'

'And will it truly make you happy if I say yes?'

'Above all else. How can you doubt it?'

She looked at him, eyes alight with mischief. 'I can't be an ordinary wife, Geoffrey. I shall sometimes be a dreadful handful. Are you prepared to have a businesswoman as a spouse?'

'As long as she never stops loving me.' He paused. 'It will tickle me no end to watch my wife making rings round those old fogies in the city and building up a business empire any man would be proud to own.' He had Thomas Wistonby to thank for telling him that Sarah Jane was at her wits' end trying to raise capital and Thomas was a willing conspirator when it came to suggesting to her that a visit to *Benson & Benson* might be worth their while. Old Sam Benson could be trusted to keep the secret and Sarah Jane would never know where the money had come from. And he had no intention of interfering in the business; it was hers.

She reached across to kiss his cheek. 'She will never do that.'

He took her into his arms and kissed her lips, gently, tenderly, half-afraid of her reaction, but she responded with a warmth and lack of inhibition which delighted him, kissing him back and awakening a passion he thought never to feel again. 'My dearest Sarah Jane, my love.'

She pulled herself from his embrace at last, smiling through the tears which lay on her lashes and made her eyes sparkle like emeralds. There was still something of the innocent child about her. 'If anyone had told me, when I stood in your library all those years ago, quaking in my shoes and expecting to be dismissed, that I would one day return to Chevington, that you and I—' She stopped and looked at him intently. 'Do you know, my one ambition then was to become a lady. I never dreamed how that would be brought about.'

'My own dear darling lady.' He put up a hand to touch her hair. 'I think I've known for some time how much I loved you, but I wouldn't admit it, even to myself. It began that day when I met you outside your school and you talked of nothing but the navvies. I certainly realised I loved you after the riot when we travelled back to London together and talked about so many things. Did you not guess?'

'No, never. I thought you looked on me as a servant, that is all.'

'A servant? Oh no, my darling, you are no one's servant.' He paused to kiss her tear-wet cheek. 'You are the loveliest thing that has ever happened to me.'

She sighed and relaxed in his arms, leaning her head on his shoulder. 'I still want the navvy schools, you know, Geoffrey. Amelia has been an enormous help and we've made great headway.'

'Of course, I want those too. And will it also please you if we make it a firm rule that the navvies are to be paid fortnightly in cash and the tommy shops are to stock only good quality merchandise at a fair price?'

'Yes, oh yes – but it will have to be enforced. You can't just leave it to the subcontractors, you know what they are like. You must have an inspector.'

He laughed and kissed her again. 'Now I know what Henry Carter feels like when you bully him.'

'I don't bully.'

'Oh yes, you do, you're frightening when you get the bit between your teeth, do you know that?'

'I'm sorry, it's the only way I know to get things done.'

'Don't be sorry because without you and people like you, life would be very dull indeed. You have a way of making things happen.'

'And not always good things,' she said, suddenly serious. 'There is so much I regret.'

'Never regret what you have done, Sarah Jane, because you have accomplished much and there is still more to be done. It all began at Chevington House, and it will go on from there, but we will do it together, you and I.'

'And Jason.'

'Of course. I love the boy; he is part of you, part of me too.' He smiled. 'And you never know, there may be others.'

She blushed. 'I still can't believe this is happening.' She stopped speaking as he traced the outline of her slightly parted lips with his finger, then slid his hand round to the nape of her neck and pulled her forward to kiss her mouth and then bury his face in her neck. She shivered.

'Perhaps you will believe it when we are married, and I can show you exactly what I mean,' he murmured.

She felt the tug of desire contract the muscles of her belly and thighs and put out a hand to trace the outline of his jaw. 'You may be prepared to wait, my lord, but I am not so patient.'

He laughed. 'Now, my lady?'

She nodded and took his hand, pulling him to his feet and leading him into her bedroom, where she turned and tilted her head up to be kissed. 'Are you sure you will have no regrets?'

He kicked the door shut as he took her into his arms.

'None, now or ever. And you?'

'None.'

Slowly, very slowly, he began undressing her, until a trail of clothing led from door to bed, and by then they were locked together in a naked embrace which took them from the tenderest caresses she had ever known to passionate fulfilment. The wonder of it took them both by surprise and afterwards they lay and giggled like children.

Three weeks later, in a simple ceremony at the little church on the Chevington estate, attended by Jason, preening himself at his own importance, and witnessed by a handful of close friends, Sarah Jane became Lady Chevington. Afterwards, leaving Jason in the care of Thomas and his new tutor at the Oxford Street apartment, she and Geoffrey went on to the house in Cumberland Terrace, where they spent an idyllic three weeks, making a token appearance at their respective businesses each day and spending the rest of the time getting to know each other.

The only thing that marred Sarah Jane's complete happiness was that she had no idea of what had happened to Billie. If she could only know that he was safe, it might have helped, but Thomas had not been able to find a single trace of him. It was left to Rifleman Harker to have the last word. It came with the correspondence forwarded to Cumberland Terrace from Oxford Street.

'This isn't a business letter,' she said, shuffling through the letters which had been brought to the breakfast table. It was late and both were still in dressing gowns – Geoffrey's was a burgundy satin and hers a gossamer of pale-blue silk – but neither cared about the time; the joy they had found in each other could not be hurried and if their lovemaking of the night extended into the day, then they would rise when they felt like it. It was the nearest thing to a honeymoon she would allow herself. 'Second-hand envelope and my name hardly legible.' She paused. 'There is a note from Thomas. He says it was found slipped down behind the mantelshelf and the chimneybreast when workmen came to install a new fireplace in the Oxford Street apartment. Someone must have put it there for me when I was at Chevington and it missed being sent on.'

Geoffrey left his own mail to look at her; he could not get over the fact that he had found such contentment so late in life and not only contentment, but a passion fulfilled beyond his wildest dreams and an unbounded joy. The cool-headed businesswoman was completely uninhibited when in the privacy of their bedroom and he could not have enough of her. He smiled. 'Are you going to open it or do you think staring at the outside will reveal its contents?'

Laughing, she broke the seal. The letter had been scrawled in an almost illiterate hand, but the news it brought, though brief, was plain enough. The writer had seen Billie and had persuaded him to emigrate to America. *"Tis his onely way out, there bein no futur fer him in this land, wot with him bein surched for and onely the lash at the end of it. In the New World he can mek a new lif. He is a good felow, is Bill, and he will mek it, I'll tek me oath on it, so do not greeve fer him.'* She assumed it had been written by Rifleman Harker though he had not dared to sign his name in case the letter fell into the wrong hands and he was punished for befriending the runaway; he had simply ended it, *'His frend.'*

Ever since they had taken that long road to the workhouse, she and Billie, their lives had followed separate paths, but every so often fate had decreed that they should be in the same place at the same time; they had been on the same stretch of road on the opening day of the Great Exhibition and at Hailey Common they had been within a few yards of each other, only to be torn apart again by circumstances neither had been able to control. Had it been ordained at the very beginning? Had their lives been set on separate courses from the day Geoffrey had seen them playing in the stubble? Were they destined never to meet again?

'Must I accept that this is the end?' she asked, after handing the note to her husband and watching him read it. 'Will I never see him again?'

'Never is a long time, Sarah Jane.' He didn't want to raise her hopes but he could not leave her with none at all. Neither did he want the boy found and her happiness marred by a court-martial of her brother for shooting Timothy; knowing how she had felt about both men it would tear her to shreds. 'The soldier is right. Billie has to find a new life for himself and if he is also right in his confidence that the lad will make good in America, then, perhaps, you should be happy for him.'

'I let him down badly.'

'Stop blaming yourself, my darling,' he said tenderly. 'Billie had choices to make about the way he lived his life, just as you had. You can't make yourself responsible for the things he did, any more than he should feel responsible for you. You were children when you arrived at the Union, and what happened afterwards was no one's fault. Perhaps, one day, when he's settled, he'll write to you.'

'I hope he'll be happy,' she said, reaching across and covering his hand with her own. 'I hope he finds the joy I have found.'

He picked up her hand and put the palm to his lips. 'Darling Sarah Jane, you'll see him again one day, but you must let him go now. His is a free spirit, just as yours is, and he will find his own wings to fly with.'

Sarah Jane smiled at the man who sat opposite her and held her heart and her happiness in his hands; safe hands, she knew it. It had been a long, long road, that road from the stubble field at Penny Drift, but she had found her home at last – a secure haven with the man whose love would sustain her for the rest of her life, because that was how it was always meant to be.